HIGHLAND DESIRE

"It angers me to think my father and your father gave you to a boy." Ian held fast to her braid, twisting it around his finger as if he could somehow possess it. "You deserve a man, Kara." His voice was tight, full of emotion.

She felt her chest tighten. She had never evoked such sentiment in a man before.

"You deserve a man who can love you as you deserve to be loved. A man who can give you children."

Kara had no time to think. She felt Ian's breath warm on her lips. The next thing she knew, he was leaning over her, drawing her into arms that seemed all-encompassing. She tilted her head, mesmerized by the scent of him, by his power, by the atmosphere within the castle ruins.

Kara was shocked by the warmth of Ian's lips, shocked by her own desperate need to feel his mouth against hers.

This is wrong. A sin . . . The words pulsed in her mind. But she couldn't stop herself, not any more than she could prevent the English from invading her beloved Scotland, or prevent the sun from rising each morning.

"Kara." He breathed her name against her lips like a chant. A prayer.

She wanted to pull away. Run. But instead she pressed her body against his, drawn to his warmth and his strength . . . .

Books by Colleen Faulkner

FORBIDDEN CARESS
RAGING DESIRE
SNOW FIRE
TRAITOR'S CARESS
PASSION'S SAVAGE MOON
TEMPTATION'S TENDER KISS
LOVE'S SWEET BOUNTY
PATRIOT'S PASSION
SAVAGE SURRENDER
SWEET DECEPTION
FLAMES OF LOVE
FOREVER HIS
CAPTIVE
O'BRIAN'S BRIDE
DESTINED TO BE MINE
TO LOVE A DARK STRANGER
FIRE DANCER
ANGEL IN MY ARMS
ONCE MORE
IF YOU WERE MINE
HIGHLAND BRIDE

Published by Zebra Books

HIGHLAND BRIDE

Colleen Faulkner

Zebra Books
Kensington Publishing Corp.
http://www.zebrabooks.com

ZEBRA BOOKS are published by

Kensington Publishing Corp.
850 Third Avenue
New York, NY 10022

First Printing: January, 2000
10   9   8   7   6   5   4   3   2   1

Printed in the United States of America

PART I

"The Trees They Grow High"

An English Ballad
Author Unknown

The trees they grow high,
And the leaves they do grow green.
Many is the time my true love I've seen.
Many an hour I've watched him all alone.
He's young but he's daily growing.

Father, dear Father, you've done me great wrong,
You've married me to a boy who is too young.
I am twice twelve and he is but thirteen,
He's young but he's daily growing.

Daughter, dear Daughter,
I've done you no wrong.
I've married you to a great lord's son.
He'll make a lord for you to wait upon.
He's young but he's daily growing.

Chapter One

Highlands of Scotland
Grampian Mountains
Spring, 1636

Kara pulled the heavy tartan blanket to her chin as her gaze settled apprehensively on the bedchamber door. Despite the warmth of the blaze on the hearth, she was chilled to the bone. Her teeth chattered, clicking together in an unsettling rattle. Naked, she shivered beneath the mountain of woolen blankets.

When the maids had led her to the tower room they had removed her gown and refused to bring her sleeping garments, or even a dressing gown. It was wedding tradition, they had told her, but she guessed it was to deter her from attempting to flee.

Kara waited.

At any moment, through that door, her groom would emerge. He would come to her bridal bedchamber perhaps with laughter on his lips and scotch on his breath, expecting his husbandly rights. Kara had known him all of six hours, and of that, they had spent most of the time at the wedding feast separated except for the brief ceremony. She didn't even know the color of his eyes.

Her gaze fixed on the rough-hewn door that appeared to have previously been splintered by an overly anxious bridegroom. Kara's lower lip trembled and she bit down on it until she tasted the metallic tang of blood.

She set her jaw with determination. She would not give herself to her husband. Not tonight. Not tomorrow night. Her father could beat her, he could force her to marry the Lord Dunnane, he could even send her far from the only home she had ever known, but he could not compel her to have carnal relations with his lordship.

This was where her father's authority over her ended. Here, in this castle at the foothills of the Grampian Mountains, in the unfamiliar bedchamber where she was surrounded by strangers, Kara finally had a wee bit of control over her own life.

Nae. Short of rape, there would be no consummation tonight, and she'd be damned if she cared what anyone thought on the morn.

Kara heard a sound in the passageway outside the bedchamber and she involuntarily flinched. Here she was naked beneath the covers and he was coming . . . they were coming.

Her gaze again locked on the door.

At least Harailt Gordon, Lord of Dunnane, called Harry to his intimates, would not rape her. Of that she was fairly certain.

A satisfied smile crossed her bruised lips as she thought of getting the best of her father just this once. It was a minor victory in the face of a vast defeat, but she held it dear to her heart just the same.

Harry wouldn't rape her because he couldn't. She outweighed him by a stone and towered over him by a full head. In a wrestling match she'd have the best of him in less than a minute. Short of knocking her unconscious, he would not get his way with her.

The sound of raucous laughter filled the outside passageway, and Kara shrank back under the edge of the tartan. The door was flung open and she lifted the blanket higher, lying back on the duck-down pillow.

"To the bride," a wedding guest cried with gusto as raucous men burst into the room.

"Aye, to the bride," another reveler echoed.

More Scotsmen poured into her bridal chamber, all drunk and merry, their attire in disarray. Some wore bonnets and cloaks, clad to make their departure, while others were half-dressed. One fellow with a tangled red beard was missing a boot, another his stockings. A rosy-cheeked piper playing a cheerful jig brought up the rear of the entourage. Fierce clansmen lifted their goblets in salute while others drank from the earthen jugs just come from the bowels of Dunnane Castle. The Highlanders stank so of damp wool, Scotch, and armpits that Kara had to swallow against the bile that rose in her throat.

The wedding guests surrounded her brocade-curtained bed, seemingly unaware that she was a human being laid out between them. Much as she would someday be laid out upon her death, she thought ironically.

"To the bridegroom!"

"The bridegroom!" The men lifted their vessels and drank again.

"May his rod always remain straight. May he always strike home."

The clansmen burst into coarse laughter as they lifted their drinks in salute again.

"Where is he? Where is the groom?" someone shouted. "Bring in the groom!"

Kara wanted to close her eyes and shrink under the blanket. She wanted to retreat from the bed, from the chamber, from the dark, lonely Dunnane Castle into nothingness. But she knew there would be no retreat this night.

"Lord Dunnane! Lord Dunnane!"

The wedding guests began to stomp their feet and clap their hands so loudly that Kara wanted to cover her ears. Only her pride kept her staring straight ahead at the doorway.

"Lord Dunnane!"

The bridegroom appeared in the doorway and Kara's breath caught in her throat. Her heart tripped and set off pounding again. Here he was at last, her husband, Harry. Her husband until death parted them.

Harry was the great lord of Dunnane Castle and all the vast lands it encompassed. He was the clan lord of the Gordons, a man of great influence and wealth, a man admired by many, perhaps even feared by a few. He held a position most men only dreamed of aspiring to.

It was a pity he was only thirteen years old.

"Step aside, aside, men," a giant of a black-haired figure announced with authority as he filled the doorway behind her husband. His speech held the whisper of the burr of a Highland brogue heard only farther north, but he sounded well educated, better than most in the room.

Kara didn't know who this huge man was but she had noticed him right away when she'd arrived this morning in time for the ceremony. There had been a great deal of confusion in the great hall upon her arrival, but then, too, he had taken command and all had fallen into place as he directed. As the day had progressed, she had gathered he was some sort of adviser to her husband, someone close to him. But none had spoken to her so that she might ask and no one had apparently thought her worthy enough of introductions.

"Step aside, McCulver," the dark stranger demanded in a deep, booming voice. "You stand between a man and his virgin bride."

Again the chamber filled with crude laughter. The black-haired man laughed, but there was something about his laughter that made her think he was not laughing with them, but at them.

Kara felt her cheeks color with embarrassment. Her gaze strayed beyond her husband with his eyes downcast to the adviser. To her surprise, he was staring directly at her, and despite his gruff speech, she found his dark eyes filled with compassion. He seemed to be the only man in the room who understood her vulnerability at this moment . . . her fear.

Something in the Highlander's eyes gave Kara the courage to take another breath. *I am not afraid. I am not afraid,* she chanted silently. *There is nothing for me to fear from this child.*

Kara's gaze returned to her husband standing halfway between the door and her bed. Her lord and master gazed at his feet, his thin, boyish face obscured by shadows. He was dressed from head to toe in a silk brocade dressing gown and robe, garments made in the Orient. On his head was perched a tiny silk cap.

He looked so ridiculous that had it not been for the circumstances she might have laughed. Instead she felt sorry for the man-child. He seemed as out of place at this moment as she did.

The witnesses who filled the bedchamber were lords themselves, warriors all. And though she heard words of goodwill from their lips, she saw no respect for Lord Dunnane in their eyes. Young Harry might, in name, serve as lord over these men, but no one saw him as lord. Rather than allies, Kara saw each man as a hawk waiting to fly in, lift up young Harry and take the kill, and his lands, his title, his monies with it.

The adviser leaned forward over Harry's shoulder and whispered something. Harry glanced up at her and for a moment she thought he might burst into tears. He was more frightened than she was.

The adviser gave him a gentle nudge. "Abed with your wife and I will clear the room, my lord."

Kara had no desire to lie beside the boy, and yet out of pity she lifted the edge of the coverlet, taking care not to reveal her own nakedness.

The crowd cheered.

The boy slipped into bed beside her, bed slippers and all.

"Out, out, allow his lordship to be about his business," the adviser called merrily in the same commanding voice. "Down below where there is more to drink, my friends."

Still clinging to the bed tartan, Kara watched the crowd file out of the room, calling bawdy well-wishes over their shoulders as they went. Finally the fiddler took up the rear and Kara was alone in the chamber with her husband and his dark-haired guardian.

The Highlander closed the door and walked to the hearth. "Is there anything I can get you, Harry?" he asked quietly as he took up an iron cane to prod the fire.

Sparks leaped and the room was immediately filled with the sweet scent of apple. Apple wood burned on the hearth.

"N-nae, Ian."

Ian . . . He was called Ian.

"My lady?"

Ian kept his gaze so politely averted that it took Kara a moment to realize the handsome, dark Highlander spoke to her. She was not certain anyone had spoken directly to her, save the priest, since her arrival.

"Nae," she whispered, touched again that he would take her wants or needs into consideration.

"I have left wine on the table should ye wish to partake," he told her, crossing toward the door.

Kara could not drag her gaze from his. Now she wanted desperately to know who he was, but she didn't have the nerve to ask.

Ian glanced at the boy. "Ye must come and bolt the door behind me, else they'll be back before the next strike of the clock."

Harry, needing no further invitation to escape the bed, leaped from the bedcovers. "Ye won't stay, Ian?"

The man smiled tenderly. "I told ye, Harry. I canna stay. 'Tis your wedding night." His gazed strayed to Kara. "But I have no doubt your wife will take care of ye. I will see ye on the morn."

Still, Kara could not separate herself from Ian's compelling gaze. He was asking that she look after Harry. Perhaps even pleading. Kara nodded and she knew that Ian understood. In that moment she knew he realized what a child Harry still was and how ridiculous was this entire situation.

He looked back to Harry. "Good night then, my lord, my lady." Ian backed out of the door. "Latch it," he said from the passageway.

Harry slid the bolt home and then stood there a moment, his back to Kara before he had the nerve to turn to her. Then he just stood there.

Kara watched him for a full minute, waiting to see what he would do. Finally she realized that unless she said something he would probably stand all night.

She lifted the corner of the bedcovers again. "Come, sir. You'll catch your death if you stand there any longer."

"I . . . I could pull a chair to the hearth and sleep there," he said hopefully. His voice was still high in pitch, the voice of a boy who had not yet reached the physical maturity of manhood.

Kara couldn't resist a smile. "Nae, 'tis your bed as well. I'll stay to my side and nae snore, I promise you."

Harry looked longingly at the space beside her in the bed. He appeared tired; it had been a long day for him as well. She knew he wanted nothing more than to slip between the warmth of the wool and sleep, but obviously something else was on his mind.

The men, of course. Harry couldn't help but be thinking of all the things they had said—what they expected him to do.

"It's all right," Kara said softly. "Because if it's husbandly duties you worry over, you've nothing to fear from me, my lord. I won't tell.'' She made the assumption that he didn't want to lie with her, praying she was right.

He swallowed, his Adam's apple bobbing. ''My . . . my men, they expect—''

''*I* expect nothing. We have many years to be wed, my lord. Many nights to share a bed as man and wife.''

His gaze met hers for a fraction of a second and then he bounded to the bed too much like a little boy and not at all like the great lord of the castle.

Harry yanked the bedcovers up to his chin and lay back on his pillow, his body rigid. Kara leaned over and blew out the candle beside the bed, leaving the room in the glow of the firelight. She stared at the bed linens draped overhead.

Harry lay absolutely still, barely breathing. After a moment she heard a little sound. Then again.

The child was crying.

Kara exhaled slowly. She wanted to go to sleep. She didn't want to comfort the boy. She didn't want to touch him—give him any encouragement he might interpret wrongly. Who was she to comfort him? Right now she could use a little comforting of her own. But of course there was no one to comfort her. Never had been.

A little sob escaped his tight lips.

''My lor— Harry, it's all right,'' she whispered.

What did she do now? Her first thought was to go to him, draw him into her arms and comfort him as she would any child. But she was naked, for heaven's sake!

Another sob.

With a sigh of concession, Kara rolled onto her side toward him and draped her arm over his abdomen. This was not a man in a position to be demanding husbandly rights; this was a little boy in need of a mother or a suitable substitute.

Harry's thin body was trembling with cold and fear. When she drew near, she felt not the body of a man in her bed, but the body of a little boy, a frightened little boy.

"There, there," she whispered. "All will be all right. Shhh." She had no need to ask him why he was crying. She felt like crying herself, and she was an adult. She could only imagine how frightened and confused he must be.

"It's all right, Harry," she soothed, rolling close to him to share her body heat beneath the covers. "Go to sleep." She reached up with one hand and stroked his silky blond hair as she would any child's. "Sleep and all will look brighter on the morrow."

After a time Harry began to relax against her. His crying subsided and eventually he drifted off to sleep in Kara's arms.

This is certainly not how I imagined my wedding night, she thought sleepily as her own eyes drifted shut. She had once imagined lying in the arms of Harry's brother, William. It was he, fifteen years older than Harry, a son of the deceased earl's previous marriage, to whom she had been betrothed. It was only upon William's death in a skirmish with the English that she had found herself the intended of a child.

A tear fell from the corner of Kara's eyes. She wanted to roll over on her own side of the bed but she was afraid to move for fear of waking the boy. Instead she drifted off to sleep, her thoughts heavy with the day's events and the uncertainty of her future with the boy-husband who slept in her arms.

Kara woke to the sound of the bedchamber door swinging open on its creaky iron hinges. Instinctively she yanked the covers up higher. The boy was gone from the bed and she was alone. "Harry?"

Crisp daylight filled their bridal chamber. They had slept late, she realized with embarrassment. She had been more tired from her previous day's journey and the wedding than she realized. What would everyone think? What did anyone think of a bride and groom who slept late on the morning following their wedding night?

Harry was at the door still in his Chinese dressing gown. "It's all right. It's just my brother, just Ian."

His brother? She pushed her hair from her face, confused. How could Ian be Harry's brother? William had been his elder brother, and William was dead. Then Kara vaguely recalled mention that William and Harry's mother had been previously married as well. Ian had to be a half-brother and therefore not a Gordon, not an heir.

Ian walked in before Kara could protest. It was bad enough having the boy in the chamber with her stark naked, but his brother as well? She opened her mouth to protest, but she couldn't find adequate words. He entered her bedchamber as if he belonged there.

"Good morning, my lord; sleep well?" Ian spoke in the same commanding voice as the night before, almost as if reciting lines from a performance.

To Kara's horror she heard the sounds of others in the passageway behind him. Whispers, footsteps. Was this the audience Ian played for?

"Step back," Ian called back through the doorway. "Allow his lordship and lady a moment of privacy."

Again laughter, though more subdued than last night. No doubt the previous day's festivities would bring a certain amount of hushed speech to the household, as well as headache droughts.

Ian closed the door firmly behind him. "How did you sleep?"

Harry smiled, almost proudly. "Good, Ian. Good."

Ian's gaze shifted to Kara, half sitting in the great bed, the woolen blankets pulled to her nose. "And you, madam?"

"As well as was to be expected," she said softly.

He nodded slowly, again seeming to understand her position, her fears.

"We haven't much time," he said, speaking directly to her and not Harry. "They're bound upon coming in and inspecting the sheets."

"The sheets?" Kara's eyes widened.

"The sheets?" Harry said, panicky. "But, Ian, I . . . I dinna—"

Ian scowled. "Of course ye didn't." He started for the bed in such a direct manner that it scared Kara. She slid over toward Harry's side. Surely to God he didn't expect to resolve the fact that her virginity was still intact?

At the bedside he lowered his gaze, allowing her meager privacy. That simple, compassionate gesture surprised her even more than his advance on her bed.

Had this man fallen from the heavens? A gift sent from God, for surely he was an angel.

"Forgive me, my lady, but you must be up at once. If I do not take the sheets to the men they will surely come for them."

Kara glanced at the bed, then up at Ian, releasing her breath. She still didn't know what his intention was, but she knew it wasn't rape. "If there was no consummation," she said, past the point of embarrassment, "what shall I do?"

He came to the edge of the bed, speaking softly so that Harry could not hear. "I can remedy the problem. I need only have the sheets, my lady."

She found it ironic that she and her brother-in-law should be resolving this intimate matter, and not she and her husband. But of course she and Ian were the only adults in the room.

A strained pause seemed to stretch between them.

Ian rested one hand on the corner of the top sheet, while she gripped the opposite corner. "Urgency is most important."

He wanted her to get out of the bed, but she didn't know how to do it gracefully without revealing herself. "I would step from the bed, sir, but I've no clothing," she confessed. "The maids took it all last night."

Ian muttered something under his breath that did not sound favorable and turned away. "Slip from the bed and take the blanket with you. I'll have garments sent right away. This will not happen again, I assure you."

Harry stood by the fireplace, smiling. By the light of the morning, he was a handsome blond boy. A comely boy who would no doubt grow to be an attractive man. "Ian will take care of the matter," he said pleasantly. "I'll warrant that. Ian can take care of anything."

With Ian turned away, Kara climbed out of bed, dragging the heavy woolen blanket with her. She didn't care if Harry caught a glimpse of thigh. He was just a child.

She crossed the chamber to stand near her husband, who was stoking the fire and adding more wood.

Ian ripped the bottom sheet from the tick and pulled it toward him. Balling it up, he dropped it onto the bed and pulled a knife from his sporran. Kara didn't understand what he was doing until he nicked his little finger and smeared the sheet with his own blood.

She turned away, feeling her face grow warm.

Ian was providing false proof that she was no longer a virgin. He was protecting her and Harry with his own blood. *God bless him.*

Chapter Two

Kara took her time entering the great hall. She had postponed her morning appearance as long as possible, but now she could no longer dally. Her husband had summoned her.

Alone, she approached the great hall from the dark passageway. Her miserly father had not sent even a single maid to serve her after she was wed. He had declared that her wealthy husband could supply her with a bevy of maids should he wish.

After Ian and Harry left the bedchamber, Kara had asked a serving girl to help her into her underclothing and an overgown. But because the servant was only a kitchen maid delivering chocolate and a biscuit, Kara had not detained her. Kara had brushed and arranged her own hair, found a light woolen cloak from her trunk that Ian had ordered delivered to her tower room, and now she could stall no longer.

Kara peered around the corner apprehensively. Ordinarily the hall would have been the castle's heartbeat, with common men and women coming and going, arguments breaking out and being settled. Here, Lord Dunnane would also hold court sessions to hear the complaints of the citizens under his authority. Today, however, the tapestry-lined room still served as a banquet hall. It was presently filled not with common folk but with wedding guests both male and female who had remained overnight.

From her hiding place in the doorway Kara spotted young Harry seated at the dais before one of the two stone fireplaces that stood in opposite walls, eating heartily of sausage pie. Several spotted hounds lay at his feet beneath the table. He nodded absently as a tall, thin, bearded man spoke into his ear. Kara recognized the man from the previous night's banquet, but didn't know who he was.

"Tsk, tsk, ye canna hide all the day," came a voice from nowhere.

Startled, Kara peered directly around the corner to find her brother-in-law standing guard at the doorway. He had, no doubt, been there all along and caught her in the act of spying.

"I do not hide," she said quietly, pulling back into the passageway so that neither the guests nor her husband could see her. "I merely survey my surroundings before entering them."

She heard a deep chuckle. "A wise warrior, worthy of the Gordon name."

Kara was glad to see Ian again and have the opportunity to thank him for what he had done for her that morning. But now she was unsure of how to broach the subject. She realized that he had done it for Harry, but it had saved her great embarrassment just the same.

Apparently it was as unfathomable to her brother-in-law as it was to her that the Gordons should expect a boy of thirteen to consummate his marriage. He wasn't even old enough to grow hair on his chin, for sweet Mary's sake!

She had no intention of lying with a child; he would grow soon enough. But in the meantime she knew she and Harry must hide the fact that they were indeed not truly husband and wife. It was obvious she now had a dependable ally in the ruse.

"He's a good man, our young Harry," Ian said, his words still meant only for her ears. "Will be."

"Aye, I'm sure. But for now—"

"He's still a boy," Ian finished quietly, seeming to know what she was thinking.

Kara couldn't resist the hint of a smile. Perhaps her life here at Dunnane Castle would not be so dreadful. If there were others as compassionate as Ian, perhaps women, she might find companionship, friendship even.

"I suppose I should make my entrance," Kara said after a moment.

"His lordship is waiting."

"Waiting for more pie, I think." Kara giggled and then was immediately ashamed of herself. She was speaking of her new husband, the powerful Earl of Dunnane. She had no right to disparage him.

To Kara's relief, Ian chuckled with her. "Wait until someone brings him a plate of sweets. Then you will see the true width and breadth of his appetite."

Kara shifted her weight from one foot to the other. A servant passed with a trencher of more meat pies and ale, and she shrank back out of his way.

Ian waited to speak until the servant had passed. "Do you wish me to escort you? It's always easier for two to enter an uncertain room than one."

She peeked around the corner at him again. He appeared unbelievably tall even in the great hall with its domed ceiling and massive stone walls. A giant even to Kara, who was quite tall for a woman. And he had massive hands; she had noticed them this morning when he had smeared blood on her sheets. Strong, masculine hands full of power and control, but kind hands. Hands that would soothe and protect a woman.

She straightened her back and pressed her fingers to

the girdle she wore at her waist. "I can enter a room alone, I assure you, sir."

Again he chuckled. "Aye, no doubt ye can. Tell me first what you see, though."

Ian's voice was so gently probing, so personal, that it made her feel as if she were doing something she shouldn't be. Yet she couldn't resist his warmth, not in the cold world she lived in. "What I see?"

"What have ye observed lurking in the shadows, my lady? What is your perception of the room and its men?"

She peered around the corner, her gaze shifting from one group of clansmen to the next, to the dais, and to another gathering of men bearing arms. A cloud of smoke from the double fireplaces hung over their heads, the scent of sizzling meat and sweet apples heavy in the air. Someone played a few notes on a pipe, ceased, and then started up again.

"Your clansmen are nervous," she observed. "They are unsure how the dice will fall with the new Lord Dunnane. Some are afraid, while others are anxious to find what power they can gain."

"Not my clansmen. I am a Munroe. But you are quite perceptive."

"My husband is hungry," Kara continued, seeing this almost as a game now. "He delights in the pie and the pup he feeds with his fingers beneath the table, but nae in what the man in the beard says to him." Her eyes narrowed, studying the black-bearded stranger closer. "Who is he?"

"A wise man to spot and assess immediately. That is Dungald, my brother's cousin and next in line to Dunnane, should death befall Harry before he fathers a son."

His words hung ominous in the smoky air.

Kara touched the single pearl choker at her neck. "I do not like the way he speaks to my husband. He looks to be giving orders."

"*Guidance*, I am certain he would say."

Kara peered up at Ian, studying his dark eyes. She had caught the hint of sarcasm in his voice. "You do not care for my husband's cousin?"

Ian smiled wickedly. "I adore Dungald, though I would not trust him any farther than my lady could toss him."

Kara nodded, making note to avoid Dungald Gordon. She had lived long enough in her father's castle to understand the alliances men and women made. They could sometimes mean life or death.

"Come, I believe Dungald has chatted long enough in my liege's ear. Let me formally introduce you." He moved into the doorway, offering his arm. "My lady."

Kara stepped out of the relative safety of the dark passageway and laid her hand lightly on Ian's elbow. He towered over her, yet his size did not intimidate her. Something about the ability of such a large man to speak so gently led her to believe she had nothing to fear.

As Kara and Ian entered the great hall, clansmen stepped aside to make way for her. They lowered their gruff voices, some taking the time to scrutinize her more carefully through dark eyes and thick red beards. There were a few women, wives of her husband's kinsmen, but even they appeared judgmental.

"Kara." Harry spoke through a mouthful of pie. "Come sit." He tapped the chair Dungald sat in to his left.

Dungald scowled, his pointy black beard twitching as his pale lips moved. "I beg your pardon, my lord, but wouldn't the Lady Dunnane prefer to sit with the ladies?" He indicated a lower table set near the far corner of the hall and far from the warmth of the two great fireplaces. There, three women dressed for traveling sat drinking and talking.

Kara noticed that Dungald's hand trembled with a palsy when he gestured. Harry thrust another forkful into his mouth. "I think I should ask her, don't you?" The boy smiled at her, flaky pastry caught in the corners of his mouth. "Kara, would you sit with the women or with me?"

Without hesitation, she released Ian's arm and circled

the table to claim the chair beside her husband. "With you, of course, my lord."

"Good choice." Harry swallowed a great gulp of ale, seeming genuinely pleased to see her. "I'm quite sure the conversation is better here. Men talk of fighting English, blood and gore while women talk of nothing but babies and spinning." He waved his fork. "Out of her seat, cousin. My bride wishes to sit."

Kara waited to the right and rear of the padded chair, taking notice of how differently her husband behaved now compared to the previous night. One would hardly believe this handsome, confident young man had cried himself to sleep only hours before.

Dungald glanced up, his gray-green eyes meeting hers in challenge. He was an elegant man with black hair and pale skin, more handsome than any in the room perhaps, but his eyes were cold like the gray stone of the castle walls.

Kara said nothing, keeping her expression free of any emotion, though she felt as if she were prey being stalked. Something told her, some sixth sense, that this man was evil, and she had to suppress the urge to cross herself. She was afraid not just for herself, but for Harry, too.

Dungald paused only a moment, not daring to deliberate any longer, but his point was obvious to her. He thought himself above her and he did not approve of her place at his lordship's table.

Harry missed the exchange altogether, his mind as well as his stomach still focused on the pie.

"My lady." Dungald slid out of the honored chair and offered it to her.

Kara felt the stares of clansmen in the room as they followed the activity at the head table. She heard their whispers.

"Sir." She nodded regally but did not make eye contact with Dungald again. *"The serpent was more crafty than any beast of the field the Lord God had made,"* Kara thought, recalling

Scripture memorized from childhood. *A serpent in the garden, indeed.*

"Munroe." Dungald nodded a greeting, his tone patronizing.

"Dungald."

"Here, sit here, brother." Harry tapped the chair to his right occupied by an elderly, graying man who slept, his head resting in his arms on the table.

Ian moved to stand behind Harry and rested one massive hand on the back of Kara's chair as if his mere presence could protect her from Dungald. "Nae, my lord. Let Red Eye sleep. He's in need of a place to rest more than I."

He chuckled and several men who had apparently been listening chuckled, too.

"My lord, I hate to take ye from your celebrations, but when you finish dining, I must have words with you," Ian said to Harry. "We have much to discuss." He glanced over his shoulder at Dungald, who still hovered. "Privately."

"Aye, aye. Council. Clansmen to speak with. That land dispute to settle. So many things to think about. They make my head ache."

"I know ye wish to enjoy the festivities, but many of the men must return home. It would be a pity not to meet with them before they return to their holdings."

Kara wondered how Ian could speak seriously to Harry when the boy had food on his face. It was certainly unbecoming of an earl.

As inconspicuously as possible, she slipped her handkerchief from her sleeve into Harry's hand.

He glanced up at her questioningly.

She touched the corner of her mouth, hoping no one else caught the exchange. No one but Ian did.

"Oh." Harry wiped the pie from his face. "Aye, brother. Let me see my bride fed and then we will meet with whomever you see fit."

"At least see Grey Gordon about his cattle. His mount is saddled for his departure. His wife is ill."

"I've no need of anything, my lord," Kara assured Harry. "Please go, sir, about your business. Don't worry over me."

Harry frowned. "But you're new here. And I wanted to show you my castle." He looked over his shoulder at Ian and pointed at Kara. "Can she come?"

Harry's request obviously took him by surprise. "To council?"

Kara tried to protest, but Ian interrupted, recovering. "As ye like, my lord. She is your wife and certainly at your bidding. It might be good for the Lady Dunnane to see the importance of your lordship's position."

"Want to?" Harry passed her back her handkerchief. He lowered his voice, speaking to her as if she were a playmate. "Mostly I find these meetings boring, but at least you would not be alone on your first day at Dunnane. It can be a frightening place, especially if you meet my cousin Dungald in a dark passageway." He smiled at his joke.

Kara lowered her gaze, hiding her own smile. She could see that she could quickly grow fond of Harry Gordon. "As you wish, my lord husband."

Harry climbed from his chair and every man and woman seated rose immediately. Harry flapped his arms. "Sit, sit. Be about your business. Ian." He started off across the great hall, a new green wool cloak about his shoulders.

Ian waited for Kara and they both fell into step behind his lordship. All eyes were on the three as they entered a smaller room, which served as Harry's private chamber. She could not help but notice the serpent Dungald standing in the shadows of the smoky hall, watching them go, his animosity for her clear on his noble face.

Ian made a conscious effort not to watch the tall, regal Kara take her leave when she excused herself from Harry's private chamber to return to her rooms. He found her entirely too distracting in ways he preferred not to explore.

Kara was barely out the door before Harry jumped from his chair and began to chatter.

"I like her, don't you? My father made a good choice in marriage for me—well, for my brother," he corrected himself as if it were a small detail.

Ian couldn't help but smile. He liked to see Harry happy. After the death of his brother in battle followed only six months later by the death of their father, Harry had had little to be jovial over lately.

So great a change so quickly for such a young man. One moment he had been a younger son, living in Edinburgh with his mother, taking lessons in French and Latin, and the next moment an earl and heir to great lands and responsibility, as well as a husband. He had not been prepared as his brother William had for this position, and his age compounded his unreadiness for the task.

It was Ian's responsibility to see Harry through until he matured. Appointed by Harry's father during his brief but fatal illness, it was his responsibility to advise Harry, guide him, protect him, and mold him to be the man his lordship had known the boy could be. Though Lord Dunnane, his mother's second husband, had been Ian's stepfather, the man had been kind to him. He had given him many of the opportunities he need not have provided his wife's child and had even confessed as he neared death that he wished Ian would be next in line to inherit rather than his brother's hawkish son, Dungald.

"She's pretty, too, isn't she?" Harry continued feeding cake morsels from a plate to a hound that licked his fingers and whined.

For two hours Lord Dunnane had been meeting with clansmen in need of advice or his lordship's approval, and the boy was growing bored and tired. It was Kara who had shyly suggested a brief recess, and Ian had agreed that she was right.

"I have never seen red hair like hers, all red and golden like the setting sun."

Ian noted that his half brother's observation was accurate. Kara was indeed pretty, beautiful even, though perhaps not by the standards of the day. She was tall, neither slender nor heavy, but hardy in appearance, as if she could hold a sword if need be. Her skin was fair and slightly freckled. And her eyes were the most intriguing color, sometimes blue, sometimes green.

"My lord, you sound severely smitten with your wife," Ian teased, remaining seated, sifting through documents Harry needed to sign and set his seal upon.

Harry's face reddened at his remark but he did not address it. "It's Harry. I understand why you must call me that in front of others, but can't I just be Harry with you?"

Ian looked up from his recorder's table. "If you like, Harry. But I would suggest you not give others the same allowances. They will forget too quickly who you are and thus diminish your power over them."

"Except Kara, of course. That's all there is; away with you." Harry shooed the dog, wiping his hands on his breeches. "I may allow my wife to call me by my Christian name, may I not?"

Ian smiled again, but he felt a twitch of jealousy in his chest. What need did a thirteen-year-old have for a woman like Kara? She was the kind of woman, in different circumstances, he might have married.

"Do ye think she likes me, Ian?"

"I think she likes you as well as she can, considering she has known you less than a day," he answered more coolly than he had intended.

Harry nodded, pacing the small room. "Of course you're right. I just want her to be happy. I want her to like it here at Dunnane. I want her to like me."

Ian flipped through several documents. "Ye want her to be happy, do you? Then perhaps you should delay our mother's arrival a little longer. I don't suppose it would be possible to arrange another washed-out road?"

Harry laughed. "Mother will like Kara. I know she will."

Ian lifted an eyebrow doubtfully. "Come, now. Sign these documents. There are still men who wait to converse with you."

Harry flopped down in the chair that had been his father's only a few short months ago. "Must I? I'm tired. And I want to try my new bow." He rested his chin on the heel of his hand, a blond lock falling forward over his face. "Did you see the bow Dungald gave me as a wedding present?"

At the mention of his cousin, Ian's mood darkened. "An unusual wedding gift."

"I thought he was trying to make peace after the things he said about me not being fit to hold the title." He glanced down. "About my father."

"I am certain those were words spoken in haste in an emotional moment and soon regretted."

Harry twisted his mouth one way and then the other. "Perhaps, but I fear he doesn't like me."

Ian set down the documents to give the boy his full attention. "Harry, ye must understand that many men will not like you, if only because of who you are and what you represent."

"It shouldn't be like that."

"Nae, it shouldn't."

Harry jumped up. "I'm going to find Kara and show her the castle."

Ian rose. "My lord, your men—"

Harry passed him, fluttering one hand in a gesture Ian had often seen the previous Lord Dunnane make. "Take care of the matters or tell them to wait, I care not." He set his jaw, meeting Ian's gaze, taking a childish tone. "It's my wedding celebration and I'm going to do as I please."

Ian lowered his gaze, trying hard to keep his position in mind. Though he was Harry's adviser, he was still his servant. "Aye, my lord."

Harry pushed on the stone wall near the rear of the

chamber and a nearly invisible door swung in. He hesitated in the doorway. "Ye may come if you like. Try my bow."

"No." Ian lowered himself onto his stool again. "Take some time alone with your wife, my lord. Get to know her better. It will only serve Dunnane. Just be certain to stay inside the walls."

As Ian watched his half brother go, he could not suppress the unwelcome wish that he was in the boy's place.

Chapter Three

"This way." Harry motioned from the end of the dark passageway. "Hurry, before someone comes."

Kara glanced behind her, then at Harry, unsure of what to do. The corridor was narrow and dank and the walls sweated with moisture. It smelled of musty soil, rodents and something rotting she dared not attempt to identify.

She felt utterly ridiculous running down dark hallways following a boy, but what was she to do? He was her husband, and lord over her. He wanted her to come. And he certainly didn't belong in the catacomb of cellars beneath the castle alone. Again her mothering instinct surfaced. What if he slipped on the wet stones and injured himself? How long would it be before someone found him here?

She held up her sputtering candlestick. "Harry, I really think we should turn back."

"Nae, not yet. We're almost there," he said excitedly. "I just want you to see the nest."

She batted her lashes, glancing heavenward in a silent plea. What had she done to her father as a child that he should punish her so as an adult? Surely a woman in her mid-twenties, well into her childbearing years, should not be running about her castle in search of baby rats!

Impatiently, Harry waved the torch he carried. "Please, just a little farther. Then I promise we'll go back. We'll go to the kitchen and find a warm treat. A cup to warm your insides."

She hesitated a moment, then gave in, thinking it would be faster than standing here and arguing with him. "All right, a little farther. I will see your treasure, but then it's back to the great hall. Your men await you, my lord." She lifted a handful of her skirt, the hem wet against her stockings, and hurried to catch up with him. "You cannot take your leisure when your clansmen wait for you."

"Ye sound like Ian now. Both of you talk only of responsibility and never of fun." He stomped off ahead of her, gesturing. "Ye don't understand how hard this is for me. *He* doesn't understand. He's the big hero, fought in the war, killed men. Everyone respects him—they're afraid of him. No one respects me."

She thought to disagreee, but he was probably right, and she would not be dishonest with him.

"No one asked me if I wanted to be an earl," Harry finished.

It was on the tip of her tongue to counter that no one had asked her if she wanted to marry a child, but she did not voice her thoughts because she knew it would serve no purpose. Her situation was as it was, and she had to make the best of it. "I think I do understand how hard this is for you," she said, tempering her urge to speak as if she were his mother. "At least I understand some of it. I, too, tire of my duties sometimes."

He stopped, lifting his torch to see her face better. "Ye do?"

"Aye. But I have found that I can have both."

"Ye have?"

"With a little planning, aye. And I'm certain you could do the same. Why not set time aside for your duties to your people, and time aside for yourself and your own pleasures?"

He nodded thoughtfully. "Perhaps you're right."

She went on quickly while she had his attention. "I'm certain that your brother could help you schedule time for yourself if you express your wishes."

He grimaced. "Ian thinks of nothing but duty. He doesn't understand. He doesn't know what fun is." He studied her again, thoughtfully. "But you could make him understand, couldn't you? He would listen to you."

"My lord—"

"Harry." He stomped his foot. "Call me Harry, at least when we're alone. I don't like all that 'my lord' nonsense. It's still hard for me to see myself as the Earl of Dunnane." His voice filled with emotion. " 'Tis my father who is the earl, not me." He looked down at his fine leather shoes.

"Harry then," Kara said gently, brushing his shoulder with her hand. "I shall speak with Ian on the matter of some free time for you if you wish."

He glanced up again, his sorrow passing. "I wish it. Now come on, come see my rat's nest!" He took off into the darkness and Kara had to run to keep up with him.

"You should not have permitted him to go down there." Ian held a huge finger beneath her nose, speaking through clenched teeth.

"I should not have permitted?" Kara flared.

"Do you realize the danger of traipsing about in the darkness in those dungeons? He could have fallen and struck his head."

"I was with him to see him safe. Besides he would have it no other way. He was going with or without me. Remember, thirteen years old or nae, he is my lord and I am under his command."

Ian paced before the fireplace in the great hall, which was empty save for an elderly clansman slumped asleep in a chair pulled up to the opposite fireplace. Several of Harry's dogs dozed at his feet. "I see," he went on, obviously not hearing a word she said. His tone took on a caustic air. "You were there to catch his fall. You were there to defend him should he come upon a blade in the darkness."

She pressed her fingers to her girdle. "Come upon a blade? What are you talking about, sir?" She knew she should not speak so to her husband's brother but she would not be bullied. Not in this house. She had lived too many years under her father's bullying. "There are no knives lying about the cellars, waiting for boys to fall upon them."

"Nae." Ian whipped around, his broad face strained with barely suppressed hostility. "But there are knives in men's hands."

She opened her mouth to retort, then clamped it shut, staring at him in horror as she realized what he implied. She lowered her voice. "You mean there are men who want to see Harry dead?"

"There are always men who want to see others in power dead. It is human nature." He lowered his face close to hers. "Dead men leave land, and land is what men have been fighting over since Genesis."

Kara struggled to understand, divided by her concern for Harry and Ian's nearness. Ian made her uncomfortable standing so close to her, his breath on her face, but she didn't know why. She was certainly not afraid of him. "But Harry is just a boy. Surely no man would—"

"Just a boy whose father amassed great wealth, land and even some popularity with the king."

Kara turned away from Ian to face the crackling fire. The light and warmth spread across her face. "Is this general apprehension," she asked softly, "or do you have reason to believe someone actually plots to see him dead?"

Ian was at her side in an instant. He caught her arm,

placing pressure on her soft flesh with gripping fingers. "I speak of real men, with real daggers."

At his grim tone, she was suddenly afraid for the boy she had known only one day. She was surprised by the overwhelming urge to protect the young earl washing over her. Why did she care if the boy died? Left a widow she could return home to her father's castle or remarry, taking a small portion of Harry's monies with her. What did she care who the castle Dunnane fell to? She was not a Gordon, but a Burns from far to the west.

But she did care. She cared because she'd become quite fond of Harry in the few hours she'd known him. She cared because he was an immature boy trying to be a man, expected to be a man. She cared because she could not help but care for the sobbing child she had held in her arms last night.

The pressure from Ian's fingers on her arm made her intensely aware of how close he stood to her again. How intimately he touched her. She swallowed, the heat in her face coming from within now, rather than the flames. Something about this man made her heart beat irregularly and her stomach flip-flop.

She carefully disengaged her arm, confused by her emotions. "Ye did not tell me he was in danger from his own men," she said softly, stepping back a safe distance from him. "Does he know?"

"I have tried to make Harry understand, but I'm not sure he does. He is very innocent in the ways of the world, Kara." He chuckled, but without humor. "All that concerns his lordship right now is that his men like him . . . and his new wife."

At mention of her, she glanced up expectantly. "Me?"

He held her gaze, no laughter in his eyes. "Aye. His lordship is quite taken with you." He hesitated, as if he wanted to say something else, then glanced away.

She couldn't help but wonder what he had wanted to

say. Did he mean to say that he, too, was taken with her? "And . . . and I am taken with him."

A strange silence hung between them, at once filled with electricity like just before a storm. What was this feeling, Kara wondered, both fearful and anxious at the same time? She had never felt a bond like this with anyone before, not even her mother.

"My lady," Ian said, seeming to feel the spell and the need to break it. "We both realize that these circumstances are not the most desirable—your marriage, I mean. But, should his lordship live to adulthood, he will make a good husband. A good provider. A good father."

At the mention of children, Kara immediately thought of the way that men and women made children. Somehow, the longer she knew Harry the less she was able to imagine doing that with him, even when he grew older. Already she saw herself more as a surrogate mother, a protector, a friend, but not a wife in the true sense of the word.

"I would do anything to see him safe," she said, and she meant it. "I did not mean to encourage his foolhardiness, and it will not happen again."

"It's a fine line I walk here, my lady." Ian yet again drew closer to her.

Why was this man so set upon being so near her? Didn't he know how uncomfortable he made her? Why was he so intense? Why was she so drawn to him?

Kara could not back up. She was already too close to the fire.

"He is a boy trying to do a man's job." Ian smoothed his green woolen *leine chroich*. "I must teach him to be a man, but I cannot entirely ignore the fact that he is still a boy. What was he doing in the cellars?"

"He wanted to show me a nest of baby rats he had discovered." Just saying it out loud made her feel foolish.

To her surprise he smiled. "His lordship has a soft heart for animals. Should he want to show you baby rats again, you need only to seek me. No man would dare draw a knife with me near."

Kara's gaze lifted from his belted leine chroich to his chest, as broad as a bronze shield, to his compassionate eyes. "With that I cannot disagree."

Again he smiled, but this time the smile was not for Harry, but for her. Strangely, it warmed her to her toes.

"Very well, should we have the need to hunt rats, I will call you."

"Should you have any need," he said, full of seriousness again. "You must call me. I do not mean to fill your head with my importance, but I am all that keeps some men from killing our Harry in his sleep. Do you understand?"

Our Harry. A bond between her and Ian that could not be broken.

She folded her hands. "I understand."

"We are allies, my Lady Dunnane."

"Kara, please call me Kara, at least in private."

Again that broad smile. "Allies, *Kara.*"

"Allies."

She offered her hand and he accepted it, squeezing it in his much larger one.

Kara didn't know if it was her imagination, but it seemed that he held her hand a moment longer than he should have. And it seemed to her that she let him.

Flustered, she backed away, bobbing a half curtsy. "His lordship is in the kitchen eating cake. I'll fetch him and send him to his office."

She turned away and hurried off, feeling Ian's gaze on her back as she retreated.

"Wonderful! Wonderful!" Harry clapped his hands enthusiastically as the players brought their tune to an end. "Wasn't it wonderful, wife?" He lifted a cup of ale to his lips.

Kara forced a smile. It was late and she was tired, but

Harry had wanted her to remain at his side for the evening's entertainment after the meal, which she had barely touched. There were still wedding guests at Dunnane, and Harry insisted upon being a good host. He had served another banquet and hired traveling entertainers to juggle, sing, and recite poetry.

" 'Twas wonderful."

He grinned at her, then turned to the minstrel. "Another. Play something so my wife and I may dance."

Kara's gaze fell to her goblet, still full to the brim with wine. "No, Harry, 'tis quite all right," she said softly.

"My lord is right," Dungald interrupted loudly from two chairs down. "The earl has not danced with his lady wife all evening."

Kara's gaze met Dungald's and he smiled wickedly. She looked away.

Harry jumped up from his seat. Tonight he wore a garish purple and green cloak and matching short English breeches. "A dance, Kara. I want to dance." He held out his hand as the players stepped back from the head table and began to play.

Reluctantly she rose from her chair. Did no one but she see how ridiculous this was? She and Harry calling each other husband and wife. She seriously doubted the boy was even physically capable of being a husband.

As she took Harry's elbow and passed Ian, she realized one person in the hall saw the absurdity of her situation. Ian. Only Ian.

Harry released her elbow and clapped to the music, backing up to begin the old country dance. Kara had no chance to escape without making a scene. She rested both hands on her hips and began to dance.

She felt like a strumpet. All the men in the hall, many in their cups, began to clap and stomp. Even the servants bearing trays turned to watch the earl and his lady dance.

They were laughing at her and her boy-husband. She

could not hear their laughter, but she could feel it. Didn't Harry?

The music's tempo quickened and Kara danced faster, wishing she could melt into the floor. The hall was hot and smoky, overwhelming her with the smells of roasting meat, ale and bodies.

Harry caught her hands and spun her. He was a full head shorter than she. They looked ridiculous. She felt ridiculous.

The tune came to an end and Kara curtsied, red-faced.

"Another!" Harry shouted. "Another."

"No, my lord, really, I . . ." She didn't want to stay. She didn't want to dance with a child pretending to be a man. She didn't want to make a spectacle in front of the Gordons. She didn't want the men making fun of Harry behind his back.

"I want to dance again," Harry said, stubbornly meeting her gaze.

Yet again, like an angel from the heavens, Ian appeared between them.

"My lord," he said diplomatically, his voice intended only for the two of them, "I believe your lady wife tires. Perhaps it is time you said your good nights."

Harry set his jaw. "But I want to dance and she has to do what I say, doesn't she?"

His words startled her so that she didn't know what to say. She was thankful Ian was quicker of mind.

"She is your wife, Harry, and that relationship is more complicated than I can explain to you at this moment. Let it suffice to say that a happy wife is a happy castle, a happy lord. An overtired, cranky wife is an overtired, cranky keep and therefore an unhappy lord." He stared at Harry like a disapproving father. "Do you understand what I say?"

Harry twisted his mouth, glancing begrudgingly at Kara. "Do you truly tire?"

She exhaled, knowing they had him convinced. He would dismiss her. "Aye. I'm quite tired. I fear I have not your stamina." She fluttered her hand in front of her overheated face for effect. "Feel free to stay, my lord, but I really wish to retreat to my chambers. It's been a long day."

Harry thought a minute.

Kara saw that a few clansmen watched curiously, but no one could tell what was being discussed. The musicians had started another tune. Interest in the couple in the center of the hall was beginning to wane.

"Very well." Harry threw up his hands. "Be abed, wife. I'll come shortly."

"Yes, my lord. Thank you, my lord." She dipped a deep curtsy, not daring to look at Ian, and then made a hasty retreat before Harry changed his mind.

Kara took her leave of the hall and followed the dark corridors, carrying her own candle to her tower room. Just as she turned into the last corridor, she saw a shadow. A man appeared suddenly out of the darkness.

"My lady."

It was Dungald.

She had barely exchanged a word with him, but she already knew his voice. She pressed her hand to her chest. Her heart was pounding. He had startled her.

What was he doing here in the dark when the other men were still in the hall? What did he want?

She lifted her candle to illuminate his face. His face was handsome, but his eyes were so cold, so inhuman. Either the man had no feelings, or he kept them buried deep inside him. He was absolutely eerie in the cold darkness. "Sir."

"You return without your husband, I see."

She wanted to look away, but she didn't. She would not be intimidated. "He comes shortly."

"To your bed?"

His implication was obvious.

Her first impulse was to tell Dungald it was none of his concern. No man who was not a husband should speak to a woman of her bed. But there was something in his tone that frightened her. "Aye. He comes to my bed. I . . . I anxiously await him," she stammered.

Dungald chuckled, taking his time, studying her with his stony eyes. "Do you, now?" He put out his hand and lifted a ringlet of hair from her bosom. "And does my lady find his lordship's bed . . . adequate?"

She stiffened. "Let me pass, sir, or I shall—"

He let the curl fall. His tone took on a sharp edge. "You shall what?"

She met his gaze, her own as hard as his. "Or I shall call my husband *and* his man."

Dungald flinched.

She had found his weakness: he was afraid of Ian. She saw it in his eyes. It was only a flicker, but most definitely fear.

"I meant my lady no harm. I only asked of your comfort."

"Of course." She walked past him and did not halt until she was inside her chamber, the door latched.

Chapter Four

Kara crawled from her bed, taking care not to disturb Harry. He lay curled on his side, his back to her, snoring softly.

She'd gone to sleep as soon as she had returned to her room, but when Harry arrived near midnight she'd had to rise to unlock the door. Unable to drift off to sleep, she'd grown more restless as the night progressed. She couldn't stop thinking about her run-in with Dungald, about the boy she now slept with . . . about his brother, whom she could not get from her mind.

And she was hungry. She had not eaten when the others dined because she had been uncomfortable pretending to be the happy bride and hating herself for it. She'd hated those who forced the ruse upon her. Now she wished she'd swallowed her pride as well as some bread.

Shivering in the icy draft that crept around the closed window hangings, Kara threw a cloak over her sleeping gown and lit a candle with coals from the fireplace. She debated what to do now. Read? Stitch?

Her stomach growled. What she wanted to do was eat.

She glanced at the locked door. Dared she go down to the kitchen in the middle of the night?

Why not? Dunnane was her home now, wasn't it? She would most likely live here until she was carried out in a pine box. As mistress of the castle it was her prerogative to take food from the kitchen. She could even wake a servant and have him cook for her. She had no desire to bother anyone, though. A bit of bread and cheese would be enough.

Kara tiptoed back to her side of the bed and located the pair of French silk mules she'd left there the night before. They were a wedding gift from one of the Gordon families. She slipped her cold, bare feet into them and moved noiselessly toward the door.

She slid the lock and slipped out. Only once in the corridor did she think of Dungald. He'd accosted her here last night. Perhaps leaving her room alone at this hour was dangerous.

No, if she were truly mistress here, she'd not cower in her chamber.

She stiffened, pressed her back to the closed door and lifted her candle. If she did come upon Dungald in the darkness, she'd strike him with the candlestick. He'd keep his distance after that, wouldn't he? She peered into the darkness.

Nothing but a dark hallway.

"Don't be a goose," she whispered beneath her breath.

Hearing her own voice calmed her. Surely Dungald had not stood in the hall all night. Someone would have seen him. Whatever his reasons for wanting to torment her, she knew he wished the torment to remain private.

Boldly, Kara walked down the center of the hallway into the tower's circular stairwell. Her footfall was so loud on the stone steps that she wondered if she might wake someone on a floor below.

She pressed on.

She reached the ground floor and followed the main

corridors, still unfamiliar with the layout of the castle. Harry had told her that, like many of the castles in the Highlands, it had been constructed in stages, adding structures to the original tower, which dated back to the twelfth century. There had been an even older castle built before the tower. Some of the catacombs of rooms below ground were actually part of the ancient fortress—the same rooms Kara had passed through the day before looking for baby rats.

In a center hall she came to several portraits of unsmiling Gordon men wearing stiff ruffs around their necks. She wondered if their eyes would follow her as she passed. She held up the candle suspiciously. They did not. Something told her that she need not be wary of ghosts at Dunnane, but rather of its living occupants.

Reaching the iron and plank door to the large kitchen, she pushed through and was surprised to see light coming from around the corner. The fireplace? No, the fireplace would be banked at this time of night. It was candlelight.

"Who is it?" came a terse voice.

Kara knew that voice. Her first impulse was to bolt. But how far would she get before he caught her? Besides, what reason did she have to run? This kitchen was more hers than Ian Munroe's.

Kara turned the corner to find Ian rising from a stool pulled up to a worktable before the banked hearth. His hand rested on his dirk, which rested on the table close at hand. He had been eating. A fat tallow candle illuminated his makeshift dining table.

"It's me," she said, her voice seeming strangely intimate-sounding within the whitewashed walls of the kitchen that smelled of baked pears and cinnamon. She'd said it as if he would know who *me* was. "Kara."

He eased back onto the stool. She had surprised him; she could see it in his expression, though he covered it well. "What are you doing here?"

The sight of the crusty dark bread and rich, soft cheese

on the table was more than her grumbling stomach could bear. She set down the candlestick and reached for the bread knife to saw off a piece for herself. "I came with the same intentions as you, I see." She stuffed a bit of crust into her mouth and was pleasantly surprised to find it warm.

How intriguing. A no-nonsense man like Ian warming his bread before he ate it? So, despite his tough outer shell, he was a man who liked his simple comforts.

He sliced a bit of pungent, white goat cheese for her and pushed it across the table. "Ye should have called for a servant. A tray could be brought up. It matters not the time. You are now the Countess of Dunnane, a lady of title and rights."

She wrapped the cheese in bread and settled on the stool opposite him. Had it been day, the six-foot-long table would have been cluttered with rolling pins, biscuit cutters and piles of vegetables to be washed and chopped. Tonight it was still dusted with flour and smelled of cloves and cinnamon.

"One of those being the right not to call a servant." She bit into the warm, hearty bread, noting that Ian must have bathed before partaking of his simple meal. His inky hair was damp, and strands curled at his ears. "What of you who calls the kettle black? Surely someone could have brought you a tray. I doubt Harry would deny you anything."

" 'Tis my place to serve my brother, not use those who serve him."

She studied his massive, square-shouldered frame, exaggerated by the small stool he perched on. The man was a mountain. She was amazed by how comfortable she felt in the dark kitchen alone with him. She wasn't even at ease alone with Harry yet. "You know, you can nae keep coming to my rescue," she said softly.

He did not glance up. "Offering bread is hardly rescue."

"You know that I speak of last night. The dancing. I

was mortified to be making such a spectacle of myself. Mortified for Harry. Didn't he know they were laughing at him, at us?"

"It's my place not to serve only my lord, but my lady." He cut another piece of cheese and wrapped it in bread for her. "But to answer your question, no, he does not know."

Their fingers brushed as she took the food, and she found the physical contact strangely comforting. "Make what excuses you like for yourself. It was kind of you to handle my husband as well as you did, and I won't forget it."

Ian glanced away under her scrutiny and cut another large slice of bread for himself. "I followed closely behind you when you took your leave. I came upon Dungald at the bottom of the tower stairs. He denied seeing you, but he is a liar. Did he disturb you?"

"I find his mere existence disturbing."

Ian's mouth twitched into a smile, and she took note of what a sensual, full-lipped mouth it was. The moment the thought passed through her head she checked it. What was wrong with her that she entertained such wanton thoughts of her husband's brother?

"Humor is an admirable quality and will serve you well here. Be certain you keep it."

She smiled back. "To answer *your* question, he was waiting for me in the corridor near our chamber. We briefly exchanged words." She hesitated, feeling her cheeks grow warm. "He inquired of my bed."

Ian cursed beneath his breath as he pushed his goblet toward her. Without forethought, she lifted the cup and pressed her lips to its rim, sharing his wine.

As the cool, fruity wine touched her lips she thought of his lips touching hers. Shocked, she set down the goblet with a rattle.

Ian did not seem to notice her distraction.

"What did you say?" Ian's tone had taken on an edge but she knew he wasn't angry with her.

She tried to concentrate on the conversation. "I . . . I lied." She brushed her fingertips across her mouth but she couldn't wipe away the taste of the wine or the thought of his lips on hers. "I said I awaited my husband in bed . . . anxiously."

"Good. That was the right thing to say." He pushed the cup toward her again with one large, strong hand.

"Well, what else was I to say?" She felt a flare of irritation. "Do ye think me a fool? I understand the importance of this union. I understand Harry's need to get an heir."

"I did not mean to—"

"I should go," she interrupted, not letting him finish his thought.

Kara was no longer comfortable in the kitchen alone with Ian—not because he gave her reason to be uneasy, but because she made herself uneasy. What were these thoughts running in her head? Sweet Mary, she was another man's wife. How could she be thinking about Ian's mouth, or worse yet, his mouth on hers?

She pushed off the stool, not accepting the wine he had offered. It burned on her lips now, and the harder she tried not to think about his mouth touching hers, the more she thought about it.

Ian rose from the stool. "You must continue to give all appearances that the marriage was not only consummated, but that his lordship is bent on getting an heir. Should Dungald believe otherwise, I would not put it past him to petition to have your marriage annulled or something else equally as dangerous."

Kara took a step back as Ian came around the table. It was on the tip of her tongue to ask him what they would do as time passed and she did not become pregnant, but she didn't want to broach the subject. Not tonight. "I . . . I'll say good night."

"I will walk you up."

He was so close that she could smell his clean hair and the damp wool where it brushed his back. They were ordinary scents, but somehow on him, disturbingly pleasant.

She lifted her palm. "No. Sit and finish your meal. I can find my chamber quite well on my own." She grabbed the candle and made a quick move for the door.

Ian remained where he was. As she turned the corner, she saw him lift the goblet to his lips and brush where hers had just been. That image kept her warm all the way back to her bed.

A week later, Kara stood beside Harry, who was seated in his father's chair in the private chamber off the great hall. Beyond the closed door, she could hear men's and women's voices. Harry's hounds barked and raced back and forth outside, adding to the commotion. She could have sworn she heard the bleating of a sheep.

"You've nine matters to deal with this morning, my lord," Ian said from his stool at the desk, where he was putting documents in order.

Harry glanced at Kara and rolled his eyes. "I thought you told my brother I wished for more free time."

She patted his hand. "Aye, and free time you've been granted. After the nine cases, you've much of the afternoon to do what you please. Hunt, ride, play cards if you like. The master builder does not arrive to speak with you until four."

"If I hurry, that should give me three or four hours before I meet with the builder." He glanced at Ian and frowned. "Why am I seeing the builder again?"

"He'll be directing necessary repairs to the footing of the south wall, remember? We talked about this a fortnight ago. And I thought we would see about connecting the rooms in the tower so that you might be more comfortable now that you are a married man."

Harry shrugged and picked up a stick from his lap. With

a small blade, he whittled and flipped shavings onto the floor. "I'm comfortable enough in my father's chamber."

This was the first Kara had heard of the intended improvements for the tower bedchamber she shared with Harry, but she was excited by the idea. With the rooms connected, maybe there would be a way to discreetly sleep separately . . . only until Harry was older, of course.

Ian rose from his chair. "Aye, I'm sure you are, Harry, but a woman needs more space than a man. A place to keep her clothing, her sewing, female trappings. And should there . . . *when* there are children," he corrected himself, clearing his throat, "you will be in need of a nursery. Your wife should also have a maid at her disposal. A girl could sleep in the small room at the end of the hall."

Harry gave a snort. "My mother was satisfied enough with the master bedchamber."

"If you recall," Ian said pointedly, "our mother spent less than two weeks a year at Dunnane. It's not as if she resided regularly with your father."

Harry frowned, apparently trying to remember, then shrugged. "Whatever."

He flipped another wood shaving airborne and Kara considered picking it up. He was making a mess on the floor. Who did he think would clean up the shavings? "Talk to Kara. Whatever she wants." Harry jumped up and more shavings fell from his lap to the floor. He made no attempt to clean up after himself and Kara found herself annoyed. But she held her tongue. After all, it was his floor to leave untidy and his servants to bid clean it up.

"Let's go. The sooner we can get this over, the sooner I can go riding."

Ian stepped aside to allow Kara to pass. As she did, he whispered in her ear, "His is not exactly the attitude I would want the man who stood in judgment of me to possess."

She frowned in agreement. Ian was right; Harry was

acting childish in a position where he had great authority, and one he had to take seriously. "Can you listen in and advise him?"

"Aye." Ian lifted his chin. "But I see my cousin has already settled in to *advise.*"

Kara glanced up through her lashes to see Dungald seated at the table where Harry dined. Most of the chairs had been drawn away and tables had been moved to the outside walls to make way for the men who approached his lordship. Dungald was seated to the right of Harry's chair.

"Sit on the other side of Harry," Ian instructed quietly.

Kara shook her head. "Nae. It was not my intention to sit court with him. 'Tis not a woman's place—"

" 'Tis the mistress of Dunnane's place to see her people fairly judged and protected by his lordship's power."

"What good is it for me to hear the cases?" she whispered. "Harry will no more listen to me than—"

"Presently, you are one of the few he will listen to." Ian moved from behind her to beside her. "Please, Kara, just this once. Perhaps a few more times until he feels more comfortable. This is a great responsibility for such a young man."

Kara found herself watching Ian's lips rather than hearing his plea. She thought of the goblet they had shared that night a week past. She knew it wasn't rational, but how could she argue with that sensual mouth? "All right, but just this once." She raised a finger.

He flashed her a smile that was worth the concession and she glanced away, embarrassed by her pleasure at his attention. She didn't know what had come over her since she arrived at Dunnane. Where had these lustful thoughts come from? She needed to go to the chapel and pray for her soul.

Harry, as always, was oblivious.

"My lord." Dungald half rose from his chair.

"Cousin." Harry nodded, taking his position at the head

table. He looked over his shoulder at Kara. "You're staying. Good." He lowered his voice, covering the side of his mouth with his palm. "You can tell me what to say."

"I'm just here to support you," she whispered back, sitting beside him as Ian had instructed. "To see what challenges your lordship faces each day."

"I believe the Earl of Dunnane is ready to commence," Dungald said with authority he didn't possess. "Munroe, bring the first case before us."

Ian and Kara exchanged glances over Harry's head. Neither wanted to see Dungald at Harry's side, but they didn't have the sanction to dismiss him.

Ian called names. "Robert Burr and George Campbell."

A bearded man in his mid-twenties stepped from the crowd and hurried forward. He was followed by a man slightly older . . . leading a sheep.

Harry sniggered at the sight of the sheep in his hall, but had the good sense to cover his mouth.

"My lord."

"My lord."

Both men bowed nervously.

"State your business," Dungald declared, leaning back in his chair and pouring himself a cup of ale.

The two men looked at each other. The younger spoke first. "See, my ram, he wandered off, cut through a fence and got with Georgie's best ewe. When she got pregnant"—the man cut his eyes toward Kara—"excuse me, my lady." He returned his attention to the young lord. "See, when she got pregnant, we agreed we'd just share the lambs."

"But then Maddie only had one lamb," Georgie offered.

"Now's my ewe's croaked, so I think this one be mine."

"I dinna think that was fair," the older man said. "But she be half mine."

"So now what's to be done, my lord?"

Harry rose up in his chair and peered over the table at the sheep.

Kara watched his expression. She could tell he was thinking. She could also see that he wasn't certain what to say.

Dungald shrugged, sipping from his goblet. "Cut it in
half. Butcher it and be done."

Harry's face lit up. Kara looked at her husband. He
looked at her. She knew he was relieved to be offered a
solution, any solution. She also knew he wanted just to
repeat what Dungald had said and make it so. Perhaps not
because he thought it was the right decision, but because
he wanted some sort of decision. He didn't want to look
foolish.

Harry cracked his knuckles. "What would you do, wife?"
He lifted one shoulder casually. "I am merely curious."

Kara thought before she spoke. "Of course, I am only
a woman, my lord, but . . ."

"Speak on," Harry urged, leaning forward in his chair.

She flashed him a shy smile. "Your cousin's solution
would indeed work, but . . ."

"But?" Harry leaned toward her. "Aye, but what?"

Kara made eye contact with one crofter and then the
other. They were obviously poor. A sheep might seem
meager to Harry or Dungald, but one sheep could make
a great difference in the lives of these men.

"I think," she said slowly, "were it my decision, I would
see this sheep bred once it's of age Then the lambs could
be shared."

Harry's face lit up. "Then they would both get more
sheep!"

Kara lowered her gaze, not daring to meet Dungald's,
though she knew he was staring at her.

Ian moved behind her to rest one hand on the back of
her chair and one on Harry's. His presence could not
be ignored. She knew he had not missed a word of the
exchange.

"Aye. Very clever, wife. I see you and I think much alike."
He returned his attention to the crofters. "I have made my
decision. You, sir, shall keep the sheep." He pointed at the

man with the sheep on the rope. "You, sir, shall breed your ram to this sheep. When lambs are born you may share them. Keep a tally. This sheep is jointly owned by both of you until . . . till death do you part."

Kara smiled behind her hand. It was an interesting notion to use wedding vows to settle a quarrel over a sheep, but it seemed to work.

The crofters exchanged glances and nodded.

"Excellent." Harry clapped his hands together. "Next!"

Kara feared Dungald would criticize Harry's decision, and public criticism was the last thing he needed right now. She was thankful Dungald said nothing, only downed his ale.

Kara let out a sigh of relief.

Ian leaned over. "Good job," he said softly, then aloud called for the next petitioner. "Next, Isla Beattie. Bring her forward."

One of Harry's men stepped from the milling crowd, leading a young woman bound at the wrists. She was no more than sixteen years old. She was filthy, with snarled blond hair and ragged clothes. She also appeared to be well with child.

The clansman tugged on the rope that bound the girl and she jerked back on it, sending him a threatening glare.

"Step forward before his lordship," Ian announced in a clear, loud voice.

The woman walked to the head table, holding her head up proudly.

Harry shrank back in his chair and wrinkled his nose. She smelled.

"This woman was caught stealing from your own kitchen, my lord," Ian said. "She took bread, milk and apples. It's believed she has stolen before. It's only taken until now to catch her."

Harry looked at her, seemingly a little intimidated by her stare. "Did . . . did you steal from Dunnane?"

"Aye."

Harry looked startled. Kara supposed he had expected her to deny the charge.

Kara's gaze met the young woman's. She stared back in defiance. Kara's hackles immediately went up. What right did this woman have to steal from Harry? Thieves had to be punished, not only to prevent their continued thievery, but also to serve as a warning to others.

But there was something in the woman's defiant blue eyes that made Kara want to ask her why she had stolen. Where was her husband? Her father? Her family? Something told her this ragged girl had a story to tell.

"Simple enough," Dungald declared loudly with a flip of his wrist. "The punishment is routine. Cut off her hand and she'll not thieve again." He looked to Ian. "I'm in need of more ale. Fetch someone to bring it, will you, Munroe?"

Harry opened his mouth to speak. Kara feared he was going to repeat what Dungald had just said. "Harry," she whispered.

He did not seem to hear her, and panic rose in her chest. She couldn't let him cut off the girl's hand! At least not without further inquiry. But what could she do? How could she stop him without making him lose face in front of the others in the room who watched him so closely?

Kara reached under the table and laid her hand possessively on Harry's knee.

Chapter Five

Harry's eyes widened and he let out such a gasp that Ian, Dungald and Isla all stared at him.

Harry gulped, his eyes still round as plates.

"Harry," Kara repeated softly.

This time he turned to look at her. He swallowed yet again, his Adam's apple bobbing.

Perhaps in her haste she had placed her hand a little higher than his knee . . . a little too high. But what did it matter? She had what she wanted—his attention.

"Aye, Kara?" Harry's voice came out breathy.

She lowered her head to whisper. He lowered his to hear every word.

"I do not believe it is wise for a man to always bring down his fist harshly," she said, choosing her words carefully. She in no way wanted to diminish his authority or give him or anyone else the impression that she had. But she could not allow these men to cut off this young girl's hand without a fair chance to explain herself.

He nodded, his attention completely hers.

"Sometimes it is mercy that shows a man's true

strength," she continued. "You do not know why she took from your kitchen. Was it to sell your food or was it to nourish the child she carries? Why is this woman homeless and so big with child? Where is her husband? Has she been abandoned? Is she a victim of rape?"

Harry licked his lips. His face was taut with concentration. "You would not cut off the thief's hand?" he whispered.

"I would be certain it was the right thing to do."

He lifted his head, seeming hesitant to suspend their private conversation. "Woman." He used his best earl's tone of voice. "Tell me why you took from my kitchen what was not yours."

The girl stared hard at him. "It matters not, my lord, do it? Your punishment will be the same."

Dungald gave a snort of derision.

Harry glanced at Kara as if to say *Now what?* Now both women had him flustered.

Kara had to think fast. Why had the girl answered that way? Didn't she want to hold her child with two hands? Didn't she realize the chances she would take by having a limb removed? Fever, gangrene, even death?

"She is probably overwrought, my husband. Afraid. We have all said the wrong thing when we have been confused and afraid."

"I'm confused a lot," Harry confessed under his breath.

Kara couldn't resist a little smile. Ian was right: beneath the surface of this gangly boy was a good man. He needed only time to emerge.

Harry lowered his head to draw Kara further into his confidence. "What now?"

"Ask her if she has a man to speak for her, a husband or a father."

Harry sat upright again. "Have you a husband who can speak for ye?"

The woman with the wild hair gave a laugh. "Husband?

Nae. Nor father, nor brother, nor anyone who knew me as a child."

"And you will not tell Dunnane why ye stole from his coffers?" Harry demanded.

Isla's hard gaze met his and yielded. Beneath her mask of haughtiness was stark fear. "I had not eaten a meal in a great time, my lord. Not since my stepfather put me out a moon ago, big with the babe he forced into me."

There was a collective gasp from the crowd of men and women who waited to make their pleas to Lord Dunnane.

Again Harry looked to Kara for advice.

She was so appalled that she didn't know what to say.

Ian moved behind her, leaning on her and Harry's chairs. He lowered his head between them. Anyone who observed them would think he spoke to his lordship, but Kara knew his thoughts were as much for her as for Harry.

"Extenuating circumstances, my lord. You were smart to question the lass."

"What now?" Harry whispered.

"Great galloping God!" Dungald protested, striking the table with his empty goblet. "Cut the bitch's hand off and be done with it." He pressed his hands close to Harry's, demanding his lordship's attention. "Do ye want everyone to think you weak, cousin?" he hissed beneath his breath. "You set the wench free without punishment and the word will be out in days. Crofters from all of Scotland will be stealing from your larders." He spit ale with his last venomous declaration.

Harry looked to Ian. "Will they think me weak?"

Ian eyed Dungald dangerously, warning him to back off. Dungald took the warning and rocked back in his chair.

"The countess is wise, my lord," Ian said, still keeping an eye on the unruly Dungald. "I believe a man must rule with strength, intelligence and compassion. Worthy men respect compassion. It is an honorable trait seen rarely in politics these days."

Kara wanted to look up at Ian, to thank him, but for

some reason she felt she didn't dare. She didn't want him to see the respect for him she knew shone in her eyes. Respect and something else she didn't quite comprehend yet.

"Cut off her hand," Dungald repeated. Jumping up, he yanked his own dirk from his belt, his hand trembling slightly. "Hell's witness! I'll do it myself, if it pleases your lordship!"

Again those in the hall gasped.

Isla recoiled instinctively, but then held her head high. No tears welled in her eyes.

Kara brushed her hand against Harry's arm, not daring to touch him beneath the table again for fear of giving him heart failure. It had never occurred to her to touch him in a sexual way. He was just a boy, but after this she knew she would have to be more careful.

"Ye said earlier I should have a maid," she said quickly. It was a lie—Ian had said it—but she hoped Harry would remember it as his own idea.

He listened.

"Let me take the girl and clean her up and feed her. She can serve me, my lord."

Harry thought. "But she is a thief. She—"

"I will take full responsibility." Kara clung to his arm. This woman was no one to her, and yet she could not see her punished. Perhaps in some small way she saw herself in Isla's eyes. "Please, my lord, please, Harry."

Harry gazed into her eyes with adoration that both surprised and frightened Kara.

"Anything for you," he whispered.

She drew back, not sure what to make of his words, yet afraid that she did. The boy was becoming smitten with her. But she had what she wanted. That was what was important right now; the girl's hand would be spared.

"I have made my decision," Harry declared loudly. "Release the prisoner to my wife so that she may serve my household and thus repay what she has stolen."

A murmur rippled through the great hall. Sunburned faces turned to their master in wonder.

Harry's man removed the rope from the girl's grimy wrists, and she rubbed them where they had worn her skin raw.

"Would you lead her to my chamber?" Kara asked one of the clansmen quietly. "Have a tray of food sent to her and a bath drawn. Wait for me there," she told Isla. "I'll be up directly."

Isla stared with astonishment at Kara for a long moment, then dipped a low curtsy, bowing her head in reverence. "Thank you, my lady," she said humbly, her tone passionate. "My lord. I will not forget your mercy, not for all my born days."

"Weak," Dungald muttered beneath his breath as the thief was led away. "Weak mama's-tit boy—"

"Sir," Ian addressed Dungald. "Have you something to say?"

Dungald rose, lifting his upper lip in a sneer. "Nae, I've nothing to say. If you'll excuse me, I've . . . other duties to attend."

Harry gave a nod, dismissing his cousin. Either he did not recognize his cousin's sarcasm, or he didn't care. He poured himself a cup of ale and reached for a sweet biscuit Kara had ordered for him from the kitchen. "Next case, step forward."

Hours later, when Harry had completed his morning's work, Kara excused herself from the great hall to return to her chamber to see to the pregnant girl.

She met Ian on the tower stairwell. He had to have been waiting for her. He blocked her passage, one sinewy hand gripping the rope that wound up the steep staircase. He was so big in the small, cylindrical stairwell that he seemed to fill the space.

A part of Kara wanted to dart beneath his arm and race up the stairs, but a part of her wanted to stay here with him in the shadows. Be with him, hear his voice. Was it her imagination or was there a bond forming between them, a bond greater than the one related to Harry?

"God's teeth!" Ian exclaimed. "What did you do to that poor lad? Two hours later and he's still walking bow-legged."

Kara was embarrassed by his insinuation, but she couldn't resist a grin and a chuckle. "I meant only to gain his attention, not—"

"Stimulate him?" Ian teased.

Kara covered her mouth to muffle another giggle. She knew she should have been mortified. Such a conversation with her brother-in-law was entirely inappropriate. Yet with whom else could she talk about the incident? Who else could see the humor but his elder brother?

She lifted her palms to him innocently. "I assure you, I had no such intentions. I wanted only for him to hear me out."

His laughing eyes met hers. "You know my little brother has been infatuated with you since your wedding night, but now there shall be no living with him for you or me."

"For you?"

He gripped the stairwell rope. "When we are alone he cannot concentrate on his duties for declaring your attributes."

Kara ran her hand over her face, still amused. He was a child, for heaven's sake! "He does appear to be growing enamored, doesn't he? So what am I to do?"

Ian lifted a dark, bushy brow. "Do? Madam, he is your husband." He smirked.

"And a little boy," she corrected.

"Aye, but boys his age are beginning to notice women."

"I don't know what I've done to draw his attention." She rested her hands on her hips. "As soon as I realized he was watching me, I became more modest in our bed-chamber."

"The only way you can end his infatuation at this point would be to shear your hair, blacken your teeth, and take to wearing sackcloth and ashes, and even then . . ." Ian's sentence hung in the air as he reached out to brush a bit of hair from her eyes. He lowered his voice. "Even then, he would still smell your sweet skin, hear your voice, see the laughter in your eyes."

Kara swallowed hard. Ian was talking about Harry, of course, but she had the feeling he was also talking about himself. She lowered her gaze to her hem, struggling to come up with a way to change the subject, which was becoming all too personal too quickly. "I . . . I want to thank you."

"Again?" His tone was playful once more.

Another side of Ian Munroe revealed.

"For what now? Did I offer you water? Perhaps make way for you in the hall?"

"The girl. You saved her hand, perhaps her life."

"Nae, that was you." He reached out to touch her again, but pulled back and grabbed the rope instead, as if for safety. "So I thank *you*, my lady, not just for being there for the girl, but the other cases as well."

"No thanks are necessary. You were right. My duty is to my husband"—the word stuck in her throat—"and his people."

"Duty, hell. Hearing you in the hall today made me think you should be the lord of Dunnane and not my little brother."

"You embarrass me with your undeserved flattery," she said, avoiding eye contact. In her mind she could see Ian's dark brown, penetrating eyes.

"Not at all undeserved. Ye have a knack for justice, Kara. And I am greatly relieved. This was one of Harry's duties I was most concerned with." He leaned toward her, drawing her into his confidence. "I feared he was not old enough or wise enough to make life-and-death decisions for the people, but your abilities exceed my expectations."

She laughed. "Ian, let me by. I must see to the girl."

He moved to prevent her passage and she looked up. "Please let me go," she begged meaningfully.

He was immediately contrite. He stepped aside. "You've no need to fear me, Kara. I would never—"

"I am not afraid of you. I'm afraid of—" It was on the tip of her tongue to say she was afraid of her feelings for him. Feelings that were still in their infancy stage, but feelings she knew were wrong, harmful, even dangerous. But she couldn't say it.

Afraid of what?"

She passed him on the bottom stair tread and grasped the rope just above his hand. The heel of her hand brushed his knuckles, and she had a strong urge to cover his hand with hers, feel its size, its warmth, its strength.

"Kara?"

She shook her head, unable to say more. "Good day, sir." She lifted her woolen skirt and ran up the steps.

She was thankful Ian did not follow.

Kara entered her bedchamber to find Isla curled up in a chair in front of the fireplace. She looked cold, though she was wrapped in a woolen blanket, covered from neck to toe. She looked up expectantly when Kara entered the room, but did not move from the chair.

"I see you got a bath," Kara said kindly. "And did someone bring you a meal?"

Isla nodded. "Aye. Soup and bread and buttermilk." She drew the blanket closer. "I had nothing clean to put on, my lady. My skirt and shift was torn and soiled past savin'."

The girl was naked beneath the blanket; no wonder she was cold. "Let me get you something to wear." Kara knelt at the trunk at the foot of the bed and retrieved a shift and woolen stockings, followed by an old plaid skirt and a cotton bodice. She rose, the clothing bundled in one arm. "Dress in these. I'll turn away."

Isla stood and accepted the clothing. "Ye don't have to look away. My stepfather, he took away my modesty long ago."

The young woman's words were matter-of-fact, but Kara heard the pain in her tone. Her heart went out to Isla.

"How far gone are you?" Kara busied herself straightening the bedcovers, giving the girl a little privacy to cover her swollen abdomen.

" 'Bout seven months, I'm guessin'."

Kara turned to her, a blanket folded in her arms. "If you tell me where you came from I could send men to your stepfather. He should be punished for what he has done to you."

Stepping into the old but sturdy woolen skirt, Isla shook her head, her damp blond hair swinging at her shoulders. "Nae. Harm him, and me mother and little brothers would starve. What's done is done. I never want to see that Satan's son again." She glanced up quickly. " 'Scuse my words, my lady."

"Bedeviled is right," Kara said.

Isla met Kara's gaze and grinned. She picked up her filthy clothes left in a pile near the bathtub at the hearth. "What should I do with these?"

"Toss them in the fire. Burn them with your past."

Isla hugged the dirty clothes. "Ye got a good heart, my lady."

Kara turned back to the bed. "I thought you could help me dress, do a little sewing for me, for my husband."

Isla tossed the clothing in and watched the flames flare up. "Pardon me for bein' so bold as to ask, but why are you married to that boy? Was it my choice I'd take the big bear man who was standin' behind his lordship."

Kara didn't dare face the girl for fear Isla might read something in her expression. "Ours was an arranged marriage," she said. "We were wed only last week."

Isla nodded, looking around the small, cozy chamber. "So ye want me to sleep on the floor? I could pull my pallet right up here to the fireplace. I won't disturb you and your lordship." She covered her ears. "I don't hear nothin' once I'm asleep."

Kara laughed. "Have no fear of hearing anything." She didn't know what made her make that comment. She had told Ian she would keep their lack of consummation a secret. But somehow Kara knew Isla would not betray her. Something told her that she would find a friend in Isla.

Isla chuckled. "Ye need not say more. My lips are sealed." She ran one finger across her full, rosy mouth. "There's a builder coming. The other two chambers on this floor will be joined. You can sleep in the small one."

"Anything ye wish, my lady. I told ye: I'm grateful."

The bedchamber door opened and Harry burst in. "Kara! Ye have to come out. Ian's going to let me fly his best hawk." He ran to her and took her hand.

Kara didn't know what to do. He'd never been so bold before. Had he taken the wrong meaning from her actions this morning, or was he just an excited boy?

"Won't you come?" He tugged on her arm.

"Aye, let me grab my cloak."

As Kara reached the door with Harry, she turned to Isla. "I've some wool there to spin if your hands are idle. I won't be long."

"I'll be fine here by the fire," Isla said. "Ye go with your husband and pay me no mind. A woman needs to spend time with her new laird."

Isla said all the right things, but when the women's gazes met, the young girl winked mischievously, and Kara smiled as she let Harry lead her out the door.

It felt good to have a woman to confide in.

Chapter Six

"How many head stolen?" Harry cracked a chestnut with a small wooden mallet and picked the meat from the shell.

After the evening meal, Kara, Harry and Ian had gathered in front of the fireplace to relax before retiring. This had become their regular routine, and Kara looked forward to it each day. She found it awkward being alone with Harry in their private chamber before bed, but here with both men she was comfortable, almost content. Tonight she had roasted chestnuts on the hearth and placed them in a bowl to be shared by all.

"At least three dozen head," Ian intoned. He sat straddling a straight-backed chair, his back to the fireplace, watching Harry struggle to crack another nut. "We ignored the first dozen or so; my guess is that they came back for more."

Chewing with great gusto, Harry thrust out his hands to Kara. "Can I have some more nuts?"

"Ye think it's the same thieves?" She passed another handful to her husband.

Near the fireplace it was warm and cozy, and the air smelled of roasted chestnuts. Shadows cast by the blaze on the hearth danced on the stone walls of the great hall, making the lighted space she shared with the two men seem intimate and far removed from the rest of the castle.

"Aye, it's the same rogues. That I'm sure of. They're bold as Satan himself," Ian said with disgust. "They butcher a cow where she stands and take the choicest cuts, leaving the rest to rot on the ground."

"I don't like men stealing my cattle." Harry tapped on a nut, but the shell didn't break. "We can't let them steal my cattle, can we?"

Ian took the nut from his brother and cracked it in his palm. He handed the broken nut to Harry. "Nae, we cannot tolerate cattle reivers at Dunnane. They will only grow bolder as the season passes. This time they took from far afield, but next time it might be from our own paddock."

Kara lowered the red wool stocking she was knitting for Isla to her lap. "What must be done?"

"We've little choice but to go after them. We must round them up like the swine they are." Ian cracked another chestnut and passed it to Kara. "They can surrender and take their chances with the sheriff or hang where they stand."

Kara popped the warm nut into her mouth. For the last half hour her husband had been eating nuts she had roasted for him, yet he had not offered her one. Ian had not eaten a single nut before first cracking one open for her. She knew the difference was only that Harry was still young. When did children not think first of themselves? She knew it was a minor incident, but Ian had thought first of her and it felt good. No one had ever put her first before.

"We hang them ourselves?" Harry asked, wide-eyed. "I've never seen a man hang." He chewed excitedly. "Once I wanted to go to a hanging in Edinburgh but

Mother wouldn't permit it. She said it would give me nightmares.''

Ian's and Kara's gazes met. His mouth twitched into a smile; then it was gone as quickly as it had come. She hid her smile behind her hand. It wasn't even that amusing—the great Earl of Dunnane's mother controlling his actions for fear of nightmares. It just struck Kara as funny, and Ian as well, apparently.

"Aye, 'tis not a pleasant sight, one I would wish upon no one," Ian told Harry stoically. "But justice must be served, else there would be anarchy in these hills. Hanging is the price a man pays for stealing another man's livelihood.''

"Hanging? Who are we hanging?" Dungald entered the circle of firelight as if appearing magically.

Kara had not heard him approach nor seen his shadow. Not even Harry's dogs in the entryway had stirred. She wondered if Dungald had sneaked up on them on purpose. What could he possibly be hoping to hear by eavesdropping?

"We were talking about the cattle thieves," Harry told his cousin. "I think it's time we go after them."

"Do ye, now?" Dungald perched on the arm of Harry's chair, placing himself between Kara and the other men.

"I received word as to where it's believed they're camped," Ian advised.

He cracked another nut in his palm, and Kara noticed that his movements were stiffer. He had been relaxed a moment ago, but now the muscles in his neck stood out and he gripped the mallet more tightly. She realized now that Ian was always on guard in Dungald's presence.

"Want to go, Dungald?" Ian did not look up. "You always enjoyed a little bloodshed."

"I want to go." Harry jumped from his chair, sending nutshells skittering across the floor.

Annoyed, Kara lowered herself to her knees and began to retrieve the shells, dropping them into her skirt. She knew she must speak to Harry about constantly making messes for others to clean, but she hadn't yet found the right time. Here in front of his cousin and Ian was not the right time.

"Leave those, Kara," Ian said absently. "I'll get them." He looked to Harry. "No, ye should stay here . . . with your wife," he added as an afterthought.

Harry rested his hand on his hip petulantly. "They're stealing my cattle. I should go, too. I want to go. I'm the earl and I'm in charge. I can go if I want."

Her husband sounded as if he were on the edge of a temper tantrum, and Kara found it rather unbecoming. Harry was too old to be behaving like this, his responsibilities too great. But wasn't that like a boy his age, mature one moment, childish the next?

Dungald settled into Harry's chair, the chair that had been Harry's father's. Dungald crossed his leg over his knee, leaning his head back to relax as if the brocade-upholstered chair was his rather than Harry's. "Aye, let the boy go if he wants. He's right. They are his thieves, too."

Ian eyed Dungald, warning him to back down. He returned his attention to Harry. "For safety reasons, I believe it would be wise for you to remain here, my lord. We may be gone overnight and be forced to camp. And our mother is scheduled to finally arrive tomorrow. You should be here to greet her."

"You're always telling me I need to make decisions." Harry strutted back and forth before the stone hearth that was as long as a dining table. "Then when I do make decisions, you tell me they're the wrong ones."

Kara moved behind Ian to dump the shells into the fire. "I believe Ian is right, Harry," she said quietly. " 'Twould be safer if—"

"Safer!" Dungald exclaimed. "Christ's bones, he'd be better guarded if he stayed attached to his mother's tit, too! But if the boy wants to be a man, let him be a man!"

Ian rose from the chair, gripping its back in an obvious attempt to control his anger. "Dungald, that language is not appropriate before Lady Dunnane."

"It's all right," Kara murmured. She was flustered, not because of Dungald's language, but because Ian had spoken for her, not Harry. She was embarrassed for her husband. "My father used far worse in my presence."

"It's not right," Ian said. He glanced at Harry, who was occupied picking through the bowl of nuts looking for the biggest. "My lord, it's not fitting."

Harry sighed. "Dungald, shut up," he threw over his shoulder.

Surprisingly, Dungald sat back in the chair and was silent.

Harry turned to Ian. "What would my father do?"

Ian did not hesitate. "Your father would tell you to remain at Dunnane with your new wife, greet your mother, and see to your duties. He would tell you that your men could take care of this small annoyance whilst you dealt with more formidable matters."

Kara smiled to herself. She knew that what Harry was asking was what his father would do in his place, not what his father would tell him. Ian was clever. Very clever.

Harry took the last nuts in his hand and pitched them into the fireplace. "You never want me to have any fun!" he snapped. "Fine. Go round up the thieves yourselves. But if you get to hang anyone, bring him to Dunnane. I always wanted to see a hanging." He stomped out of the light. "I'm going to bed. You coming, Kara?"

She turned her head to reply, but unintentionally caught Dungald's gaze.

He lifted a bushy, black eyebrow questioningly. He said nothing, and yet the lascivious look in his eyes said so much, as if he was thinking of her naked body in bed with Harry and he wished it was himself instead. The idea of it sickened her.

"Aye," she snapped, whipping away from Dungald. She

wanted to say something to him, but what could she say? A woman could not make accusations against a man for thoughts. "I'm coming, my lord," she called to Harry.

"Sweet dreams," Dungald mocked as she passed him. "Don't stay awake too long. Get plenty of rest."

Kara followed Harry, ignoring Dungald when what she really wanted to do was hit him so hard that she wiped the smirk from his face.

"I should think you'll be comfortable enough in here," Kara said, covering a pallet with a wool blanket.

Isla hung in the doorway. "I never had no room to my own," she said proudly.

"There's no fireplace, of course, but the stone from the fireplace in the next room should heat this one just fine."

Isla tugged on an old shawl Kara had given her. "I'd say I'll be more than warm, my lady. Some nights in my cottage, ice would form in the water bucket."

Kara smoothed the blanket on the bed. "And when your baby comes, we'll get you a cradle to put right there." She pointed to the corner of the room. "That way the babe will be close at hand in the night."

"I can't say words to thank ye," Isla said.

"Ye needn't thank me. Just serve Dunnane well." She walked past her, touching her arm as she went by. "Harry has ordered a door cut between each of the three rooms so they'll all be connecting. When your labor comes, I'll only be in the next room. You have only to call out."

Isla leaned against the doorjamb, her brow furrowing. "Ye mean ye won't be sleepin' with his lordship in the master bedchamber?"

Kara hesitated. She glanced up the short hallway. The tower was the Earl of Dunnane's private chambers, so there were rarely servants about. There was never any reason for anyone to be here on the third floor of the tower unless they had direct business with the lord or lady of the manor.

"If you're to be my handmaid, I suppose you will know much of my private affairs anyway," she said softly. She paused and then continued. "His lordship has a great deal on his mind presently, and I just think he would be more comfortable sleeping alone."

Isla's rosy lips turned up in a sly smile. "I wouldn't tumble with no boy his age either," she said. "I got a brother, Timothy, the same in years, and he wouldn't know a woman's teat if he fell over one." She crossed her arms over her bosom, her tone softening. "But he'll grow up soon enough, your earl, I warrant you that."

Kara lowered her gaze. "I would ask that you not mention this to anyone else, nor refer to the situation to his lordship."

"Ain't nobody's business," Isla chimed in. "Nobody's but yours and the earl's." She ran a finger over her rosy lips to seal them. "That ain't nobody's business. Not that nor anything else. Me, I don't know nothing that goes on here, nothing that goes on in this whole castle for that matter."

Kara smiled. The girl might be a thief, a liar, maybe even a harlot if her sad tale wasn't true, but somehow she knew Isla would not reveal her secret. Woman's intuition.

"Well," Kara said. "Why don't you go through that basket of cloth and see what can be salvaged for making new garments? I'm going to go find Harry and see what he wants prepared for the evening meal. His mother is expected today."

Isla frowned. "Mistress, his lordship, he done rode off an hour ago. I seen him myself from the window."

"Rode off?" Kara's heart tripped. She was supposed to be keeping an eye on Harry while Ian was gone. He and Dungald and a dozen men had ridden off at dawn to round up the cattle reivers. They were not expected back until tomorrow. "Rode off with whom?"

"Rode off with nobody. With himself."

Kara stood for a moment in indecision and then bolted for the door. She ran down the stairs and into the great hall, where she found several of Dunnane's men gathered about one of the fireplaces playing cards. "You, sir," she called to the nearest man. A small but muscular man with a short-trimmed beard turned to her. She recognized him as the same man who had brought Isla to Dunnane's hall.

"Me?"

"What is your name?"

The clansman looked away from her in obvious disregard. He glanced at the other men, amusement on his face.

Kara was suddenly aware that she was alone in the castle without the protection of Ian. Even when he wasn't in the room, his presence in the castle made her feel safe. No clansman would look at her with such disregard in Ian's presence.

She spoke louder. "Rise and give me your name, sir."

He rose from his chair, but took his time. "Gilean McClean, my lady." He bowed, but his movements were exaggerated, mocking.

"McClean, I am in need of assistance. I would ask that you have a horse saddled for me and one for yourself as well. I'm in need of an escort."

" 'Tis not safe for you to go riding, my lady."

"I do not wish to take a leisurely ride. The earl has gone out unescorted and I must find him."

"Pardon, my lady," McClean said entirely too casually, "but my orders were to remain within the walls of the castle."

"Even if I order differently?"

His dark-eyed gaze met hers defiantly. "Even if the Lady Dunnane orders me so."

She dropped one hand to her hip, her temper rising. She didn't have time for this nonsense. Harry had left the castle unescorted. There were a thousand dangers for a boy riding alone. Anything could happen; he could fall from his mount, he could be robbed, he could even accidentally come upon the reivers. "These orders were given by whom?" she demanded.

"From the master."

Kara immediately thought of Ian. But of course Ian wasn't the master of the household. Harry must have told the men to stay put. Of course it was Harry. He wanted no one to follow him. "Lord Dunnane may have told you to remain behind," she said carefully, not wanting to discredit her husband before his men. "But he is young and impulsive. He doesn't realize the dangers—"

"It was his lordship's wish, my lady."

"You heard him speak these words yourself?"

He lowered his gaze. " 'Twas Dungald Gordon who spoke to me directly, but 'twas the earl's order, to be sure."

She glared at McClean. The earl's order? She doubted it. It was more likely that Dungald knew Harry wanted to go with the men so badly that he suspected he might try to follow them. She guessed Dungald had given that order in Harry's name. Dungald might even have encouraged Harry to follow them.

"Sir, I demand that you see two horses saddled and that you escort me north in the direction my husband, the Earl of Dunnane, has taken."

The Scotsman shifted his weight from one leather boot to the other, lowering his gaze. "Again, my apologies, my lady, but I must not disobey. 'Twould be a flogging I'd get for my troubles. Perhaps 'twould be better if you returned to your quarters and—"

Kara swore under her breath as she turned away. Didn't anyone here understand the danger of the young heir riding out alone? Didn't they care? If the other men in the room served Dungald like McClean, perhaps not.

She ran out of the hall. If no one would ride out after Harry with her, she would blessed well ride alone.

Chapter Seven

"Isla, I cannot allow you to ride in your circumstances," Kara said, tightening her mount's girth.

Isla threw a saddle over the other horse in the same stall. "My circumstances! I mean no disrespect, mistress, but my circumstances ain't kept me from workin' in the fields nor scrubbin' floors on my hands and knees till they ache."

Kara stood in debate as her stubborn young companion continued to saddle the horse. If Isla didn't accompany her, she would have to ride alone. She had been unable to find any other man in the castle willing to escort her. The stable boys would not even saddle the horses. Apparently anticipating her attempted departure, Dungald had passed word to everyone in the household that the Lady Dunnane was not to be aided in any way. What he had not anticipated, she guessed, was that she would dare ride alone.

"Isla, really, I can go myself," she argued lamely.

"Ride where?" Isla caught her mount's reins and led it out of the stall. "Ye told me yourself you're not from here. Me, I know these hills like I know my lye-burned hands.

Now come on with ye, mistress, time's a'wasting. We got to find the young sir before he's hurt or lost."

Kara's gaze met Isla's. The girl was right. There was no time to waste. Harry was Kara's responsibility and she had to find him. "Have you got the supplies?" Kara followed Isla out of the barn.

The women walked past the gawking stable hands. None of them dared try to stop them from departing, but no one dared help them mount either.

"I got the food, blankets and some other things I thought we might need. If we don't make it back tonight, we'll be cold and hungry by nightfall." Isla walked to the closest fence and used the lower rail to climb astride.

Kara did likewise, mounting her horse. She was thankful she had dressed sensibly in boots, two woolen skirts and one of Harry's heavy riding coats. Though it was April and the sun was warm on her face, spring came harshly in the Highlands. Should they be out after dark, she would be thankful for the weight of the wool clothes and the thickness of her knitted stockings.

Once astride, Kara reined the horse around and started in the direction Isla had seen Harry go, praying she would find the boy before trouble found him.

By luck and the aid of a few scattered hoofprints, Kara and Isla came upon Harry late in the afternoon. He sat on a rock, huddled under his cloak, dejectedly hitting stones into the air, using a tin whistle as a baton. His horse was nowhere to be seen.

Relief washed over Kara as she saw from a distance that the boy was unhurt. He was missing his bonnet, his cloak was torn and his brow was swollen, but he was safe.

She rode up to him and dismounted on her own when he didn't offer his hand. "Harry, are you well?"

The boy stood and kicked at a stone, his eyes downcast. "I couldn't find them. Ian said they were coming this way.

The reivers are supposed to be camped right around here. I even found lots of tracks." He twisted his mouth. "But I couldn't find them. Then my stupid horse stumbled and I fell and hit my head." He touched his brow. "Then he ran away."

Kara reached out to gently wipe the dried blood from above his lordship's eye.

He flinched. "Ouch. That hurts, Kara. Don't."

Isla walked up beside her. "Water, my lord?" She offered a skin bag she'd wisely packed.

"Thank you. I've been dying of thirst. I forgot water." He lifted one shoulder as he drank from the skin. "Usually someone brings water for me when I travel."

Kara watched the boy drink greedily. Now that she knew he was safe, her fear was turning to irritation. "You should not have left the castle, Harry. Do you know how dangerous it is for you to be out here alone?"

He wiped his mouth with the back of his hand. "I just wanted to see the cattle reivers. I just wanted to go with Ian. But he doesn't want me with him."

"That's not true. But your brother's first priority is your safety." She turned and walked away. This was not the place to have this conversation, not here in front of Isla. When they got home, when Ian returned, the three of them would sit down and discuss Harry's making wiser choices concerning his safety. "Come. You mount up behind me and we'll start back for Dunnane. It will be getting dark soon."

"Mount behind you?" Harry frowned. "You're my wife. You mount behind me; better yet, ride with your maid." He tapped his undeveloped chest. "I'm the lord of the keep. I should ride alone."

Kara eyed him as she would any insolent boy. "Ye've lost one mount today, sir. I think one is sufficient, don't you?" She brushed past him, grabbing her horse's reins. Without glancing back, she walked to the rock he'd been sitting on and used it to give herself a boost into the saddle.

Isla mounted her own horse.

"Ye riding or walking, Harry?" Kara asked impatiently. She'd had enough of Harry's immaturity and lack of respect for her and the others who depended on him. She understood that she couldn't expect from a thirteen- year-old what she could from a man, but she expected him to at least attempt to behave maturely.

"You, girl." He pointed his finger. "Move forward and I'll ride behind you."

Isla reined in her horse. "Isla, my name is Isla, my lord."

Harry ran and leaped up behind Isla in the saddle.

"Nice mount," Isla said.

Harry grinned. "Thank you."

"Have you any clue where your horse went?" Kara asked, scanning the horizon. She was tired and hungry and wanted to start for the keep, but she couldn't leave a valuable horse behind without attempting to search for it.

"He just ran off," Harry declared with a sweep of his hand.

"How far up?"

"Here."

"Here?" She turned back, riding up beside Isla's horse. She stared incredulously at her husband. Harry's story was getting better by the moment. "Your horse threw you and you didn't start back for the safety of your castle walls?"

"Well, I certainly wasn't going to walk!"

"Ye weren't going to walk?" she spit angrily. "You were just going to sit here and wait for the wolves to devour—"

An explosion of pounding hoofbeats came from behind, taking them by complete surprise. As Kara sharply reined her horse around, she prayed it was Ian and Harry's men, but her hope was short-lived.

The riders who quickly surrounded them were rough men with haggard faces, weighed down heavily with fire-arms. Their mounts were dressed for traveling with blanket rolls and saddlebags.

The cattle thieves, she thought.

"Look what we've found, lads." A wild-bearded redhead rode directly up to Kara.

Kara backed her horse up a little within the confines of the circle, trying to shield Harry. Her gaze met the leader's. It was odd, but she wasn't really afraid, not for herself, at least. She feared only for Harry and Isla. She lifted her chin. "Move aside, sir, and allow us passage."

His broad face widened in a grin. He was probably a handsome man beneath the shaggy beard. "Allow you passage? Ye speak as if we detain ye, my lady, when we but attempt to greet fellow travelers." He spoke like a gentleman, odd for a thief.

"Have you any idea who I am?" Harry declared loudly.

Out of the corner of Kara's eye she saw Isla elbow Harry so hard that it took the wind out of him. He bent forward with a gasp.

"We're bound for home sir, and in a hurry. Unfortunately we haven't the time for fellow travelers."

The redhead's gaze shifted from Kara to Harry, then back to Kara. "Who is he?"

Kara held the man's gaze. "An insolent brother who knows not when to keep his mouth shut."

The man stared hard at her for an instant, then tipped his head back in jovial laughter. "Clever, ye are quite, my lady . . . whoever you are." The redhead passed his reins to one leather-gloved hand and offered her the other. "Robert the Red, my lady, at your most humble service."

Kara didn't want him to know who they were for fear they would take them for ransom or worse. The Earl of Dunnane would certainly bring a high price, in the right man's dungeon.

"A pleasure to meet you, Robert the Red," she replied. Every muscle in her body was tense. Every fiber of her being was focused on getting Harry away from these men. "Now I beg you, allow us to pass." She lifted her reins. "I must be getting my little brother home."

He leaned forward, drawing unacceptably close to her.

"Who are you?" he cajoled softly. "For surely you are the bravest, most beautiful traveler I have ever encountered in the Highlands."

"I'm a woman who, should she not return in a timely manner, will have an angry husband," she lied smoothly. "An angry, violent, vengeful husband."

He sat back in his saddle, chuckling. "I must tell ye, you are the most refreshing—"

"Riders!" one of the men in the band cried in warning. "To the north!"

The other riders immediately reined south in alarm, but Robert the Red did not react. Instead he sighed. "Alas, I suppose I must be off. Your husband, mayhap?" He lifted one red brow.

"I'm quite certain."

"Well, give Ian my best," he said, reining his mount around. "And do get your young husband abed before he takes ill . . . Lady Dunnane."

Kara gasped. He knew who she was. Who Harry was. "You will not get away with stealing our cattle," she hollered after him as he broke into a gallop.

He lifted his plaid bonnet from his red head and waved it in salute. "Until we meet again, my lady. 'Tis been a pleasure."

The cattle reivers thundered off in a stampede of flying grass and pounding hoofbeats. What seemed like only seconds later, Ian appeared out of the brush to the north, followed by Harry's men. They shot past Kara, Isla and Harry.

"Ian!" Harry cried, waving his hands. "Wait! I want to come with you!" He waved wildly as they crashed past them. "Ian, wait!"

"Phewee!" Isla remarked, brushing her brow. "I thought we was mutton stew there for a minute." She turned to Kara in the saddle. "But I'd put ye up against cattle reivers any day, mistress."

A single man turned back from the riders from Dunnane. It was Ian. He could be mistaken for no other purely by size.

"Are you all right?" Ian shouted, riding hard toward them. His question was meant for all three of them, but his gaze was fixed on Kara.

She felt a flush of heat. Her heart gave a little kick. Heavens, she was happy to see him.

"We're fine," she said, trying to keep her voice calm. Though now that the danger had passed she could feel her body trembling. Those men could easily have cut all three of them down and they would have been defenseless. "Harry . . . his lordship," she corrected, "attempted to ride after you. His horse threw him. We found him and were returning to Dunnane."

Ian leaped from his mount and charged toward them. "Ye let him leave the castle walls unescorted!"

Her eyes narrowed. She was not in the mood for this. "I am not my husband's keeper, sir."

The moment the words came out of Ian's mouth he regretted them. He'd just been so damned scared when he saw Kara alone amidst the cattle thieves. She could have been kidnapped, raped or even murdered. He knew his first thought should have been for his liege, his little brother, but as they'd cleared the ridge and he had seen Kara's bright hair rippling in the wind from beneath her cap he had thought of nothing but reaching her, driving the thieves off. He had thought of nothing but drawing her into the safety of his arms.

The moment his gaze met Kara's he knew he was in trouble.

"He is the lord of the keep," she shot back angrily. "And I am only his wife. I have no authority to lock him in his chamber!" Her blue-green eyes flashed in challenge.

He couldn't help but admire her. Because of his sheer size and reputation, both real and imagined, there were few men bold enough to provoke him in the best of times.

Ian sat back on his heels at arm's length from her. She put out her hand to dismount and he rose to help her.

"Ye should have known he would try to follow you," she chastised. "He thinks the sun rises and sets on you. He would follow you to the gates of hell."

Ian lifted her easily down from the saddle and was caught between wanting to feel her on his arm just one moment more and wanting to get as far from her as possible. He had little experience with women, at least women of Kara's station. And he'd certainly never met a woman with this kind of fire in her heart.

"Harry, are you all right?" Ian released Kara's hand, stepping away.

Harry jumped down off Isla's horse. "I'm fine. I was just about to run the thieves off when you came upon us," he boasted, throwing back his thin shoulders.

Kara stared at him, shocked by his bold-faced lie.

Surprising all three of them, Harry offered his hand to help Isla down. "Where have my men gone?" Clasping Isla's hand, he looked in the direction the men had ridden in. "Are they coming back?"

"Dungald and our men will catch up with the thieves. They'll not get away."

"You think not?" Kara, too, looked in the direction the men had gone. "Ye think Robert the Red won't outsmart him?"

Ian turned sharply. "So it is old Rob." His brow furrowed. "How did ye know?"

"He told me," she said tartly.

Ian almost smiled. He didn't know why. Her tone just caught him off guard. Amused him. She caught him off guard often.

He cleared his throat. " 'Twill be dark soon. I fear it's not safe to travel until morning. I know a place we can camp."

"Camp!" Harry exclaimed excitedly, taking the water

skin from Isla's saddle. "I've been wanting to camp out. Shall we cook our meal over the fire?"

Ian snatched the water skin from Harry's hand and took a long pull. The last thing he wanted to do after a hard day of riding in circles in pursuit of the cattle thieves was to stay awake all night watching over women and children. He wiped a droplet of water from his mouth with his sleeve. "I should like to roast you over the fire right now, little brother," he said under his breath.

"Aye," Kara said softly, her words meant only for Ian as she brushed past him. "But I should like the first opportunity."

Ian threw back his head and laughed long and hard. Perhaps this would not be such a bad night after all. . . .

Chapter Eight

Daylight was failing over Kara's left shoulder as she rode behind Ian up the hill to the castle ruins. "How beautiful," she breathed, reining in to take full advantage of the better view.

Only half the stone curtain wall of the thirteenth-century castle remained; two of its four lofty towers had crumbled to the ground. The massive granite walls were jagged in places, blackened by smoke and weathered by time. The enormous structure stood as merely a shell of what it must have once been. Yet still it was a spectacle of grace and power against the backdrop of dusk.

"What strength this fortress must once have possessed," she mused quietly, fearing the sound of her voice would somehow lessen the castle's nobility.

"Aye." Ian's voice was strangely reverent as well. "I thought the same myself when first I laid eyes upon her. She is called Barclay. Some say she was once held by clansmen to Robert the Bruce. Her size and fortitude were once said to be rivaled by none but the Bruce's own castle, Kildrummy, up the road a piece."

Kara could hear Isla and Harry chattering away as they came up the path behind them. Lost in their conversation, they took no notice of the beauty of the castle ruins.

"We'll sleep here tonight?" she asked. She was no longer angry with Ian, only weary and eager to dismount and stretch her tired legs.

"Aye. From the top of the hill we can hear and see anyone who approaches. The walls will offer some shelter from the winds."

"Do you expect our men?"

"Nae. If Dungald has not returned by now, he's still on the chase. I gave him orders to rendezvous at Dunnane on the morrow. At dawn's first light we'll head home, for surely there are those who worry for his lordship's safety."

Kara clamped her hand over her mouth. "Oh, no, your mother. She's arrived at Dunnane with no one to greet her but Harry's hounds."

He smiled lazily. "Have no fear; our dear mother is probably sitting before the fire in the great hall as we speak, eating and drinking our finest port."

Kara hunched her shoulders and shivered. "Don't say fire. I'm chilled as it is."

He whipped off his woolen cloak with one smooth motion.

"No, it's all right. I'll be warm soon enough."

Ignoring her protest, he backed his mount and laid his mantle gently over her shoulders. "Nonsense. Surely you don't think your husband will offer his."

Kara wanted to protest. It was unseemly for her to be wearing her brother-in-law's cloak. But it was so warm. And it smelled so good, of hickory smoke and him. She lowered her gaze. "Thank you."

Isla and Harry overtook them on the path that led upward to the castle's dry moat. "God's teeth! Look at the size of that gatehouse," Harry said, still riding behind Isla. "Can we explore it?"

"Aye." Ian nodded. "But take care with your footing.

It will grow dark soon, and I've no desire to fetch your broken body from the dungeon below."

Harry grimaced. "Gads, you worry too much, brother."

"I'll keep an eye on him for ye, mistress," Isla said as the two rode by.

The young girl winked and Kara smiled.

"They seem to have taken to each other," Kara remarked as she and Ian started up the hill again, at a pace slower than Isla's. "I'm surprised. I would think his lordship and a pregnant serving woman would not have much in common."

He shrugged his massive shoulders. "Aye, but remember they're much closer in age." He glanced at her when he said it, his face lined with regret. "I did not mean to say—"

She lifted her brow, amused. "That I was an old crone in my husband's eyes?" She laughed merrily, waving one hand. "I know exactly what you meant. I take no offense. It's true enough. There is too great an age span between us presently. You know it and I know it." She watched Harry and Isla dismount at the imposing gatehouse. "And my guess is that he knows it, too. He's just trying to be gracious, now that he's burdened with me."

Ian sighed heavily. "I sometimes question the wisdom of my father."

" 'Twas pure politics. The Gordons and my father's family have been marrying for hundreds of years. We're said to be good breeders." She chuckled, her tone dry. "Little good that will do either of us anytime soon."

Kara was surprised when he made no response to her joke. A moment ago he had seemed to be enjoying their conversation. Now he was suddenly silent, hunched over his mount as if she had said something wrong. Ian didn't seem to be a man of proprieties, but perhaps she had crossed the line with him this time. But how could she know, if he didn't say?

And men said women were moody.

Kara frowned as a full minute passed and still he spoke
not a word. "I think I'll find a good place to start a fire,"
she finally said, choosing not to question him over his
sudden change in humor. Maybe it was better that he
remained distant from her, anyway. Distant was safe.

"Isla packed some bread and cheese and apples," she
continued, "though I don't know what Harry expects us
to roast. He brought nothing but a tin whistle." She trotted
her horse past Ian, through the gatehouse, into the courtyard. Her horse's footfall fell hollowly over the ancient
cobblestones.

She glanced over her shoulder at Ian but he did not meet
her gaze. "I'll call you when we've a fire and something to
eat."

He nodded but did not speak, his face shadowed by the
deteriorated ceilings that yawned over their heads some
three stories into the darkening sky.

Kara turned away, shaking her head at the vagaries of
men.

"I believe that was one of the best meals I've had since
returning to Dunnane," Harry declared, lying back on
Ian's bedroll as he patted his stomach.

After their arrival at Barclay, Ian had surveyed the area,
making sure they were alone. Then he had ridden off
toward a copse of trees half a mile from the castle gatehouse. Less than an hour later, he had returned with three
partridges on a string, a feast for hungry travelers.

Isla had cleaned the partridges and set them to roast
over the open fire Kara had built against a wall in the area
that must have once been the great hall. By the time the
sun fully set and they were surrounded by velvet darkness,
the birds were cooked and they were supping on poultry,
bread and cheese.

Kara finished the last of a piece of partridge and tossed
the bones into the fire. She accepted the water bag Isla

offered. "Thank you for thinking to bring the food," she told the girl. "Remind me not to go anywhere without your clever practicality."

The girl spread out her own bedroll across the fire from Harry. "Can you play us a tune, your lordship?" She eyed Ian. "Unless ye think it unwise. I wouldn't want to draw unwanted attention."

Ian rose from where he crouched by the fire. "There's no one for miles."

Harry sat up, pulling his whistle from inside his cloak. Isla drew closer to the fire to watch him through the dancing flames. "Do play then, my lord. Your skills are quite good."

If Kara hadn't known better, she would have thought Isla was smitten with her husband. Not that she cared as long as no proprieties were broken. If Isla was keeping Harry busy, he wasn't getting into trouble.

Kara washed her hands with a tiny bit of water from the bag. "I think I'll walk a bit before I retire," she said, strolling out of the ring of light.

She was not ten steps from the fire when she heard someone behind her. She didn't have to look back to know who it was. She crossed the center of the open courtyard and walked toward a trio of lancet windows that had earlier caught her eye.

Ian followed quietly. Kara halted directly below the three windows, their glass long gone, but their majesty still intact. She could hear Harry's whistle behind her, faint on the night air. "A chapel?"

Ian came to stand beside her. She felt a heavy warmth fall over her shoulders as he again placed his cloak over her.

"Aye. She was such a magnificent edifice that she held her own church. Men could lay siege against Barclay for fortnights, yet she was so self-contained that it was naught but a slight annoyance."

Kara stared up at the oval windows. A tall one in the center reached twenty-five feet over her head, flanked by two shorter ones. "This has to be one of the most peaceful, most beautiful places I have ever been." She turned to him. "Thank you for bringing me."

"I knew you would like it." His voice was gentle, yet still filled with the strength of his masculinity. "I confess that's partly why we came. We probably could have made it home safely."

"Ian?"

"Aye?"

"Why did you become angry with me tonight? When I made the jest about children?"

He paused.

Kara knew from experience that this was difficult for a man. She waited patiently.

"Not angry. Not with you. Not ever."

She breathed deeply. This conversation was too intimate. She needed to take a step back. She needed to change the subject to something less personal. She was another man's wife.

Yet she couldn't.

"No?" she asked. "But you acted as if you were angry."

He reached out to catch a tiny braid that had fallen from the loop of braids she wore down her back.

Kara's breath caught in her throat. Ian shouldn't touch her like this. She shouldn't let him.

But she wanted him to touch her.

"It . . ." Ian struggled to speak his thoughts.

She waited.

"It angers me to think my father and your father gave you to a boy." He held fast to her braid, twisting it around his finger as if he could somehow possess it. "You deserve a man, Kara." His voice was strange, tight, full of emotion.

She felt her chest tighten. She had never evoked such sentiment in a man before.

"You deserve a man who can love you as you deserve to be loved. A man who can give you children."

Kara had no time to think. She felt Ian's breath warm

on her lips. The next thing she knew, he was leaning over her, drawing her into arms that seemed all-encompassing. She tilted her head, mesmerized by the scent of him, by his power, by the atmosphere within the castle ruins.

Kara was shocked by the warmth of Ian's lips, shocked by her own desperate need to feel his mouth against hers.

This is wrong. A sin . . . The words pulsed in her mind. But she couldn't stop herself, not any more than she could prevent the English from invading her beloved Scotland, or prevent the sun from rising each morning.

"Kara." He breathed her name against her lips like a chant. A prayer.

She wanted to pull away. Run.

She pressed her body against his, drawn to his warmth, his strength. She parted her lips. No man's tongue had ever passed between them, and yet she opened, beckoning.

He tasted fresh. Hot. Powerful. Yet in no way did he make her feel as if he overpowered her. She kissed him of her own free will. She touched her tongue to his, glided it along his even, smooth teeth.

Kara's pulse raced. Her heart pounded. She was breathless, growing dizzy for want of air. Yet she couldn't bear to end this kiss. Not when she knew this intimacy could never, ever be shared again.

The castle wall spun around her. The sound of her husband's tin whistle faded. Kara reached up to thread her fingers through Ian's rich, silky dark hair, wanting more of him. Needing more.

It was Ian who broke the kiss.

He breathed her name again. She clung to him, breathless, still dizzy, in an utter state of confusion.

He smoothed her hair with one big hand and rested her cheek on his broad chest. She could hear his heart pounding, its pace matching her own heart's.

As she caught her breath a heavy sense of loss overcame her. The kiss she had shared with Ian was the most wonderful thing that had ever happened. Yet it could never happen again.

"Ian," she whispered. She did not look up, for fear she couldn't resist his mouth again.

"Aye?"

His voice sounded in her head, almost as if it were her own voice.

"Ian, I should not have—"

"I'm sorry." His breath was still short, ragged like her own. They spoke in unison.

"I don't know what came over me."

"I had no right."

They said all the right things and yet he still held her tightly in his arms. She made no attempt to move away.

Kara began to tremble. She was afraid for herself, for Ian. To kiss another man not her husband was a sin. Yet how could anything so glorious be sinful? How could her loving God deem anything so perfect a sin?

She wanted to move away, but her legs were still weak.

"It won't happen again," he whispered, his warm breath on her ear.

"Nae." She looked up at him, into his dark eyes reflecting the moon's light, just rising in the night sky. "Not again."

But he lowered his mouth again, and she was unable—or unwilling—to protest.

This kiss was not one of passion or desperation. It was a kiss of regret, of sorrow for what could never be.

He brushed his mouth lightly against hers and she yearned to part her lips, but she resisted. If she didn't resist now, she might not be able to. If then she didn't resist, if he laid his cloak out for her here at the foot of the chapel windows she might lie with him. She might make love with him and then surely their souls would both be doomed.

"Go back to the fire," he said gently.

As he lowered his arms, she wanted to cry. She had never felt so safe, so loved, so alive.

She wrapped his cloak tightly around her shoulders and ran toward the campfire, leaving the only man she knew she would ever love alone.

"Where have you been?" Harry jumped up as Kara entered the ring of firelight. "I was worried about you. Where's Ian?"

"I . . . I only went for a walk," she said shakily.

"I thought I heard wolves," he said, a tremor in his voice. "I don't like wolves."

"You're safe enough, Harry. They're a mile off, in the hills."

Ian remained just outside the firelight, making a conscious effort to keep his tone even and unrevealing.

He had wanted to remain at the foot of the chapel window longer, to collect himself and his thoughts. But he wanted more to see Kara in the firelight. To see the expression on her face. He feared she hated him now, and that he couldn't bear.

Ian didn't know what had come over him. He had fantasized about kissing her, but he had certainly never intended to do so. He hadn't meant to do it until he was already in motion, until she was tipping her mouth up to his, looking into his eyes.

Kara was right, of course. It was wrong. She was his brother's wife. A married woman. To cuckold his own brother would be the worst of crimes. Not only could a dalliance with his sister-in-law put Kara in danger, but also Harry's position. Dunnane could not stand such scandal now, with Harry still so young and vulnerable.

Ian knew all this to be fact and yet still he had not been able to stop himself. And the kiss had been better than he imagined. Her lips had been sweeter, her tongue more tantalizing. Ian had kissed many women, but never had anyone given so freely of herself, of her very soul.

"A mile away?" Harry peered into the darkness. "You certain?"

Ian tried to concentrate. He tried not to look at Kara. Her face was flushed, her eyes downcast. The serving girl was watching her carefully. Did she know, with some woman's intuition, that something had passed between them?

"I'm certain," Ian said, trying hard not to be short with his brother in a moment when he had no tolerance for his childish fears. "We leave early in the morn. It's best you get some sleep now."

As he spoke, Ian watched Kara walk around the fire and lower herself to the bedroll between her maid and her husband.

Her husband. Even the word angered him.

Ian loved Kara; he knew he loved her. But naught could be changed.

He turned away from the fire. "I'll keep watch. Sleep, all of you." He strode off.

If he loved Kara there was only one thing he could do. Once he returned his brother safely to the walls of Dunnane he would ask permission to take his leave. The only way to save his soul, the souls of all the men and women at Dunnane, was to go far from the Lady Dunnane now, while he was still able.

Chapter Nine

"Why do I have to go now?" Harry whined.

Kara and Harry entered the castle through the guarded yett. They had made good time this morning returning to Dunnane, encountering no adversity. It was not yet noon.

"You must greet your mother before retiring to your bedchamber," Kara said beneath her breath so the Scotsman at the gate would not hear her. "Because she is your mother and deserves that respect."

"And what of respect for me?" Harry muttered under his breath. He halted, crossing his arms over his chest, his voice growing louder. "I'm supposed to be the earl around here. This is supposed to be my castle."

Kara massaged her temples with her thumb and forefinger. Her head was pounding and her nerves were on edge. She was not in the mood to deal with Harry this morning. She had too much on her mind.

She'd barely spoken to Ian since their kiss last night, and then only in a perfunctory manner. But she'd not stopped thinking about him, not for a moment. She was so confused. She was Harry's wife. She felt responsible for him, felt a duty to him, and yet her heart called in another direction. Her heart yearned for Ian, and she knew at the moment as surely as she knew her name that Harry would never have her love. Not that kind of love, no matter how mature, how handsome he grew to be.

So what was she to do?

"Harry, your mother will hear us," she said softly.

"Oh, all right. Have it your way." He scuffed his boot on the flagstone, letting his arms drop to his sides. "I'll go speak with Mother, but you have to go, too. Otherwise she'll be asking me all kinds of intimate questions I don't want to answer."

The tone of Harry's voice drew her from her own concerns. He was saying he needed her. How could she not go? It was odd how they had been married such a short time, and in such circumstances, and yet she still felt a devotion to him. But it was the devotion of a big sister, perhaps even a mother. Not the devotion of a wife. "I'll go with you," she conceded, "though I look a fright." She tucked her hair behind her ear. "Your mother will think you've married a crone."

Harry walked through the hall ahead of her, immediately brightening. "Nonsense. She'll think you're as beautiful as I think you are. Mother will love you." He caught her hand. "Come, I'll introduce you."

Kara smoothed her hair and then her gown, but to little avail. With a resigned sigh, she allowed her boy-husband to lead her into the great hall.

Harry's hounds burst into frenzied barks of greeting and raced toward them. He patted one after the other, scratching behind their ears and rubbing their muzzles. The dogs leaped excitedly, red tongues lolling.

"Good girl. Good Matilda," Harry said. "Down, Edward. Charles, really, you must behave. Get off Kara before she sends you packing!"

"Harry, dear!" A woman in her early sixties rose from a chair pulled in front of one of the fireplaces.

Kara was surprised that she suddenly felt nervous. She'd been betrothed to marry into this family since she was fifteen. But she'd never met the dowager of Dunnane, and for some unknown reason she wanted the woman to like her. She wanted her approval. Perhaps because she had never had the approval of her own mother.

The older woman came to her son with open arms. She was tall, thin, but not overly so. Her white hair was fashionably coiffed, her gown subdued but well stitched. She was the epitome of what Kara thought a mother-in-law should look like.

"Mother!"

Harry released Kara's hand to meet Anne Gordon and throw his arms around her. He hugged his mother hard, his embrace genuine.

Kara couldn't resist a smile.

"You look wonderful, dear." She smoothed his cheek, which had yet to need shaving. "I believe marriage agrees with you."

He grinned. "Mother, I want you to meet Kara." He held out one hand graciously.

Kara accepted her husband's hand and bobbed a curtsy. "Lady Dunnane."

Anne laughed and fluttered her hand in front of her face. "Nae, you are now the Lady Dunnane, dear. Call me Mother Anne."

She took Kara's face between her palms to look into her eyes, then wrapped her arms around her. She smelled of peppermint. "Welcome to the family. I'm so sorry I wasn't here for the wedding. But first there was the washed out road and then my gout."

Kara stepped back, squeezing Anne's hands before releasing them. "Are you feeling better?" She gestured to the chairs pulled up to one of the fireplaces. "We should sit so you can rest."

"I'm fine. Fit as fennel. I'm just glad I could make it to Dunnane now. Ian has assured me in his letters that Harry is doing well in his father's place, but I wanted to see for myself." Her tone softened. "I needed to see."

The mention of Ian's name sent a thrill down Kara's spine. How could she have forgotten? Harry's mother was Ian's mother. When she hugged Harry's mother, she was hugging Ian's as well. If Harry's mother liked her, Ian's mother liked her. Somehow that seemed important.

"Ian has been wonderful," Kara said, taking care with her tone of voice. She couldn't let anyone know her secret. And she knew that she would have to be especially careful around Anne Gordon. Women could see things in matters of the heart where men could not.

"That is because Ian is a wonderful man. Both of my sons are wonderful men." She walked back toward her chair, leading Harry by his hand. "Now come sit, both of you, and tell me how married life is. You both look so happy."

Kara hesitated. She had told Harry she would stay if he wanted her to, but he seemed comfortable enough now with his mother. She really needed to be alone for a short time. She needed to bathe, brush her hair and her teeth, and collect her thoughts. She needed to figure out how she was going to deal with Ian. They spent so much time together that she had to have a plan. She couldn't keep ignoring him. She couldn't keep kissing him, either.

Kara pressed her hands to her girdle. "Harry, if it would be all right, I'd like to retire to our chamber for a short time. You could have some time alone with your mother."

Harry glanced up. He started to protest; then the expression on his face changed. He nodded. "Very well. I wanted to show Mother the new falconry anyway. Will you order supper? A feast for my mother's homecoming."

"Isla is already seeing to it. Anything else, my lord?"

He rose, seeming older before his mother. "Nothing else. Go rest." Then, to Kara's complete shock, he rose up onto his toes and kissed her cheek.

She felt her cheeks grow warm as she bobbed a quick curtsy and hurried out of the room.

Kara was so flustered by Harry's gesture that she didn't see Ian until she ran right into him in the corridor. "Oh!" she cried, glancing up, knowing who the human wall was even before she saw him.

Ian caught both of her arms to steady her. "Kara." He spoke her name as if he were breathless from running . . . or kissing her.

She glanced up at him, met his gaze and looked down. "I . . . I . . ." She took a breath, trying to calm her pounding heart. She didn't want to sound like a simpleton. "I left Harry in the hall with his . . . your mother. She's very kind." She scrambled to find something to say that would keep her thoughts from his mouth and how badly hers ached for him now. "I . . . was just going to my chamber to clean up. I've ordered a banquet feast to welcome her home."

"Kara—"

"I'm a mess." She swept loose hair back over the crown of her head. "I was embarrassed for your mother to see me like this, but Harry insisted—"

"Kara, I need to talk to you."

He didn't touch her. She knew he didn't dare.

She could feel that familiar tightening in her chest. She, too, was breathless. This was madness. She held up her hand to stop him. "Not now, Ian."

"But—"

She pushed past him, running for the steps and the sanctuary of her private bedchamber. "Please, Ian. Not now. I can't. I just can't. We'll talk tonight."

Before he could say anything more, she was up the steps, taking two at a time. She was thankful he did not follow.

Kara bathed, then allowed Isla to help her sweep up her hair and don a clean gown. Then she sent the girl to rest in her own room. With Isla tucked into her bed with a cup of herbal tea, Kara slipped down the stairs, through a rarely used corridor and into the tiny chapel some previous Lady

Dunnane had built. She and Harry had not married here, but in the great hall, because the chapel was too small, and truly meant only for private devotions.

Privacy was what Kara needed right now.

She passed the four dusty, wormholed pews, two on each side, and approached the altar. It was bare except for a silver Celtic cross. She knelt on the stone floor before the altar and clasped her hands.

She squeezed her eyes shut. "Please, God," she prayed fervently. "Help me to be a good and virtuous wife. Help me to preserve my husband's name. Help me to not love Ian so much," she whispered.

Kara opened her eyes and waited. She thought her prayers would lift the burden she felt, but there was no lightening.

What if she was praying for the wrong thing? What if she was demanding too much from God?

She closed her eyes again.

"Help me," she prayed silently, her lips moving. "Help me to do the right thing, God. Help me to do my duty to my husband . . . and to myself. To you. Give me strength. Guide me to do what is right. Forgive me for what I do that is wrong." She paused. "Amen."

She opened her eyes and stared at the cross. Now she felt better. She still didn't know what to do or how to handle Ian and her feelings for him. But she felt better. Stronger. She rose from the altar, a satisfied smile on her face.

She would remain friends with Ian. She would continue to rely on his counsel to help Harry become more self-sufficient. She would just avoid personal conversations. She would avoid being alone. Maybe these feelings for Ian weren't real, weren't lasting. Perhaps with time they would fade, she told herself. With time Harry would mature and eventually take her to his bed. They would have children and she would forget her infatuation with her brother-in-law.

She sighed. Aye. And perhaps with time she would also become the queen of England, Scotland and Wales.

"I need to talk to you." Ian stood in the doorway of Harry's bedchamber. He had waited in the shadows of the corridor below stairs until he had seen Kara heading for the kitchen. Only then had he dared come to her bedchamber, to the room where she slept, where she undressed.

Avoiding her was the only way he could deal with her right now, with his feelings for her. She'd taken him completely by surprise in the hall earlier. He'd thought to tell her he was leaving, but she hadn't given him a chance. Instead he would bring the matter up with Harry alone. It was probably better this way.

"Do you like the red coat?" Harry held up a handsome scarlet wool coat. "Or the blue? The blue matches my eyes." He held it up, studying himself in a large oval looking glass that had been a wedding gift from the MacDonald clan. "I really can't choose. They're both so wonderful."

"Harry, are you listening to me?" Ian wanted to get this over with. He wanted to speak his piece while he still had the courage. He had to get away from here before he did something he would regret. Worse, something he feared he would not regret.

Harry tossed both coats onto the bed. "I'm listening, but make it quick. I've hired a traveling magician to entertain us tonight and he's promised to teach me a card trick so I can perform. Kara will be impressed, don't you think?" He perched on the edge of the bed, on top of the two new coats.

Kara's hairbrush lay on the table beside the bed, and for a moment Ian couldn't take his eyes off it.

"Well?" Harry asked, crossing his arms across his chest. "What is it?"

Ian took a deep breath, dragging his gaze from the

hairbrush. He chose his words carefully. "With your permission, I would like to take my leave, my lord."

"Take your leave?" The young man wrinkled his nose. "Of my chamber?"

"Nae! Not your chamber. Dunnane!" Ian took another deep breath. He couldn't lose his temper. Not with the boy. Not over this. "Aye," he said more quietly. "I'd like to go to my land holdings to the north. Stay the summer there. Perhaps the winter."

Harry rose off the bed. One of the coats slipped to the floor, but he paid it no mind. "Take your leave of Dunnane?" he questioned incredulously. "Take your leave of me?"

He said it in such a way that Ian felt only two feet tall. His brother spoke as if even the mere suggestion was a betrayal.

"You are doing well on your own. And you have your cousin Dungald—"

"Dungald!" Harry spit. "Do you know that Dungald ordered men—my men—not to assist my wife whilst we were gone?" He threw up one hand. "I've yet to figure out how I'm to deal with that matter."

Ian felt like a young boy being scolded. He stared at Harry's feet, wishing he were anywhere but here. Wishing he'd kept his mouth shut. Wishing he'd kept his mouth off the mouth of his brother's wife.

"I am not an idiot, Ian, that I do not know the game my dear cousin plays."

"We don't know for sure—"

"No, we don't know for sure!" Harry snapped, approaching him.

Ian stared at his own boots. He felt so torn. His allegiance was to his brother. Didn't Harry understand that it was for that sense of duty that he wanted to go? That he must go?

But of course Harry didn't know that because Harry didn't know how his brother felt about his wife. Harry didn't know about the stolen kisses last night. He didn't know that secretly Ian lusted for his wife.

"I know that Dungald is next in line to Dunnane should I die," Harry continued. "I know that a part of him wants this land for his own. A part of him that might be willing to harm me or mine to have land."

"As I said, we have no proof," Ian said lamely. He felt like an ass. Like a traitor. It was true; they had no proof. Harry had no factual reason to send his cousin Dungald from his service. But he had plenty of reasons to hold him suspect.

Harry rubbed at his eyes. Ian could have sworn he saw tears. "I cannot do this alone, Ian. Please don't leave me."

"Harry—"

"Nae." Again he wiped his eyes with the back of his hand. But this time his tone was firm. "Nae. Permission denied. You will not take your leave. You will not return to your holdings. You will remain at Dunnane and assist me until I decide you are no longer needed." He paused. For an instant he had sounded like a true heir of Dunnane. "I have that authority, don't I?"

Ian turned away. He felt his heart sink in his chest, then rise in his throat until it threatened to choke him. "Ye have that authority, my lord."

Harry followed him into the hall. "Please understand. I want to make my father proud. You, our mother, Kara. I want to do what is right. I want to serve as a good and fair lord over these lands. But I can't do it alone." He beseeched with a hand much smaller than Ian's. "Please don't hate me."

Ian halted at the top of the winding staircase and raised his hand to rest it on the frame overhead. "I don't hate you."

"If there's anything I can give you to make you happier here . . . coin? I have plenty of money. Cattle? Tell me what it is."

Your wife, Ian thought. *Can you give me your wife?*

He didn't say it, of course. He wouldn't hurt Harry like that. He wouldn't betray Kara like that. But the thought hung in his mind just the same. It prevented him from thinking clearly. From knowing what he would do now.

To remain here within these walls with Kara so near. To see her, but not touch her. He didn't know if it was humanly possible for him to resist his desire for her. He didn't know if he could keep himself from making love to his brother's wife.

"No, Harry," he said quietly when he had found his voice. "There's nothing I want. Only to serve you. I apologize. I didn't realize what I was saying."

Harry pressed his hand to Ian's back. "I want you to be happy, brother. I want you and Kara to be happy. I would do anything to see you two happy."

If only the boy knew what he said.

"I must change for supper. Mother will be waiting."

Harry lowered his hand. "So it's settled. You're not leaving me. You'll never leave me."

Ian started down the tower steps. "Nae. I'll not leave you, little brother," he said beneath his breath. "Not so long as your Lady Dunnane draws breath."

Chapter Ten

"How dare you give such an order," Ian hissed.

Dungald took a step back farther into the shadows of the empty corridor.

Ian had waited for Harry's cousin outside his chambers. Everyone had gone to the great hall for the evening meal, or was busy serving there. There was no one near to hear or see them.

"I don't know what you're talking about." Dungald took another step back, pressing his back to the wall.

"The hell you don't." Ian slammed the wall with the palm of his hand, striking it just to the left of Dungald's ear.

Dungald flinched and threw up his hand as if to deflect Ian's blow should he attempt to strike him.

"I'm certain there's been a miscommunication," Dungald said.

Ian stepped closer, throwing back his shoulders, knowing he was intimidating the man. Wanting to intimidate him.

Ian was angry enough with himself over the situation he

had gotten himself into with Kara. But after he'd found out what Dungald had done, how he had endangered Harry and Kara, his anger now bordered on rage.

"Miscommunication, my ass." Ian ground his teeth. "You knew Harry would ride after us."

"I knew no such—"

Again Ian struck the wall just by Dungald's ear and the man fell silent.

"And you knew that Kara would go after him."

"I was merely considering her ladyship's safety."

Ian leaned down, his face close to Dungald's, so close that he could smell the fear on his breath. "These excuses might work with the boy, but they won't with me. I know what you did and I know why. Were I a betting man, I might even wager that you suggested to your cousin that he follow us after we rode out."

Dungald opened his mouth as if he intended to protest, but the look in Ian's eyes must have frightened him into silence again.

"I'm warning ye, Dungald. I catch wind of any more of your antics and you'll be banished to the northern isles with no one but the seagulls to warm your bed."

Dungald's eyes narrowed. "You can't do that. You can't send me from here. I have a right to live in this castle. I'm a Gordon. My uncle was the Earl of Dunnane before that boy. You, you—you're nothing," he spit.

Ian almost smiled as he tightened his hands into fists at his sides. In the mood he was in right now, he had a mind to kill Dungald here and be done with him. He could choke him, maybe slit his throat and dispose of the body before anyone knew he was missing. Who would go looking for him? Who would care if he rotted in some remote ravine? Then the threat to Harry and his seat would be gone. One less thing for Ian to lie awake at night worrying over.

The thought was tempting.

Ian flexed his fingers and closed them into fists again.

Tempting, indeed. It wouldn't be the first time these stones had witnessed cold-blooded murder. Nor the last, he'd wager.

"If I tell Harry to send ye away, away ye shall go," Ian said softly, stepping back.

"You have no proof I've done anything wrong. The boy won't banish me. He likes me. I've brought back one of the reivers. One of the thieves who stole his cattle."

Ian's expression changed. "You caught one of them?"

Dungald slid along the wall in the direction of the great hall, his back and palms against the cold stone. He broke into a grin when he was far enough away that Ian couldn't reach him without taking several steps. "Caught one. Nae, even better than that."

Ian watched Dungald make a hasty retreat.

With that matter taken care of, at least for the time being, he knew he now had to make an appearance in the great hall. Right now that was the last place he wanted to be.

"He wanted to what?" Kara unintentionally raised her voice.

They were seated in the great hall at the dais. The evening meal was just being served.

"He wanted to go to his land. Land his father left to him." Harry waved his fork. "Somewhere up north. I don't know exactly where."

Kara swallowed the lump in her throat. *Because of me?* she wondered. *Was it because of me?*

Of course it was.

She fought the panic in her chest. Ian couldn't go. He couldn't leave her. "What did you tell him?" She lowered her voice, leaning in toward her husband.

"I said no, of course. I forbade him to leave Dunnane." He glanced at her, his brow furrowing. "Ye don't think I should have let him go, do you?"

Kara didn't know what to say. If Ian left, she didn't know that she would be able to bear living within these walls. Ian was her companion, her adviser, her comfort. She didn't know how it had happened, or when, but it was true.

On the other hand, if Ian left, there would be no temptation. There would be no chance she might betray her husband with another kiss . . . or worse.

When Kara didn't respond immediately, Harry continued. He picked up a drumstick from his plate and began to eat. "I couldn't let him go. I depend on him to help me. I still don't know what my duties are here. What I'm supposed to say. What I'm supposed to do."

Her gaze met the boy's. Harry was right; he did need Ian. And she was proud that Harry recognized it. "I think you're doing quite well, my lord." She didn't know what else to say.

"Certainly I'm doing well. For a thirteen-year-old." He gnawed on the bone. "Speaking of which, I meant to ask you about my birthday. You know my birthday is next month. I'll be fourteen."

She blinked, wondering how the conversation had changed so abruptly. "Nae. I didn't realize it."

"How do you think we should celebrate?" He spoke excitedly. "A festival? I was thinking of a festival. You could have one in my honor. Horse races, traveling musicians, a hunt, perhaps."

Kara's head was spinning. How could Harry go from discussing such a serious matter as Ian's possible departure, to birthday festivities in the same breath? She reminded herself that he was still a child in many ways. In his mind, perhaps one was just as important as the other.

But Kara wanted to draw the conversation back to Ian. She wanted to know why he wanted to go. Or at least the reason he'd given Harry. She wanted to know exactly what Ian had said. If he had dared mention her. But she didn't know how to return to the previous conversation without making it obvious.

"Well, what do you think?" Harry waited, drumstick poised in midair.

His mouth was slick with grease and she had to suppress the urge to wipe it with her napkin.

"Well, aye. Yes," Kara stammered, keeping her hand in her lap. "I think a festival is an excellent idea. But perhaps we should discuss it with Ian."

She scanned the room filled with Gordons. It was noisy and smoky. Candlelight flickered in the drafts so that it was difficult to make out who was who on the far side of the room. Ian had not yet made his appearance; nor had Dungald.

"The preparation of the roast duck is lovely," Harry's mother said from the seat on the far side of Harry. She had been in conversation with an older man, distant kin to her deceased husband, but the man had wandered from the table.

"Thank you, Mother Anne." Kara forced a smile, then glanced around the room for Ian again. She didn't know if she wanted him here now or not. A part of her wanted to ask him why he wanted to leave. A part of her wanted to avoid him into the next century.

"I must have the recipe to take home to my kitchen in Edinburgh."

"Mother, you can't go home before my birthday. Kara's going to arrange a festival in honor of my birthday!"

"What an excellent idea!" Lady Dunnane clasped her hands. "I do love a festival. Everyone loves a spring festival."

Again Kara forced a smile. "I'm certain the cook—" Out of the corner of her eye she saw Ian enter the room. She made herself return her attention to her mother-in-law. "I'm certain the cook will give you the recipe."

"Ian!" Harry half stood and waved to his brother.

One of Harry's hounds circled Ian as he slowly made his way to the dais.

Kara couldn't take her eyes off him: his dark eyes, the way his hair fell to nearly brush his shoulders. The more she saw him, the more she wanted him. The more she reminded herself that she couldn't have him, the more she wanted him. It was lust, pure and simple, she tried to convince herself. It would pass.

"Harry, Mother." Ian nodded. "Kara. Good evening."

"Sit, sit," Harry said. "You're always late. You always miss the choicest meats."

"Only so that you may have the choicest meats," Ian answered, rounding the dais table to take his seat beside his mother.

"The magician is about to start." Harry waved his hands, glancing at Kara, who was making a point now not to look past Harry and Mother Anne at Ian. "Then I have a surprise." He laid his hand over Kara's. "A surprise you're going to love."

Harry's touching her like that in public made her uncomfortable, but she didn't know what to do. She didn't want to hurt his feelings. Nor did she want his hand on hers.

"My lord," a voice called from the doorway.

Everyone looked up to see Dungald entering the great hall. And he wasn't just entering; he was making an entrance, dressed handsomely in blue and gold, his beard and hair freshly combed, still damp. He was carrying a small sack, speaking to be certain everyone heard him.

A hush fell over the room as everyone looked up with curiosity to see what Dungald was about.

"My lord, I have returned from pursuing the cattle thieves and I've a gift for you."

Harry sat back in his chair. "A gift for me?" He waved his cousin forward. "Approach and tell me of those insolent reivers. Did you catch them?"

"Nae, not all of them, I fear to say. They got away, my

lord." Dungald reached the dais and turned so that his back was to Kara. Now he faced the room of clansmen and the earl at the same time. "But one thief was not so fortunate."

With a great flourish Dungald shook the bag and something rolled out onto the table before Harry.

Something bloody.

Kara stared, her mind not registering what it was for a moment. Something the size of her fist, bloody, fleshy, almost heart-shaped.

Kara clamped her hand over her mouth just as she and the others in the room realized what it was.

It seemed as if everyone in the room gasped at once.

Harry stared for a moment, his eyes wide. Then he broke into a broad grin. "Saints alive!" He poked the object with his fork. "Is it real?"

For a moment Kara thought she would be ill. A heart. It was a man's heart.

"Ye killed him and cut out his heart?" Harry exclaimed, still wide-eyed.

"He would not surrender, my lord." Dungald splayed his hands as if he were an actor reciting his dramatic lines. "What else was I to do?"

Lady Dunnane made a sound on the other side of Harry, and Kara looked across the table to see her mother-in-law pressing a napkin to her mouth, as pale-faced as she felt. Lady Dunnane began to fan herself with the napkin.

Ian leaned and whispered into his mother's ear, supporting her back with one broad hand.

Kara didn't know what to say. Slowly she slid her hand from her lips, her gaze falling to the heart again. It was so offensive, and yet she couldn't take her eyes off it.

Now Harry was poking it enthusiastically, rolling it in front of his dinner plate. A dog under the table began to whine, perhaps at the smell of blood.

"A real human heart?" Harry breathed, still amazed, fascinated.

"That is obscene," Kara said, jumping to her feet. "Gruesome and inhumane."

Dungald turned slowly to face her. "The reivers are stealing Dunnane's cattle, madam. Surely you know the price of this kind of thievery is death."

Kara threw down her napkin, disgusted with Dungald for doing such a horrendous thing as killing a man and cutting out his heart. At Harry for being so fascinated. At Ian for not coming to her defense and agreeing with her.

The room was abuzz with men's voices again. Shockingly, no one else seemed repulsed or even upset. Several men were actually chuckling. The Gordons were returning to their meals, their ale and their pipes, as if their earl were regularly presented with the human hearts of his enemies.

Without another word, not even to the Lady Dunnane, Kara rushed out of the great hall.

She reached the tower steps before Ian caught up with her. Again she knew it was him without even having to turn around.

"Kara!"

She threw up one hand, starting up the winding stone steps. She was close to tears. She certainly felt nothing for the man who had committed the crime. She understood the need for swift and severe punishment. But to take his heart and make a spectacle of it? What kind of men resided beneath this roof?

But it wasn't just the heart. It was everything. Last night's kiss. Ian's request to take his leave. She felt as if her life, her emotions, were spinning out of control and there was nothing she could do to prevent it.

"Leave me alone," she said over her shoulder, taking the steps as quickly as she could.

"Kara, wait, let me explain," he hollered up.

She grabbed a handful of her woolen skirt and raced faster up the steps. "Let me be. You want to rip out men's hearts? You want to go from Dunnane? Go! Go right straight to the gates of hell, for all I care!"

Ian came up the steps after her. "Kara, listen to me. That was not a human—"

Kara turned on the curved staircase, blocking out the sound of his voice, the pounding of her footsteps. She passed the second floor, breathing heavily, tugging hard on the twisted guide rope. The stairwell was dark, but she knew her way even in the darkness. If she could just get to her chamber, she could lock the door. If even she couldn't lock him out of her heart, she could at least lock him out of her room.

He caught her hand just as she reached the top of the stairs.

"Kara!"

"Let me go!" She pulled hard, but he wouldn't release her.

At the landing she threw herself against the wall. The corridor was dark too, lit only by a single candle sconce near her door.

She thought to call to Isla, who was most likely in her room, but she didn't.

Ian held tightly to her hand. "Did you hear what I said?"

She panted, winded from the run up the staircase. "I don't want to know what you said. I want you to leave me be. All of you!" She turned her face away so that she wouldn't have to look at him.

"It wasn't a human heart."

It took a second for his words to sink in.

She looked at him. "What did you say?"

He loosened his grip on her wrist, but did not release her. "I said it wasn't a human heart. Dungald caught no reiver and cut out his heart. What kind of a man do you think I am that I would stand for such sacrilege?"

"But the heart. 'Twas the right size for—"

"A deer's heart." His tone lightened. "A prank."

"A prank?" She stared at him, still not certain she understood. "Dungald pretended he cut out a man's heart?"

He lifted one shoulder. "No one in the room thought it was a human heart, not after the first moment."

"No one but Harry. But me. Your mother."

"I told Mother."

"And Harry?"

"He'll figure it out in a moment or so. And even a deer's heart is fascinating to a boy his age."

Kara closed her eyes for a moment, resting the back of her head against the wall. "I don't understand. What sickness in a man would lead him to . . . to think this was funny? Or appropriate or . . . or . . ." She let her sentence die, too stunned for words.

"The thieves escaped. Dungald was embarrassed." Ian shrugged his broad shoulders. "Rather than just walk in and say he let the reivers go, he added a little drama to diminish his failing."

She opened her eyes to look up into his dark ones. "A little drama?"

"It worked. Harry didn't berate him in front of the men."

She shook her head. "And this makes sense to you? To bring a deer's heart and say it was a man's?"

"It makes sense," he conceded, "in a roundabout way."

She exhaled, the pounding of her heart slowing and her breath coming more easily. "Men," she said.

"Pardon?" He lifted a brow.

"Men. Mad. They're all mad." She gestured with her free hand. "All of you!"

He chuckled. "Aye. At times. That I canna disagree with."

"I live in a household of madmen!"

Now he was grinning. And he was so blessedly handsome when he smiled. His whole face lit up. His dark brown eyes sparkled. She liked it when he smiled. Loved it.

For some unknown reason she found herself smiling. Laughing with him. It was completely inappropriate and yet she couldn't stop herself.

When her laughter was spent, she gazed into his eyes. He was still holding on to her, but he had slid his hand down until his thick fingers laced through hers.

"You asked Harry to allow you to leave Dunnane." It was half question, half accusation.

He, too, sobered. "Aye."

"Why?" Her tone sharpened. "Because of me?"

"Nae." With his free hand he gently brushed her forehead. "Because of me. Because of this. Because I want you," he whispered fiercely. "And I cannot have you. Not ever. Ye understand, not ever, not even if, God forbid, something should happen to Harry."

"God forbid," she breathed, unable to tear her gaze from his. "Because you are his brother."

"The church would never allow it," he said. " 'Tis forbidden. You would be married off to another."

"Dungald, even." Her last words came out as a breath.

"It could be so ordered."

Lost. Hopeless. Kara wanted to speak but she was too filled with emotion to form any words. It was hopeless and yet still she couldn't bear the thought of him leaving her. Couldn't bear the thought of what might happen if he stayed. She wanted to tell him that she didn't want him to leave. She wanted to tell him he had to go.

"Harry says he has forbidden you to go," she said when she found her voice.

His gaze remained locked with hers. "Aye."

"So ye stay here . . . with me, with us."

He leaned over her. "Aye."

His lips were nearly close enough to kiss. She had only to lift onto her toes and they would be hers. "So what now?" she breathed.

He shook his head ever so slightly. "I do not know."

Kara took a deep, shuddering breath. He was going to kiss her again and there was nothing she could do to prevent it. Nothing she could do, because she didn't want to stop him. Suddenly his mouth against hers seemed more important than the breath she drew. Certainly more important than the punishment of everlasting hell she knew was impending.

Kara pressed her hand to his chest, smoothing it upward, over his shoulder, around his neck. Like some tavern wanton, she caressed the nape of his neck and drew him closer.

When Ian captured her lips with his, once again the sensation was even stronger, greater than she expected. Something electrical arced between them. Something magical and, on some level, mystical. His arms slipped around her waist, his tongue between her lips, and she was powerless to resist.

"This is wrong," she whispered. But even as she exhaled the words, her tongue touched his in the enchantment of a lover's dance.

Ian pressed his hand to her waist, slid it over her bodice and brushed against the underside of her breast.

A sound came up out of her throat, something of a sigh. A moan.

He backed her up against the wall until the hard, cold stones cut into her back.

She didn't stop him.

She couldn't.

His mouth set hers on fire. His hand scorched her bare flesh as he slipped his fingers into the neckline of her bodice, beneath her linen shift, flesh against flesh.

She threaded her fingers through his thick, sweet-smelling hair. She was utterly overwhelmed by his size, his power, and yet she felt completely in control.

Their mouths parted and his wet, hot lips grazed over her chin, down her neck to the valley between her breasts.

Every nerve in Kara's body seemed to be awakening. She felt his touch where he touched her not. At her waist. Her knees. The place between her thighs that had known no man.

He's going to take me here and now in the hall and I cannot stop him, she thought wildly. *I will not.*

A sound in the stairwell below jerked Kara back to her senses.

Footfalls. Someone coming fast.

Ian heard the footsteps at the very same instant. His hands fell to his sides as if he'd been burned.

"Kara! Kara are you up there?" rose a voice from below. It was Harry. Her husband.

Kara looked up at Ian. His face was stricken with guilt, fear, perhaps not for himself, but certainly for her.

As she pulled up her shift to cover her breasts, she pointed to the end of the hall where Isla's chamber lay.

Ian's gaze met hers for one fleeting moment, and then he hurried noiselessly down the hall.

"Kara?"

"H-here," she called weakly, readjusting the woolen folds of her bodice. "Here, Harry."

A moment later he came bounding up the steps. At the same moment that he turned the corner onto the landing, Ian disappeared into Isla's chamber.

She stood with her back against the wall, still feeling the heat of Ian's hand on her breast.

"Please come back," Harry said, halting before her. "I want you to see the magic tricks." He lowered his gaze, suddenly seeming shy. "I'm sorry about the heart. It wasn't really a man's heart, you know."

"I know," she whispered, not yet ready to trust her voice. She brushed her mouth with the back of her hand as if she could wipe away the feel of Ian's mouth against hers, the taste of him.

Harry worked his jaw. "Will ye come? Please? It won't be a celebration without you."

Guilt washed over Kara. She couldn't meet his wishful gaze. "I'll come," she said.

When Harry offered her his hand to lead her downstairs, she took it.

Chapter Eleven

Isla stared at Ian. Ian stared back.

She glanced at the doorway that led from her servant's chamber into the hall. He glanced at it.

He could hear Harry talking to Kara, but he couldn't make out what his brother was saying. Maybe because his heart was pounding too fiercely.

Their conversation was short; he heard them descend the stairs.

Only then did Ian move toward the door, away from Kara's maid, who seemed neither uncomfortable nor overly surprised by his sudden intrusion into her tiny private chamber.

She crossed her arms over her protruding belly, almost as if she waited for an explanation. There was something about the look on the girl's face that made him think he actually owed her one.

"Harry," he said, pointing toward the door.

She nodded. Waited.

"Kara. She . . . I . . ." He was at a loss for words, confused by what had just happened. He had sworn to himself he wouldn't kiss her again, and this time he had both kissed her and touched her. He just couldn't stop himself. Even now he could still taste her sweet mouth on his. He could still feel the warmth of her breast in his hand.

So now what? He was so confused by his feelings. He loved her. He knew it as surely as knew his own name. But he loved Harry, too. And his duty was to Harry first, wasn't it?

Ian balled his hands into fists at his sides. He wanted to shout something, anything, to release his frustration. Maybe hit something, even someone. But his hands just hung lamely at his sides. He pointed again.

The girl's mouth slowly turned upward in a smile of obvious amusement. "My lady sent you here?"

He nodded.

She studied him thoughtfully. "Is it true what they say of ye?" she asked, finally breaking the silence of the small room.

"And what is that?"

"That you have killed Englishmen with your bare hands? That ye could face a regiment and still come walking home? That ye have?"

"Exaggerations," he said simply, wondering at her point.

She nodded as if his explanation was satisfactory. "Let me check the stairwell, then, and see that it's safe to pass below."

He stepped out of her way, deciding his best choice of discourse was just not to say anything at all. At this moment it would be the least incriminating.

Isla went down the dark hallway and entered the stairwell. She came up the stairs minutes later. "It's safe to pass. They've returned to the great hall."

Ian hurried past her. At the top of the stairs, he halted and turned back.

Isla stood in her doorway, hand poised on one hip.

"Tell your mistress . . ."

"Aye?" She lifted one brow. She was a saucy wench.

Tell her what? he thought. *Tell her I love her? Tell her we're doomed?*

The serving girl waited patiently, so patiently that he found her irritating. She looked so smug. As if she could possibly understand what was between him and her mistress. What could not be between them.

"Never mind." He hurried down the winding stone stairs and pretended not to hear her retort.

"Men . . ."

The word echoed in his head all the way down the tower stairs.

Harry made a deep, exaggerated bow, first to the dais; then he turned and faced the hall and his men and bowed again.

They clapped their hands, stomped their feet, and struck their goblets on the wooden tables scattered throughout the hall.

Harry's face was flushed with pleased self-consciousness as he rose and tucked a purple scarf into his sleeve with a flourish. "So you liked it?" He turned to the raised head table, speaking both to Kara and his mother at the same time. "Bet you didn't realize I could do magic."

Kara attempted a smile.

She had returned to the great hall with Harry because she didn't know what else to do. If she had remained upstairs and sent him away with an excuse of a headache or women's ailments, she knew what would have happened. She would have led Ian into her bedchamber, locked the door, and made love to him on Harry's bed. Nothing could have stopped her. Nothing but coming downstairs.

"Wonderful!" Anne Gordon clapped her hands. "I'm so impressed, son. I never knew you were such an expert at sleight of hand."

"Which one did you like better, Kara?" Harry leaned

on the table, still grinning broadly. "The card trick or the disappearing duck egg?"

Kara took a sip of wine to delay answering him, to delay coming up with a reasonable response. To delay any thinking at all.

To her surprise she found the wine unwatered and strong and a little bitter to her tongue. She wondered what servant had neglected his or her duty.

Kara knew she shouldn't drink the wine like this, not on an empty stomach, for she hadn't touched her meal. The strong drink would hinder her thinking, but to think was the last thing she wanted to do right now. She didn't want to think about Ian, or about Harry, or about the dreadfully tangled web she now found herself in.

She took another drink.

Musicians struck their first notes, tuning their instruments. Momentarily music would begin. Beyond Harry, clansmen were moving tables to make room for dancing.

"Which trick?" Harry insisted.

"I . . . the cards," she said as her gaze strayed to the hall's entrance. She wondered where Ian was. Had Isla been in her room when he slipped in? What had the girl said? Done? She prayed he hadn't frightened her. He could be frightening to those who didn't realize how gentle a man he really was. "Aye, the cards. 'Twas my favorite."

A maidservant moved unobtrusively behind Kara, picking up dirty plates, clearing the table, and serving more wine. Kara thought she recalled that the girl's name was Meg.

"I was thinking of hiring the magician to stay on and teach me a few more tricks. I fancy myself as being quite good, had I the opportunity," he said proudly. "What do you think?"

Her mouth was dry. She drained the pewter goblet and made no protest when Meg refilled her vessel.

The serving girl took Lady Dunnane's plate, then moved on to Harry's. At his lordship's place, she hesitated.

"He's done," Anne said pleasantly. "You can take it, child."

Harry frowned. "I am not done! I want another tart." Meg dropped the plate with a clatter.

The Earl of Dunnane turned to his mother. "How dare you say I'm done when I'm not. How dare you tell my servant when to take my plate. I'm lord around here now and I say when my plate shall be taken!"

Anne glanced at her son in puzzlement. "Harry—"

"I'm sick to death of people making decisions for me," he said too loudly. "I am the lord here and I will make my own decisions. I will decide when I'm done eating!"

Harry was so busy with his self-absorbed temper tantrum that he was unaware that many of his men were staring at him. They whispered. Some smiled with amusement.

Kara was embarrassed for Harry, for his mother. And she was angry with her husband. Where was Harry's sense of respect? Surely his mother and father had taught him better behavior. What man could be respected who showed no respect where it was due?

She pushed the heels of her hands against the table and rose suddenly. The wine had made her warm from the inside out. "Would you like to dance, my lord?" she asked, tight-lipped.

He looked at her in surprise. "Dance?"

"The first set has begun." She gestured to the musicians, who had struck up a Scottish country dance from the Lowlands.

His young brow furrowed. "I thought you said you didn't like to dance."

"That was another evening, my lord." She stared at him hard. "I would like to dance now."

His mouth dropped open, then flapped shut. "Of course, of course, wife." He held out his hand.

"My lady." Kara bobbed a quick curtsy to her mother-in-law, who sat still apparently perplexed by what had just passed between her and her son.

"Go, go," she shooed. "You young people should enjoy yourselves and each other. I need not be coddled."

Kara rounded the dais to accept Harry's hand. The moment they faced each other and Kara was certain no one could hear them, she unleashed her disapproval. "What on God's green earth has gotten into you, Harailt James Gordon?"

He blinked.

She turned in his hand, still easily able to follow the complicated dance steps despite the strong wine she'd consumed. It hadn't made her drunk, only bold. "Your mother does not deserve to be treated thusly and I will not stand for it." As she spoke, she kept a slight smile on her face for appearance's sake.

"I . . . well, she . . . she . . ." he stuttered.

"You wanted to be treated like a man? Respected for your position? Then it's time you began acting like a man!"

Harry worked his jaw up and down as if he wanted to say something, but no words came forth.

"That woman carried you in her womb for nine moons. She pained to give you life. She fed you on her breast, she caught you when you fell taking your first steps." Kara drew nose-to-nose with him. "She wiped your soiled bottom, Harry."

He swallowed hard. "I didn't mean to—"

"I'm certain you didn't." She lifted her skirt and danced around him. The minute they were face-to-face again, she picked up where she left off. "My suggestion to you would be that you apologize to your dear mother, offer to dance with her, and spend the remainder of the evening seeing to her. She says she need not be coddled. I suggest you *coddle* her."

At this point Harry was so astonished by her diatribe that he could say nothing. Do nothing but copy her dance steps.

"She wants to see you succeed, Harry. Show her you are

the man she and your father prayed you would be." Kara released his hand abruptly and started for the door.

"Where are you going, Kara?" Harry ran after her.

"To my chambers." She kept her tone low. "To move my belongings to the center room. The doorway is nearly cut. We can pass easily back and forth."

His hands fell to his sides in bewilderment. "You're not going to sleep with me anymore?"

"Nae. No one will know but us." She met his gaze in challenge. "But I think it best, at least for now. Don't you?"

He bit his lower lip. "Aye. Yes. Whatever you think. Do . . . do you wish me to escort you upstairs?"

"Nae. Tell your mother my head aches and I've gone to bed. Make my apologies and see to her. There's no need for you to retire early."

"Of course." He clasped his hands. "Good night. I . . . I hope you feel better."

Kara left the great hall, her cloak fluttering. She didn't know what had possessed her to tell Harry that she could no longer sleep with him. She would have liked to have blamed the wine, but she knew better. She had left Harry's bed because she knew in her heart where her relationship with Ian was leading. The wine had only given her the courage to admit it to herself.

Ordinarily Ian would take one of the horses from the stables into the village, especially so late at night. But a man who wanted to be inconspicuous did not ride one of the master's horses through a cottagers' square. He walked quickly, quietly past thatched-roof, single-family dwellings and the occasional lean-to shed. Light shone through some of the cottage windows, but few. A dog barked occasionally. He heard the bleats of sheep, once a horse, but for the most part the village of Dunnane was peaceful.

Ian halted at a cottage door, and the scrawny brown dog

that lay across the threshold tilted its head and gave a low growl. Ian made a sound and offered a tidbit of meat and biscuit from his pocket. Leftovers from the supper he had eaten standing up in the kitchen.

He gave the dog a friendly scratch behind the ear and then tapped on the plank door. Lamplight shone from the tiny window near the door.

She was waiting for him.

He didn't have to knock again. The door opened and, taking a quick look up and down the deserted road, he slipped inside.

"I brought ye some cheese and sugar." He set a brown sack on the table that sported a single straight-backed chair. "Some ale and a little peppermint."

The dark-haired widow, Ruthie, brushed her hand across his shoulders as she walked behind him. She picked up the sack with interest and peered inside. "Ye be a good man, Ian."

"It's cheese, Ruth, nae gold coin."

She walked to a dry sink, where she began to empty the sack on the sideboard. "And 'tis a good thing, because were it coin I'd toss ye out on your handsome arse." She grinned over her shoulder.

Ian settled in the chair with a sigh. Tucking his hands behind his head, he watched her pull one gift after another out of the bag. He liked to see her smile.

Ruthie was a beautiful woman with inky dark hair that fell in waves over her shoulders and down her full, pale breasts when he undressed her on her rope bed. She had a tiny waist that had never borne children, but shapely hips and thighs. And her lips always appeared berry-swollen to him, as if she'd been eating wild strawberries in a meadow. Kissable lips.

She hummed to herself as she put away the food, her hips swaying slightly to and fro, her skirt brushing her ankles in a way that once would have tantalized him.

Her task complete, she walked back to his chair and

rested her hands on his shoulders. She kneaded the knotted muscles, and he let his eyes drift shut with a groan.

"Ye be sullen tonight."

"I am not sullen."

"Pouting?" she teased.

"Men do not pout."

She laughed, digging her fingers deep into his flesh, massaging, rubbing, and releasing his tension.

"Fancy that."

"Enough of your female wit," he growled. "I'm not in the mood tonight."

Again she chuckled. She was not intimated. Couldn't be. That was one of the reasons he liked Ruthie. She could not be frightened or bullied. She knew what he was and what he was not and accepted him at face value. He liked Ruthie because she liked him for who he was, not what he could do for her. Not even when it came to her sheets.

"Want to talk about it?" she questioned softly.

"Nae!" Again he spoke more sharply than he intended, and the moment the word came out of his mouth, he regretted it.

She was silent.

He let a minute pass. "I'm sorry. My head is full to cracking." He brought his hands to his temples and pressed hard. He could almost feel the tension building, swelling, threatening to burst in his head.

"I've a couple tricks to relieve that pain," she said. Her tone was coy, but she was not a tease. She came around the chair and sat on his lap.

He lowered his hands to rest them comfortably on her waist. That was Ruthie. Warm, comfortable, sensual.

He leaned forward to rest his face between the valley of her breasts. She always smelled clean, though a little of the wool she spun.

Ordinarily he would have nuzzled her breasts; he would have sought a brown nipple with his mouth. He was disappointed to realize that tonight he wasn't interested. Not in *her* breasts, at least.

He thought of the scent of Kara's hair, the feel of her small, firm breast in his palm.

Ruthie brushed her lips across his forehead.

He did not lift his head to meet her lips with his.

She cradled his head with her hands, ran her fingers through his hair. But it didn't feel the same as Kara's touch. Didn't feel as good. Not as right.

Ian sighed.

Ruthie lifted her head, let her hands fall to her sides. "Ye didn't come in the mood for lovin' tonight, darlin'?" It wasn't an accusation. He was thankful her tone was kind.

He, too, let his hands fall. He would not pretend what he did not feel. He respected the widow too much. "I don't know why I came."

She got off his lap. "Our boy-lord wearing on ye?"

Ian covered his face with his palms. It wasn't the boy who was wearing on him. It was the boy's wife. He couldn't tell Ruthie that, of course. No one could know his secret. No doubt Isla was already suspicious. He could let it go no further than that.

"Harry is bright. His heart is good. He'll grow into his seat."

Ruthie backed up and leaned against the table to face him. She crossed her arms over her breasts. "And the wife? I have heard the boy seems infatuated with her. That against all wagers, the marriage has taken."

Ruthie's comment struck Ian wrong and he glanced away. He didn't want his little brother to be infatuated with Kara. He wanted her all for himself. He knew the thought was preposterous, but he couldn't help it. He didn't want to share her, not with anyone, not even her husband.

"The adjustment has been difficult for her, but she is managing," he said carefully.

Ruthie moved to the kitchen sideboard and opened one

of the bottles of ale. She poured half into a pottery cup. "They say she is very beautiful, with baskets of red, rippling hair and a rosy mouth. They say very wise, a good judge of character and the law." She pushed the cup into his hand. "Better than the earl."

Ian drank. "He is young, but his heart is in the right place. He will do what is right for Dunnane."

"Ye sound as if ye've spoken that speech more than once." She tipped the dusty ale bottle to her lips. "Keep saying it and perhaps even ye will believe in time."

Ian frowned. Finishing the cup, he pushed it onto the table and rose. "I shouldn't have come tonight. I'm preoccupied. I'm sorry."

She smiled, still leaning against the table. "Do ye wish to tell me who the woman is or not?"

He couldn't meet her gaze. Was he a man so easily read? That could be dangerous.

"Nae?" She raised a shoulder in a shrug. " 'Tis all right, Ian. I knew ye'd not warm my bed forever."

He walked toward the door. "It's not you, Ruthie."

"I know," she said warmly.

He halted at the door and turned to her. "Thank you."

"For what?" Her dark eyes sparkled but they were nothing in comparison to Kara's.

"Listening."

She chuckled. "It's not hard. Ye don't say much." She opened the door for him. "I hope ye figure it out, Ian, because you'd make a woman a damned fine husband."

He kissed her on the cheek and stepped into the cool night air. "Good night, Ruth."

"Night, Ian, love. Good health, good life."

"Good health, good life." He gave a wave and disappeared into the shadows of the cottages.

Coins jingled in a sack. "This be not the amount we agreed upon," a rich, burred voice accused.

Dungald pressed his back to the stone wall, holding up his candle. He hated these catacombs. They were dark and cold and rodent-infested. But they served his needs well. In a copse of trees west of the castle was an opening that had once led into the bowels of the old castle built before Dunnane. Now it served as a clandestine entrance to the catacombs beneath the present structure. He never had to pass through the gates to meet with the men he hired.

"Give me time. I'll have the rest."

"Ye'll have the rest or ye'll have a blade to yer throat."

Dungald gave a snort. He was not afraid. He was not afraid because he had the righteousness of God on his side. "Must everything be about money?" he snapped. "What honor is left in this world?"

The man chuckled. "I wonder the same."

Dungald stared into the velvety darkness. He couldn't see the man but he could feel how close he was. He could see the glisten of his eyes, hear him breathing. "Ye know not what ye speak of. I should have been the earl, not that whining brat. His father was not worth the pot he pissed in! My father defended this castle! My father saw to its day-to-day running. The late, great earl was too busy marrying and getting brats by one woman after the next to be concerned with Dunnane."

"Tsk, tsk, ye sound bitter. Bitterness is not a draught well taken to the table," the man warned.

"Shut up. If I want your opinion, I shall pay for it. Until then keep it to yourself!"

The man jingled the coins in the bag. "As ye wish, master."

"Now go before you're seen." Dungald turned away, anxious to get to his warm bed and the even warmer wench who waited for him. "Continue with your orders."

"Need another heart?" the voice taunted.

Dungald stalked off. "Nae, not unless you can bring me the boy's."

Chapter Twelve

"Aye, this fabric for his lordship's coat, to match the green-and-brown plaid for his kilt," Kara said, fingering the rich forest green brocade. "And a length of the plaid for my gown as well."

She sat at a table in the corner of the great hall, making the preparations for Harry's birthday festival. There were so many decisions to make, too many. After a while she chose fabrics, food and guests by what was easier, faster. She certainly wanted Harry's birthday celebration to be a fine one, but she didn't want to turn into a raving lunatic for the sake of a boy's fourteenth birthday, either.

"Aye, my lady." The tailor bowed and backed away, his fabrics draped over his shoulders like a Roman toga.

"Thank ye, sir," Isla told the tailor. "Tell me when ye need his lordship for the fitting. Next!"

Isla had been a godsend this last fortnight. Kara could never have organized such a large celebration without her. The girl learned quickly and was amazingly adept at dealing with servants and merchants, as well as with Harry. She had undying patience for the most mundane chores. She helped Kara focus on each task at hand, knowing when to offer suggestions and when to remain silent.

"How many partridges?" Dunnane's sour-faced game-keeper asked. The man had to be in his seventies, walked with a cane and squinted, but he was a master of his duties. He kept Dunnane's tables laden with meat, and the surrounding fields and forests devoid of poachers. "I must know how many partridges ye need," he grumbled.

"Depends on the number of guests, James." Kara flipped through the sheets of paper scattered on the table. They were all notes taken in her own sprawling handwriting. She located the guest list lined with clan and family names, checks, and names crossed off. "I believe we're up to a hundred and thirteen men and women. Plus children and servants."

The gamekeeper tapped his cane impatiently. "How many partridges?"

Kara tried to think, but she couldn't. She pressed her hands to her temples.

When Harry had brought up the idea of a birthday festival, she had thrown herself completely into planning the event. She thought it would be a good way to keep her mind off Ian. In the last weeks she'd been too busy planning for the party and overseeing the tower renovations to see him at any other time but the evening meal.

But, in spite of her busy schedule, Ian was constantly in her thoughts: when she ate, when she sewed, when she lay awake alone in her bed at night and listened to Harry's soft snoring. As she chose the menu, the guests, even the entertainment for Harry's birthday, she imagined what Ian would like. She secretly pretended he was her husband and she was planning a surprise for him. Then she spent half the hours of the day pining for him and the other half feeling dreadfully guilty.

Ian, too, seemed to be going out of his way to avoid her. And when they did meet it was always in the presence of others; he stayed away from the tower, away from the staircase where they seemed to run into each other.

They were both trying so hard to avoid what she feared could not be avoided that her nerves were raw. She was jumpy, tired, couldn't sleep at night, and had no appetite. She could only imagine how he was holding up, because he was always so stoic. But Kara knew how she felt: like a pot on the edge of boiling. Simmering, not knowing at what moment she would spill over.

"The partridges, my lady," the gamekeeper repeated.

Kara glanced up at Isla, who stood at her right hand.

"I'll check with the cook," Isla said smoothly, "and tell ye how many blessed partridges we need. Next!"

Kara groaned. Shadows were lengthening in the great hall. The sunlight coming in through the windows high on the walls was beginning to fade. She'd been at this for hours.

"How much more?" Kara whispered behind her hand.

Isla leaned over her mistress's shoulder, still seeming to be unencumbered by her growing abdomen. "The weaver, the dairy mistress, and a gentleman wishing you to hire his minstrels." She drew her lips taut in an attempt not to smile. "Also a man with monkeys."

"Monkeys?" Kara gathered her notes.

"Aye." Isla grinned. "He says they're performing monkeys. Swing on little swings, drink from ale bottles, spit and scratch, I suppose."

Kara glanced at her maid. "Sounds the perfect entertainment for our Gordon men, don't ye think?"

Isla snickered. "Ye want me to see the last few while you take a walk in the garden?"

Kara rose, thankful for the offer. Despite the girl's age, she trusted Isla implicitly. "You would do that for me?"

A man who looked a wee bit like a monkey, and most definitely smelled like one, hovered in front of the table, waiting to be recognized.

"Would ye take a barefoot slut of a pregnant girl into

er house?" Isla questioned. "Would ye feed her, clothe
her, treat her kindly, and give her a reason to think she
has a place on this earth?"

Kara patted Isla's arm. "We'll hear the musicians
tonight. We'll take the monkey man, and ye deal with the
dairy mistress the best ye see fit." She looked into the
young girl's warm eyes. "Thank you."

Isla slipped into Kara's chair. "Next!"

Kara walked out of the hall and out of the castle by the
guarded yett. Once outside, yet still within the walled bai-
ley, she walked to the south side, where there was a small
garden.

She took a deep breath as she walked under an archway.
It was May and the garden was just finally beginning to
turn green. Trees were sprouting new leaves, bushes were
budding, bulbs were poking their heads up from the
thawed ground. Everything in the garden seemed so fresh
and new, as if just awakening from a long slumber. Kara
admired the garden's fresh vitality and yearned to feel the
way the garden appeared: hopeful.

She walked down a stone path, deeper into the garden.
A bird sang in the ivy that grew up a trellis. Insects chirped.
There was a large stone fountain that stood in the center
of a bed of green vines. Water trickled from a cherub's
pitcher into the pool.

"Beautiful, isn't it?"

Kara glanced up, surprised to see her mother-in-law
seated on a stone bench beside a sundial on a pedestal.
Kara had been so lost in her own thoughts that she'd not
realized she wasn't alone.

"Mother Anne."

"Just out for a walk?"

"I needed a breath of fresh air, I think." Kara clasped
her head. "I'm swimming with so many details. I want
Harry's birthday to be special for him, but I fear I've bitten
off more than I can chew."

"Nonsense. I see you at work. You are a perfect mistress

for Dunnane. Better than I ever was.'' Anne tapped the place beside her on the bench. "Will you sit with me?"

Kara accepted the invitation. She liked Anne and had enjoyed her companionship these last weeks. She was thankful that spending evenings with her mother-in-law took away from time Kara would have ordinarily spent with the men in the great hall. With Ian.

"Ye look troubled," Anne said.

Kara avoided the older woman's gaze.

"You're pale and ye seem to be thinner than when I first arrived. You're not by chance with child, are you?" Anne's tone was gentle, but she couldn't hide the hint of hope in her voice.

It was all Kara could do to keep from laughing aloud. Since the night she'd argued with Harry, she had slept alone. Not that it would have made a difference. She had no intentions of having sexual relations with a boy. "Nae, I am not with child, Mother Anne."

Anne sighed and patted Kara's hand. Her touch was oddly comforting.

"Ye know, it's not easy, the lives we women lead," Anne said, folding her hands in her lap. "We are here to serve, to protect, to comfort, to love. To bear children for our lords, raise them to be lords themselves. 'Tis a large pair of slippers to fill at times. And so easy to lose ourselves."

"I'll manage. 'Twill only take time to grow used to my new duties."

"Aye." Anne squeezed Kara's hand. "You've a good attitude. I admire a woman who does not shrink from her duties." She paused. "The question is: what if fulfilling our duty is not all we desire out of life?" Anne looked sideways at Kara.

Kara felt that Anne could somehow see through her, know what she was thinking.

"Duty is not always where our hearts lie. Husbands are not always where our hearts lie." She paused, glancing away. "And sometimes what we believe, what we know to be the truth, is not."

Kara was feeling more uncomfortable by the moment. What was Anne trying to tell her? What did she know? Kara had been so careful around Ian. He had been so careful. Surely Anne didn't suspect there was anything between Kara and her elder son.

"Ye understand, Kara," Anne went on, her tone suggesting she meant more than she said. "I think that if ye fulfill your duties, ye be entitled to some happiness of your own. Ye'd be amazed how easily a husband will turn his head when he is well fed and a son sleeps in a cradle on his hearth."

What did Anne mean? Did she mean what Kara thought she meant? That it would be permissible to have a lover? Would she say the same if she knew it was her other son Kara loved?

"I married Harry's father because he was a good prospect for a husband. He needed my father's name at court to get him out of a wee bit of trouble. I needed his name to protect myself, to provide stability for Ian." She lifted her hand from Kara's and tightened the tartan shawl she wore on her shoulders. "Once I provided his lordship with a son, I was free to do as I pleased. He even allowed me to return to Edinburgh for most of the year."

Kara was silent. She could feel her heart ticking in her chest.

Anne rose. "What I'm trying to tell you, and saying badly, is that I understand your marriage to my son has not been easy. Is not easy. Will not be easy." She softened. "He seems to care a great deal for you. . . ."

Kara lowered her gaze, her guilt slipping over her like a widow's veil.

"But he is young and at times immature. Not a man a woman dreams of marrying." Anne was quiet for a moment as she gazed over the garden.

The sun was slipping over the horizon, below the west

wall of the garden. The sky was a muted shade of pink and mauve with strokes of red. The breeze was slight; new leaves rustled.

"Take my words of age and wisdom, Kara." She turned to the younger woman. "If you do your duty, as all women must, you could find some happiness in this world. You could make a place for yourself. A place acceptable to both you and your husband. Just remain discreet."

Kara studied her fingernails. She could not believe Harry's mother was saying these things. And yet she was thankful. It did her heart good to know that someone knew how she felt.

"I appreciate your advice, Mother Anne," Kara said quietly. "I—"

"Kara!" Isla appeared in the garden archway. She waved a hand wildly. "Come quickly! His lordship has been injured!"

Kara leaped off the bench and ran across the garden, her woolen skirts bunched in her hands. Anne followed.

"What happened?" Kara demanded as she ran beside Isla and cut in front of her.

"He and Master Ian were dueling, mistress." They ran out of the garden, past the entrance to the house, to the outer courtyard.

"Fighting!" Kara exclaimed. Her heart was pounding. Not Harry. Not her dear Harry. Why in God's name would Ian be fighting with Harry? Had the man no sense at all?

"Practicing, mistress. For the duels at the birthday festival."

"No one told me he was dueling! Whose idea was this? The competition was for guests, not him!"

Isla darted along the wall. Kara could see a crowd of men, along with Ian, down on their knees circled around a prone body. It had to be Harry.

What would she do if Harry died? She would be expected to marry Dungald. She'd sooner run a sword through her own heart.

"It was supposed to be a surprise." Isla clasped her red cheeks. "Please don't be angry, mistress. His lordship wanted to surprise you with his abilities."

Reaching the huddle, Kara pushed a burly Gordon aside. "Harry!"

Ian was kneeling to the boy's left, pressing a cloth into Harry's thigh. The cloth was soaked with blood. Harry's eyes were closed.

"Harry!" she cried, her voice shriller than she had intended.

She was thankful when his eyes blinked open. "Kara?" he said.

Softly she brushed her hand over his cheek. He was so pale.

"My son," Anne begged. "Does he live?"

"He lives," one of the men muttered.

"A flesh wound," said another.

Isla held Lady Anne's hand, keeping her back out of Kara's way.

Kara lifted her gaze to look Ian straight in the eye. "Was he injured elsewhere?"

"Just my leg," Harry said weakly, lifting his hand to point. "Don't worry yourself, wife." He smiled a crooked, boyish grin.

"Don't worry!" Kara flared. "You're struck by one of your own men! Your own brother. Run through, and I'm not to worry!"

"My lady," Ian said gently.

She raised her head again. "What is wrong with you, fighting with real swords?" she spit. "Ye could have killed him!"

"Kara," Ian said again, this time more forcefully. "That is enough."

"Enough! It is not enough! You're supposed to be protecting him. Keeping him safe from harm, not running him through with swords!"

Ian rose. "Take him into the hall," he barked, wiping

his hands on his plaid kilt. "I'll send for bandages. Isla, my medicinal basket. Fetch it from my chamber."

The men moved to follow Ian's bidding, lifting Harry gently between them.

Kara stepped back. "Are you certain he should be moved? Shouldn't we summon a surgeon from Aberdeen?"

Ian grasped her arm tightly. "Kara, hush," he said sharply. His face was hard and lined.

"Let go of me," she hissed under her breath. "Let me go to Harry."

The men carried the boy off, his mother trailing behind.

"Not like this."

"Like what?" She squirmed to get away from him. She didn't care if she made a scene before the men. She didn't want Ian touching her. She didn't want him touching her because a part of her wanted so badly to be touched by him.

"You cannot behave like this," Ian said between his teeth. He dragged her along the stone wall, away from the others.

"Let go of me!"

He pulled her behind a half wall that extended from the main wall that circled the castle. "Kara, you're embarrassing him. Demeaning him in front of his men."

She yanked and he released her so quickly that she nearly tumbled.

She glared at him, rubbing her forearm where his fingers had bruised her flesh. "What do you mean, demeaning?"

"Ye want him to be the lord of the manor, so treat him like the lord."

"A dead boy cannot be a lord!"

"He is not dead! He is not even greatly injured. Injuries occur during practice. It's the only way the boy will learn."

Kara turned away, feeling hot tears rise behind her eyes.

"He shouldn't be dueling." She folded her arms, hugging herself. Suddenly the air was cool. The sun had set. "He doesn't know what he's doing. He's only a little boy."

"He is not a little boy. He is nearly a man, a man with a wife and responsibilities, and men must know how to fight."

At the mention of the word *wife,* she inhaled sharply. "He could have been killed," she managed.

"Ye think I don't know that? Ye think I wanted to hurt him?" Ian's voice cracked with gruff emotion. "Ye think I wouldn't give my own life for that of my brother? If ye think that, lass, then ye don't know me as well as I thought ye did."

Ian walked away and Kara let him go. Tears slid down her cheeks. He was right. She knew he was right. The injury wasn't so bad. Harry was conscious, talking. Men were often wounded in dueling practice. Her brothers had all been wounded when learning the art. She had just forgotten.

Kara stood at the wall another few moments, collecting herself, and then went to the great hall to see how Harry was doing.

She found Harry sitting up in a chair in front of the fireplace. His leg was propped on a stool, where Lady Dunnane could get a better look at his wound. He was drinking some wine and eating a sweet biscuit slathered in jam. Color was returning to his face. It appeared he would live.

"Harry." She went to his side and squatted, taking his hand. "I'm sorry," she said quietly. "I didn't intend to be the hysterical wife."

Harry's men wandered about the hall, talking among themselves. Servants ran back and forth fetching bandages and food, and adding to the general disorder. She saw neither Ian nor Dungald.

Harry smiled up at Kara. " 'Tis all right." Bright spots

appeared on his pale cheeks. "I rather liked having ye come running to my side."

She rubbed his hand between her palms. It was dirty and smelled of sweat and soil but still a comfort to her. She loved Harry; she knew it when she'd run through the garden, fearing for his life. What pained her now was the knowledge that what she had suspected was true. She loved him as a brother and nothing more. There would never be more. "Nae, it was wrong of me to behave thusly before your men. I promise ye it won't happen again."

Anne pressed an herbal compress to Harry's bare leg thrust from his green kilt, and he flinched and closed his eyes.

When he opened them again, she asked softly, "Would ye like to sup in our chamber tonight? In private. There ye could rest in your bed and be more comfortable."

"Ye'll stay with me?" His blue eyes searched hers. "Stay until I go to sleep?" he whispered.

Kara lowered her forehead to rest it on the back of Harry's hand. "Whatever it is ye wish, my lord."

Kara hummed softly, her cheek pressed to Harry's pillow, her body stretched in the bed beside his.

Harry's breath came evenly. He was asleep.

Careful not to wake him, she slipped out of bed. She was still fully clothed.

Once Harry's wound was cleaned and bandaged properly, Kara had had her husband carried to his chamber. She had ordered a light supper and she and Harry ate it picnic-style in the great bed they had once shared. Then she helped him into his nightshirt, read to him, and tucked the woolen blankets beneath his chin. At his request she lay beside him until he drifted off to sleep.

Kara moved quietly about the room, cleaning up the supper dishes. She had dismissed Isla. The girl had done enough work for one day, and she was, after all, far gone with child.

Kara felt drained. After she had seen for herself that Harry's wound was not terribly serious, she had wanted to speak to Ian privately. She wanted to apologize. But she hadn't found a chance in the hall, and then when the men brought Harry upstairs, Ian had not accompanied them.

The dishes stacked on a tray by the door, the fire stoked and the candles put out, there was nothing left for Kara to do in Harry's chamber. She wandered into her own, then Isla's, where candlelight still burned. The girl sat up in bed stitching a tiny gown.

Kara leaned on the doorjamb that did not yet have a door. The workers were building the doors that would go in each of the doorways that had been recently cut into the walls.

Isla glanced up. "Ye look tired, mistress."

Kara smiled. "Probably not as tired as I feel."

"His lordship?"

"Sleeping. I think he'll be fine."

Isla took another stitch and looked up at Kara again. "If ye were to lay in your bed, my lady, sleep might find ye."

Kara smiled. "I'm too jittery to sleep just yet."

Isla bowed her head. "Ye were awful angry with Master Ian. Ye know, he didn't mean to hurt young Harry."

Ordinarily it wouldn't have been appropriate for a serving girl to refer to her lord in such a familiar manner, but between the two women, when they were alone, it just seemed right.

"I know he didn't, Isla. I handled myself poorly."

"Ye were distraught over your husband."

"I was angry with Ian."

"Fer duelin'?"

Kara closed her eyes. "For being alive, I think."

"Ye know, he sometimes walks the parapet this time of night."

Kara opened her eyes. "What did ye say?"

"Master Ian. I seen him going up the tower stairs. He passes this floor. Goes all the way up to the old parapet. Girls in the kitchen say he probably howls at the moon." She grinned.

Kara smiled. "I suppose I could go up and apologize."

"Ye'd be alone," Isla offered.

Kara's gaze narrowed. She knew that the girl knew there was something between her and Ian, though not how much she knew. Still, she trusted her. "What are you saying, Isla?"

"Not saying a thing ye didn't hear." She shrugged. "Only that Master Ian be alone. Ye could . . . talk alone."

Kara ran a hand through her hair. Much of it had come undone from the tortoiseshell pins and hung over her shoulders. She knew she must look a sight.

"I'll keep an eye on his lordship. Listen for him."

Kara stared at her leather slippers peeking from her skirts. Did she dare go above with Ian . . . alone?

But she knew she wouldn't be able to sleep without making things right between them. She had spoken harshly and out of turn. She owed him an apology. He was right; she did know him better than to think he would ever intentionally harm or allow anyone else to harm Harry.

Isla climbed out of bed. She wore one of her mistress's old sleeping gowns, which swept the floor as she walked. "Take yer cloak, mistress; it's windy above."

Her woolen mantle thrown over her shoulders, Kara walked slowly up the tower steps toward the door that led out onto the parapet. She carried no candle, but she knew the staircase well enough by now to find sure footing with each step.

At the top she pushed open the heavy door. Cold wind struck her as she stepped out onto the palisade four and a half stories above ground level. A flag bearing the Dunnane colors flapped somewhere out of view.

She closed the door behind her and turned to study the dark horizon.

She immediately spotted a hulking, dark form illuminated by moonlight.

Ian.

Chapter Thirteen

He didn't turn as she approached behind him. "Ye should not be here," he said sharply.

" 'Tis my home now, too." She stood beside him and leaned on the wall, not daring to look at him. "Mine more than yours, if ye have no wish to mince words."

He made a sound in his throat.

"I came to apologize."

"How is he?"

She pressed her bare hands to the waist-high stone wall that kept her from tumbling to her death. The stones were cold, rough on her palms. "Harry is fine." She glanced at him, then into the dark abyss again. "Did you hear what I said? I wanted to apologize for the way I treated you today."

"I heard ye."

She sighed. He wasn't going to make this easy. "I was scared, Ian. When I heard Harry had been injured, all I could think was that he could die."

"Ye came running."

She wondered what he meant by his observation. "Aye.

I came running. But I would have done the same had it been you or Isla."

"Ye came running because you love him." His tone had become flat and intentionally devoid of any emotion.

"Aye," she answered firmly. "I do love him."

He was silent.

She could see only the silhouette of his face, so she couldn't make out any expression. He was wearing a calf-length cloak that was dark and formless and made him seem even taller, broader than he was—not a man anyone would want to encounter on a dark night.

"Ye should go," he said quietly.

It occurred to her what he meant about her running to Harry's side. "I don't wish to go. I want to stay here with you."

"I will not come between a man and his wife."

She almost smiled. He was *jealous*. He thought she meant that she loved Harry in a romantic way. Didn't the man understand how many ways a woman could love?

She slid her hand across the top of the wall to cover his larger hand. "I am a woman of age and of sound mind. I have a right to make my own choices." She smiled wryly. "Choose my own sins."

"I don't understand you, woman."

She turned to him to stand so close that she could feel the warmth of his body. "I think ye do."

He groaned as he turned to her, as if he were battling some invisible spirit. His conscience, she guessed.

"Kara, do ye understand what ye say?" He spoke in anguish. "What it would mean?"

"I love Harry." She spoke quietly but adamantly. "But only as a sister loves a brother. I have already made up my mind that I will not sleep with him as a wife sleeps with her husband. Not ever."

"He will grow," Ian said lamely. He still did not touch her. Did not look at her.

She stared at his face, close enough that she could see

his inner turmoil reflected in the tightness of his lips, the squint of his eyes, the hard lines around his mouth.

"It doesn't matter. In my mind, he will always be a boy."

"I could not share you." He lifted his gaze. "Ye understand that? Not with anyone. Not even my brother."

"No more than I could share you." She took both his hands in hers, lacing their fingers. She felt as if she were standing atop the wall, about to jump. "Yet I can see no way to divorce or to annul."

He was quiet, listening.

"Nae," she whispered, amazed that the two of them could stand here and discuss the matter so logically. "I must remain married to Harry until death comes to one of us. And if he should die, I would be married to another." She paused. "Ian, I can give you my heart . . . my body, but never my hand."

" 'Twould be dangerous. If Harry discovers—if anyone discovers the truth, ye could be tossed in the dungeon. I would be hanged."

She stepped closer, pressing her chest to his. His open cloak fell around her, enveloping her. "What is worth more risk than love?"

"Aye, what indeed?" he breathed as he swept down, taking her mouth with his.

Their lips met so abruptly that he took her breath away. She clung to him, shocked by the fierceness of her desire for him. Their tongues met, hot and wet, tangling, thrusting. She molded her hips to his and he drew her even closer. Inside his cloak the two became one. "Not here," he groaned. "I will not make love to you here. Not like this. I want us to have time. I want to see you, to touch you. To hold ye."

"Nae," she agreed, kissing his cheek, his ear, the side of his neck. "Not here." His words made sense somewhere in the back of her mind, but her desire for him was suddenly so desperate that had he said the word, she would have stepped out of her skirts here in the cold darkness and given herself to him on his spread cloak.

"Where can we go?" She sucked in a breath of cold air, her heart pounding. "Harry sleeps, but my chambers have yet to gain a door."

His hands brushed her waist, her breasts, burning a trail of heat through her layers of undergarments and Dunnane plaid.

"We should wait. Think," he breathed hot in her ear. "Be certain this is what we want."

She wrapped her arms around his neck, lifting on her toes to look him in the eyes. "It's what I want if you want it."

He groaned and kissed her again. "Ye do not know how long I have dreamed of you. Dreamed of taking you in my arms, to my bed. You are on my mind so greatly that I have begun to fear I would perish without you."

She laughed, her voice husky with passion. His words were a song in her ear. And not for one moment did she doubt him. Ian was a man of few words, but when he spoke she knew she could believe him.

"Where?" she repeated. "Where can we go? Your chamber?"

He shook his head. "It's dangerous, so close to Dungald's."

"I'll come to you, quiet as a mouse."

He pushed away the hair that had blown in her face. "Kara, hinny, are ye certain this is what you want? We take this path and there is no turning back. No matter what the courts or my brother say, you will be mine, forever. Ye understand?"

She squeezed his hand and let go of it, then walked away. "Wait for me," she whispered. "And I will come to you."

* * *

Kara crept down the velvety dark corridor without the assistance of a candle. Ian slept in the south wing, where some of the other single men of Dunnane resided. Somewhere along the length of hall was Dungald's room, but she didn't know which. She knew only Ian's. Third door on the left.

Though spring had come to the Highlands, it was still cold at night and she was thankful she had thought to wear a light cloak. The hallway was drafty, eerie, but she pressed on.

After meeting Ian on the parapet she had returned to her rooms. She had checked on Harry and Isla and found both sleeping. Then in her own room she had brushed out her hair, washed her face and brushed her teeth, and changed into a sleeping gown. She chose the one she liked the best.

Kara waited more than an hour before leaving the safety of her room to be certain all in the castle had retired for the night. It was after midnight. As she'd waited before her fireplace, her hands clasped, she had been nervous. It had been her chance to change her mind. But she knew in her heart that she would never love another man as she loved Ian. She would not turn away this chance at a few moments of happiness. She didn't know where her future lay, but at least she would know that she had this love, if only once. If only tonight.

Now, reaching Ian's room, she was nervous again. But not about having made the right decision. She was nervous about making love. He said he wanted her so desperately that he had dreamed of her. What if she wasn't what he had imagined? What if she couldn't live up to his expectations? She had no experience at lovemaking. She had little experience at kissing.

She was tempted to turn and run.

The door creaked open.

"Kara?"

Step in or run? Last chance.

Kara slipped into his room and pushed the door shut with the heel of her slipper.

Ian's room was illuminated softly with candlelight. It was a tiny chamber, sparse, clean and utilitarian, seeming hardly fit for an earl's brother. There was a small stone fireplace, a narrow wooden bed, a table and one chair. It looked like a room Ian would sleep in. No mess. No fuss. But it smelled good. Like lavender. His special touch.

"Wine?" he asked her.

Before she could answer, he pushed a goblet into her hands. She didn't need the wine—she was already dizzy—but she drank anyway.

Ian stood in front of her and drank from his own cup. He had stripped down to his kilt and a linen shirt, barefoot without his stockings. He looked like a husband just about to turn in for the night. At least he looked the way she had imagined a husband would appear. Harry still wore those silly sleeping gowns and a cap on his head.

"Ye don't have to stay if ye don't want to," Ian said, walking three steps to the fireplace.

She came to stand beside him. She was bubbling inside. Anxious, fearful, joyful. "I want to stay."

He slipped his hand around her waist as they both stared into the flames in the hearth. This all seemed so natural to her, the two of them alone late at night in private chambers. Him touching her casually, in a loving way. This was how she had once imagined marriage.

Ian took her goblet from her hand, setting both on the narrow mantel, then drew her into his embrace. He gazed into her eyes, brushing away the hair that fell over her cheek. "Before I make love to ye, hinny, I must make a vow."

She shook her head adamantly. "I ask for no promises. Only the truth." She studied his dark eyes that seemed to penetrate her very soul. "Do ye love me, Ian Munroe?"

He took her hand and pressed it to his breast. She could feel his heart pounding.

"I love ye as the eastern sky loves the sunrise," he murmured, "as the western sky loves the sunset."

Her lower lip trembled and she felt the burn of tears in her eyes. Tears of happiness, mingled with sorrow. "That's all I ask of ye."

" 'Tis not enough." He held her hand firmly to his pounding heart. "I vow to love ye, protect, honor ye whilst I live in this world as well as the next." He took her hands in his and kissed them. Then her lips.

At that moment she knew she was the happiest woman who breathed.

"I love ye, Kara," he whispered in her ear. "Always, forever."

"I love ye," she returned.

His mouth met hers again, this time with greater insistence. Her tears dried as the burning in her middle began to spread outward, seeping through her limbs. His mouth set hers on fire. He tasted so strong, so confident. How could she not be confident of herself?

He pushed her cloak from her shoulders and it fell in a puddle at her feet.

Locked in his embrace, he kept her from swaying as her knees grew weak. He drew his hand up her thigh, over her hip, her waist, taking his time, burning a path of desire with every passing moment.

He skimmed his palm over her abdomen and she inhaled, awash in the sensation. The fabric of her clothing seemed not to deter his touch but to invite it. As he brought his hand up under her breast she let out a strangled sigh. His thumb found the bud of her nipple and she groaned. All the while he was kissing her, his tongue stroking hers.

"Will ye come to my bed?" he whispered.

Again he was asking. Again he was giving her the chance to change her mind.

She wrapped her arms around his neck, pressing her mouth to his. She would not turn away now, not if Satan were breathing down her neck. Maybe he was, but she didn't care.

"Aye," she whispered. "Your bed."

To her surprise he lifted her into his arms. She smiled up at him. Perhaps it was foolish of her, a romantic notion, but she was flattered that he would lift her, carry her.

She rested her cheek on his shoulder as he took her the short distance to his bed. He lowered her slowly, gently, never taking his gaze from her for a moment. He sat on the edge of the bed, lifted her foot and removed her slipper. He stroked the instep of her bare foot and she sighed with contentment. He removed the other slipper, tossing it to the floor.

Ian stretched out beside her and took her in one arm, rolling her toward him so that they faced each other. He stroked her arm, her waist, and the rise of her hip. He nibbled on her lower lip, her earlobe.

Kara's breath came faster. She could feel her blood racing in her veins. Her heart was pounding, her entire body quaking, yearning.

He slipped his hand under her gown and she sighed, then groaned. His hand was big, so warm. As he stroked her bare flesh he left behind shivers of delight.

Never in Kara's wildest dreams had she imagined making love would be like this. All she knew of the union between a man and a woman was of duty. Of tolerance. Why had all the women in her life failed to tell her the truth?

Growing more confident of herself as Ian whispered sweet words of encouragement in her ear, Kara dared to put out a hand to touch him. At first she just stroked his chest through the linen of his shirt. He half sat up and skinned it off his back. He lay beside her again, his chest bare and such a wonder that she could not resist touching . . . kissing.

The hair that fanned between his breasts and narrowed to a line disappearing beneath his kilt was almost black, soft, springy beneath her fingertips. To her amazement, his nipple hardened as she brushed it with her fingertip. At first she touched him only gingerly, to see what his reaction would be. But his groan of pleasure made her bolder.

Ian drew her gown up slowly, baring first her calves, then her thighs, then higher. The air in the small room was warm and felt liquid as it glided over her flesh.

Shyness washed over her as he removed her gown, but then he drew her into his arms and whispered that he loved her, and she felt safe and confident again.

They kissed, first gently, then deeper and harder. He stroked her bare breasts, taunting them into ripe peaks. As he took her nipple between his lips she cried out, then covered her mouth with her hand.

He glanced up at her, smiling. She laughed at herself. "I promised I would be quiet," she whispered.

He stretched out over her. "I promise nothing more than a soft mew will escape these lips."

She moaned with delight and pulled him closer. Her entire body pulsed, ached for the pressure of his body pressed atop hers.

She fumbled with his kilt.

"Ye want me to take it off?" he whispered.

She knew her cheeks colored, but she felt assured enough in his embrace to speak up. "Aye, I want . . . I want to see all of ye."

"Sassy wench," he teased.

Her eyes grew round and she backed away a little as his hand found the closure of his kilt.

He grinned. "And a sassy wench is just what I like."

His smile was contagious. It had never occurred to her that there could be smiles and laughter between the sheets. The thought delighted her.

Ian shed his kilt and his man's rod sprang up, hot and hard against her bare leg. Again they kissed, and as their kiss deepened she moved closer to him, molding her groin to his. She liked the feel of his hardness against her. She wanted more. . . .

Ian rubbed her bare thigh; first the top, then the inner flesh, and with each stroke the heat in her middle grew hotter. Of their own accord, her legs parted.

She was breathless with anticipation before he ever touched the curls of red hair between her thighs. And as he finally did, she stiffened, her muscles flexing, then relaxing. Glorious. His touch was glorious. How could anything that felt this good inside and out be sinful?

Kara felt dampness between her thighs. She felt her body moving to the rhythm of his, as if it had a life of its own.

She rolled onto her back. "Please," she whispered, panting.

He stretched over her, his hair coming loose from its leather tie to fall to his shoulders, to tease her chin. "I love ye, sweet Kara. Always. Forever."

"Always. Forever." She panted.

"Now what is it ye want?" He ran his fingers through the cascade of red hair that fell on his pillow. "Tell me, lass."

"You." She closed her eyes, moving her hips against his. "I want you."

"And I you," he whispered.

As their mouths met in a lover's dance, he pressed his hips to hers and she felt his stiff rod probe between her thighs. She opened up to him. If she did not have him soon she would burst.

With the aid of his hand, he slipped into her. She arched her back, cried out.

"Are ye all right?" Ian whispered, his face immediately lined with concern.

She lifted her heavy eyelids and smiled. "Ye did not hurt me."

He smiled and kissed her gently. "To be the first to love a woman is a great gift. I thank ye for this gift."

She let her eyes drift shut. Of their own accord her hips lifted, fell and lifted again.

She felt consumed by him, possessed. And yet the way that her flesh captured his gave her possession as well. He moved slowly inside her.

Kara grew light-headed as their movements became more urgent.

"We have plenty of time," he whispered teasingly in her ear.

She rolled her head back and forth. No. She had waited her whole life for this. For Ian. She would not be delayed now. She was too anxious, too desperate for . . . for what?

Ian's breath came heavier in her ear. Faster. He pressed his palms to the bed on each side of her and lowered and raised his massive body, taking care not to put his full weight on her.

She felt like a vessel washing closer and closer to a rocky shore, rising and falling with each swell of the sea.

Suddenly she felt a burst of pleasure that ran so deep, it touched her soul. Light flashed behind her eyelids; every fiber of her being felt the surge of pleasure. She was shocked . . . amazed. It took her breath away.

Ian halted for an instant, then with a groan stroked again. Once, twice and then he, too, cried out. He called her name and then came to rest atop her.

Kara struggled to catch her breath, her eyes still squeezed shut as little aftershocks of pleasure rippled over her. He rolled off her and onto his side. When she opened her eyes he was watching her.

She raised her head to reach out and brush his lips with her fingertips, smiling. She thought she'd be smiling the rest of her born days. "I liked that," she whispered timidly.

He threw back his head and laughed long and hard, and she fell back onto the pillow, laughing with him.

PART II

The trees they grow high,
And the leaves they do grow green.
Many is the time my true love I've seen.
Many an hour I've watched him all alone.
He's young but he's daily growing.

At the age of thirteen he was a married man.
At the age of fourteen, the father of a son.
At the age of fifteen, his grave it was green,
And death had put an end to his growing.

Chapter Fourteen

Kara felt Ian stroke her hair and plant a kiss on her temple. He whispered her name softly, in a way no one had ever spoken her name before. She knew he was trying to wake her, but she kept her eyes closed and snuggled against him. She didn't want to wake up. She wanted to lie in this limbo between sleep and waking and drift in his warmth, his love.

"Ye must rise, hinny," he murmured. "Dawn will come and ye cannot be here when the castle awakes."

Still she didn't open her eyes. She was too comfortable, too content. Ian held her in his arms, she on her side, he on his back, both naked beneath the woolen blanket. The fire on the hearth had died in the middle of the night and she could feel the chill in the air.

"Kara."

She smiled. "What if I don't want to go? What if I want to stay here with you forever?"

He kissed her forehead. "Would that I were a magician and could make it possible."

Her eyelids fluttered open and she gazed into his dark brown eyes. "Did you sleep?"

"A little. But I didn't want to. I wanted to lie awake and hold you."

She sighed with contentment as she ran her hand over his bare chest. She liked the feel of his muscular frame under her palm; she liked the tickle of his crisp, dark hair that was so different from her own. "Ye should have wakened me and we could have done something else."

He chuckled. "Who would have thought my sweet Kara would be so brazen?"

She lifted her lashes. "Not brazen. Honest. We have no time for anything but honesty between us, Ian."

"Truer words could not be spoken." He patted her bare bottom, his hand cupping one cheek. "Now, come, rise and dress and I'll escort you upstairs."

With a moan of resolve she sat up in his bed. "Nae. It's safer if I go alone." She frowned. "What time is it?" It was still dark in the room, with only the glow of light from embers on the hearth. After she had fallen asleep Ian must have risen and extinguished the candles.

"Near four, I think." He slid out of bed.

She sat on her knees, the tartan blanket drawn around her. She watched as he strode across the room to stoke the fire and add another log.

Ian's naked body was a magnificent sculpture, massive and muscular. She could see the outline of muscles and sinew down his legs, his arms, across the wide expanse of his chest and back. They flexed and rippled when he walked.

She watched as he lit several tallow candles. Her gaze drifted below his navel, and heat suffused her cheeks. His manly part fascinated her. Just thinking about it sent ripples of pleasure through her. She had heard women in kitchens and around the sewing table remark what an ugly abomination the thing was, but she disagreed. Not ugly, only different from her anatomy, and certainly intriguing in its own way.

Ian wrapped his kilt around his middle and reached for last night's discarded shirt, which lay crumpled on the floor. Half-dressed, he retrieved her gown and slippers and brought them to her. "Come, hinny, if you do not dress I will not be able to stop myself from making you mine again."

She accepted her gown and dropped it over her head. "And this would be bad, why?"

He chuckled. "Out of my bed, wench, and to your own."

She climbed out and faced him, the gown falling down her back until the hem brushed her calves. "All right, I'll go," she conceded. "But I will be back."

He kissed her full on the mouth. "Promise?" he whispered.

"Promise." She kissed him again and reached for her slippers on the edge of the bed.

He watched her. "Ye know, Kara, we will have to be very careful, you and I."

"I know."

"To cuckold a man in his own household is dangerous."

She turned to him, running her fingers through her unbound waist-length hair, attempting to put it in some order, knowing it would be impossible. "I understand the seriousness of the sin I have committed."

"Nae, nae, not a sin," he hushed, taking her into his arms again. "The sin was in marrying you off to a boy who could never be a husband to you."

She studied his worried frown. She wanted to believe what he said. She wanted to feel absolved, but right now she didn't. She traced the worry lines across his forehead with her fingertip.

"You know, I would have married you, had you been free," he said.

She smiled sadly. She would not think of would-haves or could-haves right now. It would only make her realize how unfair her lot in life was.

"The first time I laid eyes upon you in that great hall, I knew I would never love anyone but you."

She looked at him doubtfully. "Ye mean to tell me you were virgin as well?" she teased.

"I mean to say I have never loved anyone but you and will never love another. Remember that when you must sit at my little brother's right hand."

The mention of Harry sobered her. "I don't know how I will do it." She broke from his embrace and went to the fireplace to lace the ribbon of her gown.

"You will do it as you do every task, with grace, confidence, determination."

She stared at the flames in the hearth. "I just don't want to hurt him. I am very fond of him."

"I know." He came up behind her and snaked his arms around her waist. She leaned against him and closed her eyes.

"I would not hurt him either," he said. "Unfortunately he is not old enough to understand affairs of the heart."

"As if any of us do." She breathed deeply, her eyes still closed. She wished she didn't have to go, but she knew she must.

Ian rested his cheek against her head. "Last night I said I would not share you. That was unfair. Harry is your husband. Should you become with child—"

"We will cross over that stile when we come to it," she interrupted. She turned in his arms. She didn't want to talk about this, not now. Maybe not ever. She didn't want to think about it. To become pregnant would surely be a calamity. "Now kiss me and I'll be on my way." She turned up the corner of her mouth. "I'll be on my way before I toss you onto that bed and have my way with you."

He kissed her again, this time as a husband kisses a wife. Then he lowered her cloak to her shoulders and let her out his door.

Kara returned to her chamber and her empty bed.

"Kara, are you awake?"

She rolled over in her bed and opened her eyes. It was barely daylight. "I am now," she answered sleepily.

Harry perched on the edge of her feather tick. He was already dressed in his new kilt and wearing a bonnet adorned with the Gordon cockade. Isla had had it stitched for him as a birthday gift. "Today is my birthday," he announced, as if she didn't realize the fact. As if she had not been preparing for today for the last month.

She blinked the sleep from her eyes and shifted to sit up a little higher against her pillows. "Good wishes."

He slid closer to her, his hand behind his back. "And . . . and I know it's my birthday, so people will be giving me gifts," he said hesitantly, "but I wanted to give you something."

"A gift for me?" He had taken her completely by surprise.

"I have one for Mother, too." He lifted one shoulder in a half shrug. "You know, because she gave birth to me." He offered the small object from behind his back. "It's nothing big or costly, but I made it myself."

Kara stared at the small bundle he placed in her hand. It was wrapped in a brocade fabric scrap and tied with a pretty green ribbon. She didn't know what to say.

Guilt washed over her. In the last fortnight she had gone to Ian's private chamber five times. She had wanted to go more often, but had not dared. She had gone to make love to him, to betray Harry, who now sat beside her and offered a gift.

"Open it," he urged with a shy smile.

She tugged on the ribbon and the cloth fell open. Inside was a small wooden box. Inside the box was a wooden cross. It was half the length of her index finger, made of rosewood and polished with some type of wax.

Across the intersecting pieces of wood, Harry had carved the leaves of a vine. It was simple, yet utterly beautiful.

"Oh, Harry," she breathed, fingering the delicate charm. It smelled faintly of freshly carved wood. "It's beautiful."

He beamed. "You like it?"

She hoped he did not see the single tear that gathered in the corner of her eye. These last weeks she had felt so torn. So happy and yet so dreadfully unhappy. "I love it."

"I thought you could put it on this." He picked up the ribbon he had tied the gift with. "Green to match the gown Isla said you were wearing today."

She studied him in wonder. "You asked Isla what I was wearing today?"

He slid off her bed, obviously pleased with himself. "Aye, well, I know how important it is to you ladies to have everything, you know, match."

She stared at the cross in her palm. It truly was beautiful, and what was even more beautiful was that it was obviously a gift from Harry's heart.

What a cold, ruthless woman she must be to cuckold the husband who would carve a cross for his wife with his own hands.

She slid out of bed, dressed in only a thin gown. "I will wear it today proudly," she told him. "And treasure it always." She leaned to kiss Harry, who had grown taller since they had wed.

He took her by surprise by turning his head at the very instant she was to press her lips to his cheek. Her mouth met his. She drew back, startled. He looked into her eyes, making no attempt to step back.

He had done it on purpose; she knew he had.

Kara lowered her gaze and turned away. Instinctively she

raised her fingertips to her mouth. She did not want Harry's mouth touching hers. She wanted to share no such intimacy with anyone but Ian. She didn't care if Harry was her husband or not.

"Well, um, I guess I'll go down to the hall to break the fast with my men," he said awkwardly. "Guests will be arriving soon."

"Aye, yes," she stammered. "I suppose you should go. If you don't mind, I'll just have a little bite here and finish my preparations for the day. I still have to speak to the cook, and the man with the monkeys is nowhere to be found."

"Very well, then." Harry halted in the open door to his chamber and rested his hand in the doorway the way she had seen Ian do so many times. Harry had most definitely grown taller in the last two months. He still didn't look like a man, but he didn't look like a boy anymore either. "I'll be going. I . . . I'm glad you liked your gift."

She didn't look at him. She heard him pause in the doorway, and then he was gone.

Kara let out an exasperated sigh of relief.

"Looks to me like you might be in trouble," Isla said from her doorway.

She must have seen Kara and Harry's exchange, or at least heard part of it.

Kara groaned and held up the cross. She had not told Isla that she and Ian were lovers, but she knew Isla knew. She didn't know how; maybe she had woken and realized Kara was gone one night and figured out where she was. Maybe it was just women's intuition. "He gave me a gift. This cross." Kara held it up. "He . . . he kissed me."

Isla smirked.

"It's not funny!"

Isla came into the chamber, her belly entering before the rest of her. "I know it's not. But the boy is only spreading his wings, becoming a man like we all want him to."

Kara left the cross on the end of her bed and walked to

her window. Her own room was smaller than the one she had shared with Harry, but she liked it. It was cozy, the furniture simple, the bed linens and draperies less impressive. It reminded her of Ian's room. "First a kiss, next he'll be wanting to ... to ..."

"Exercise his husband's rights?" Isla offered. She walked to the fireplace and picked up a poker to stir the embers. "And then what will I do?"

"What will ye do, or what should ye do?"

Kara turned to face the serving woman who had become her friend. "What should I do?"

"Ye're asking me?" She gestured with the iron poker.

"Aye." Kara crossed her arms over her chest. The thought that she might become pregnant weighed heavy on her mind.

"Ye should seduce the boy. Give him his rights, regularly, once month whether he needs it or not. Then go about yer business."

Kara knew her business meant Ian. She could tell by the look on the girl's face. Kara groaned and turned away. "I don't know if I can do that. Harry ... he ... he's still just a boy."

"Ye asked me what would be the smartest thing to do. What's smart ain't always what we do, mistress. Had I been smart, I'd have laid out my stepfather with a poker the first time he slipped under my sheets." She swung the iron rod to demonstrate. "I wouldn't be lookin' like the cow that I am now, if I had."

Kara studied the girl with sympathy. "Has life always been this difficult for women?"

"Always." Isla set down the poker. "Since Eve ate that apple. We got to fight for every lick of fairness and every bit of happiness we can get." She started back toward her small chamber. "I'll dress and get your gown directly. 'Twill be a long day. I already sent for a food tray." She waggled her finger. "Now you be sure you eat. Won't nobody have time today to be carryin' you up these stairs if you fall out from hunger."

Kara couldn't resist a smile. Isla's language was always so colorful.

Someone rapped on Harry's door, and Kara passed from her chamber into his. It had to be a kitchen maid with the food. "Come," she called.

The door swung open. It was Ian. She glanced up in surprise. In the last weeks he had purposely avoided the tower just to be certain he didn't encounter her alone.

"Harry here?" he asked gruffly.

She shook her head. Her stomach fluttered and she pressed her hand to it. Every time she laid eyes on him she felt light-headed. She had read of how love could be felt in a physical way, but she had never believed it until she herself fell in love.

She tried to speak casually, as if they were merely brother and sister-in-law and not lovers. Not beloved. "Harry has gone down to break the fast."

He lowered his voice, glancing through the doorway into her chamber. "Anyone else here?"

"Nae. Just Isla. She's dressing."

He broke into a broad-faced grin, reached out and grabbed her around the waist, nearly lifting her out of her slippers. "Good, because if I don't get you in my arms methinks I will shrivel and die."

She laughed, pushing at him. "Oh, you will not. Where do you get this romantic nonsense?" she chastised him, but secretly she was pleased. She liked his poetic sweet talk.

"I will." He kissed her neck, the pulse of her throat. "As God is my witness."

She struggled, but not too hard.

"I missed you last night," he murmured in her ear. He nipped at her lobe.

"Harry wouldn't go to sleep. He was too excited about his birthday. We played cards for hours. I think I fell asleep first."

He kissed her lips and let her go. " 'Tis all right. You need your rest. You're beginning to get circles under your eyes from lack of sleep. Too much love, not enough sleep."

She walked to the floor-length looking glass framed in an oval of copper. "Ye think so?" She rubbed under both eyes, staring at her face. She was pale and did look tired. But she thought her face reflected her guilt more than lack of sleep. "Heavens, I do look like a hag."

He crossed his arms over his chest. "Ye look beautiful to me."

"Would you please leave?" Her tone was playful as she pointed to the door. "Leave before you get us both into trouble."

He glanced into her chamber again. He could see her bed from where he stood. "Ye said we were alone. Want to . . ." He indicated the bed with a nod of his head.

Her entire body went warm. "I would love to." She clasped his arm and dragged him toward the door. "But I must dress and find the monkeys."

He frowned. "Monkeys?"

"Don't ask. Just go. I'll see you downstairs later, at the festivities."

He stepped into the hall and she followed. "Why were you looking for Harry so early?"

He gave a wave of one broad hand. "Oh, 'twas nothing. A feud that's been going on between two families has escalated again. I wanted to warn him."

"You'll find him in the great hall."

He started for the staircase. "I know."

"You know?" She leaned against the door. "What do you mean, you know? You said you came up in search of him."

"Just an excuse to see you." He winked and then he was gone.

Kara smiled, returning to her bedchamber. "All right." She clapped her hands. "Come, Isla, let me dress. I've got to find those blessed monkeys."

Chapter Fifteen

Kara laughed and clapped as she watched a black spider monkey toss a bright red ball into the air and catch it in his tiny paws. Harry laughed too, delighted by the monkey and Kara's good humor.

It was the most wonderful birthday Harry had ever had. Servants had carried tables and chairs from the great hall into the courtyard for the many guests at the festival. There were boards laden with food, tables for gambling, and stalls for entertainment, just like a village festival. One of his guests could try to toss balls into a jug, strike a bull's-eye with a tiny spear, or guess which nutshell would reveal the halfpence. Kara had even hired a fortune-teller from the village to read tarot cards and toss rune stones. There was music, horse racing, even wrestling. Tonight men and women would dress in their best gowns and kilts, dine and drink until they were satiated and then dance until dawn— all in honor of his fourteenth birthday.

Dungald came up behind Harry and leaned on the table. He smelled of scotch. "Fine fete you've thrown, my lord."

Harry glanced at his cousin. Kara was busy talking with

his mother. The monkey was standing upright on its rear legs, playing a tin drum. "I've my wife to thank," Harry said, watching the performing animal. He always felt awkward around Dungald. His cousin said and did all the right things, but there was something in his tone that scared him sometimes.

"Aye, she's become quite the little wife." He sipped from a goblet. "A fine piece."

Harry forced a smile and reached for his watered wine. That was a compliment, wasn't it? When a man's wife was a fine piece?

"She as talented between the sheets?" Dungald questioned over the rim of his goblet.

Harry choked on the wine that slid down his throat. He coughed and his cousin struck him on the back.

"Easy there. We'll not have you drown on your birthday!"

Tears came to Harry's eyes as he tried to clear his throat. He set down the goblet and wiped his mouth with his sleeve.

"Why, my lord," Dungald whispered in his ear. "By the redness in your face, a man would almost think you had still not slipped her the rod."

Harry felt his cheeks grow hot. He squirmed in his seat. He didn't like Dungald speaking to him about Kara in such a crude manner, but he didn't know what to do to stop him. Did Dungald really know the truth or was he just guessing? How could he know? He had to be guessing. But Ian had warned that no one could know Harry was not sleeping with his wife in the intimate way. It was dangerous, his brother said. Dangerous for them all.

Harry cleared his throat. "I . . . I will not have you speak of my wife thusly," he whispered under his breath. "Mind your own sheets!"

Dungald cackled, sinking the bony fingers of his hand into Harry's shoulder. "Tell me you're not shy, cousin! 'Tis a simple enough act. One she should enjoy thoroughly." He lowered his mouth to Harry's ear. "I could show ye myself, if you wished."

Harry glanced over his shoulder at Dungald in shock.

"Only for the sake of Dunnane, of course," his cousin amended.

Harry waved a hand. "Get your drunken self from me before I have you tossed in the dungeon!"

He spoke loudly enough that several people heard him, including Kara. Heads craned to see what was passing between the earl and his cousin.

"Trouble with the peasants, my lord?" Ian appeared out of nowhere to stand behind Harry's chair.

Thank God for Ian. Harry didn't know what he would do without his dear half brother.

"No trouble," Dungald said innocently. "We were just jesting, weren't we, my lord?"

There it was again, Harry thought. The way Dungald said "my lord." He was mocking him.

"My lord?" Ian questioned Harry directly.

"No trouble," Harry mumbled. "Just get him away from me."

Ian stared hard at Dungald and the man backed away, laughing as he went.

Just then the performing monkey leaped onto the table. Harry clapped his hands, pushing aside thoughts of Dungald and his unconsummated marriage. "Kara, I have to have a monkey," he exclaimed. "Sir, will you sell me this monkey?"

The monkey picked up a piece of bread from Harry's plate and nibbled on it.

"It looks so human, don't you think, Kara?" He peered into the creature's white-framed face.

Kara turned to Harry and smiled, pleased he was having such a good time. She was feeling lighthearted today. She had prepared so well for the festival that she was actually finally able to sit back and enjoy herself. Isla kept her abreast of any minor problems and solved them smoothly.

"Well, sir? Will ye sell me this fine monkey?" Harry asked the monkey man again.

"Nae, my lord, not this monkey, for he is my finest friend, but another could be arranged."

Harry beamed at Kara. "Do you hear that? This fine man will sell me a monkey."

Kara rolled her eyes. "Aye, my lord. That was precisely what I was thinking this morning when I awoke. I thought, what Dunnane needs is a monkey!"

Ian, standing behind them, chuckled.

The monkey man put out his arm and the little creature ran up its length and onto its master's shoulder. The monkey man bowed.

"Come back and talk to me later," Harry told him as he backed away from the dais. Then he rose and offered Kara his hand. "Shall we stroll through the courtyard and see what's about?"

She slid from her chair and accepted his hand. Harry kissed the back of it with a graciousness she'd not seen before in him. Out of the corner of her eye she caught Ian's gaze. He was watching the exchange between them, stone-faced.

She could tell by the look on his face that their situation was as difficult for him as for her.

Kara hated living this lie that her life had become. She hated pretending it was Harry she cared for when it was Ian. She hated taking Harry's hand when it was Ian's she wanted. And where would this end? How could it end but badly? If she were smart, she would end her love affair with Ian now, before her heart was broken. But she knew it was too late. She could not stop herself from loving him, or even from going to his bed. She felt like a sword already thrust, hurtling forward. Now she could only wait to see where it would fall.

"The fortune-teller," Harry chattered. "I think we should try our luck with the fortune-teller." He waved Ian toward him and they waited for him to catch up. "Brother, come with us; we're bound for the fortune-teller's stall."

Ian came reluctantly toward them and Kara watched as the crowd of men and women separated to allow him a wide berth. She found it interesting that a man's reputation could make such an impression on people. After all, few, if any, had ever witnessed Ian Munroe's fury or fighting ability, and yet they all feared him on some level. Most of these people didn't even know for certain if the rumors were true of the number of men he had slain in battle. It was his sheer size and the stern look on his face that convinced them, rather than facts.

"I've no need to have my fortune told," Ian said, walking beside Harry. "I don't wish to know my fate, and if ye had a lick of sense you wouldn't either."

"Surely you don't think it real?" Kara teased. "No one knows the future but God." She squeezed Harry's hand. " 'Tis only for fun, for our own amusement."

Ian waggled a finger. "The Bible warns us of false prophets, of evil spirits occupying the bodies of soothsayers."

Harry rolled his eyes. "Could we expect anything else from my droll brother?"

As they arrived at the fortune-teller's booth, the old woman looked up expectantly. She seemed pleased that the earl of the manor had come to see her.

"Cast your fortune, my lord?" she asked, her voice low-pitched and gravelly.

She did not look the way Kara had imagined a fortune-teller would look like. She was neither shriveled nor sharp-boned, and her gaze had no penetrating light to it. Instead she was round and roly-poly, with pursed red lips and graying hair tied up in a scarf. She looked like someone's grandmother.

"Nae, first my dear wife." Harry pulled a stool out across from the rickety table the old woman sat behind.

"It's your birthday," Kara said. "You should go first."

"You first, then Ian, then me."

Ian made the sign of the cross with two fingers as if to ward off evil spirits. "Nae, I told you. I'll have no part of witchcraft."

Kara laughed and pushed past him to take the seat Harry offered her. "Come, Ian, it's just for fun." She looked at the old woman. "Should I show you my palm?"

Harry slid a coin across the table to the fortune-teller and she tucked it quickly into the bodice of her sacklike gown.

"Aye, give me your pretty hand, dearie, and let Mother Ella tell you what is already cast in the stars for you."

Kara extended her palm.

The woman smoothed it between her own hands and then studied it carefully. She made clicking sounds between her teeth and sighed an occasional "aha."

"Well?" Kara asked. "Will I live to be a grandmother?"

Mother Ella rubbed Kara's palm, causing heat from the friction. "I see much happiness in love," she croaked with a toothy grin. "Great happiness." She knitted her fuzzy brows. "But also great sorrow." She stared at the lines on Kara's palm. "But aye, ye will grow old amidst these walls. A great-grandmother you will be, with many red-haired sons, grandsons and great-grandsons to keep your belly full and your heart happy."

Kara popped out of the chair, satisfied. "Next."

"You certain you won't try your luck?" Harry asked Ian. Ian scowled.

Harry took his seat across from the old woman and offered his palm. She took it between her own plump palms and rubbed it as she had rubbed Kara's. This time she did not smile.

She studied his hand for only a moment and then released it. Harry looked up at her in disappointment. "What of me? Will I be a great grandfather?"

"The runes," she mumbled. "I must consult the runes, my lord."

Kara suddenly felt uncomfortable, though she didn't know

why. "Come, Harry," she said. "Let's see the puppet show. It's about to begin."

"Nae. I want to see what the runes say."

The old woman tossed the rune stones from a bent tin goblet and lowered her face until her eyes were only inches from the tabletop.

"Well?" Harry asked impatiently.

The old woman glanced up past Harry to Kara, then quickly down at the runes again.

Kara didn't like the way the old woman looked at her. She didn't believe in fortune-telling. And she wasn't superstitious, but there was something about the woman's eyes that made her uneasy. Perhaps this wasn't such a good idea after all. "Harry." She touched his arm.

"I want to wait," he declared.

"I see . . . I see much happiness, many children," Mother Ella said, not totally convincingly.

"And a monkey? Do you see a monkey in my future?"

Kara grabbed his hand. "Harry, Ian and I are going to see the puppets. You coming?"

Harry tossed the old woman another coin and rose from the stool. "Lead the way, wife," he said, swaggering gallantly. "I am yours the rest of my days."

The strum of stringed instruments rose in the tower stairwell as Kara descended from her private chambers.

"Mind your skirts," Isla warned, catching the hem of the emerald watered silk as Kara hurried. The gown had been a belated wedding gift from Mother Anne, brought from Edinburgh, and Kara adored it. It was the kind of fashionable garment she imagined a mother would give her newlywed daughter, and she would treasure it always.

"The ale and wine casks have been brought from below to refill our guests' cups?" Kara asked.

"Aye."

"And the cake, doves in place?"

"Yes, mistress. All fourteen. His lordship will be thrilled."

At the very bottom of the winding stairs Kara halted and smoothed the laces of her tight-fitting bodice. "What have I forgotten?"

Isla handed her mistress a lace kerchief. "To smile, my lady."

Kara blotted her lips with the handkerchief. "It's almost over and it's been a great success, hasn't it?"

Isla licked her finger and smoothed one of Kara's stray strands of hair. "His lordship has had a grand time; he told me himself."

"Did he?" She studied fresh-cheeked Isla, who was also sporting a new gown in honor of the earl's birthday. "And when did he tell ye this?"

"Late in the day. When you were in the kitchen. We talk sometimes, the master and I. Ye don't mind, do ye, because if you do—"

"Of course I don't mind. You are here to serve us both."

"Aye, but my loyalty must be to you, my lady, always." She ran a clean hand over her swollen abdomen. "It was you who saved my hide and my baby's."

Kara took Isla's hand in hers. "You have already paid your debt twofold. I could not have gotten through this without you. Any of it," she said meaningfully.

"I am only glad I could be of service. Now go, my lady. I'm certain the birthday boy awaits you."

In the great hall the celebration had already commenced. The tables and chairs had been returned to the hall, and the room was lit with hundreds of blazing candles. Music played and men and women laughed and danced merrily.

Kara spotted her husband standing before one of the twin stone fireplaces, drinking with his men. She approached the group, curtsied and greeted them.

Each man spoke respectfully and bowed. Harry brushed

his lips against her cheek. He smelled of scotch and sounded a little tipsy.

"I thought I would have to come for you myself, wife," he exclaimed, curling one arm around her waist.

The spirits had made him bold. He did not usually handle her with such familiarity. She flashed a smile, wondering if he would make it through the entire evening without passing out, or if he would have to be carried to their private chambers by his clansmen.

"We were just remarking how well his lordship has recovered from his wound," one of the men said.

"Not even a limp," commented another.

Harry grinned and tipped his silver drinking cup adorned with ram's horns for handles. It had been his father's cup before him, presented by Dungald earlier in the day.

"Better yet, I've learned my lesson," Harry said cheerfully. "When my opponent feigns right—" he demonstrated—"I must be certain not to move left."

The men laughed, probably harder than they should have, but they were all indulging Harry today, in honor of the special occasion.

"I wondered myself," Kara said pleasantly, "if—"

The sound of a crashing table cut her off in midsentence. She spun to face the room in time to see a chair fly through the air, hit the northern stone wall and shatter.

"Ye gods," one of the group groaned good-naturedly. "It's George Gordon and Matty MacFae at it again."

"Will they never settle this dispute?" someone asked.

"Haven't in over a hundred years!"

Another chair glanced off the same wall and split. Kara charged toward the middle of the hall, her husband stumbling after her.

"Where are you going?" Harry had to run to keep up.

"I will have no fighting in my hall," Kara said, pushing her way through the crowd that was gathering around the two brawling men. "It's barbaric!"

"It's Scotland," a bearded redhead commented, laughing.

"Not in my hall," Kara snapped.

"Kara, wait." Harry grabbed her shoulder. "I'll not have you in the midst of that. You're liable to be injured."

She hesitated. She didn't want him hurt, but she realized this was an opportunity to show the Gordons who was indeed the rightful heir to Dunnane. She turned to face her boy-husband. "All right," she said quietly. "Then you settle it."

Harry's jaw worked up and down as she took the scotch from his hand. He swallowed hard, tugged on his shirt and gave a decisive nod. "Aye. You're right, wife. We'll have no brawling in our hall." He swept one hand, his voice filled with bravado. "They can well take their fight into the courtyard or be tossed in my dungeon."

Those around Harry stepped back to let him through. Kara took a deep breath as he passed.

"Stand back, wife."

By the time Harry reached the inner circle, four men were fighting, two against two. "Gentlemen," he bellowed as loudly as he could. Luckily his voice did not crack. "Gentlemen, there will be no fighting in my hall!"

As if to punctuate their defiance, Matty MacFae threw a punch, George Gordon ducked and Matty's fist accidentally caught Harry's shoulder.

To everyone's surprise, Harry reacted instantly, swung and struck Matty square in the jaw.

A cheer rose among the clansmen.

Kara cringed. Suddenly she was in a sea of men pushing to get a closer look. Two more men added to the ring, three, then four. Fists were flying. Shouts of encouragement rose and fell with the tide.

Harry caught Matty again, this time on the chin. Matty drew back his bony fist, and before Kara could cry out a warning, MacFae's fist met Harry's nose squarely. His face flowered red as he stumbled backward, flailing his arms.

Kara had enough good sense to know it was too late for her to step into the middle of the fray now. The men were beyond the point of reason. They no longer even knew who they were hitting. Her great hall was quickly turning into a dockside tavern.

"Ian!" she cried, pushing out of the crowd to circumnavigate the fighting men. Where was he? She hadn't seen him in the hall when she entered. "Ian Munroe!"

She reached the entrance to the hall just as he was entering.

"What the hell's going on?" he demanded.

She threw up one hand. "What's it look like? A fight! George Gordon and the eldest MacFae started it, but it's becoming worse."

Ian strode toward the center of the melee, pushing men aside with his elbows and hands.

"Harry's in the middle," she called after him.

"George Gordon!" Ian boomed. "Matty MacFae! What in bloody hell makes ye think you two dogs have the right to—"

Kara never heard the last words out of Ian's mouth. One of the new brawlers slammed a chair against Ian's back and he spun around in fury. Reaching out to lift the man with his bare hands, he shook him until his teeth chattered.

Men cheered. Women covered their mouths and gossiped, but made no attempt either to draw their husbands away from the fight or to move to safer ground.

Ian tossed the man aside and reached for another. He caught a punch to his left cheek, spun his attacker around and sent him colliding with another. The men were in such a frenzy that they seemed to have forgotten who they were fighting or why.

Ian swung one thick fist after the next, catching two men in their jaws, one after the other. He stuck out his leg and tripped another man bent on reaching Harry.

Harry jumped on the fallen man's back and began to

pummel him. The two flipped and suddenly it was Harry being beaten.

He was enjoying it, for heaven's sake! Harry was enjoying the fight.

"Enough," Ian shouted, demonstrating incredible strength by literally lifting the man off the bloody-nosed Harry. "Enough, gentlemen, else you'll all be in the dungeon. I swear by all that's holy, I'll carry ye down there myself."

Kara watched as he plowed through the men, his face bright red with anger and exertion. As she watched, a strange sense of fascination was added to her anger and fear. While the other men in the brawl staggered and swung unevenly, Ian was like a dancer in some macabre performance. Every move seemed well rehearsed. He swung his fists rhythmically, dodging blows from one man as he sank a punch into another man's stomach. Slowly they were beginning to fall and not get up.

Harry lay on his back, panting. His nose was bleeding, his shirt torn, but he appeared to be unharmed. The wound on his leg had not reopened. Recalling the incident in the courtyard and Ian's previous warning concerning her behavior in the presence of the men, Kara suppressed her urge to run to her husband.

Another man fell, and soon it was only Ian and George and Matty left fighting.

"Do the two of ye not realize when enough is enough?" Ian demanded.

Matty swung one fist, then the other, but Ian dodged left, then right, and managed to come around his back and grab him tightly by his linen shirt. Ian twisted the shirt until it tightened at the man's neck.

"Let go! You be choking me!" Matty protested.

"Stop struggling," Ian answered, "and you'll breathe well enough."

George attempted to take a swing at Matty, but Ian caught his arm with his spare hand and twisted it behind

George's back. George shot upright immediately, bending backward, knowing his arm would snap under the pressure of Ian's grasp if he moved.

Harry dragged himself off the floor, grinning. He wiped at his bloody nose with his sleeve as he approached the men Ian held at bay.

"I have had enough of this feud," Harry announced, strutting up to them. He seemed exhilarated by the drink or the fight—perhaps both. "I will settle it here and now or arrest you both. Am I understood?"

Matty's head lolled, his face bright red. George glared.

"Understood?" Harry demanded. He glanced quickly at Ian. "I've that right, don't I?" he whispered.

"Aye," Ian answered, panting. "The land is under your jurisdiction."

Harry spun on his heels and headed for the dais. "Lady Dunnane, my cup."

Kara watched with astonishment as he strode toward the head table. "Now. I will settle this matter now."

Kara followed him and handed him his silver cup, which he downed. She didn't know what had gotten into him and she wasn't certain she liked it.

"Let them make themselves presentable," Harry ordered. "And then they may come before me and I will hear the argument." He clapped his hands with an authority no one had seen previously. "Musicians."

And they began to play.

Chapter Sixteen

"You think this wise?" Kara whispered in Ian's ear.

He had taken his customary position behind Harry's chair, but had leaned over her shoulder to hear her.

"He's been drinking," she murmured. "He's too full of himself."

"Let him stretch those new long legs of his. He can make no worse of the matter than our father did before him."

Kara met his gaze. There were rumors in the castle, women's gossip that the previous earl had not been the best manager of the land and its people. But this was the first time she had ever heard Ian hint that there might be some truth to the matter. She didn't know why, but she had naturally assumed that Harry and Ian's father had been a man worthy of his position.

"The two families have been fighting for more than a hundred years. Perhaps men will admire our Harailt for taking a stand." Ian straightened and returned to his guardian position behind Harry's chair. He tucked his hands behind his back and stood like a mountain in his Gordon kilt, a silver-handled dirk strapped to his waist.

Kara cast her gaze in the direction of her husband. Harry had ordered a plate of food. He drank from his horned cup and stuffed bread into his mouth as he awaited the appearance of the men he had ordered before him.

The musicians still played but there was no dancing. Party guests gathered in knots, spoke in hushed tones and tried to speculate how their young earl would rule on the land dispute. The knots were divided down the center, with approximately half the guests on one side of the hall and half on the other. Supporters of each camp, no doubt.

"A map," Harry said over his shoulder. "Ian, I need a map of the land they're arguing over."

Ian stepped closer and leaned over Harry's right shoulder. His shoulder brushed Kara's, the physical contact putting her on edge. It was difficult for her to suppress her natural impulse to reach out and stroke his arm.

"We've no map, my lord," Ian said. "But I could sketch one quick enough. I know the lay of the land."

Harry nodded. "Make it so. I do not want either of the men offering the sketch; how will I know if he tells the truth?" He made a sound between his teeth, calling to the young spider monkey that perched on the edge of the table. The creature he had purchased earlier in the day from the traveling monkey man came running for the tidbit he offered.

Ian disappeared into Harry's private chamber off the hall. He reappeared just as George Gordon and Matty MacFae approached the dais. Both had washed the blood from their hands and faces, run a comb through their hair and attempted to straighten their rumpled, torn attire.

Harry pulled the monkey into his lap and waved for the two men to step forward.

Kara thought to quietly suggest to her husband that perhaps he should set the pet aside while he made this important ruling. After all, what would two men, each twice his age, think of a lord who played with a monkey while making a decision that would alter their lives forever? But she thought of what Ian had said about allowing Harry to grow up and she bit her tongue.

"Gentlemen, I understand this dispute has been going on for quite some time."

Matty MacFae, a redhead with blue eyes, opened his mouth to speak, but Harry held up a hand to silence him.

Someone gasped at Harry's unprecedented assertion of his authority. Kara had to cover her smile with her hand as she silently cheered for him. Ian was right; Harry was trying his legs.

"This dispute has been going on for a century, a century too long." He eyed both men as he stroked the monkey in his lap. "Now, as I see it, you men have two choices: you may agree to the settlement I will make, or you can be escorted to the dungeon below." He opened his hands. "What shall it be?"

The rivals glared at each other.

Matty MacFae spoke up. "My lord, I do not mean to question your authority, but—"

"Then don't," Harry snapped.

Again Kara had to hide her smile.

Harry raised his hand to Ian. "The map."

Ian leaned over the table to smooth out a bit of parchment he had sketched upon. " 'Tis a rough illustration, but self-explanatory." He pointed with his finger. "Here and here lie the borders of their properties, and here is the land in dispute."

Harry studied the map. "How much land?"

"A small parcel." Ian calculated in his head. "Perhaps twelve, fifteen acres."

" 'Tis not the size of the land," George interrupted. "But—"

Harry glanced up, locking gazes with his distant Gordon cousin.

The men fell silent.

182 *Colleen Faulkner*

Harry returned his attention to the drawing. "And what is this squiggly thing?"

"A narrow creek."

"That runs approximately down the middle?"

"Aye."

Harry pushed aside the map and looked up. "A hundred years? Ye've been fighting over these rocks for a hundred years?"

" 'Tis a fine meadow," George Gordon mumbled.

"Excellent water supply," Matty said.

" 'Tis a complicated matter—"

"My father—"

"Gentlemen! Gentlemen!" Again Harry raised his hand. This time not only the men before him grew silent, but so did the entire hall.

All eyes were upon the young Earl of Dunnane.

"Today is my birthday. Do you think I want to spend the rest of my evening discussing this matter when it's already been discussed a thousand times?"

No one answered.

"I do not," Harry said. "So here is my decision. Abide by it, or you'll be residing in Dunnane's dungeons." He grabbed the map and spun it around so that the two men could see it. "This stream now divides your property, gentlemen. MacFae's land here, Gordon's land here."

Matty MacFae's jaw dropped. "But my lord, my grandfather died upon—"

"I have made my decision, MacFae; now be silent or take your leave to the darkness below!" Harry was quiet for a moment and then went on. "MacFae land here, Gordon land here. The stream divides the land. Both men may share the water that flows, but the division of property lies down the center of the stream. My decision is final. You are dismissed, gentlemen. Should I hear of bickering between you or your families, I will see you here before me again and I will not be in such a pleasant mood next time. And now I think I would like to dance with my wife.

Go before I change my mind and send you to the dungeon anyway."

Both men stared at Harry for a moment, then bowed and backed away.

Harry nodded in the direction of the lead musician, and he launched into an old country tune.

Harry lifted his goblet and leaned toward Kara, smiling behind his cup. "I almost sent them to the dungeon anyway. Just so I could say it. I've always wanted to send someone to the dungeon." He chuckled and drank.

Kara glanced over her shoulder, wide-eyed, at Ian. His face was immobile but his eyes sparkled with amusement. Amusement and pride. Their Harry had done well.

"Want to dance?" Harry said, jumping up and seating his monkey in his chair.

Kara offered her hand. "I would love to."

The entire room was abuzz with Harry's decision. Kara could hear them humming, feel them staring as she walked out into the center of the room with her husband. They were all shocked that Harry had made the ruling. The question now was whether they agreed with it. She couldn't tell by their faces. All she could see was their surprise. Apparently no one had expected this from their young earl.

Kara and Harry took hands and danced. As she turned and dipped, lifted the skirt of her gown and curtsied, she took in the faces of her guests. Many she knew now, some she did not. The knots of men and women had broken up. Some were beginning to take their leave for the night; others were moving toward the casks of ale and wine, intending to stay until dawn.

Harry clasped Kara's hand, turned her and pulled her close. As she spun away, fingertip to fingertip with him, she caught a glimpse of a smiling face in the crowd. A face familiar, yet not familiar. Who was that man with the bright red hair? Why was he watching her?

She had to turn away to meet Harry again. As she turned

back, she saw that the man was gone. Red hair . . . bearded. Like so many Gordons, and yet different.

Then she realized who the man was.

"Harry," she whispered.

"Aye?" He was grinning at her.

"Harry, 'tis Robert the Red."

His forehead creased. "What?"

"Robert the Red, the cattle thief, he is here."

Harry halted in midstride. "Where?" He turned slowly in a circle.

"I don't know. He was here a moment ago. There by the cask."

Other dancers had joined them on the hall floor. They spun and turned around them. Onlookers clapped, and some stomped their feet.

"I see no one but old Edgar the blind drunk by the cask. Wait, there's Dungald, refilling his cup." Harry craned his neck. "Nae, he's filling my cup." He grinned. "That's kind of him."

Kara caught Harry's hand and started for the head table. "Ye should tell Ian. The men should check the perimeter at least. What if the thieves are here beneath our roof, Harry?"

He frowned. "Ye gods, woman, what thief would be so foolish? We've more than a hundred Gordon clan swords within these walls tonight."

She spotted Ian near the door to Harry's private chamber and headed toward him. "Tell him or I'll tell him myself."

Harry sighed. "All right. But you return to your seat. Have something to drink. You look flushed. I'll take care of the matter."

Reluctantly, Kara let go of his hand. "Well enough, my lord," she said quietly. "Just be certain to tell him *I* spotted Robert the Red."

"You worry too much," Harry said, smiling up at her; then he leaned forward and kissed her.

Kara had nowhere to go, no way to avoid his mouth. She shut her eyes as their lips met. They were cool, dry.

She lowered her gaze and walked away, her emotions in a jumble again. Had she encouraged his behavior? More important, what was she going to do about it?

Would this day never end?

"Tired?" Ian asked Kara.

They were alone at the head table. It was past midnight, but there was no indication that the birthday festivities were slowing down. Many of the women who were spending the night had given thanks to Kara and then retired to one of the many chambers throughout the castle. The great hall was now almost entirely occupied by men who were growing louder and more boisterous by the hour, thanks to another cask of ale that had been brought up to the hall.

"Tired and weary," she said.

"Your monkey, madam?"

She laughed. Asleep on her lap lay Harry's new pet. "You see, even the poor wee monkey is exhausted."

He touched her lightly on her back.

She let her eyes drift shut for just an instant. She needed so much to feel Ian's touch right now. But of course it was impossible. The room was full of Gordons, of witnesses.

Because Ian stood behind her, no one could see him caress her back with the pad of his thumb. "Tell him you're tired and wish to retire. Ye've done your wifely duty, more than your duty," he said quietly.

She watched two men arm wrestle. Spectators stood in a ring around the table, tossing coins in wagers. Harry was cheering the smaller man on.

"I don't suppose there was any sign of the reivers."

"Nae."

"I saw him, Ian. I'm certain of it."

"I don't doubt ye."

"Harry doubted me."

"Harry does not know you as I know you. It sounds like one of Rob's tricks. To sneak into the castle with the crowd, not to make trouble, just to see if he could get away with it. He's taunting us."

"Will he take cattle tonight?"

" 'Tis likely. I'll gather a group of men now, ones I can find sober. We'll divide into patrols. We cannot protect all of the herds, but at least the larger ones nearer to Dunnane."

He was no longer stroking her back, but she could feel the warmth of his presence behind her. "Be careful," she whispered, stroking the monkey's fine, downy fur.

"I wish you could come tonight."

"With so many in the castle?" She laughed aloud. No one noticed them. It was too late at night, too many were in their cups. "Ye might as well come up the tower steps and announce yourself."

"I might surprise ye some night. I don't like you leaving the safety of the tower."

Kara thought of the doors that now stood between her chamber and Harry's, between hers and Isla's. Would they dare? Were they completely mad? Was this what love did to a man and a woman? Drove them mad?

"I think you're right. I'm tired." She rose from her chair. "I'm going to sleep."

He stood back from her chair. "Sweet dreams," he whispered.

"Sweet dreams," she returned.

"Only of you . . ." His voice was so soft that it was a whisper in the warm, smoky air of the hall, but she did not miss his reply as she passed him.

Kara carried Harry's monkey under her arm as she crossed the great hall. She found Harry near the door that led out into the passageway. "I'm going to bed," she said.

He smiled crookedly. "Then I shall come, too."

"Nae. It's not necessary. It's your birthday. You should

stay." She didn't want to deal with Harry another minute. She wanted to climb into her bed and sleep. "You should stay with your men."

The monkey blinked drowsily at her as Harry took it from her and nestled it safely into the crook of his arm. "I'd rather be with you."

He gave a wave to Ian and followed her out of the hall. Kara groaned. Now she would have to see to his nighttime ablutions, order him a cup of chocolate, find one of his missing slippers.

"My lord?" a voice called from behind as they retreated down the corridor.

It was Dungald.

"Just a moment with you, my lord. I see you're retiring with your lady wife. 'Twill take only a moment."

Kara kept walking. She would not speak to Dungald; she hadn't the stomach for it.

Behind her she heard Dungald's voice, low and rumbling. Harry said something. Dungald spoke again. By the time she reached the stairs, Harry had caught up with her.

They entered their chambers through his door. "I was thinking I might call him James. What do you think?" Harry carried the monkey to his bed and placed it on his pillow. The monkey curled into a ball and went back to sleep.

"After the king of England?" She shook her head. "You'll be lucky if you're not hauled to London and tossed into the Tower."

He laughed. "Methinks His Majesty has better things to do than worry what a boy calls his monkey in the northeastern foothills of the Grampians of Scotland."

She presented her back to him. "Unlace me, will you?"

When Isla was asleep or not available, Harry always helped her out of her gown. Kara had sent Isla to bed long ago.

She felt him tug on the ribbons at her back. She dropped

her chin to her chest. She was so tired she thought she could fall asleep upright.

"I took care of the possibility of the reivers being nearby. I sent Ian and a patrol of men. They won't dare strike."

She rested her hands on her hips and turned her stiff neck one way and then the other. He was taking too long to unlace her gown. She could feel his cool fingers on her back through her shift.

"It was a bold move to rule on the MacFae-Gordon dispute." She pressed her hands to her waist. "I was proud of you."

He stepped closer to her, his warm breath on her bare back. "You were?"

"Aye. Your men will respect you for making a stand. For not tolerating their childish behavior."

"I hope. More likely they'll just all hate me. The MacFaes for not giving all the land to Matty—George Gordon's band for not granting it all to him."

Kara thought a bath would be nice and relaxing, but it was too late. "Are you through unlacing me?"

She stiffened as his hands slid around her waist. He didn't normally touch her this way when he unlaced her.

" 'Tis done."

She felt his mouth close to her ear. His breath was thick with the bite of scotch.

She tried to move away, but he resisted, tightening his arms around her. He pressed his mouth to the side of her neck. His movement was awkward, but his intentions undeniable.

He had taken her completely by surprise. "Harry!"

He kissed her shoulder, his lips wet and soft.

She shuddered, on the verge of repulsion. "Harry, please don't do that."

Holding her with one arm, he came around to face her, surprising her with his strength.

"Why shouldn't I?" He leaned forward to kiss her collarbone, bared by the shift.

She pushed his head away. "Because I don't want you to!"

He looked up, still not releasing her. "It's my right, you know," he declared boldly.

She looked him straight in the eye. "Is this you talking, or your cousin?"

Color flared on his cheeks.

She had hit it right. This must have been what Dungald was talking to him about downstairs in the hall. He had put Harry up to this. Anger rose in her throat.

He let go of her, but did not back up. "I . . . I am your husband. You are my wife." He made a fist. "I have a right to—"

"You have a right to force yourself upon me?" she demanded. "You have a right to take me against my will? Hurt me?"

His gaze fell to his boots, which were spotted with splashes of ale. "Everyone wants me to be the earl. They want me to act like a man. And a man . . . a man . . ." He gestured toward the bed, not having the vocabulary to say what he meant. "He . . . he *exercises* his rights with his wife. He gets a son."

Kara ran a hand over her eyes. She'd known this would come eventually; she just hadn't expected it so soon. Not tonight. She tried to calm herself. "Harry, you are fourteen years old," she said quietly.

"I'm old enough to—"

"You are not old enough to understand what it is to love a woman. You are not old enough to take a woman into your arms and make love to her." She met his gaze.

His lower lip trembled and his gaze fell to his boots again.

"You are not old enough to love me the way I deserve to be loved."

He drew back his foot and kicked a small table, sending a vase of white flowers crashing to the floor. The painted

Chinese vase shattered, the flowers sprayed, the water pooled.

Her gown hanging off her shoulders, she stared at the broken vase at her feet, wondering if his childish reaction had made him feel any better. It was a silly thought, but she hoped so.

Fat tears ran down his cheeks as he was transformed from a young man to a boy again. "You don't love me," he whispered.

Kara felt drained. She put out her hand to touch his shoulder. "I love you," she said quietly. "Just not in that way." She took a deep breath. "And it has to be in that way between a man and a woman for it to be right, do you understand?"

In truth, he looked a little relieved.

"I just want to do what's right." He wiped at his face, embarrassed. "I don't want you to hate me."

"I don't hate you, Harry." She wrapped her arms around him and hugged him. "But you have to do what you know is right. Let your own mind, your own heart, be the final judge. Not Dungald, not me, not even Ian."

He sniffed as he lowered his head to her shoulder. "I know you wish we hadn't had to marry, but if I had to marry someone . . . you know, older, I'm glad it was you."

She smiled sadly, stroked his hair, and said nothing.

Chapter Seventeen

The following week Ian glanced over his shoulder to see what delayed Harry. He had been beside him when they left the courtyard, headed for the mews to see the new falcon that had just arrived.

Dungald. Who else? The man was worse than a flea.

Dungald was talking to Harry. Harry walked along, balancing his pet monkey on his shoulder, making a good effort of watching his boots and nodding periodically.

"What do ye speak of that you can't share with me, Dungald?" Ian called over his shoulder in challenge. He didn't trust Dungald, not as far as Harry could toss him, but he had no tangible proof the man was anything but what he appeared be—an annoying relative.

"No concern of yours. Only busy making plans to overthrow Dunnane," Dungald said cheerfully. He flashed even, white teeth with his handsome smile. "Actually I've no need to bring in soldiers. My cousin and I have struck a deal, haven't we, Harry?" He slapped him on the shoulder.

Harry glanced up, offering a lopsided smile, as if amused, only Ian knew that smile. Harry was not amused.

"My cousin says he will grant me title to Dunnane and all her holdings for three fine stallions, a hundred head of cattle"—Dungald counted off on his fingers—"a bottle of two-hundred-year-old scotch brewed upon the premises, and a red-haired whore."

"If I am as well informed as I believe I am, methinks you've no holdings to offer but your piss pot," Ian said. "His lordship holds possession of all the horses, cattle and scotch upon these lands. In fact, correct me if I am wrong, but your cousin Harry, the Earl of Dunnane, even owns *your* piss pot."

Dungald didn't like being reminded that he was a poor relation. He had once held a small land plot and some monies, but had gambled them all away years ago. He lived here by the grace and goodwill of his younger cousin, and everyone knew it. The men who served him, served only because they had nowhere else to go and by his name could also reap the benefits of the castle walls.

Dungald glared.

Ian returned a grim smile.

Harry missed the exchange between the two men.

"And besides, what would I want of a whore when I have a beautiful red-haired wife?" Harry asked.

"Harry, leave Kara out of this," Ian said quietly.

"Aye, how can one forget the Lady Dunnane?" Dungald said as they reached the mews.

His hackles raised at the barely discernible sneer in Dungald's voice, Ian lifted the latch and stepped inside, the small structure not much larger than the smokehouse. Three of its four walls were lined with cages, two or three high, depending on their size. The outbuilding was warm and smelled of sawdust, bird droppings and feathers. Light streamed in through the door and the single louvered window.

"Did our falcon arrive safely?"

One of the caged hawks screeched. Others made cooing sounds, almost like the doves they hunted.

"She arrived safety, my lord, from the shores of Iceland," Ian said to Harry, ignoring Dungald, hoping he would go away.

He did not.

"Tell me, how is your dear wife?" Dungald asked, sidling up to Harry.

Harry peered into the cage at the gyrfalcon. "Well enough, sir."

He handed his monkey to Ian, who irritably sat it atop an empty cage. Since when had he become the monkey keeper? The monkey, wearing a green coat similar to Harry's, sat staring at its small front paws with great interest.

"Is she?"

"Aye, she . . . she's quite well," Harry repeated stiffly.

"No, no, I mean how *is* she?" Dungald cackled and drove his elbow into Harry's side. "Between the sheets, I mean."

Harry's face reddened. He swallowed, his Adam's apple bobbing up and down.

The hair prickled on the back of Ian's neck. "Dungald, this is not appropriate."

"Certainly it's appropriate. It's what men do." He threw open his arms. "We talk of our bedchamber conquests and we scratch our stones." He demonstrated, then leaned in to Harry again. "Ye know, I'll bet she's a screamer," he continued without taking a breath.

Ian flexed his fingers and drew them into a fist at his side. He had a good angle on Dungald. He could punch him in the nose and lay him flat.

"She is, isn't she? A screamer." Dungald waggled a finger. "Ye know, I've found that the bossy ones, the ones who flutter about the castle by day giving orders to men, are the loud ones by night." He arched a dark eyebrow. "I'm right, am I not?"

Harry glanced quickly at Ian, then concentrated on the latch of the falcon's cage. Only the bright red of his cheeks showed he had any inkling at all of what Dungald meant.

"Dungald," Ian warned softly. The only reason he had not yet stopped this was that he knew he must let the boy defend himself and his own. His first instinct was to come to Kara's defense. It was only his love for Harry, his sense of duty to him that made him bite his tongue. Besides, to defend Kara might cast suspicion in Dungald's eyes, and that was the last worry they needed right now.

"What? Ye gods, boy, don't tell me you've still not ridden her?" Dungald plucked at his chin. "What of our little talk on your birthday? Surely you've—"

Ian ground his teeth, but still held back.

"Aye," Harry blurted suddenly. "Of course I have."

Ian looked to the boy, surprised by his outburst. He was lying, of course. Ian knew that. Still, he didn't like to hear the words come out of his mouth.

"Aye . . ." Harry stammered. "Of course I've . . . we've . . . consummated. Don't be ridiculous."

"Well, thank God! Ye know, there are those who were beginning to talk."

Ian's gaze fell to the mew's dirt floor. His anger spread through his limbs like the white-hot heat of a branding prod. He wondered if anyone would miss Dungald if he killed the bastard now. If he buried him at his feet, would anyone even know he was gone?

Still, Dungald would not let up. "Not me, of course but others within the castle walls. There should soon be signs of pregnancy, they say," he mocked.

"Dungald!" Ian snapped. "A woman . . . a man," he quickly corrected himself, "has a right to some privacy."

"Privacy, privacy, ye say." Dungald turned on Ian. "Is that why that little slut comes so late at night to your chambers? For privacy's sake?"

Ian stiffened. He and Kara had been so careful, so quiet. Surely Dungald could not know . . . and yet he did know something.

"Who is she?" Dungald wheedled.

Ian exhaled in relief. Dungald didn't know who came to his room. Of course he didn't.

Harry released the latch on the falcon's door and slipped his hand inside to stroke his new acquisition.

The new falcon was a gyrfalcon, brought in from the shores of Iceland. Some two feet high, she was an impressive bird with white plumage and a few spots of gray. A gyrfalcon was not as easily trained as a peregrine, but most definitely more desirable and far costlier. There was something about the way the falcons held themselves, the way they flew, that gave them a regal aura no peregrine could claim.

"Who is she?" Dungald repeated. "Do tell. Surely not the blond wench, Kara's maid? Doesn't her belly get in the way of—"

"Dungald!" Harry snapped, gripping the spindles of the cage. "Will you shut up?"

Dungald stared, wide-eyed.

Ian had to suppress a smile of pride. So the boy had some stones after all.

"If ye haven't something constructive to say, then for God's sake, say nothing at all!"

It was all Ian could do not to give the boy a cheer. He had known he had it in him. He had known all along.

"Go make yourself useful for once," Harry ordered Dungald, waving him away. "I tire of your constant, senseless chatter."

Dungald stood for a moment, silent, still stunned by Harry's outburst. He was completely taken off guard. "I . . . I'll see to that work in the catacombs you ordered. Should . . . should be nearly complete."

Harry nodded and turned away.

"My lord . . ."

Ian watched Harry glance at Dungald again. It wasn't often he addressed him with the respect he deserved.

"Aye?"

"I . . . I want you to know, I only inquire of your bed because of my concern for Dunnane. For you, my lord."

He turned to go and Harry made a response under his breath. At first Ian thought he had misunderstood his young brother. Then he broke into a wide grin as he realized there could be no misunderstanding. When Dungald had said his only concern was for Dunnane, young Harry had definitely and bitterly said, "My ass."

Kara lay back on her bed and waited, her entire body trembling with delicious expectation. The room was dark, lit only by the feeble light that came through the open window. As she lay naked upon the sheets, the cool night breeze swept over her body, making her skin tingle with sensation.

Tonight Ian would come to her.

They had passed earlier in a hallway and she had whispered under her breath that she would come to him tonight. But he had shaken his head no. "Me to you," he had whispered.

Now she waited.

Ian had never come to her chamber before. They had both thought it too dangerous. After all, Kara, as mistress of the household and keeper of the keys, had a right to be in any part of the castle, even the men's wing. Ian had no right to the tower. No one did, without Harry's permission.

Kara didn't know what had changed to make Ian say he would come to her, but she could not stifle the shiver of anticipation as she thought of his coming here to her bed. When she went to his chamber, all she could think of on the long trip down that last corridor was of being caught. She imagined being hauled into the dungeon, stripped naked and beaten. She imagined Ian being dragged into the courtyard and hanged for the greatest crime known to a Scotsman—treason.

But even her haunted thoughts could not keep her from Ian's door. No matter how dangerous their situation was, she knew she could not, of her own free will, give Ian up. Not any more than she could, of her own free will, cease to breathe.

And now, wicked, fallen woman that she was, all she could think of was being able to fall asleep in Ian's arms and not have to rise in the darkness to return to her own cold bed. All she could think was: One more night together. One more night together and she honestly thought she could live in everlasting hell. It would be worth it.

The unmistakable sound of a creaking door caught Kara's attention and she sat up in her bed.

Was it Ian? Was it really the door or just her imagination?

Her bedcurtains swayed in the cool breeze.

She glanced at Harry's door ahead and to the right of the foot of her bed. Even in the silky darkness she could see it was closed. To her right, behind her headboard, Isla's was also closed.

She stared into the darkness at her hall door.

Again it creaked. Did she hear footsteps?

The thought of Ian lifted goose bumps on her bare flesh. It had to be him and not her overactive imagination. He was here. She could sense him.

She heard another creak of the door, and though she could barely see its movement, she knew it opened a crack. Yes, Ian. She heard his footfall on the floorboards; she smelled his freshly washed hair on the night air.

The door creaked closed.

"Ian," she whispered.

"Expecting someone else?" His voice was as silky and sensual as the black night air.

He came to the side of her bed, and she heard him step on the heels of his leather boots and slip out of them. A shiver of anticipation crept up her spine as she heard his kilt fall to the floor with a swish and the muffled thump of the pin that held it closed. It was followed by the rustle of his linen shirt, woven on Dunnane's own loom.

Kara slid over in her bed and felt his weight lower onto the edge. She rose up on her knees and pressed her bare breasts to his bare back. The coolness of the night air and the warmth of his skin made her tremble with desire for him.

He sighed the sigh she knew so well.

"Do you know how much I love this?" he whispered. "How much I love you?"

She pressed a kiss to his bare shoulder, a shoulder so broad that she could cover it with a hundred kisses. "How much?" she breathed, pressing her cheek to his back so that she could feel him breathe in and out.

"Let me show you." He turned toward her and slipped one hand around her waist to bring her onto her back on his lap. He cradled her head and lowered his mouth to hers.

She slipped her arms around his neck and sighed his name against his lips. It was worth it. All of it. Pretending to be the obedient wife. The stealing about the castle in the darkness. The fear. This was worth it. Ian's love was worth it.

"Kara?"

"Aye?" She brushed her fingertips against his lips, reveling in the feel of them, imagining how they would feel elsewhere on her body.

"Harry said something."

"What did he say?" She stared up at him. With no candles burning she could barely make out the outline of his face, though it was so close she could feel his breath on her mouth. She stroked his hair, which was still damp from his bath. It was silky and cool between her fingers.

"I want you to know I would not blame you. It makes more sense. 'Twould be safer—"

She slid her arms over his shoulders.

He rested his hand on her breast.

"Ian, tell me."

"Harry . . . Harry gave the impression that he . . . that you and he had—"

Instantly she knew what he meant. "Nae," she answered sharply, her fingernails biting into the flesh of his shoulder. "We have not. I would not. He has not touched me that way."

She had chosen not to tell Ian about Harry's attempted seduction the night of his birthday because she didn't want him ever, for one moment, to think she would betray him, even to save her self. "He is a child," she said firmly.

"He is your husband."

"He is a child, and I love you." She smoothed his beard-stubbled cheek, loving how masculine he was, loving how feminine he made her feel. "Only you."

Ian let out a long breath that made her believe he had been thinking about this for a while. Perhaps days.

"Do you believe me?" she whispered.

"Aye." He smoothed her hair in a caress that told her all was right and well between them. "He was cornered when he spoke the words. He said the right thing. It was the safest response for him. For you. He was only trying to protect you, not boast," he reassured her.

Suddenly Kara felt cold, and she reached for the light counterpane to pull over them, as if the counterpane could protect them from the evil that lay beyond their bed. "Dungald?" she whispered.

"Of course."

She was quiet for a moment. "Does this have something to do with why you came here tonight rather than me coming to you?"

"Nae." He wrapped his arms around her and pressed his mouth to hers.

Kara wanted to question him further, but as he slipped his tongue between her lips, as he slid his hand from the fullness of her breast, lower, she lost all sense of conscious thought.

Suddenly nothing mattered but Ian's hands, Ian's voice and her love for him.

Chapter Eighteen

Kara walked along the rocky stream and tossed a smooth stone to watch it splash and hop. She turned back to see Ian still on the picnic blanket, propped against a tree, his eyes closed.

She smiled and started along the streambank again. Behind her she could hear Harry's voice, which had grown deeper in the last four months. Isla's laughter echoed.

In the first days after Kara had gone to Ian's bed, she'd thought certain time would not pass, but stand forever still. She'd thought everyone in the castle was looking at her, that somehow everyone knew she was an adulteress. But time did indeed pass, just as it always had: days, weeks, months. And as the days went by she became more relaxed, less concerned that she and Ian would be caught. They were always discreet in private, and in public took pains to be certain their relationship continued to appear as one suitable to a brother- and sister-in-law.

In June, Isla had given birth to a beautiful daughter whom she named Margaret, after Kara's middle name. Meggie was a sweet, good-natured babe with rosy round cheeks and a gurgle that no one in the castle could resist, Harry least of all. Since Isla's lying-in, the two had become close. Close enough to cause talk in the kitchen of the master and the mistress's maid. Kara almost had to laugh the first time the well-meaning cook had warned her that her husband might be dallying with Isla. Kara knew for a fact there was no such dalliance. What worried her was that Harry might fall in love with Isla. Such a love would be as tragic as her own. Like her and Ian, they could never marry. So far, at least, Harry seemed to be satisfied to have Isla for a friend. Isla seemed to enjoy his companionship as well, and was thrilled that he was so taken with her little bastard baby. Aye, for the moment life seemed to be good at Dunnane, so good that Kara wished it could on like this forever. So good that she knew it couldn't.

Lost in her thoughts and enjoying the last of the mild weather before the cold set in, Kara followed the bend in the stream. It felt good to be out in the open, away from the confining walls of the castle and all its duties. It had been Harry's idea to go for a ride and a picnic. Ian had joined them as their escort.

She thought of Ian lying under the tree asleep and smiled tenderly. She was worried about him. He often looked tired, troubled. She knew their clandestine relationship was wearing on him, but they had no other choices. They could love secretly or not love at all. Running away together to England or France was out of the question and had never even been discussed. They could not abandon Harry.

Since his ruling on the Gordon-MacFae land dispute on his birthday, the political climate in the area had grown hot. Everyone was taking sides, either with George Gordon or Matty MacFae, but as Harry had predicted, no one was taking his side. There was grumbling about the poor decisions of a boy master. Kara knew this worried Ian even more than their personal tribulations. When she had first arrived at Dunnane, he had warned her of the dangers to

Harry's position, to his life, and though he did not speak of it, she feared that the danger had increased.

In the last months, Dungald had remained relatively quiet, mild for his usual behavior. He was so quiet that that worried Kara as well. Despite his lack of any obvious aggression, she felt him watching her, watching Harry. After a while his mere presence became unnerving.

Kara glanced behind her. Ian and his tree were out of sight. She could no longer hear Harry and Isla. She knew she ought to turn back. But the stream was so peaceful. A glimmer in the water caught her eye and she crouched on the bank. Tiny fish swam downstream, the sunlight reflecting off their silver skins. She put her fingers into the cold water and tried to catch one, but they were too fast and shimmered away.

"Fishing for your supper?"

Kara spun around, coming to her feet. Only six steps from her sat Robert the Red, the cattle reiver, perched on a large rock, a blade of grass between his teeth.

She glared at him.

He made no attempt to approach her but twirled the blade of grass in his mouth. "How have you been, my lady?"

"I was quite fine before you appeared," she said coolly. She thought of calling for Ian, for surely she was still close enough to him to be heard, but her curiosity got the better of her. Why was Robert the Red here? He was still stealing Dunnane's cattle, not a great many, just enough to be a constant annoyance.

" 'Twill be cold soon. You are wise to stroll now before the snow flies."

"Why are you here?"

He lifted one broad shoulder. "To see you. To see how close I could get."

Her heart gave a trip. She slid her hand downward to her abdomen. Her first and immediate thought was of the secret she feared she carried. Until this moment she had denied the possibility. But now, faced with danger, she knew it to be true. She was pregnant. She was carrying Ian's child, and her first thought was to protect that child. What if the cattle reiver meant to kidnap her for ransom? Could she protect the child she might carry from the likes of such a man?

"Do not fear." He lifted one broad palm. The breeze kicked up and his orange-red beard fluttered. "I would not harm you, my lady. I only wish to worship you from afar."

She didn't believe him. It made no sense. Why would a man risk his life to see a woman he didn't know, another man's wife? "You are a fool to come here. When you're caught, my husband will hang you."

His smile was so broad that she wondered if the man was mad.

"If I am caught."

"Why are you stealing our cattle?"

"Coin, pure and simple. That which drives most men . . . and women."

She frowned. "I don't care about coin. I care about those I love, those I am responsible for."

He regarded her carefully, still twirling the blade in his mouth. "Ye know, you speak so sincerely that a man could almost believe ye."

She studied him, still wary, but not afraid. Whatever this thief was about, it was not kidnapping, and somehow she knew she need not fear for her own life or that of the child she could barely admit to herself she might be carrying. "Why would I care if a thief believed me?"

"Ye would not. I only state my opinion."

"If ye want to know my opinion, it's that you'd best go before I call for my men and they string you to the nearest tree limb."

"Your men? I saw only the boy, your maid with a babe, and Munroe. Munroe's first concern would be the safety of the earl, as it should be. He would not dare take off after me for fear of leaving the boy vulnerable."

He was right. They were less than a mile from the castle walls; Ian had thought there was no need for further escort. But in a dire emergency situation, his first priority would be to protect Harry, not to chase down a cattle thief.

"You had best go," she said, lifting her skirts to head back upstream.

"It was good to see you, my lady."

"Take care that we do not meet again," she answered, "at your hanging."

His cheerful laughter echoed in her ears as she hurried back around the bend in the stream, putting Ian back in sight. As she reached the blanket and sat down, he opened his eyes.

"Where were you?" he asked sleepily. He slid his hand along the blanket to touch hers.

Kara looked for Harry and Isla, but they were not in sight.

She smoothed her hair, hoping she didn't appear too flustered. "Just downstream. There were little fish." She didn't know why she didn't tell Ian about Robert the Red. Some fanciful romantic notion, she supposed. She knew he was no Robin Hood. He stole from the rich to line his own pockets, but there was something about the look in his eyes that did not give her the stomach to bring him to the hanging tree.

"Where are Harry and Isla?"

He gestured upstream. "There through the thicket; I can see Isla's red cloak." He leaned forward to kiss the nape of her neck. "Which means we are alone for a moment."

She closed her eyes, then opened them. Robert the Red. What if he was still watching them? She stood up suddenly.

"Where are you going?" Ian called, holding out his hand to her.

She walked toward the flash of red cloak in the brush

beyond the clearing where they picnicked. "It's getting cool. Isla should get Meggie back. Isla! Harry! Let's go!"

Kara picked her way over the rocks and clumps of tall grass, thinking of the child she suspected grew inside her. She had missed only one bleeding; she was barely late. She had told herself in the last two weeks again and again that she mustn't panic. Not yet. There were explanations for the irregularity of a woman's body. All this worry could be for naught. Yet she knew in her heart of hearts that she carried Ian's babe.

Of course life could not remain the same.

"I don't understand." Harry sat before the fire and bounced four-month-old Meggie on his knee.

Ian paced nervously before the hearth while Kara sat in a chair across from Harry, repairing the sleeve of one of his shirts. Isla had gone to the kitchen to see to the following day's meal.

"What is there to understand? They're angry, and when men are angry they become like small children, stubborn, resentful."

"I offer them my protection, not just from each other but from the Crown as well. I am owed this impost."

"I agree."

Harry brought his nose to Meggie's and muttered some inaudible baby gibberish, then returned his attention to Ian. "I have not demanded coin. I will take it in cattle, sheep, even scotch. And the sum is not unreasonable; it's nothing more than a token."

Ian crossed his arms over his chest. "Again, I agree."

Kara listened quietly to her two men, wishing she could do more than just sit there and stitch. She knew Ian was worried about this matter. The delay of neighboring families in paying the Earl of Dunnane his annual duty was obviously an act of defiance. The men did not approve of a boy leader and they were expressing their disapproval.

They were also backing Harry into a corner. No matter what he did now, he would gain more enemies. If he ignored those who had not paid, those who paid would be angry. If he tried to enforce the fee, he would be accused of being brutal.

The baby fussed.

"If they don't pay, what do I do? I can't let them get away with this." Harry bounced Meggie again, but she continued to fret.

"I see little choice."

The baby opened its pink, toothless mouth and let out a wail.

"Want me to take her?" Kara asked Harry, opening her arms.

"Nae, you sit," Ian said. "I'll take her."

Kara watched Harry pass Isla's baby to Ian. The child looked so tiny in his arms, as if she might be swallowed up by bulging biceps and folds of tartan plaid. His hand was almost as large as her head. Yet he did not appear awkward with her.

Kara couldn't resist a sad smile at the sight of Ian cradling a baby. It tugged at her heart. He would make a good father . . . if only he was permitted to be one.

Ian brought the fussing baby to his shoulder and patted her swaddled bottom. "What can you do? You've little choice."

Meggie's cry became a gurgle once more as she settled against Ian's thick neck.

Harry thought. "Seize goods? Take them by force?"

Kara noticed Ian using this tactic more and more often. He no longer told Harry what to do, but tried to lead him in the right direction. He asked him questions but attempted to allow Harry, with guidance, to come to the correct conclusions on his own.

Harry shook his head, coming to his feet. "Fight my own clan? I hate the thought of it."

"Some who drag their boots are Gordons, but there are

other families as well." Swaying with the baby in his arms, Ian took Harry's empty chair. Meggie was drifting off to sleep. He tucked her blanket under her chin.

"My guess is that you would need to make an example of only one or two families. No one should be injured. We ride in with a couple of dozen men, talk mean, take a couple of head of cattle and ride off," Ian thought aloud. "The countryside will be in a great uproar for a couple of days, and then those remiss will show up at our doors swearing they had meant to pay all along, but were merely delayed."

Kara gave up on her stitching to watch Ian rock the baby to sleep. She loved this time of night when they were all together like this—just her and Ian and Harry—the other men gone from the hall for the night. Sometimes Dungald, but more often not. He seemed to have other, more pressing business these days, though where, Kara didn't know.

"That my babe who fusses?" Isla entered the circle of firelight.

Kara laughed. "She appears to be sleeping peacefully to me."

"Who would think she'd take to such a big bear of a man, eh?" Isla asked proudly, her hands settled on her hips as she gazed lovingly at her daughter.

"Who would guess," Kara mused.

She was almost two months late on her bleeding. She knew she was pregnant and yet she couldn't yet think about it in any way but abstractly. She wasn't yet ready to deal with Harry or the fact that she was obviously pregnant by another man. She could not yet deal with even telling Ian. It was funny, but she felt no sense of panic, not yet. Just this strange, warm feeling of acceptance.

"Let me take her," Isla said, putting out her arms.

Ian seemed almost reluctant as he handed the sleeping Meggie to her mother.

Kara's gaze met Ian's. This was what he wanted for them. She could see it in his eyes.

Kara wondered how far she could carry her deception. Could she bed Harry and make him think the baby was his, just born early? If she could do it, if she could complete the deception, this time next year Ian could be rocking his own babe before this hearth. Of course if she brought herself to do it, she would have to do it soon.

But in her heart of hearts Kara knew she was only fooling herself. She could not bed Harry.

"If there's nothing else you wish, my lady, the babe and I will be abed."

Kara heard Isla speak, but she didn't hear her words. She couldn't tear her gaze from Ian's.

Out of the corner of her eye, Kara saw Harry staring at her. At Ian.

Kara blinked.

Ian looked away.

Kara's gaze met Harry's. His face was awash in some emotion she couldn't quite identify. Hurt? Jealousy?

She felt like a thief, caught with the loaf in her hand. "H-Harry. I think I'm tired, too. Are you ready for bed?" She rose, taking his shirt with her.

Harry turned away, gazing into the fire's blaze. "Nae," he said, his tone echoing with what could only be interpreted as loneliness. "I think I'll stay here awhile with my brother."

Kara didn't dare look at Ian. She didn't dare hope he would come to her. Not tonight.

"All right then," she said softly. On impulse, she went to the hearth and kissed Harry on his cheek. She had to lift onto her toes to reach him. "Night."

He brushed the small of her back as she walked away. Not as a man touches his lover, but as a man touches one he loves. "Pleasant dreams."

Kara left the hall and took the tower stairs in the darkness. Her calm, peaceful manner was beginning to crumble. Pregnant with another man's child. What was she going to do?

                              * * *

Dungald laughed heartily and tossed the dice onto the
scarred wooden table again. Someone walked behind him
and spilled ale down his back. He glanced over his shoulder, but in the smoky, dim light of the low-ceilinged ale-
house, he could not distinguish one drink from another.

The Bull's Horn was a drinking house for the common
man, settled on the edge of the village of Dunnane.
Though it had been established to satisfy the thirst of
working men, there were others in the area who frequented
it: tradesmen, herders, landholders, even thieves and swin-
dlers. Dungald liked the ale house; he liked its stench and
the red-haired whore who, for coin, would take a man into
the loft above and ride him like a bucking mare. Dungald
knew she only pretended to enjoy the futtering. He knew
that she wasn't really the mistress of the manor, that she
wasn't Kara. But sometimes if he was drunk enough, if he
kept his eyes closed and her body odor wasn't too strong, he
could almost convince himself for a few fleeting moments.

A man intentionally bumped into Dungald's shoulder.
"Ye lookin' for me?"

Dungald glanced up from the dice on the table.
"Maybe."

The man glanced at the table. "Looks like you're losing
your pants, anyway. 'Tis now or never."

Dungald frowned. He didn't like being treated like a
strippling boy, like Harry. "I'm out!" Dungald threw up
his hands and stepped away from the crowd of gamblers.
He had to nudge his way through the crowd. Faces were
fuzzy, his step unstable on the dirt floor. He had had too
much to drink . . . again. He slipped into a chair across
the table from him.

"What is it?" the man asked. He drank ale from a bat-
tered pewter cup.

Dungald licked his lips. His mouth was dry, and the
man's ale looked cool and wet, but Dungald had no more

coin and his credit was at its limit. Even the proprietress, Bessie, would not give him more ale without coin.

"Our deal. I have thought to make it more . . . rewarding, for both of us."

"That right?"

" 'Twould take more men than you have." He belched from deep in the pit of his stomach.

"I can get more men, if the price is right."

"Excellent. I thought so. Excellent."

The man stared at Dungald, plucking his beard. "I take it this involves the same party we are presently involved with?"

He nodded.

The man thought. "Some say he is not as weak as what was first thought. Some say there are those who should be more careful."

"Some say, some say," Dungald muttered, wiping his mouth with the back of his hand. His tongue was thick and tasted stale. He wanted to go back to Dunnane to sleep on a clean tick, but he wasn't sure he could make it there on his own. "Some say Christ is coming this morning, but do you think we'll actually see his blessed face?"

The man looked away as if disgusted. "You're drunk. I do not make deals with drunk men."

Dungald met his eyes. "I am not that drunk, sir."

He crossed his arms over his chest. "Tell me what you wish and I will think on the matter."

Dungald nodded. "Well enough." He pointed to the man's cup. "But first I'll have your ale."

Chapter Nineteen

"Take care. Be careful. Listen to Ian."

Ian sat astride his restless mount, struggling to avoid watching Kara say her good-byes to Harry.

Harry had decided it was time to respond to the refusals to pay the levies due to him as the Earl of Dunnane. This morning they would ride out to the property of one of the men who refused to pay and demand Harry's due. Chances were, no weapons would have to be drawn, but to be on the safe side, they were traveling with two dozen armed men, eager to defend their lordship should it become a necessity. Truthfully, Ian didn't know if they were eager to defend their master, or just bored and eager to get into a skirmish. Either way, it didn't matter so long as they were there.

Kara continued to speak to Harry in a hushed, wifely tone. Ian couldn't tear his gaze from her hands as she fiddled with Harry's stirrup, or from her face as she peered up at him with genuine concern.

Ian knew that jealousy was an evil monster that ripped

men apart, that crumbled empires, that broke women's hearts. But he couldn't help himself.

Kara should have been standing beside him, whispering her farewells to him. It was only fair. She loved him, not Harry. Ian wanted her to smooth *his* kilt, to gaze up at *him* with those eyes filled with a mixture of fear and pride.

What right did Harry have to be her husband? He was only fourteen years old, for sweet God's sake. He knew nothing of a wife, of love. He was too young to understand just how much he should cherish a woman. But how could he know?

Ian gazed downward at the reins in his gloved hands. His horse backed up a step, shied to the right, as restless as his master.

How could Harry know how precious love was when he had not yet really lived? The boy had fought no battles, never watched a man's lifeblood pour onto the moors. He had not held his best friend in his arms as he sucked in one last wet breath. He had not buried any loved ones but his father, and him he had not known well. Harry had not lived long enough to realize what a brief time he would be upon this earth. He had not the years, not the wisdom, to know what was important in this life and what was not. So innocent.

Ian was jealous of his innocence as well.

"Do we leave today, my lord?" Ian asked irritably.

Harry had leaned over in his saddle to speak privately to Kara.

What did he have to say that he could not say aloud?

Kara touched Harry's cheek and Ian closed his eyes for an instant, imagining it was his own cheek she stroked. He wished she would come to him and say good-bye. Even a chaste, sisterly kiss would be nice.

But of course she wouldn't dare.

Of course he had no right to feel her lips upon his cheek.

Logically, Ian knew he held Kara's love, but as time went

on he became more and more resentful that their love had to be kept a secret. He wanted others to know he loved her, that she loved him. He wanted her to bear his children. He wanted to grow old beside her, to hold her in his arms in their bed when they were both gray-haired, their joints creaking with age.

Harry and Kara were still talking, whispering. She was smiling.

Ian spoke sharply. "Harry! 'Tis not the Crusades we are set upon. Ye'll be home by the evening meal. Let us go."

Kara kissed Harry's cheek and the boy pulled up on his reins and urged his mount forward to the head of the line of men.

Ian brought up the rear.

"Take care of him," Kara said to Ian, folding her arms before her.

He glanced down. She looked so small standing against the castle's stone wall. So vulnerable.

In that moment Ian thought he might sell his soul to the devil himself to be able to lean over and kiss her hard on the mouth.

He was thankful the devil did not appear.

"He'll be fine," he said.

Her gaze searched his and he immediately felt guilty for being so short with her, with Harry as well. But he was in such turmoil these days, his gut so twisted, his head pounding with the weight of their secret, of the impossibility of their love.

Kara lifted a hand in farewell and stepped back.

"Let's ride!" Ian commanded, and the horses bearing the Gordon men sprang forward, headed for Matty Mac-Fae's.

"To success," Ian said with a crooked grin.

Harry pushed his pet monkey onto his shoulder and raised his horned drinking cup high. "To success."

Ian knocked his goblet against Harry's and took another swallow of the fine Dunnane scotch. Ordinarily Ian didn't imbibe. He didn't like the idea that he might not be entirely in control of his faculties. He didn't like the thought that he might do or say something he would regret later. But tonight was an exception to his rule.

They had ridden over to Matty's, and though he had appeared to be surprised to see them, he had welcomed them into his keep. He had apologized for being remiss and paid his levy without further ado. No blood had been shed and there seemed to be no hard feelings.

"And now to . . . to Matty," Harry toasted. He was only drinking ale, but had already had a wee bit too much.

The monkey climbed onto Harry's head and the boy laughed, trying not to move and send the little creature flying.

Kara had gone to bed an hour ago, but before she retired she had commented that when it came to ale, Harry shouldn't be trying to keep up with his men. She said she didn't want to see him ill in the morning.

The woman was no fun. She probably didn't want a monkey on Harry's head either.

Ian had assured her it was yet another rite of manhood. If a man didn't make an ass of himself in front of his men on occasion, then he just wasn't a true Scotsman.

Kara had frowned at him with obvious skepticism, but that saucy look on her face had only made her more appealing. It was all he had been able to do to let her part their company without placing a big fat kiss on her rosy lips.

Ian slapped his goblet against Harry's again, enjoying the clinking sound they made. Ale from Harry's sloshed onto Ian's hand and he waved it, sending droplets flying.

"I know! I know." Harry raised his cup. "To . . . to the dozen head of cattle, and . . . and . . ." He leaned across the table, his forehead creasing. "What else did Matty give me in payment?"

Ian laughed. "Two sheep and a silver spoon."

"A silver spoon." Harry cackled, slapping his thigh. "What the hell am I supposed to do with a silver spoon?"

Ian laughed, feeling as silly as the boy looked, wearing a white-faced monkey for a hat. "I don't know. Give it to James there."

Harry snorted with laughter, tried to look up, and the monkey slipped off his head and down his neck to the back of the chair. He scooped up the monkey and brought it to his face. "What do you think of that, Your Grace? Would you like to eat your breakfast food with a silver spoon?"

"Just take care, James," Ian warned the monkey, "that Cousin Dungald does not steal it from you as you sleep."

Harry roared. "As you eat, you mean."

Ian took another swallow of the smooth scotch as the monkey came to sit directly in front of him. It stared at him with great concentration, looking eerily like a little man. Catching the animal's scent, Ian waved one hand and turned his face away. "God's teeth, that creature stinks."

Harry dropped his goblet to the table and reached for the pitcher of ale, cradled in the arms of a sleeping man. "Give it up, Harold," he mumbled.

Harold snored in response, turned his head, and rested it on the table once again.

"My monkey does not stink." Harry poured himself another healthy portion of the ale. "He just doesn't smell like you or me." He straightened and lifted a haughty chin. "I rather like the way he smells."

The monkey wandered away from Ian and stopped to observe something in Harold's tangled hair.

Ian made a face. "I'm telling ye, brother. The beastie stinks." He pointed a finger. He felt a little dizzy, but the dizziness was a relief. Light-headed like this, he couldn't think; it felt good not to think. "He needs a bath."

Harry looked at Ian, creases appearing on his youthful forehead. "A bath? Ye don't give monkeys baths." He stared hard at Ian, no doubt attempting to focus. "Do ye?"

"Didn't the monkey man give ye care instructions?" Ian questioned in as serious a manner as he could muster, considering the subject.

Harry leaned back in his chair and propped one boot on the table, thinking. "Not about bathing." He glanced at the monkey now picking through the sleeping man's hair with great interest. "I was supposed to be bathing James?"

On impulse, Ian jumped out of his chair. "Fear not! Do not despair! Big brother will come to the rescue."

"Ye will?" Harry's mouth slid into a grin. "How?"

"Well, I'll help ye bathe the beastie, of course." Ian pulled Harry out of the chair by his armpits, grabbed the monkey and pushed it into his arms. "Come on. 'Twill be a worthy cause."

"I don't know about this." Harry stumbled along beside Ian, the pet tucked under his arm.

Most of the men had gone to bed. A few still sat at tables in the great hall tossing dice or having one last draught before they turned in. Several slept where they sat, snoring contentedly.

"Where . . . where are we going to bathe James?"

Ian stopped in the passageway and rested one hand on the wall. Now on his feet, he realized he'd had more scotch than he thought. "Where's that great copper tub?"

Harry's eyes grew wide. "Kara's bathing tub? I think not."

"Come, come, we could get some of those sweet soaps of hers. Yours will be the most fragrant monkey in all of Christendom."

"The tub is in my room, but empty." Harry wrinkled his nose. "I'm not certain I should wake a servant to fill a monkey's tub."

Ian thought a minute. The boy had a point. Bright boy. "All right. I've another idea, but we must have soap. The lavender bars. I know she has them; I can smell it on her."

The two brothers stood face-to-face in the dark corridor.

Harry lowered his voice. "Do we really need the soap? I don't want to wake her." He grabbed his codpiece. "And I've a great need to piss just now. Why don't you get the soap whilst I do my business?"

Ian ran a hand through his unbound hair. "Oh, no, not me. I'm not going in the mistress's bedchamber whilst she sleeps."

"Please?" Harry punctuated his request with a hiccup. "Just slip into my room, then into hers. There's soap in that little chest near the end of her bed."

"Harry, I really don't think—"

"I'm the earl; you're the brother." The monkey again climbed up on his master's head. "And I say you get the soap for my monkey." He hiccuped again. "Now!"

Ian exhaled loudly through his lips. "Fine." He threw up his hands and turned away. "Give me all the servants' duties. Treat me like a slave."

Holding his codpiece, Harry hurried past Ian and down the corridor, the monkey balanced on his head with his free hand. "You get the soap; James and I will meet you."

"Right."

The boy turned. "Meet you where?"

"In the courtyard."

"The courtyard? Of course!" He thought again. "Wait. Don't ye think it's cold to be—"

"Harry, Harry, have I ever given ye poor advice?"

Harry thought a moment, grimaced and shook his head. "Nae."

"Nae," Ian echoed. "Now go."

Harry took off at a gallop down the unlit hallway as Ian headed for the tower.

He knew it was unwise to enter the tower without Harry even if he did have the perfect excuse. His master had sent him. Actually it was too bad Harry would be waiting for him down in the courtyard; otherwise he'd be tempted to dally.

Ian took the tower steps two at a time, grasping the rope

for balance. He slipped into Harry's room, then halted in the doorway to Kara's chamber. Kara lay on her side, her head on a pillow, her hair a glorious mass that poured over the pillow, over her shoulder and onto the counterpane.

Ian ached to touch her. He could kiss her just once and be gone; she'd never know he had been there. He watched her another moment, thinking how beautiful she was.

But no, one kiss would not be enough. Trying to tiptoe in his heavy boots, Ian moved to the chest at the end of the bed. He opened it and the scent of lavender soap wafted up to his nostrils. The box smelled of Kara, of her strength and her joy in life. He felt inside. Silky fabrics, a hairbrush, a handheld looking glass. Aha! A square of soap. Soap in hand, he closed the chest and took one last lingering look at Kara. "Sleep well, my sweet," he whispered as he slipped out of the room.

Ian hurried down the tower stairs, through the castle and out into the open courtyard. He found Harry by the bare arched arbor at the entrance to the garden.

"It's cold," Harry said, hugging his monkey. "I should have brought my cloak."

Ian grabbed a handful of his brother's shirt. "Bring the beastie."

"I still don't understand where—" Harry halted in a patch of moonlight. "The fountain? Mother's Italian fountain?"

Ian pushed up his sleeves. He had thought the night air might clear his head; he had thought wrong. "Better than the wife's bathing tub, eh?"

Harry sniggered, covering his mouth. "What Mother doesn't know will nary harm her."

Ian thrust both hands into the stone fountain. In the warm months the water flowed freely, but now it was still. The water was cold, but energizing. He rubbed the bar of soap between his palms, liking the smell of it. "Come, come, bring him."

Harry gingerly placed his pet on the edge of the stone

bath. The monkey gave a little shriek. Harry glanced up. "Do ye think he likes bathing?"

"Of course." Ian held up his soapy hands. "You hold him; I'll scrub."

The instant the monkey's paws hit the cold water, it shrieked again. Harry jumped. Ian laughed.

The monkey scrambled wildly, splashing Ian and Harry with cold water. Harry shrieked louder than the monkey. Laughing hysterically, both men attempted to hold the animal partially underwater so that Ian could scrub it with Kara's soap.

"Hold him!" Ian shouted.

Harry turned his head away and the monkey splashed harder, shrieking like a wounded woman.

"Easy. Easy." Ian scrubbed the monkey's back vigorously.

"Ouch!" Harry hollered and let go of the monkey.

The monkey fell into the fountain and shot up out of the water, startling Harry. Harry lost his balance, half turned, and fell back into the fountain, squealing as he hit the cold water.

James raced across the grass, hollering in monkey talk all the way to the gate.

"What happened?" Ian called, laughing at the sight of Harry lying on his back in the fountain.

"The little turd bit me." Harry held up his thumb and then stuck it in his mouth.

When Ian didn't stop laughing, Harry splashed him, soaking what was still dry of his linen shirt.

"Fine. Wet your big brother." Ian reached over and shoved Harry's head underwater.

The moment he let go, Harry sputtered up, spitting water, laughing. Before Ian could back up, Harry caught his arm and knocked him off balance, and Ian tumbled into the fountain atop his brother.

As he surfaced, Ian thought he heard a feminine voice

from a window above. He shoved his brother. "Ouch! I hit my head on the bottom." He groaned.

"Shame ye have such a fat head." Harry laughed and shoved him backward.

"What in heaven's name are you two doing?" Kara called, leaning out the window three stories above them. "You're making enough noise to wake the dead."

Harry and Ian, side by side on their backs in their mother's fountain, waved up at Kara.

"Good even," Ian called, still laughing.

"Evening, wife," Harry followed.

"What are you doing?" Kara repeated, staring down at them. Her tone was most definitely not approving.

"Nothing," Ian proclaimed innocently.

Harry sniggered. "Nothing, dear."

They heard the paneled window shutter slam shut. Both men sat up looking at each other and burst into guffaws of laughter again.

"Soap, brother?" Ian grabbed the bar as it floated by, getting a handful of leaves with it.

"Thank you, brother." Harry then proceeded to scrub himself with Kara's soap, over his clothes.

"Hey, toss me the bar," Ian called.

Kara appeared in the garden just as they were rinsing off. "What are you doing?" she demanded.

"Why, washing James," Harry said innocently.

Ian slapped the water. "Damn. I knew we lost something." He glanced around. "Where's the little beast gone?"

Kara folded her arms over her chest. She was wearing a night robe, but Ian guessed she had nothing on beneath it. He knew for a fact that she liked to sleep naked. He wondered if he could will the gown from her shoulders if he stared hard enough. It was certainly worth a try.

"When I opened the yett, a small, wet, furry creature burst through. I think he was headed for the hall."

"Oh, good. I wouldn't want him to catch the ague."

Harry sat up, tried to throw one foot over the edge of the fountain, and fell back in.

Ian laughed and pushed him upright again.

"You two are drunk," Kara accused.

The two brothers looked at each other. "Nae," they insisted in comic unison.

She stomped over to the fountain. "I thought you might be hurt." She gestured. "That something was wrong. And here you're swimming in your mother's fountain."

Harry gripped the side of the fountain and attempted to heave himself over the side. Succeeding, he fell into the dying grass. "Not swimming, the water's too shallow for swimming."

"Oh!" Kara exhaled in exasperation. "Have you no sense whatsoever?" She glared at Ian. "And you!" she accused.

He touched his breast, making no attempt to exit the fountain. "Me?" he said virtuously.

"You, at least, Ian Munroe, ought to know better."

Harry rolled in the grass, laughing and kicking and holding his sides. " 'You, at least, Ian Munroe, ought to know better,' " he mimicked.

With a grunt of exasperation, Kara spun around and strode out of the garden.

Ian knew he was in trouble, big trouble.

He spread his arms wide and fell back into the water with a great splash, submerging himself. He remained underwater until she was gone.

Chapter Twenty

The man's voice came out of the cold darkness. "They're all drunk now and lying about the hall, I should guess. Ye want us to do it now and get it over with?"

Dungald pressed his back to the damp stone wall of the catacomb beneath the castle. "Nae," he snapped, holding up his candle to be certain there were no rats in his vicinity. "I told ye! I will not be hurried. This must be well planned, not obvious."

"Not obvious." The man whose face was shadowed sniggered. "When does a man die untimely and another inherit that it is not obvious someone has aided his own cause?"

Dungald scowled. "I told ye. Keep your twopence philosophies to yerself! I pay ye to act, not think."

"Which brings us to the matter at hand."

Dungald thought he heard something behind him and turned. Rats? Ghosts? He shuddered. Christ's bones, he hated this darkness. "I told ye, I haven't the coin yet."

"Ye promised payment regularly. Hiring men to do yer

dirty work means paying them. I intend to retire on yer *compensation.*"

"I know what I promised," Dungald spit. "An' ye shall get your money and then some. I merely do not have the coin tonight."

The man drew his dirk from his belt and began to shave at his thumbnail. The light off the candle glistened off the blade, making Dungald uneasy.

"There ... there shall be something extra for ye, of course."

"Of course," the man said. "But ye know this is not my usual game. The cost will be extra and it will be steep."

Dungald lifted the candle again, thinking of spiders. Did spiders live this far underground? He hated spiders almost as much as he hated rats. When he became the earl of Dunnane he would have these catacombs filled in. "I will pay you what you ask."

"Ye don't understand; it's not for me." The man in the shadows flicked his thumbnail toward the damp dirt at Dungald's feet. "It's for the men. The men I must hire. They don't come cheap, you know."

"When my plan comes to fruition, ye will need no men of your own. There will be plenty in this shire willing to raise arms. And once my plans succeed, I will be a powerful man. There is much I can do for you."

"Do for me?" the man growled. "What makes you think I would want ye to do anything for me? I am not interested in yer power, only yer coin. I told ye that from the beginning." He flashed the dirk. "I want no part of the rest. In truth, it disgusts me."

"I am taking what is rightfully mine," Dungald said instantly. He reached out with one hand, but when it trembled, he drew it back. He did not want the man to see his weakness.

"Whatever ye say, 'tis not my concern. My only concern is my payment. My men's payment. We've mouths to feed, debts of our own to pay."

"And you'll have yer bloody payment." Dungald lifted the candlestand to cast light on his face. "Now be gone with you!"

"Well enough. I'll be gone. But I'll be back for my money." He lifted the blade and turned it, purposefully reflecting bands of light off the smooth, shiny surface. "I'll be back for me money, or back for you."

"Move over."

"No," Kara mumbled sleepily, snuggling deeper beneath her woolen counterpane.

"Kara, move over, love. It's cold and I am bare-arsed naked."

Kara stubbornly refused to slide over in her bed. Who was he to think he could behave so childishly and then come for a quick tumble in her bed?

"You're drunk."

"I am not. I was a little silly earlier, I admit, but not drunk."

He didn't sound drunk. His voice was warm, breathy. Sensual. Still, she didn't want to give in too easily. He shouldn't have let Harry get drunk. Ian shouldn't have taken him swimming in the fountain in the cold of winter. "Ye shouldn't be here," she said begrudgingly. "Harry—"

"Harry is passed out, dead to the world. Ye'll not see him until noon tomorrow."

She kept her eyes closed, torn between wanting Ian in her bed and wanting him to know how annoyed she was with him. "I told you I don't want drunken men in my bed," she whispered.

"Good, then I shan't invite any." He pushed her over and slid under the blankets in one quick motion.

Kara rolled to the far side, not wanting to surrender all at once, though she knew she would. She needed Ian too badly. Wanted him too badly to ever send him from her bed. Even drunk, wet, and with the monkey under his arm, she believed she would have welcomed him. "You're cold," she complained.

"I told ye I was." He reached out to pull her into his arms and she didn't resist. "That's why I wanted in your bed, my countess."

"Don't call me that, and if you die of the ague"—she snuggled against him—"it will be no fault but your own."

He brushed his mouth across her forehead. "Now that's a pleasant thought."

She settled her head on his shoulder. "You ought to be ashamed of yourself, carrying on like that. And in your mother's fountain. Your mother would be appalled."

He chuckled. "My mother would probably be pleased to think I had shared in a little fun with my brother."

He was right, she knew he was right, but she didn't want to let him off so easily. After all, if he was trying to encourage Harry to act mature, he shouldn't be swimming in a fountain in late October. He shouldn't have been swimming in a fountain at all. "A grown man," she muttered.

He was already growing warm, his body radiating heat that she craved.

"Well," she said, still cool, but warming up to him, "I hope you at least saw him dried off and put to bed with something warm in his stomach."

Ian's hand glanced over her arm, down her bare hip. "Harry and the monkey," he whispered, nuzzling her neck.

She couldn't resist a chuckle . . . something akin to a purr. "You really shouldn't be here. It must be very late."

"Close to three. You're right; I shouldn't be here." He kissed her collarbone, his tongue tickling her skin. "But I couldn't help myself. I was in Harry's chamber, peeling off his stockings, thinking of you only a door away. Thinking of this."

She ran her hand over his muscular biceps. "You took off his stockings?"

"I told ye, he was asleep. I couldn't put my little brother to bed with wet stockings, now, could I?"

Kara rolled over to face him in the narrow bed, pressing her groin to his. She could already feel him hot and hard against her. She could already feel herself growing damp for want of him.

"Nae, I don't suppose you could have."

Ian kissed the hollow of her throat and she tilted her head back, her eyes drifting shut. "This is wicked," she whispered. "You're wicked to make me feel this way, to make me want to feel this way."

He rolled her onto her back, cradling her with one strong arm. With the other he drew teasing circles with his fingertips, starting between her breasts, wandering lower. . . .

"Not wicked, my love. Never wicked. Ye and I, we were meant for each other. Yours and Harry's marriage was a mere mistake, an error in fate. Ye were meant to marry me. To be mine and I yours for all eternity."

Kara slid her hands over his bare shoulders, arching her back as his hand grazed her belly.

It was still flat and taut, but how soon before it began to swell? Kara thought she should tell Ian what she suspected, tell him now. He would be so angry that she had not told him right away. But she wasn't ready to tell him. She wasn't ready to deal with their choices. Because they had no choices. In her heart, she knew she and Ian could never flee, and yet she also knew that here he could never claim their child. This would be Harry's baby. There was no choice. Harry would have to be told, and what his reaction would be, she couldn't imagine. That was why she wasn't ready to tell him, because she wasn't ready to give up Ian's claim to her child. For just a short time longer she wanted to imagine him as the father.

She couldn't deal with this now, nae, not now. Now she wanted to touch and be touched.

"An error in fate?" she whispered.

His hand skimmed lower and her thoughts began to jumble. She let her eyes drift shut again, awash in sensation. His rough fingerpads awakened every nerve in her body, leaving her shivering with desire for him.

"I . . . I thought ye did not believe in fate," she said.

He kissed her lips gently. "Open your eyes."

She gazed into his dark pupils, reflecting the firelight from the hearth. She remembered his dark brown eyes from the first night he had come to her wedding chamber. Had it been only six months ago? It seemed six hundred. Looking back now, she thought she probably loved Ian Munroe from that very first night when he had treated her with such respect, when he coddled poor, frightened Harry.

"I believe in true love," Ian murmured, holding her gaze. "I believe in God Almighty and His belief in true love. His desire for us to love, perhaps even His need. That's what I believe in. God will see us through this. It's what we must believe."

She didn't want to think right now, not about their woes. "Tell me you love me," Kara murmured.

"I love ye."

She smiled. "How much?"

He brushed the hair from her forehead in a gentle caress. "I love ye as the sea loves the salt, as the earth loves the rain."

She relaxed under him. "Ye should have been a poet."

He chuckled, bringing his mouth to hers. "Ye say ye love me?" he questioned.

She smiled up at him, reveling in the feel of his weight pressing her into the goose-down tick. "Aye, I love ye, Munroe."

He grasped her hand and guided it behind him, lowering it to his bare lower back. "Then show me, hinny, show me before the light of day shines through yonder window and sends me from your arms."

Kara wrapped her arms tightly around his waist and raised her lips to his. Their tongues met, danced. He slid down, dragging the tip of his tongue over her chin, down her neck. He cupped one of her breasts in his hand and lowered his mouth. She moaned as he caught her nipple between his teeth and gently tugged.

"So sweet, hinny," he murmured. "So beautiful."

She caught a handful of his still-damp hair and arched her back, unconsciously rising and falling to meet his groin. He teased one nipple into a taut brown peak and then the other. He kissed the valley between her breasts, her navel, and moved lower still.

She dug her nails into his back. "Ian . . ."

"Shhh," he soothed. "Have ye somewhere to be? Bread to bake, clothes to stitch? Let a man take his time. Enjoy his pleasures."

She relaxed against the pillows. He was right. They had so little time together. They should enjoy every delicious moment of it.

Ian kissed her stomach, sliding his mouth lower. As he met the bed of red curls between her thighs she cried out in amazement. Each time he touched her this way she was shocked anew by the sheer pleasure of his warm breath.

He flicked the tip of his tongue. She writhed beneath him.

Already she could feel the waves building up inside her, threatening to crash. A part of her strained to reach the crest, while a part of her wanted to extend the tortured ecstasy forever.

It was so wonderful to feel so loved. All those years in her father's house Kara had never been anything but chattel. Now, forevermore, no matter what happened, she would know she had been someone's most prized, most loved.

Ian continued to stroke her, to carry her closer to the

edge. She panted, her heart pounding, her pulse racing. Suddenly it was so hot in the room that she had to toss the blanket aside. His was such delicious torture that she resisted the building tide, wanting it to last longer. Of course she couldn't resist for long; she never could.

With little warning, the pleasure hit her hard, washing over her, sending her tossing, turning. . . .

"Ian!" she whispered, grasping him as her muscles contracted, released and contracted again.

"Kara, sweet Kara."

He rested his head on her stomach and waited for the tide to subside, for her heart to slow to a reasonable pounding.

"I don't know how you do that," she whispered, still panting, not knowing if she wanted to laugh or cry. She loved him so fiercely.

He pressed a kiss between her breasts. "You sound tired. Want to sleep?"

"In your arms?" She nuzzled his neck. "Always." She slid her hand down over his flat, muscular stomach, then lower. "But not yet," she whispered huskily.

He chuckled, too, his voice warm, enveloping. "Now *this* is wicked." He gasped as she closed her fingers around him.

She smiled in the darkness, delighting in the feel of his hot, hard, silky flesh at her fingertips. It was true that he could make her cry out in pleasure, but she had learned in the last months that she could do the same for him. While stroking him with one hand, she caressed his broad chest with the other. The sleek, hard muscles of his body fascinated her.

Ian sighed. He moaned.

She smiled in the darkness. "Shhh," she hushed. "Ye'll wake the entire household."

"Me?" His voice was throaty and filled with desire for her. "It is you who cause me to cry aloud."

She laughed deep in her throat, secretly pleased that she could reciprocate the pleasure he gave so freely to her.

"What do ye want, wench?" he whispered.

She rubbed his hard male nipple. "You know," she breathed.

"Tell me."

She whispered in his ear.

He chuckled. "Wicked, wicked woman."

"But I want to try atop."

His mouth grazed hers. "Do ye, now?"

"You'll show me how?"

He grasped her hips as she slid over him. "But of course."

But Kara needed no guidance. Making love to Ian came as naturally to her as cradling Isla's baby, as cradling her own would be.

Kara rose up and dug her knees into the feather tick. His broad hands settled on her hips, guiding her. He was so hot and hard, pressed against her woman's mound. She was becoming wet again, aching for him.

She slid over him, sucking in her breath at the sudden burst of sensation. He moaned. She pressed her palms to his, sliding his hands upward over his head, stretching over him.

Again and again she rose and fell to a rhythm that was theirs alone.

He called her name. He murmured sweet words in Gaelic, words she didn't know. Fire spread through her loins, and again she rose on the tide that only Ian could create.

Kara tried to hold back. She tried to drift on the waves, but she couldn't. She rose, then crashed down, lost to the surges of ecstasy she knew well, but could never get enough of.

Ian crashed just behind her, calling her name, driving upward.

Kara fell flat upon his chest, panting, laughing. She covered his chest with kisses.

"Ah, Kara," he breathed. "I will never have enough of you." He slid his hand over the small of her back in a gentle caress. "I do not know what I have done to deserve you, but I am thankful."

She slid off him, onto her side, and cuddled against him. He held her tightly in his arms and kissed her mouth, the tip of her nose, the arch of her eyebrows.

They were quiet for a moment, basking in the warmth of their lovemaking, of their love. When Ian spoke it was softly, seriously. "Do you think we need to consider the idea of leaving this place?"

He had never mentioned such an option before. She had thought it out of the question. It *was* out of the question. She opened her eyes to gaze into his. "I canna leave him," she whispered.

He closed his eyes with a groan, unable to hold her gaze. "I do not think I can either, not now. Not yet."

"Not now," she echoed.

He drew the blanket over them. "What if you become with child?"

She wondered if he felt her stiffen in his arms. Did he know? How could he? Only she knew . . . and perhaps Isla. But the girl had not mentioned it. Of course he couldn't know. He was only speculating.

She wondered if she should tell him now. Aye, perhaps now was better.

Kara inhaled, gathering her thoughts, trying to arrange her words in her head. She had already practiced what she would say to Ian, but now the words escaped her.

"Ian, I—"

Harry's door creaked open. It happened so quickly that neither she nor Ian had time to react. And react? React how? There was no place to run. No place to hide.

"Kara? Kara, are you awake?" Harry said, shuffling barefoot into her room. He held his hand to his stomach. "Kara, my belly hurts something fierce. Do ye think—"

He halted in midsentence, his gaze falling upon her bed, upon her and Ian lying in each other's arms.

Chapter Twenty-one

"Harry!" Ian released Kara and slid out of bed in one motion.

"W-what. . . ? H-how . . . ? Harry stammered, staring at them. The fire on the hearth cast dim yellow light across his young face, glistening on the tears in his blue eyes.

Tears sprang into Kara's eyes. She couldn't stand to see him hurt like this, not by those he loved. Not by her and Ian. "Harry—"

"Nae," he snapped, surprising her with the depth of his anger. He held up one hand to halt her. "Do not speak."

Ian had started across the room for him, unclothed, but stopped.

"Do not say a word," Harry whispered harshly. "Either of you." He clasped his head with both hands as if in pain. "I couldn't stand it. I just couldn't stand it."

He turned away from them, walked back through his doorway, and slammed the door shut. Hard.

Kara looked at Ian. All along she had known there was a possibility that Harry would discover them, but somehow she had convinced herself it wouldn't happen. Somehow she could not believe it had happened.

"Ah, hell," Ian muttered.

She slid across the bed to sit on its edge, dragging the woolen counterpane with her. Her hair fell in tangled waves over her shoulders. She felt vile. Evil. She had no regret for loving Ian. She only regretted that she had not been able to prevent Harry from finding out. She had never wanted to hurt him; she had never wanted to fall in love with Ian. It had just happened.

"I should go to him," she said softly.

Ian picked up his clothing and walked to the hearth. "Nae. This is between us, Harry and me." He dressed slowly.

She stared at him. "Between only Harry and you? I think not." She stood, taking the blanket with her. Suddenly the room was cold. Frigid. She found her night rail and slipped into it, returning the blanket to the bed. "I was certainly as much a participant as you."

"But Kara—"

"He is my husband," she whispered loudly.

"Shhh." He brought a finger to his lips. "You do not want to wake Isla or the baby."

She yanked the ribbon tie of her night rail, covering herself fully. "I will not allow you to take responsibility for this. At least not any more than I."

He sat on the edge of a chair to put on his boots. He suddenly seemed tired, older than he had when he had entered her bedchamber. "Kara, we must stay calm."

"I am calm," she snapped.

"We must be careful what we say. What we do. We still must protect Harry. Remember, he has greater enemies than you and I, than this."

Who did he mean? Dungald? Other clansmen who wanted Harry's power, even a portion of it? When clan lords fell, she knew authority and land were often divided. There were so many who could profit from the young earl's demise. A scandal like this could weaken him, cause him to lose the ground he had gained.

Kara's hand instinctively found her abdomen. Ian said they must protect Harry, but he didn't know who else he must protect. Only she knew they must also safeguard her secret, her babe. Her heart beat faster, but she forced herself to remain calm. This was no time for female hysterics. "What do you think Harry will do?"

Ian ran his fingers through his silky hair, which had now dried. His voice was edged with fear, guilt, sadness.

Kara ached to the very pit of her stomach, not just for Harry, but for Ian, too. For herself. For all of them.

"I don't know what my brother will do. Nothing rash, I think. He's matured a great deal in the last months. But just to be safe," he said carefully, "I think you should pack something."

"Pack something?" Did he mean what she thought he meant? Did he think she would flee? Abandon him, abandon them both? She padded barefoot to the hearth to stand in front of him. He suddenly seemed so large again, as large as he had seemed when she'd first come to Dunnane. Imposing, even. "Pack something for what?"

"In case I must send you off."

"Send me? You are not sending me anywhere, Ian Munroe! Do you think I'm a parcel that can be sent off?"

He rose. "This is my fault. I should have gone from here when I had the opportunity. This never should have happened," he said miserably.

She turned away, her back to him. She didn't want to quarrel with Ian. But they were of equal blame and she wanted her share. "You never had an opportunity," she said softly. She sniffed to fight her tears.

Everything was crumbling around her. She could hear the mortar cracking; she could feel the thunder of the stones as they fell. "Ye never had a chance with me, Ian Munroe. Not from the first time I laid eyes on ye."

He walked up behind her and pressed a kiss to her

shoulder blade. "What is important is that we stay calm now."

She nodded. "Let's both go in and speak with him."

Ian rested his cheek on her shoulder, slipping one hand around her waist. "Nae."

"Ian, I don't want you to do this alone."

"Actually, I think we should respect his wishes and leave him be," he said. "For tonight."

She turned in his arms to face him, studying his dark eyes.

"Let him try to get some sleep," he explained. "The excitement of the day, all the ale he drank. He's not thinking clearly and I suspect he knows it. He needs sleep. Time to think."

"And what if tomorrow he orders your hanging?" She smoothed his cheek. "I think maybe it is you who should go, tonight, now."

He gazed into her eyes, speaking fiercely. "Nae. I will not abandon my brother. Not ever."

Her lower lip trembled. How could a woman not love such a man? "He won't have you hanged, you know. He loves you too much."

He grasped both her arms. "Are ye certain ye'd not rather leave the walls of the castle, just for tonight? I know a place where you would be safe down in the village. A woman who would—"

She pressed a finger to his lips. "Whatever happens, we'll face it together." She smiled sadly. "Now go to your chambers. Try to sleep a little."

He brushed his lips against hers. "Good night, my love."

She watched him walk toward the door, hugging herself for comfort as much as warmth. "Good night."

"Leave him tonight. I'll come in the morning. All will not seem so desperate in the morning. It never does."

She turned away as he closed the door behind himself, praying silently that he was right.

* * *

Kara had not thought she could possibly sleep a wink. After Ian left her, she stood for the longest time beside Harry's door, listening. She heard him crying, then silence as he drifted off to sleep. For a time she debated whether she should go in, even though she and Ian had agreed she would not. In the end, she chose to respect Harry's wishes and leave him alone.

Cold, she had climbed into bed. Dawn would be upon them soon. She closed her eyes for only a moment, and the next thing she knew, she was opening them again. Her bedchamber was bathed in sunlight and Isla was moving about her chamber, humming to herself.

"Finally you're awake. I was wondering if you were dead, my lady."

Kara climbed out of bed, still in her night rail. "Where's Harry?" She walked toward his closed door. "Is he still abed?"

"Nae." Isla frowned, picking up one of Kara's shifts to fold. "Up long ago. I think he went hunting with his new hawk."

She looked at Isla. "Did Ian go?"

The girl halted, watching Kara carefully. "I don't know, mistress." She halted in midfold. "What's wrong? What's happened?"

Tears welled in Kara's eyes and she walked to the window to look down into the courtyard, then out over the rolling hills. The lush green of the meadows was beginning to brown. Cool weather was blowing out of the mountains, carrying the winds of winter. "You heard nothing last night?"

Isla came to her mistress. "Nae. The babe slept all night. I never woke till she fussed for her breakfast this morning."

Kara leaned on the stone sill and closed her eyes, fighting her tears. She felt so helpless, so blessedly guilty. "Harry knows," she said softly.

Kara heard Isla suck in her breath.

"My lady," the maid breathed in horror. "He found you and Master Ian abed?"

She could only nod, unable to find her voice.

"What did he say?"

"Nothing," she whispered.

Isla took a step toward her and wrapped her thin arms around Kara's shoulders from behind.

"Oh, Isla, what am I going to do?" she whispered, turning so that her tears fell on her serving girl's shoulder. "I'm going to have a baby."

"And not his lordship's, I suppose?"

Again, Kara could do nothing but shake her head.

"And now the calf be out of her pen so there's no convincing the earl it's his?"

Kara had to laugh. Isla had such a way with words. "Out of its pen and running wild, I fear."

Isla lifted the hem of her clean apron and wiped at Kara's eyes. "There, there, now, mistress. Cryin' will do no good but make you ugly."

Again Kara had to smile.

"And where is Master Ian?"

Feeling better, Kara took a step back. "I don't know."

"Long gone from here, if he has any sense." The girl studied her, hands on her hips. "But the big old bear doesn't, does he?"

Kara ran a hand through her hair and walked to the pitcher of fresh water Isla had brought for her. She poured some into a china basin and splashed it on her face. "Not a bit of sense."

"Going to be your hero, eh? Swing by his neck for ye?" Isla handed her a small linen hand towel.

"Harry would not do that."

"Nae. He would not," the girl agreed firmly. "He loves his brother too much, loves you both. That I know."

"But how?" Kara rubbed the rough fabric against her wet face. "How can you know?"

"Because I know what he tells me. How he looks at you both. His heart is nothing but goodness, my lady."

Kara felt her lower lip tremble and tears fill her eyes again.

"Now, now," Isla said. "Don't be startin' that again. Tell me what ye want to do and we'll do it. You always been a woman of action. If ye want to pack your bag and go, I'll lower ye from the tower by my own hair."

Kara would have laughed, but she knew Isla was serious. She was so fortunate to have someone so devoted to her. "I will not run," she said. "Neither of us will run. We would not abandon him."

Isla opened her arms. "So there ye have it. Neither of ye will abandon his lordship. Ye take it from there."

Kara set down the towel, feeling calmer. "Would ye find Ian for me? Find out if he's here or gone with Harry."

Isla opened the door. "I'll find him, and a draught of tea for ye as well. Ye'll have tea and biscuits."

Kara held her stomach. "I couldn't possibly eat."

"Ye'll eat anyway."

Isla was not out of the room more than a minute when she entered again. "Told ye I'd find him." She stepped back to allow Ian passage. "Be back with your breakfast, my lady."

Ian stood at the door even after Isla was gone. He had changed his clothing and was wearing a green and brown leine chroich, brown stockings, and boots. His hair was combed neatly and tied back with a leather band. He smelled of shaving soap.

"Where is he?"

"Slipped out before I could catch him," Ian said quietly.

"Alone?"

He hesitated, as if debating whether to tell her the truth. "With Dungald."

She lifted her hand to her mouth. "You don't think Harry would have—"

"Nae," he cut her off. "I do not think he would have

told Dungald. He doesn't care for his cousin. He doesn't trust him, and wisely so. I think he went hunting, as Isla said. To get his mind off this."

She sat back on the edge of her bed. "But still, he went alone with him." She took a long breath. "I wish he hadn't."

"I wish he hadn't either."

In the last months Dungald had shown himself to be no true threat, and yet Kara saw him as one anyway. "Do ye think ye should ride after him?"

"I sent a patrol, just to scout, not necessarily to check on his lordship." His gaze met hers. "But the man I sent—"

"He'll keep an eye out for him. Perhaps run into him."

Ian nodded. "I think it's the best we can do . . . considering."

She stared at her hands in her lap. "So now what do we do?"

"There's nothing we can do." His hands hung at his sides. "Nothing but wait for his lordship's return."

All day Kara tried to keep busy. She visited the dairy and oversaw a thorough cleaning. She helped Cook with an inventory in the kitchen cellar. She ordered spinners to begin making blankets for Christmas gifts for families who lived in the village of Dunnane. She even began stitching a baby gown, thinking that anyone who noticed would think it was for Isla's baby. Only she and Isla would know the truth.

Midday passed, and though Kara had a meal prepared, Harry did not return home. She began to worry. What if he had fallen from his horse and been injured? What if Dungald had killed him and was now trying to cover the crime? Would he return to say the Earl of Dunnane had met with a terrible accident? Had the cattle reivers attacked and murdered the boy?

By the time the sun began to set Kara was half-crazy with worry. She was just lighting candles about the great room, ordering bread and cheese and ale for the Gordon men present, when she heard the bark of Harry's hounds—the announcement he had returned.

She met him at the yett. Alone, he walked slowly up the stone walk, carrying a string of doves. He held them out for her as he passed, avoiding her gaze. "I brought home something for the table. If it's too late we can—"

"Nae," she said, taking the day's kill from him. "Cook can have them plucked and roasting in no time. I waited for you. I've not yet eaten."

He stepped into the entrance hall, out of sight of the yett's guard. She followed.

"I think I'll bathe and then come down to eat," he said quietly.

"I'll call for a bath."

His blond hair fell forward over his face. "Would . . . would you send Isla?" he asked.

She could not hide the pain in her voice. Pain not for herself, but for him. "You don't want me to attend you?"

"You see to the meal. I'll be down directly." He turned away from her, his voice small. "Just send Isla . . . please?"

Kara found Isla in the kitchen, baby Meggie on her hip. "He wants you," she whispered in her servant's ear. "Order bathwater."

Isla touched her breast. "He wants me?"

Kara laid the doves on the worktable—the same table upon which she and Ian had shared a meal of bread and cheese the first week she had arrived. She was amazed how much older she felt now. Since that night she had known such happiness, such sadness.

"He's always found you easy to talk to," Kara said softly, not wanting to share the conversation with the cooks in the kitchen. She took the baby from Isla's arms.

"What do I say?"

Kara's gaze met Isla's. "Be honest. It's what he expects from you. It's what he deserves."

Isla gave her mistress a squeeze of her hand and hurried out of the kitchen. "I'll be back directly."

Kara turned to watch her go. "I'll wait in the hall," she said. "Hurry back."

Harry sat on the edge of his bed, the same bed he had once shared with Kara. He smoothed the counterpane, fighting the tears that threatened to spill again now that he was alone.

He hadn't known. How had he not known?

His wife. His brother.

Fool. How could he not have known?

How could she not have loved him? How could any woman not love Ian? Strong, silent, brave Ian. And handsome, he was so damned handsome and virile.

Harry wiped his tears with the back of his hand. His monkey crawled onto his lap and pushed under his hand with his head, wanting to be petted.

"Hallo there, boy, and how is the king of all the monkeys?" he asked. He stroked its little round head. "Better than the master, I hope."

There was a rap on his door and Harry glanced up. "Isla?"

The door opened. "Nae. 'Tis your brother . . . Ian."

Harry's first thought was to send him away. Far away. Hell would be too close.

"May I come in?" Ian asked from the open doorway.

Harry rose, cradling his monkey under his arm. "Looks like you're already in, brother. Suit yourself."

Harry turned his back on Ian to pour himself some wine. He took his time in watering it down. He heard the door close behind Ian.

Harry could feel Ian watching him from near the door.

Harry searched for the courage to turn and meet him eye-to-eye, man-to-man.

"Want wine?" Harry asked finally. He felt silly the moment he said it. Here was a man in his bedchamber, a man who had cuckolded him, and Harry was offering him refreshment. If Harry was any man at all, he knew he should have been offering his brother the tip of his sword.

But of course Harry knew he was not a man. He was only a boy playing a man's part, and at this moment not playing it well.

"Aye, I'd like some," Ian said quietly.

Harry was surprised by his acceptance. He poured the wine, adding water, and then carried the goblet toward him. Ian met him halfway.

Their fingers brushed as Harry passed the wine.

"I want to tell you how sorry I am."

Harry dropped his pet onto his bed and walked to the window, sloshing the wine in his cup. He stared out the window into the darkness.

"I am sorry for hurting you," he said. "But I cannot say I am sorry for loving her. It's something I can't explain. Something so wonderful. Something I hope you will experience one day."

A lump rose in Harry's throat. He wanted to hit Ian. He wanted to slap his face. To kick him. Harry wanted to climb into his bed and pull the covers over his head. He wanted to cry. He did none of it.

"I didn't know," Harry said lamely. "I knew you two were close, but . . . I didn't know." He sipped his wine. "I never suspected she would . . . you would . . ." He was at a loss for words. He ached so inside right now that he didn't know if he would ever find the words.

"We did not intend to fall in love." Ian moved close, his footfall echoing on the polished floorboards. "And it is love. Not just bed play. You have to know that."

Harry exhaled slowly and lifted his goblet to his lips again. Listening.

"Which, in a way, makes this more difficult. For all of us."

Harry turned to face his brother, the brother he loved so much.

Ian's face was drawn. "We never intended to hurt you, Harry." He hung his head. "And for that, we are sorry."

Harry felt close to the edge of tears. He felt so lost, so afraid. He needed Ian; he needed Kara. Even now he needed them. "You . . ." He paused and began again. "Are you going to leave me?" he asked when he found his voice.

"Leave you?"

"Take her from here," Harry said. "Go away together and leave me here." A sob slipped out of his mouth. "Leave me alone with all this."

"Nae." Ian's voice cracked. "We're not going to leave you." He put down his wine and came to Harry. "Is that what you were worried about? That we would leave you?"

Harry felt his older brother's arms wrap around him. It felt strange to have another man hug him, but good. It was Ian. It was Ian, and the embrace was genuine.

Harry leaned his forehead against Ian's chest for a moment. It was like leaning on a rock. "I'm not ready to be alone. Not yet," he whispered.

"I cannot tell you man-to-man that I will not love your wife any longer, but I can swear to you, man-to-man, that I will never abandon you, Harry. Never until you send me away will I leave these walls. Not until you send us away or to our deaths."

Tears ran down Harry's cheeks, but he was beyond embarrassment. He didn't know for certain that Ian meant what he said, that Ian would be able to keep his word, but Ian said what he needed to hear. What he had to hear at this moment. What he needed to believe.

What, in spite of the truth of their betrayal of him, he knew he could believe.

"I just can't do this without you, without both of you," Harry repeated.

"And you will not." Ian hugged him tightly and then released him.

Harry lifted his gaze to meet his brother's. "You still love me?"

"I have loved you since I first laid eyes upon you as an infant."

Harry dashed at his eyes. "And Kara?"

"She must speak for herself, but I can tell you, all along her concern has been for you."

Harry breathed deeply again. All day as he had ridden at Dungald's side, talking of hunting, of horses, of things that meant nothing, all he could think of was what he would do if Kara and Ian left him. It was funny, but he didn't really even care that they were in bed together. That they had done what he knew they had done. Maybe because he already knew that would never come to pass between him and Kara. All he cared about was that they not leave him for each other. That they not stop loving him because they loved each other.

There was another tap at the door and Harry quickly wiped his eyes. "Aye?"

"Your bath, my lord," Isla said from behind the closed door.

Harry looked at Ian.

"Bathe. Then come down and we will share a meal together. As a family," he said.

Harry nodded, managed a smile. "Tell Kara I'll be down directly," he said. He glanced at the door. "Come in," he called.

Ian and Isla passed in the doorway. Behind her were several servants with great buckets of hot water. Harry stood at the window, staring into the darkness until the servants had poured the water into the tub and taken their leave.

He heard Isla moving quietly around the room, finding towels, laying out clean clothes for him. He liked being alone with her like this. She made him feel special in a way no one else did.

" 'Tis ready now, my lord, if you are ready."

He turned from the window, leaving his empty goblet. "You know?" he asked.

"I know," she said simply.

"And what do you think?" He sat on a chair and pulled off his boots. He tossed his bonnet to the bed and pulled his shirt over his head.

She turned her back to allow him privacy as he dropped his kilt and climbed over the side of the tub.

"I think that we have no choice in love. It just happens. I think they were lucky to find each other, and unlucky not to have the freedom to marry."

"You think I'm a fool to allow such a thing to happen under my roof and not hand down a punishment?" He slid into the warm, silky water.

She brought him soap and a washrag. She knelt beside the tub. "I think you are a brave man. A good man with a good heart. This is not the path you would have chosen, had you been given the choice, but you were not given a choice. None of us were."

He lathered the rag with soap. "Ian says he loves her." He looked at Isla. She was so pretty. Her blond hair looked so soft. "But he says they won't leave me."

She shook her head. "They would never leave you. They would die first."

He watched the water run off the rag. "I suppose a man could do worse. I have two people who are willing to help me. Who are devoted to me."

"Three, my lord," Isla said softly.

Then to Harry's surprise, she leaned over the tub and brushed her lips against his.

Harry squeezed his eyes shut, frozen. Terrified. Thrilled.

Her lips were softer than he had imagined, her breath more fragrant. Her mouth made his spine tingle. It made his whole body tighten and tingle. Without thinking, he rose up in the tub, pressing his mouth harder against hers. She gave no resistance.

Harry was afraid to open his eyes as she drew back, afraid he had imagined it all. He just sat there, naked in his tub, in amazement.

"Call me if you need me, my lord," Isla said, standing, walking away.

Harry opened his eyes long enough to see her disappear into Kara's room, and then he sank under the soapy water, his heart still pounding, his soul singing.

Chapter Twenty-two

Harry leaned against the fireplace with one hand, gazing into the flames. He had grown so quickly that he was now as tall as Kara, slender, and appeared far more masculine than he had when she'd arrived. His chin was even beginning to sport a few hairs.

She smiled to herself. Wasn't it funny how time passed, even when you thought it couldn't possibly? Christmas had come and gone, Harry knew the truth of her and Ian, and yet he acted as if nothing had changed. He almost behaved as if he had known all along, that or expected it. Harry, like Ian, saw no sin in what she and Ian did. Both of her men viewed the marriage as one laid down by law, but not God or heart. Her men, God bless them both.

"Alfred still refuses to pay his duty to me?" he asked quietly.

Kara glanced up from the stocking she was knitting for him. Over his head, on the mantel, rested the Dunnane horn of tenure. The ornamented cow's horn had been granted to the first Earl of Dunnane more than two hundred years ago. He who possessed the horn, possessed the title and the lands. As Kara studied Harry's tired face she wondered if the horn was worth all this.

Ian sat across from Kara in Harry's chair, one leg propped on his knee. Both of her men looked tired. Worn.

"Aye, he refuses," Ian said. "He's dug in. Last word we received this morning was that if we wanted the payment we would have to come and get it."

Harry swore beneath his breath.

Kara glanced at Ian.

As terrible as Harry's discovery of her and Ian's infidelity had been, it had most definitely matured her young husband. Though she still saw glimpses of the child she had married the previous spring, he had come out of the incident an older, wiser boy. A boy very close to becoming a man. For that Kara admired him and loved him all the more. And though she didn't know what the future held for her and Ian and Harry, she knew it was a future they would face together.

Harry turned to gaze at them both. "So I've no choice."

Kara and Ian listened, allowing him to speak, to make his own decision without their guidance. He knew what he had to do.

"I want you to gather men—four dozen," he told Ian.

"I'm not certain we have that many at our disposal presently. I will have to call men in."

While more than a dozen fighting men lived permanently within the castle walls, the others who served Dunnane came and went on a schedule. Each man who lived under the protection of the Earl of Dunnane, the Gordon clan chief, took his turn twice yearly residing within the residence for a fortnight. For years this service meant little else than drinking into the night with old friends and sleeping late in the morning. There were drills, but little true danger. Service to Dunnane was often safer work than caring for one's own cattle. Because the foothills of the Grampians had been relatively quiet for years, men actually looked forward to serving. But also because of the relative calm of the area, the service had not been enforced. Only recently had this come to Harry's attention when he counted just how many men he had at any one time to defend him.

Harry cracked the knuckles of one hand thoughtfully. "Can we send riders to bring those men due in?"

Ian nodded. "Call up a few extra as well."

"How long before we can be ready to ride?" He rubbed his temple. His blond hair fell forward over his face, obscuring his features. "I'll want men left here, of course, to defend these walls."

"Of course. Three days. Four at the most."

"And I want my own men." He glanced up to be certain no one else was near enough to hear him. "Not my cousin's cronies."

Kara knew that though all the Gordon men officially served Harry, there were several Dungald had taken under his wing years ago, and considered his own.

"So what?" Ian arched a dark eyebrow. "We leave the wolf to guard the henhouse?"

Harry chuckled, but without humor. "Nae. My cousin will ride with me."

Kara immediately glanced up from her knitting. "Ye think that wise?" she asked quietly. She hated to question Harry's authority, but she was concerned for his welfare.

Harry lifted one shoulder. "I'll be surrounded by my own men, men I know to be loyal to me." He paused. "And you know, honestly, my cousin has done nothing against me. Aye, yes, petty behavior here and there." He gave a wave. "But I begin to think we worry—*you* worry"— he smiled—"over nothing. I begin to think he's all wind and blather, but he hasn't the conviction to actually do anything to put me in danger. The man is a worm, not a snake in the grass."

Kara folded her hands in her lap. What Harry said all sounded perfectly logical. He was right. She knew he was right, and yet . . .

"And as for you," Harry said to his brother. "I have decided that you will remain here and guard my castle . . . my wife."

Kara's anxious gaze shifted from Harry to Ian and back to Harry, but she did not dare interfere again.

Ian half rose from his chair. "Harry, I understand your reasoning with Dungald. I must admit I believe I agree, but were I to come, too—"

Harry held up one hand, and the look on his face told Kara he would not be swayed. "Who else but you can I trust to protect what is mine, brother?"

Ian lowered his gaze.

Kara knew that Ian knew Harry was right. She also understood Ian's hesitancy to send Harry off alone. Not only was he still not entirely convinced Dungald was not a threat, but what of the actual task? Alfred Gordon might hand over the cattle due Harry if Harry arrived with enough fighting men, but he might just call his bluff, too.

Ian took a long time to answer. "As you wish, my lord."

"Excellent." Harry clapped his hands together. "So send riders for men and then meet me back here dressed warmly." He looked at Kara. His boyish smile had returned. "You, too, and Isla. Tell her to bring the babe if she likes. " 'Twill do Meggie good to be out-of-doors. 'Tis cold, but the sun is shining."

Ian rose to follow Harry's bidding. "Dress warmly? What are we doing? Where are we going?"

Harry smiled, tucking his hands behind his back. "I know you hate this, not knowing all, but you shall see." He shooed them both off. "Now go. You both have your orders."

Kara caught an overhanging branch and whipped around it, sliding out of control on the ice. "Whoa!" She fell back and hit the slippery surface on her bottom, sliding to a stop against a tree.

Harry, skating directly behind her, bumped into her and tumbled head over heels over her. They burst into laughter as he came up with snow on his chin.

Ian skated by on glistening steel blades, his hands tucked casually behind his back as if he were out on a summer stroll. "Need help?"

"Nae!" Harry and Kara shouted in unison and fell into laughter again.

Harry's surprise had been a half-mile walk to a small pond frozen over with ice. In his bag he carried four pairs of ice skating blades he'd discovered in a pile of refuse in one of the catacomb chambers beneath the castle. The ice-skating outing seemed to be just what they all needed.

Harry pushed himself to his feet, wobbling on the skates attached to his boots. He offered his hand.

"Methinks I would do better to crawl to the shore," she said, struggling to get to her feet.

Harry gave a tug and pulled her up, his cheeks rosy with the bite of the winter wind. "Oh, come, ye just have to get the hang of it."

She swayed, holding on to his shoulders to steady herself. "I warned you I was not a woman of superior balance and grace."

"And I—" he rocked forward, then back, steadying himself against her this time—"am a man of superior grace and balance?"

She laughed and let go of him to catch her own balance, putting out her hands as if she were about to take flight.

Ian sailed by again, turned and skated backward. He apparently skated as easily as he walked.

Harry awkwardly started after him. "Ye know, I have never liked him. Never." He put out his mittened hand to wait for her. "I've been thinking of sending him north . . . or south. Sending him to fight some English or something, just to get him out of my hair."

Isla laughed and clapped from the shore as the three of them skated by. She had started a fire and was warming cider she'd brought from Dunnane's kitchen. She wore Meggie bundled and tied in a sling over her shoulder. The baby laughed and waved chubby hands covered by little socks Kara had knitted.

"Hot cider is ready if anyone is cold."

"I'm ready for cider." Kara veered off, her cloak flapping in the bitter wind.

"I, as well." Ian followed.

Harry came to a halt on the shore's edge, arms out to keep his balance. "Isla, skate with me."

"Ye'll have to take us both," she said, coming to the edge of the pond, carrying her skates.

Kara slipped out of her skates and walked to the fire to get warm. Isla had left steaming mugs of cider on a rock. Ian approached behind her and she handed him one before taking one herself. They stood side by side to watch Isla and Harry skate around the pond holding on to each other, laughing and whispering.

Ian blew on his hot cider and took a sip. "I think Harry's found a friend in your maid," he said thoughtfully.

Kara smiled. "It's nice to see him so happy." She cradled the mug in her woolen mittens, enjoying the warmth it radiated. "Her, too."

He cut his gaze to her as he sipped from the mug. "They have seemed very . . . close as of late. Do think our Harry would . . . has . . ."

"I haven't asked him or Isla. I wouldn't dare. All that matters to me is their happiness."

"And you, my love, are you happy?"

"Depends," she said, looking down into the cup of steamy amber liquid.

She didn't know why, but she knew what she would say next. After all the fretting over when to tell him about the baby, suddenly she knew the time was now. She didn't know what made this time and place right, only that it was. Only that she must tell. The words were already out of her mouth before she could reconsider. She was already headed toward the point of no return.

"On what?"

"On how you will feel about sharing fatherhood with your brother."

There, she'd said it. At first she had been bound and determined to tell Ian by Christmas. Then the holidays had passed. Last week they had celebrated Epiphany in Dunnane's tiny chapel. It had been time to tell him, to tell him and Harry before the swelling of her abdomen became evident.

Ian was silent, so silent that she was afraid to look into his eyes. Holding her breath, she forced herself to look up. Surely he had known this was coming.

She was thankful he was grinning, grinning like a boy who had just opened his first gift of the Advent season. And this wasn't a gift of a stocking or a bonnet; this was the bow, the dirk he had always wanted. "A child?" he said softly.

She exhaled, bit down on her lower lip and smiled hesitantly. He wanted her child as much as she wanted his. She could see it in the glimmer of his dark brown eyes. "A child."

"When?"

She gazed down at her snow-covered boots. "Early June, I should think."

"June?" he growled. "You mean you've known all this time, and you didn't tell me?"

"I thought it would be better to wait until I was certain I wouldn't miscarry. That happens often, you know. Especially the first time." She paused, knowing she needed to be completely honest with him. He waited patiently for her to speak again. That was one of the reasons she loved him so much. He was such a good listener, a rarity among men.

"And because I was a little afraid. Afraid for all of us."

She gripped the mug. "I needed to keep the secret a little while. Keep it to myself."

"You should have told me sooner. This changes things."

She gazed out onto the pond and watched Harry and Isla skate past them, arms linked. They were smiling, heads bowed, whispering. "It doesn't have to."

Ian threw back the rest of his hot cider and set the mug back on the rock. "If it is born a boy, born alive and lives until his christening, he will be named the next heir of Dunnane."

"Dungald's place will slip," she said softly. "Harry's position will be solidified."

"Aye."

She looked at him over the rim of her cup, wanting to be brave, but wishing he would put his arm around her right now. Wishing he could give her the courage she knew she would need. But even though Harry knew the truth that they were lovers, out of respect for him they behaved no differently with each other in public than they had before.

"Do you think our child will be at risk?"

"You could be at risk."

"I don't care about myself," she said quickly. "Only the baby."

Standing beside her, he eased his hand around her waist; their cloaks covered his gesture. "I care for our child's safety, as well, but it is you I must protect."

She understood.

For a moment they stood in silence watching Isla and Harry skate round and round the pond. To watch them one would think Harry had not a care in the world.

"I'll tell him tonight."

"Want me to join you?"

She shook her head, leaning back against him, cherishing his touch. "Nae. 'Tis a woman's place to tell her husband she carries another man's child."

"He—"

"Or she," she interrupted.

"Or she," Ian corrected himself, "will bear Harry's name." He said the words carefully, as if they pained him.

"Of course." She glanced up at him through a veil of lashes. "But we will know the truth."

He tightened his grip around her waist in a hug, then lowered his arm and walked away. "Harry, 'tis getting dark! We'd best get that babe home."

Harry waved and skated by with Isla on his arm. "One more time around," he called, as any boy would.

Kara brushed the single tear that fell on her cheek as she watched her boy-husband skate by. She didn't know why she was crying. Happiness? Sadness?

Mayhap both.

"I suppose this was to be expected," Harry said more calmly than she knew he felt.

Kara sat across from him before the fireplace in his private bedchamber. Isla had turned in, leaving them in privacy. Kara had already dressed for bed and made them both a cup of hot chocolate.

He ran his hand through his hair, letting it fall over one cheek. "You told him."

She nodded, watching him.

"A child," he said softly, almost in wonder. "A child who will bear my name."

"As long as that's what you wish."

He rose abruptly. "You say that as if we have any choice." He opened his arms. "As if I have a choice."

She looked him directly in the eye. She was not ashamed; she would not be ashamed of the child she carried out of love. "This will be an heir. No one will be able to question your place at the head of the table."

He lifted his monkey from where it slept on a pillow on his bed, and stroked the little creature. "It's not that I'm a fool. I knew it was going to happen. I just wasn't ready to hear it.''

"I'm sorry,'' she said softly. "If anywhere along the way I could have done something differently, hurt you less . . .'' Her voice trailed off.

Harry stood a long moment in silence, stroking his pet. "Are you feeling well enough?'' he asked then.

"Fine. Thank you.''

"You should have another maid. Even with Isla's help you do too much.''

She smiled. "I'm strong and healthy. 'Twas the reason I was married off to the Gordons to begin with.''

He sighed. "I forget sometimes that this was not your choice either, to come here, to marry me.''

She rose and went to him, laying a hand on his slender arm. "I'm so glad I have you. So proud to call you my friend.''

His blue-eyed gaze searched hers. "You mean that when you say it, don't you?''

She nodded.

He smiled grimly.

"But . . . Harry, I was thinking we should wait a while longer before we tell anyone else.'' It was up to him, of course. The child would be his in name. Never completely hers and Ian's. It would be a difficult burden to bear, but one she had known all along that she must.

"May I ask why?''

"The farther along I am, the better the chances the child will survive. Men rejoice upon the birth of heirs; they lose faith in miscarriages. 'Tis ridiculous, but to question the seed of a man is to question his strength.'' She thought a moment. "And also, I . . . I'd like to keep it between us, the three of us, a little longer. Our own secret.'' She lifted a hand as if she had no true reason. "A woman's foolishness.''

He stared out into the room for a moment. "Certainly. Whatever you wish.'' His gaze returned to hers.

"Thank you," she said softly, letting her hand fall to her side.

"For what?"

"Understanding."

"I'm sure I'll never truly understand. Our lives are so tangled." He stroked the back of his neck thoughtfully. "I had never realized how tangled lives could become. Nothing is as easy as I thought it would be, nor as clear."

"Want me to read to you before you sleep?" she asked.

"Aren't you tired? You must get enough sleep."

"I'm not tired. Not yet."

"Play a game of backgammon?" He grinned.

"Better yet, I'll beat you."

He nodded, easing his monkey back onto its pillow. "I'll get the table, you the board. Best two out of three. Loser reads to the winner."

"And brings the other tea in the morning!"

He winked. "I believe you've a wager, madam."

Chapter Twenty-three

"Standing at the window will not bring him home," Kara said. She sat calmly at a small table before the hearth in her chamber, entering information into the household account book.

Ian divided his time between pacing, talking gibberish to Harry's monkey and staring out the window.

He moved away from the window. "I don't know how you sit so calmly. They should be home by now. Harry and the men should have returned."

She lifted one shoulder. "They stopped for a draught of ale in celebration of their victory."

He looked at her, not cracking a smile.

She laughed at his seriousness. "Ian, he will be all right. I doubt a sword was drawn. Alfred Gordon is a blatherskite and everyone knows it. All mouth and kilt but no stones to stand upon."

Ian smiled broadly.

"What?" She reached for the cup of watered wine they shared.

"All mouth and kilt? No stones?" He chuckled. "The Countess Dunnane speaking in such common terms?"

She made a face and returned to the column of figures at her fingertips. "I have been around you men too long. I fear my speech has become as common as yours."

He chuckled. "In truth, it rather becomes you. I would think twice of drawing my sword in your presence."

She shook her quill at him. "And well you should."

He came up behind her and began to massage her shoulders. "We should have sent you to Alfred's while we men cowered here safely behind the walls of Dunnane."

She smiled. "You flatter me only because you wish to have your way with me."

He lifted her hair to kiss the back of her neck. "That was not my intention at all . . . but now that you mention it . . ."

She closed her eyes and tilted her head forward, savoring the feel of his warm mouth on her neck. "Not here," she whispered. "Not now . . . in the light of day."

He kissed the side of her neck, then the pulse of her throat. "Why not?" he whispered. "I have never seen you naked by the light of the sun. I try to imagine, but methinks my imagination does not do you justice."

She felt her cheeks grow warm, but the warmth did not stop there. It radiated outward, pulsing through her limbs. She turned in her chair, lifting her arms to his shoulders.

He knelt in front of her.

"Ian, we shouldn't," she argued halfheartedly. "Isla might—"

"She wouldn't dare enter without being given permission, not with me here. But to be certain, I'll lock the door."

Her lips met his. A month ago—nae, a fortnight ago— she would never have dared do this. Not in broad daylight. But for some reason in the last few days she felt as if she were being hurled forward again, faster than she wanted to go. She had no idea what she was moving toward, but it frightened her. This game she and Ian and Harry played was dangerous and becoming more so with each day. That, with the unrest of the Gordon clan, made their lives seem volatile. Suddenly she was desperate for every moment of happiness she could secure.

"Ian . . ."

"Please," he begged, taking her hands in his to kiss her palms. "Let me touch you, see you."

Kara already knew she was lost to him. She couldn't say no, not ever. But she still felt the need to protest. "I thought you were worried about Harry. Waiting for him."

"What better way to pass the time?" His breath was hot, his voice husky in her ear.

She brushed her lips against his again. "Fasten the doors," she whispered under her breath.

He came to his feet in an instant and bolted the door to the hall, then the one that adjoined her room to Isla's.

"Harry's, too."

"There's no one there."

She gave him one look and he did as she bid without further argument.

Then she rose to meet him, her heart already beating faster, her pulse racing. "Straight to hell," she murmured as she looped her arms around his neck. "Ye know we are bound straight to hell for this."

"As long as you go with me, hinny, I shall be content."

He lowered his head to her bosom and she ran her fingers through his hair. She loved his hair, as dark as a crow's wing, as silky as the spun thread of a caterpillar's cocoon. It always smelled so clean, so rich with the scent of him that was his alone. At night, when he left her bed, she rested her head on the pillow where he had just lain so that she might still smell him.

"If only we could change the past," he whispered. "If only I could make you my wife."

"It can never be, Ian." She let her eyes drift shut. "I've let it go; so must you."

He tugged at the ribbon that laced her woolen bodice. It fell open, revealing her breasts pressing against the thin cotton of her shift. He slid one broad hand beneath the round neckline.

She sighed as his thumb found the nub of her nipple. His mouth met hers and he nipped at her lower lip. She swayed against him, her knees weak with the ripples of pleasure already washing over her.

He slid her bodice over her shoulders, then the shift. Kara pulled her arms from the layers of clothing to stand naked to the waist before him.

"You have the most beautiful breasts," he murmured, kissing one and then the other.

"We shall see if you say the same in a few months," she teased.

"Nae," He covered her peaked mounds with fleeting kisses. "In the years to come you will only become more beautiful in my eyes." He touched a taut nipple with the tip of his tongue and gasped softly.

"You'll have to untie me," she said, turning slowly in his arms, presenting her back to him.

He found the tie of her skirt and loosened it. She stepped out of the wool overskirt, then the underskirt, taking her time. His hands glanced over her bare shoulders, rubbing, kneading. Her undergarments fell in puddles at her feet. The air was cool in the room, but it only added to the pleasure of the feel of his warm hands on her bare skin.

She kicked off her low-heeled slippers, caught the hem of her shift and began to lift it over her head. Closing her eyes, she turned on the balls of her feet to face him. Ian took a step back to watch her.

She felt his gaze upon her as she took her time in removing the last of her clothing. She could hear his breathing as she slowly unveiled herself. She could feel his eyes burning on her flesh. She shivered, not with cold, but with pleasure at the thought of him watching her.

"Kara," he breathed.

Slowly she opened her eyes. He stood only a step from her, entranced. She lifted one foot and then the other, untying her stockings, rolling them off, stepping out of them. All the while, his gaze never left her.

"This seems unfair," she said. "You still have all your clothing on."

His husky voice caught in his throat. "We could remedy that matter easily enough."

He began to remove his shirt, but she brushed his hands aside. "Nae, let me."

She found the hem of his linen shirt, lifted it over his head and dropped it to the floor with her own clothing. Kara could not resist running her hands over the dark, crisp hair of his chest. She rested her cheek on his left breast to hear his heart beat for her. Then she took one male nipple between her teeth, licked, tugged.

He groaned. "Where did you learn that?"

"You." She stroked the width of his broad chest, running her hands down his sides over old scars. Finally her fingertips found the woolen edge of his kilt, just beneath his navel.

He made a sound in his throat. She glanced up to see that his eyes were closed. His breathing was shallow. She drew her hand over the brown and green plaid woven by Dunnane's own weavers. He sucked in his breath.

She smiled to herself, enjoying the weight of his manliness in the palm of her hand. He shifted his weight from one foot to the other, breathing heavily.

She slid her hand lower, over the hem, to his bare leg, then upward.

"Witch, ye have me under your spell," he whispered in her ear.

She took her time, cupping him in her palm, stroking. He was already hard, but grew harder with each caress. At first Kara had been timid about touching Ian, but now she enjoyed it as much as she knew he enjoyed touching her. She loved making him feel this way, and a part of her took a secret pleasure over the power she held over him in these moments.

She stroked, fondled with one hand, then both. She kissed his bare chest, teasing his nipples.

"Enough," he soon moaned. "Else there will be no loving for you this day."

She threw back her head and laughed as he lifted her into his arms. She looped her arms around his neck and he carried her to the bed and set her gently upon it. He made quick work of the rest of his clothing and lay beside her on her bed. He took her mouth hungrily.

"Let me look at you," he told her.

She lay back on her pillow, luxuriating in his approval as his gaze swept over her.

He drew his palm over her slightly rounded belly. Finally she was beginning to show her pregnancy, though it could not be noticed beneath her clothing.

Ian rested his cheek on her swollen abdomen, caressing her lovingly. "I cannot believe you carry my child," he whispered. "I am in awe."

She ran a hand through his hair, chuckling. "I don't know why men are so amazed by this feat. Women have been carrying babes in their wombs since the beginning of time."

"You have not been carrying my babe since the beginning of time." He pressed a kiss to her navel.

Kara sighed. She enjoyed quiet moments such as this with Ian, but right now it was not enough for her just to lie here. Her entire body was quivering with anticipation. She needed to touch and be touched.

Kara stroked the hard muscles of his buttocks as he nestled his face between the valley of her breasts. Hot, tingling desire flowed through her as she rolled onto her side to face him, their bare limbs entangling. Instinctively she rocked her hips forward to meet his probing. He wanted to draw out their pleasure, but Kara wanted him now, at this moment, buried inside her. She threw her arms around his neck and parted her thighs, consumed by fire.

"Kara, sweet Kara," he murmured, taking her with one stroke. "No matter what, I'll love ye till the end of time."

By the time Harry's hounds sounded the alarm, Ian and Kara were dressed again. Her hair had been brushed and returned to a presentable state. He had even gone downstairs to speak with the men before returning to Kara's chamber with a bit of meat and bread for them to share.

The dogs could be heard in the courtyard three stories below. Ian ran to the window.

"They're here?" Kara asked.

He turned back for the door. "They're here."

She stood frozen for a moment, afraid to move. "Harry, you spotted him? He's well?"

"He's well." Ian held the door open for her. "Riding in the lead. I'm not certain because of the distance, but I believe he's grinning like a cat that just swallowed a bird."

She smiled at him. "So perhaps our Harry is right. Our concern over his dear cousin is unfounded. A worm, not a snake in the grass."

Chuckling, filled with relief, Kara lifted her skirts and ran for the stairs. She beat Ian to the bottom. Side by side they met Harry just inside Dunnane's walls.

"Kara! Ian!" He waved as he rode in through the gates, past the guardhouse.

Kara waved. Ian stood still beside her but she knew he was as excited as she was, as anxious to see Harry well.

"Was your effort a success, my lord?"

Harry swung out of his saddle, tossing his reins to one of his men. "Alfred was surely vexed, even made a stand at his gate." Harry smoothed his leine chroich, holding his head proudly. "I think he was surprised to see me. But he backed down." He glanced over his shoulder at Dungald, riding through the gate. "Didn't he, cousin?"

"Aye," Dungald said with less enthusiasm. He dismounted and removed his gloves. "The boy—his lordship stood well. Alfred paid his fee when he realized it was time he took the Earl of Dunnane seriously."

Kara threw her arms around Harry and he hugged her in return. "I'm so proud of you," she whispered in his ear.

He beamed.

Ian hit him none too gently on his shoulder. It was as close to a hug as Kara had seen men exchange in public.

"All is well here, my lord," Ian said, "but 'tis good to have you back."

Harry pulled his sword from his belt and handed it to one of his clansmen. "Is supper coming?" he asked, taking Kara by the arm to lead her inside. "I'm close to starving."

Kara laughed, her voice echoing off Dunnane's gray stone walls that seemed to climb into the heavens overhead. "How did I know it would be food you would be needing?" she teased, so thankful to have him home safely again. "The tables are already being set."

Kara sat at the head table in the great hall, listening to Harry repeat the day's events to Ian. Having eaten, she sat back in her chair and listened to the men talk, content to sit between the two people she loved most in the world.

Dungald sat on the other side of Harry, well in his cups. He was obviously disgruntled about something, but she didn't know what. She didn't care so long as he was quiet and didn't bother her or Harry. Dungald had been like this often lately. Sullen, often angry. Kara guessed he was disappointed that Harry's encounter with Alfred had gone so well. She knew Dungald expected—wanted—Harry to fail at every turn. Surely it upset him when the boy succeeded.

"I honestly do not believe he thought I would come for him," Harry told Ian, lifting his goblet to his lips. He leaned closer to Ian. "Did you know my father did not enforce the annual duty?"

Ian nodded. "I have heard as much."

Harry sipped his wine and set down the cup. "I do not mean to speak ill of the dead, of my father, but I hear things. And the more I hear, the more I think he was not a good manager of his lands and monies."

Ian stared at the cup he gripped in his hand. "What your father did or did not do is not your responsibility. What you do now for your people is what matters."

Taking in what Ian said, Kara glanced at Dungald. She actually felt a bit sorry for him. She had heard him mumbling for months that Harry's father had not done his part. She, of course, had not believed a word. He was only jealous that his own father had been a younger son, and therefore had not inherited. But now, knowing what she did, she thought perhaps his father would have served Dunnane better. But that was not the way the feudal system they had followed for hundreds of years worked. Harry's father, as the eldest son, had been heir, no matter what his ability. Dungald had just never accepted the matter.

"So how are you, dear wife?" Harry asked, refilling his cup.

She smiled. "I am well, sir. Well."

He smiled back at her and then lifted his goblet, coming to his feet. "Gentlemen, gentlemen."

Slowly the clansmen quieted, all turning in their chairs to hear what their lord had to say. The atmosphere in the great hall tonight was one of joviality, victory. Everyone seemed to feel good tonight, about themselves, about their clan lord.

"I want to thank all of those who attended to me today. Well done." Harry nodded. "And also those who remained behind to protect our walls."

Everyone in the room came to their feet, including those sitting at the dais. Kara picked up her own glass.

"Hear! Hear!" Harry cried and lifted his goblet high in a toast.

"Hear! Hear!" the men echoed, their voices a roar.

The toast was followed by the pounding of feet, goblets ringing on tables, cheers of goodwill.

"And while I have you all gathered . . ." Harry said.

Again the men quieted.

"While I have you all here, I would like to make an announcement of a more personal nature."

Kara suddenly felt warm, prickly. She didn't know what he was going to say but suddenly she felt uncomfortable. Surely he wasn't going to tell them about the baby. Not yet. "Harry," she whispered.

But Harry didn't hear; he was too caught up in the moment, grinning proudly as the men waited in anticipation.

"My wife and I, the Countess of Dunnane"—he put his arm around her shoulder—"will be having a child."

A great roar of applause rippled throughout the room, echoing off the stone walls and the high, domed ceiling.

Red-faced, Kara looked at Harry.

She immediately knew by the look on his face that he knew he had done something wrong. Too angry to speak, she dropped her goblet on the table and walked away.

"Kara!" He followed her.

Out of the corner of her eye she saw Ian rise from his chair, watching her, but he did not follow them.

"I asked you to wait," she hissed under her breath.

He nearly had to run to keep up with her as she crossed the hall. Clansmen watched with interest, wondering what was about with the lord and lady of the manor.

"We agreed we would wait!"

"But Kara, I don't see why we had to wait longer. Everyone is so pleased. I only wanted—"

Kara turned on her heel to face him, still within the hall. She was so angry she could barely form her words. Harry had come so far in the last months, matured so greatly, and yet there were things he still didn't understand. Dangers he still didn't see.

"It would have been safer to have waited," she managed through clenched teeth. "Until I was farther along." Her gaze met his and tears welled in her eyes. She was overwrought. She knew, but she couldn't stop herself. "Because I just didn't want to tell! We agreed, Harry."

"I only meant to—"

"Don't say another word," she snapped, thrusting her hand in his face. "Don't say another word, Harry Gordon, or I will . . . I will . . ." She dropped her hands to her sides, too angry to think. "God's teeth," she shouted, "I wish I had never married you!"

Before he could get out another word, she turned and ran from the hall.

Harry followed Kara to the hall before thinking better of chasing her up the stairs. He halted in the dark hall, his hands falling limply at his sides. He had been so excited about his day's accomplishments, even excited about the baby, even if it wasn't really his. Now all was a mess; he had made a mess out of everything.

"They're like that, you know. Women. They can all be bitches."

Harry turned to see Dungald behind him and exhaled slowly. He thought he would give her time and then go up to the tower. He would apologize. She was right; he should have waited. He hung his head. She was always right.

Dungald sidled up to him. "I suppose congratulations are in order. Not only did you do the job, but apparently you did it right." He elbowed him.

Harry glared at Dungald. He was not in the mood for his cousin's insinuations tonight, not now.

Dungald's face fell. "It is your child, isn't it?" he asked pointedly.

Harry felt a strange sense of dread creep over him. What did Dungald know? Surely he couldn't know.

Harry felt his face grow hot. "Of course." He squared his shoulders. "Of course the babe is mine! Whose the bloody hell do you think it is?"

Dungald threw up both hands. "There, there, cousin. I did not mean to insult you."

"I know." Harry twisted his mouth, beyond annoyed with Dungald. Now he was angry. "You ask only out of the goodness of your concern for Dunnane."

"Of course."

"Harry." Ian came out of the hall.

"Here," Harry called. He was relieved to see Ian. Ian would know what to do. How to apologize to Kara.

"Well, I . . . Congratulations to you, my lord," Dungald said quickly, passing Harry, going in the opposite direction from which Ian came.

"What did he want?" Ian asked, watching Dungald hurry into the darkness.

Harry shrugged. "I don't know. Don't care." His shoulders sagged. "I think I'll let her calm down and then go to her." He looked up at his brother for support. "What do you think? She's never thrown anything at me, but there is always a first time."

Ian smiled grimly and patted his shoulder. "Wise thought, brother. I wouldn't want Kara throwing things at me either. My guess is, she's a fine aim."

"Ye appear swiftly when I call," Dungald said. He and the hired man stood just inside the entrance to the tunnel that led to the catacombs below the castle. Many years' growth of underbrush and a copse of trees disguised the entrance.

"I am not camped far." The man whose face remained obscured in the darkness scuffed a boot in the soft dirt. "What do ye want? I take it ye've brought coin."

Dungald thrust out his hand and dropped a small, clinking sack into the other man's palm. "A portion of your payment." Most he had won gambling; a few coins he had pilfered from the castle, but not enough to be missed.

The man repeatedly tossed the sack up and watched it fall to his hand. "What else have ye but this? You take me from a warm bed, a bed I do not occupy alone."

Dungald drew his cloak closer. The wind outside tonight was bitter and howling. He needed a drink badly. His hands were shaking, not just from the palsy. Shaking.

The chit, Kara, was with child. If a son, he would become the next Earl of Dunnane. Dungald's breath quickened as panic rose in his chest. There would be more children; she would whelp them like one of the castle's bitch hounds. Dungald would never hold the earldom, not if he didn't make haste.

"Have ye hired enough men yet?"

"Of course I have hired a sufficient number. What kind of man do you think I am?"

"I think you are a thief and a mercenary."

The man cracked a smile. "That I am, but one with principles." He chuckled. "Principles of my own, 'tis all." He eyed Dungald. "Now, you are guaranteeing that we fight only the men within the castle. Others will not come to the boy's aid?"

"Others? Others who? They hate him! No one in the countryside believes the boy is fit to rule."

"Word has traveled of the MacFae-Gordon settlement." The man shook his head, still chuckling. "Many are saying the boy laid down the smartest ruling he could have. It should have been done years ago. Neither side has right to complain. Some are beginning to see some merit to the child."

"Ridiculous!" Dungald scoffed. "Enough talk. I have not the time for this. You do as you're told. Gather your army and come when you are called. Serve as the diversion

you have been instructed to be and then get the hell off
Dunnane land. Do ye understand me?"

When the man did not answer right away, Dungald
jabbed a pointed finger into the folds of his Dunnane
plaid. "This is what is rightfully due to me. It is what is
best for the Gordons. The castle should have gone to me.
Should have been my father's before me. It is my father,
Henry, who kept these walls standing all those years while
that brat's father chased women and dreams." His last
words were so frenzied that his hand fell into a shaking
spasm and he had to draw it into his cloak to steady it.

The man stood for a moment, and though Dungald
could not see his face, he knew he was staring at him.
"Next time we meet, this bag will be filled with no paltry
sum. Do I make myself clear, *my lord*?"

"Ye shall have your coin," Dungald said beneath his
breath as he turned away. "And my father shall finally have
justice."

"I'm sorry," Harry said carefully.

She sank onto the edge of her bed. "Nae." She was
tired. So worn, not just physically, but emotionally. "I'm
so sorry. I should not have behaved so. I should not have
shouted at you in front of the others. That was a terrible
thing to say. I don't know what came over me." She glanced
up at him. "I didn't mean it to come out that way."

Harry walked toward her slowly, as if he feared she might
explode into another tirade, perhaps throw something at
him. "Forgotten. I take no offense. And you were right.
We agreed we would not tell of the babe. I knew that. Why
didn't matter." He splayed his hands. "But I was excited
about the day. I was full of myself; I did not think before
I spoke."

He sank a fist into his hand. "I must learn to think
before I speak. I know that. I cannot lord over these people
if I cannot be more prudent."

She couldn't resist the smile a mother smiles when her child has learned a lesson the hard way. " 'Tis really nothing to be upset about. They would all know soon enough." She laughed, hearing the tiredness in her own voice. "Look at me. I'm already growing fat."

"Not fat." He sat on the edge of her bed beside her. "I think you're beautiful," he said shyly. "I always will."

"I'm just overly emotional, Harry. 'Tis the way women get when they are with child, I'm told." She glanced at him seated beside her. "This really was my fault. I feel so bad."

"It wasn't all your fault, but let us move on. Forgotten, forgiven. Now they know, and now I must take extra precautions. You and the baby must be watched and kept safe. I could not stand to see any harm come to you because of me."

She felt a warm flush of tenderness. Harry might be young, but he was growing to be quite a man. He would make a good ruler; she was certain of it.

Harry covered her hand with his. "We need not talk of this tonight. You look tired. You should be abed."

"I am tired," she confessed. "I should have known better than to come down. I should have stayed here in my rooms and kept my mouth shut."

He smiled. "Then let me call Isla to help you into your sleeping clothes." He rose, reluctantly releasing her hand.

With him standing and her sitting, he appeared tall, almost manly. He was watching over her, watching out for her. It felt good to be cared for, after all the years of always caring for others.

She ran one hand through her hair, making no attempt to rise. She thought she might just be too tired to stand again tonight. She watched as he crossed the room and laid his hand on Isla's door. Suddenly she didn't want him to go.

"Harry?"

"Aye?" He turned back to her.

"Will you stay with me? Just until I sleep?" She didn't know why she said it, or why she felt this way. All she knew was that she needed someone. Needed him.

His gaze met hers. "I would stay at your bedside through the night, if you asked."

She smiled and lay back on the bed to wait for Isla, thinking what a lucky woman she was to call Harry her friend.

Chapter Twenty-four

Harry stood on the parapet, the wind whipping at his shoulder-length blond hair. He pressed his hands to the low wall and stared out over the gray countryside. "Looks like snow," he said thoughtfully.

But Kara did not think he was thinking about snow. His youthful face was too solemn, his lips drawn too tight.

"March snow," he mused. "My father always said he liked March snow—it cleansed the land and made the way for the green of spring."

Kara drew her cloak close over her obviously rounded belly. Six months gone, the baby was now lively; rolling, kicking, making ripples across her extended abdomen. Harry liked to lay his hand on her belly and feel the baby move. Ian loved to lie in her bed at night, his head nestled between her breasts with one hand on her abdomen. It was an odd relationship she and her two men had created, but it seemed to work. Everyone seemed to be content, as content as they could be, considering the circumstances.

Kara was relieved to find Harry here on the parapet. She had searched for him everywhere, searched long enough that she had begun to grow concerned. When she could not find him inside the castle walls, she had checked the barns and the mews. She had even sent one of the men into the catacombs below to see that he had not gone to the wine cellar or elsewhere. It was Isla who had guessed where Harry might be.

"I was worried when I couldn't find you," she said.

He gave her a half smile, though she could tell she still did not have his full attention. "Ye shouldn't worry over me, Kara, not in your condition."

"Not in my condition!" She leaned on the wall beside him to see the same view he saw, knowing she never truly could. She wondered what he had been thinking about up here alone. "I'm as fit as one of the mares in your stable. I certainly eat like one."

He rested his hand casually on her hip. "Eat through my larders if you wish, Lady Dunnane, whatever it takes to keep you and the babe healthy and happy."

She was quiet for a moment, enjoying the moment alone with Harry. He had been busy these last two months. Men had been called in to serve their duty to him, but they had not spent their time eating and drinking in the great hall. Instead Harry had ordered training sessions. The men had practiced fighting hand-to-hand, following orders. They had reviewed loading the costly firearms Dunnane possessed, and practiced firing them accurately. And Harry drilled beside them. He asked nothing of his clansmen that he did not do himself. Ian told Kara privately that he was a quick learner and would turn out to be an excellent leader. With time and experience, he would become a fighter to be reckoned with, should the need arise. Kara was so proud of him, as was Ian.

For the last few months the lands and families that fell under Dunnane's jurisdiction had existed in a strange state of unrest. The cattle reivers continued to steal, not just from Dunnane, but from other landowners as well. Families fought among themselves, constantly bringing quarrels

to the earl. The men fought among each other and they
fought Dunnane, rarely with any definitive reason for the
unrest. It was almost as if they were all in a great pot and
something or someone was constantly putting them in a
stir. The climate made Ian uncomfortable and apparently
Harry as well. It made Kara fear for the men she loved,
the life they seemed to be carving out for themselves within
these ancient walls.

"Do you know where my brother is?" Harry asked.

She shook her head. Her cloak caught on the wind and
flapped noisily. She tugged on the corner to silence it.
"Nae. I haven't seen him, but he may be in the barn.
There was a horse that needed tending."

"My cousin?"

Kara glanced at him sideways. There was something in
his tone of voice that made her wonder if something was
wrong. "In the hall, I believe."

"Are you going down soon?"

"Aye, 'tis cool."

"Would you send Dungald up?"

"Up here?" She glanced at the ground far below them.
"If you wish." She turned away to follow his bidding, then
back to Harry. "Did you want Ian as well?"

"Nae, I can handle this myself."

She started for the door again.

"Kara."

She halted.

"I want to handle this myself."

She entered the narrow cylindrical stairwell. She didn't
know what was afoot. As she took the stairs carefully, but
quickly, she wondered if she ought to fetch Ian. But Harry
had specifically said he didn't need his brother. He specifically said he'd deal with the matter on his own. He had
the right, of course; he was the earl.

Kara found Dungald in the great hall drinking from
Harry's footed goblet. She coolly sent him above stairs and
took the goblet to wash it out herself.

* * *

"Ye sent for me, my lord?" Dungald stared coldly beyond Harry, into the gray sky beyond the parapet.

It was obvious he didn't like being called before Harry, but at this point Harry didn't give a damn. Though he had done nothing Harry could interpret as a threat to his earldom, he was tired of Dungald. Tired of his whining, tired of his sulking.

"The men I just saw ride out, there were two dozen."

"Two dozen?"

Harry folded his arms over his chest. His cloak flapped in the breeze, blowing open, but he was not cold. He was too annoyed to be cold. "Where were they going?"

His cousin kept his gaze averted. "Going, my lord?"

"Are you addlepated?" Harry snapped. "Stop repeating what I say and answer me. Truthfully." He paused, emphasizing each word. "Where have those men gone and who sent them?"

Dungald swallowed. His Adam's apple slid down, then bobbed up again. "Perhaps Ian—"

"Ian did not send those men abroad! He would not do so without my permission! He knows better."

Dungald cringed. "I . . . I may have sent them, my lord."

"You may have?" Harry planted his hands on his hips. "May have? Ye don't know what you do and what you don't do?"

Dungald stared at his boots for a moment, made a feeble gesture. "I sent the patrol . . . to sweep to the south of Dunnane. I sent them looking for Robert the Red and the reivers."

"Why?"

"Because . . . because I wanted to bring them in for you, my lord. To end this matter. You've enough—"

"Do not lie to me, cousin." Harry took a threatening step toward him. "I know you better than that. I know ye do nothing that you will not profit from."

Dungald slid a step back. "All right, all right. I wanted to bring the reivers to justice to end the trouble for Dunnane, but also . . . also to show you I can be of some use."

Harry twisted his mouth in thought. "To show me you can be of some use to me, or so that I may reward you?"

Dungald gave a quick smile, then let it fall. "That, too, my lord. I fear I have debts."

"A man should not gamble more than he can afford to lose."

Dungald clasped his hands. "Aye, my lord. I ken that."

Harry exhaled, glancing out over the ground far below. "What is your monthly stipend now?"

Dungald named an amount.

It was more than sufficient, more than generous. But Harry did not want to be unkind. Perhaps if Dungald had a few more coins in his sporran, he would not be so jealous of that which would never be his.

"I will increase the amount."

Dungald looked up in surprise. "My lord, you are most—"

"But I will not hear of you giving orders to my men again. Do you understand?"

Dungald lowered his gaze in apparent gratitude. "I understand."

"We cannot afford to leave ourselves short of men. We know not what goes on around us. The men are angry, restless. Don't you understand that the castle could be attacked? That we would need those men if someone dared to raise arms against us?"

"No one would dare, not Dunnane," Dungald breathed, wide-eyed.

Harry turned away. "I pray not." He leaned on the parapet wall. "You are dismissed. But cousin, if I catch you usurping my authority again . . ." He held up a finger.

Dungald halted.

"I will send you away from here. Do you understand me? Far from here. Dunnane has other holdings, on the islands to the far northwest. Is that where you wish to live out your days?"

Harry saw a strange coldness flash in Dungald's gray-green eyes, there one moment, then gone so quickly that he thought he must have imagined it.

Harry waved a hand. "Dismissed."

But Dungald did not retreat. He slipped the hand that trembled under his arm. "Do you wish me to send someone out to bring the men back?" He hesitated. "Or would you prefer I do it myself?" He lowered his gaze. "Because I was the one who sent them."

Harry thought a second. "Aye. Go yourself. I will not spare any more men."

"As you wish, my lord, thank you, my lord."

Harry heard Dungald retreat down the steps.

Below him, over the wall, Harry caught sight of Kara. She waved to him from stories below. Ian appeared across the brown, brittle grass, his face breaking into a broad grin at the sight of Kara.

Harry could not help but smile himself. There were a hundred things in his life he wished he could change. He wished he had not been married off so young. He wished he had had a chance to be a true husband to Kara. But seeing that smile on his brother's face, how could he wish to deprive him of such happiness?

Fate. Was this all fate? He thought maybe so.

Far below, Kara caught a glimpse of Ian and stopped to wait for him.

Harry turned away and leaned on the wall, crossing his arms over his chest. If this was fate, he wondered, then what was his fate? Would he know it when he saw it?

"What the hell are you doing here in broad daylight?" the man demanded, appearing out of the rocks that hid his encampment.

Dungald slung himself out of his saddle, catching the

reins as his boots hit the hard, cold ground. "Now. Now is the time," he said anxiously. "Tonight."

"What are you talking about?"

Dungald glanced beyond the leader of the ruffians to his men. Some sat on campstools eating from wooden trenchers; others gathered around a small fire. All appeared uneasy.

"Surely you have more men than this."

"Surely ye have more sense than to come here. To allow yourself to be seen." He pushed on Dungald's chest, backing him up out of view of the reivers.

"I had to come. The opportunity was too perfect."

"I don't know that I can be prepared."

"You'll be prepared," Dungald swore hotly, "or I'll find someone who is."

The man burst into hearty laughter. "Find someone else, indeed. No one else would be fool enough." He studied Dungald carefully. "I can't help but ask." He shrugged. "Not that it makes a pence to me, but why a fight? Why not knife him in the back. 'Twould be easier. Cheaper."

Dungald scowled. "Because there will be less suspicion, you simple gowk! Who will question the death of a man in battle?" he scoffed. "Besides, what better man to inherit than a hero? If I am able to lead the Gordons into a victory, if I am able to defend Dunnane, I will be welcomed into the arms of my men, my seat undeniably established."

The man looked away, shaking his head as if in disgust.

Annoyed, Dungald tucked a lock of his black hair behind his ear. Who was this man to judge him? Who was he to understand the intricacies of politics and honor? He was nothing but a dog, a hired killer. "Can you or can you not attack tonight?"

He exhaled, ruffling his scraggly red beard. "I suppose I can. I'm ready to take my leave of this place anyway. We've been here too long."

"So ye have other men. More men."

He gave a wave. "You tell who you must. I will gather the others."

"Same meeting point?"

"The same," he agreed, not bothering to meet Dungald's gaze.

"Excellent." Dungald clasped his hands together. "Of course, I cannot be there."

He cut his gaze at Dungald as if considering him an idiot. "I would think not."

"Excellent. Excellent." Dungald strode back toward his mount. "Then I shall see you."

"For my payment. And healthy it had best be." The red-bearded man pulled his dirk from his belt. "Or you know the penalty."

Licking his lips, Dungald caught his horse's reins while keeping one eye on the thief as he mounted.

The thief stood on a rock, knife drawn, until Dungald lost sight of him on the rolling horizon.

"Kara, wake up." She heard a voice somewhere in the recesses of her mind.

"Oh, God, please, Kara. You must wake up."

She struggled to the surface from a deep sleep. "Harry?" she mumbled. "Harry, what is it? Are you—"

The moment her eyes opened and she saw his face in the candlelight, she knew Harry wasn't ill. Something else was wrong. Horribly wrong. She sat up in bed, rubbing the sleep from her eyes. "What is it?" she whispered, clasping his hand.

He climbed off her bed, pulling his shirt over his bare chest as he went to her clothing chest. "You must get up and dress quickly."

She slid her bare feet over the side of the bed. "What's wrong?"

He turned to her, stuffing his shirt into the waistband of his green-and-brown plaid kilt. "Attack," he said softly, as if still not believing it himself. "Dunnane is under attack."

Kara shot out of bed. "Attack? Attack by whom? The cattle reivers?" She grabbed the nearest gown, left flung over a chair, and dropped it over her head, over her sleeping gown.

"They haven't come for cattle." He strapped a wide leather belt meant to carry a sword around his narrow hips. His blond hair fell boyishly over one eye, but he did not look a boy to her at this moment. He looked like a man preparing to defend his castle, his people.

He shook his head stiffly. "There's too many of them to be the reivers."

"Then who?" As she jerked on a stocking, she glanced toward Isla's chamber. She could hear the girl racing about, making preparations of some sort.

"I don't know."

The sound of men's shouts seeped through the closed window, and instinctively she turned toward it. She thought she heard the sound of musket fire.

"Kara, you must hurry. We must go now."

"Go where?" She slipped on the other wool stocking, not bothering to roll it up or tie it. She stepped into a pair of shoes left under the edge of her bed.

"There's too many of them," he said, grabbing her cloak from a peg on the wall. "Men left on a patrol last night. Dungald went to retrieve them but I don't know that they have returned. We're shorthanded."

She thought she heard him swear beneath his breath. A French oath.

"You didn't say where we are going." She hurried toward the door where he waited for her, her cloak thrown over his arm.

Isla burst into the room carrying a bag, baby Meggie tied to her mother's chest in a sling. The red-checked infant was wide-eyed and shaking her hands in excitement, as if she thought she was going on an outing.

Musket fire echoed. A shot ricocheted. The sound of chipping stone could not be ignored.

Harry threw open the door. "Hurry, ladies. I believe we can hold Dunnane, but you go to higher ground. We've a safe place to hide you beyond the walls. You will escape through the tunnel out of the catacombs and no one will be the wiser."

"Us? What of you?"

Harry threw her cloak over her shoulders, ushering her and Isla down the tower steps. He held a candle to light their way. "I stand with Dunnane, wife. Where do you think I go? I stand with my men. They need me."

He said it so simply that Kara wondered if Harry knew what he said. Understood. But the look in his eyes made her realize he did.

The look in his eyes scared her. Harry Gordon would stand with Castle Dunnane, fight for her until she'd withstood the siege, or fell. There would be no discussion, no compromise. It had been nearly a year since Kara and Harry had wed, and in these months she had encouraged him again and again to stand up and be the man she knew he could be. Now he was.

Now she wished he could just be a boy again.

Men rushed by up the narrow staircase carrying firearms, bows and ammunition. Each time a group approached, Kara and Harry and Isla pressed their backs to the wall to make room for them to pass single file.

The boots pounded on the stone steps, making a deafening noise that rocked Kara to the bone.

This was real. The castle was under attack and there was a real chance Dunnane might fall. A real chance Harry or Ian might be killed.

"Harry, please." She clutched his arm desperately. "Go with us."

A step behind her, he had to look down upon her, the candlelight casting an aura of light around him. "Nae."

"Then let me stay with you."

He frowned as if she had said something completely preposterous. "Your duty is to the heir of Dunnane. Now listen to me. You will be safe until we have won the day, and then Ian or I will come for you."

"Both of you," she whispered, clasping his cloak. "Both of you will come for us. You'll take care of each other. Promise me."

He smiled, the weight of his responsibility lifting from his shoulders for just a moment. "I promise. Now hurry."

Just as they reached the bottom of the tower steps they heard a sound behind them. Something coming down the stairs fast. They heard a whine and a shriek, not human, but close.

"James," Harry said. "Heavens, I've forgotten James."

The monkey came around the corner in the stairwell and practically flew into his master's arms. Harry scooped up the pet and dropped him onto his shoulder. "Hurry, ladies," he urged. "Ian waits below."

Within the castle the sounds of gunfire and men running were punctuated by guttural shouts. Cries of battle. The sounds seemed to reverberate off the stone walls of Dunnane as Kara clasped Harry's hand and allowed him to help her down the wooden steps into the catacombs below the castle.

She was shaking all over. Frightened for Harry. For Ian. For Dunnane. This couldn't be happening. It couldn't be happening. And yet she knew it was.

Recognizing Ian's hulk in the dark shadows at the bottom of the steps, Kara ran forward, toward him. Her foot caught on the uneven dirt floor and she almost fell into his arms.

"Ian."

He held her tightly for a moment, surrounding her with his cloak, with his love. He ran one broad hand over her belly. Then he clasped her arms and pushed her back so he could look her in the eyes. "Listen to me," he said in a tone she could not ignore. "I'm going for horses."

"Don't leave me," she whispered. She wanted to say she didn't want to leave Dunnane. She wanted to stand with him and fight beside Harry and Ian, but she knew better than to even voice such a desire. She was well gone with child. Harry was right. Her duty was to protect the heir to Dunnane.

He shook her gently to get her attention. "I must go for the horses."

"Leave them in the trees and go straight to the rendezvous point. Men should be waiting there for us," Harry told him. "We'll take the enemy from behind, as planned. I will see the women safely above and astride, secure this passageway so they cannot enter the castle from here and then join you and the men."

Ian drew Kara into his embrace again. "You and Isla are to ride down into the village. There is a cottage, the sixth or seventh on the right, on the main road. A little fence before it. Put your horses in the lean-to behind it. The widow will see you hidden. Cared for. Her name is Ruthie. Give my name and you will be safe." He lowered his voice, but it was still laced with urgency. "Our babe will be safe there."

Tears ran down her cheeks but she made no sound. "Who attacks?" she whispered. "Who would dare?"

"I don't know." He kissed her quickly, a hard, hot kiss to her lips that could have been a good-bye if she allowed herself to think of it as such. He released her before she was ready to let him go.

Harry had Isla by the arm, his monkey still on his shoulder. "You go ahead, Ian," he ordered his brother with a sound of authority no one would have dared question. "We'll meet you at the entrance in the trees."

Ian ran into the darkness and disappeared. A sob rose in Kara's throat but she forced it back. She could not let Harry know how afraid she was. She had to be strong for Harry, for Isla, for the baby she carried.

Kara took the single candle and they ran down the narrow stone tunnels, the low ceiling hanging damp and close overhead. Harry held tightly to Isla's arm, supporting her as she ran with the baby. The light from the candle bounced here and there on the walls and dirt floor as they ran.

"Which way?" Kara asked.

"Left," Harry shouted.

The passageways beneath the castle were so confusing. Kara had no idea where she was. "Which way?" she shouted again and again.

Each time Harry answered immediately, confidently, without hesitation. The days he had spent hunting baby rats had become of use.

Kara made a sharp left, her heart pounding, her breath coming in gasps. She hoped it was not much farther. She held the candle up with one hand, the other grasping her skirt and pressing against her swollen abdomen.

"Right and right again," Harry called from behind.

Kara turned, and without warning he was there.

Dungald.

She stopped short.

Harry craned his neck to see around her. "Dungald," he panted.

Kara saw the look in Dungald's gray-green eyes. The look she remembered from the first night at Dunnane. Cold. Evil.

"Thank heavens you're back," Harry went on. "I need someone to go up to the parapet and check on the munitions. I think—"

Kara watched Dungald draw his sword, but even as he did, she could not believe it was happening. He seemed to be moving slower than humanly possible. Time seemed to slow down. Everything was happening at once, and yet she saw each piece separately.

She heard Harry's words as he began to give his orders to his cousin, catching his breath. She saw Dungald's sword flash in the candlelight. She saw his intention. She heard

Harry's voice grow tight and drift into silence as the boy realized what was about.

"Dungald, no!" Kara screamed, lunging forward toward him.

"Step aside, woman, and wait your turn!" Dungald shouted. "Draw, boy, and let us be done with this here and now."

Isla screamed. The baby screamed. Harry pushed Isla sideways, out of Dungald's way, as he drew his own sword.

"Kara! Take Isla. Run!" Harry commanded as sword met sword and the hideous sound of clanging metal assaulted her ears. "For my sake, Kara . . . protect yourself and my heir."

Suddenly time caught up and sped past Kara and she was helpless to stop it. Helpless to stop Dungald. "Harry!"

"Kara, go!"

The tone of her husband's voice could be construed as nothing but a direct order, an order from the Earl of Dunnane.

"Protect the baby!" Harry swung his sword again and again. "Swear to me!"

Isla cried hysterically.

"I swear!" Kara grasped Isla's arm and pulled her forward, still attempting to keep a hold on the candle, still fighting the urge to turn back, to help Harry.

"Sir!" cried a male voice ahead of her.

Someone else was coming, coming fast, carrying a torch.

Kara turned left into another arm of the catacomb, disappearing from Harry's sight, avoiding the stranger.

"Leave your torch," Kara heard Dungald shout.

Again and again swords clashed.

"Leave the torch and get her! Don't let the red-haired bitch get away. Kill her!"

"Harry, Harry," Isla sobbed. The hysterical girl tried to turn back, but Kara would not allow her to.

The baby screamed, taking great gulps of air into her little rosebud mouth.

"Hurry, Isla. The horses," Kara insisted. "For God's sake, Isla, we only need to get to the end of the tunnel."

Behind her Kara heard pounding footsteps. The man. Dungald's man. Chasing them.

The sounds of the swords had died away and there was only the thumping footfall. Maybe she was too far from them now. Maybe that was why she couldn't hear them.

Kara kept running, running, her arm linked through Isla's, dragging the maid along.

"What the bloody hell!" the male voice behind them cursed.

An instant later Harry's monkey sped past them.

Chapter Twenty-five

Dead end. Dead end, Kara's mind screamed even before she consciously realized she had made a wrong turn. They had to turn back. She whipped around, holding tightly with one hand to the candle, the other to Isla.

Too late. It was already too late. Dungald's man was upon them.

Isla screamed. She screamed so loud that her voice tore through Kara's head and echoed off the walls. One would have thought she'd already been run through.

"Stand back!" Kara shouted at the man with the torch as he entered the short passageway that had been stoned up. She glanced wildly about, looking for a weapon. A stick, a loose stone. Anything. Why had she left the castle without a weapon? How would she defend Isla and the baby? Her own child?

The man lifted his torch high, illuminating his face.

Kara stared in amazement. She knew him. Robert the Red, the cattle reiver.

But what was he doing here? Why was he in the bowels of Dunnane?

"Stand back," Kara said again, because she didn't know what else to say.

Robert the Red made no attempt to move out of her way. But he made no attempt to come closer either.

"My lady," he said, seeming as surprised to see her as she him. "I did not realize 'twas you."

Isla sobbed, her entire body shaking as she clutched her crying child. Kara slipped her arm around her companion, trying to offer some comfort. "What are you doing here?" she asked the thief. Her candle was nearly out now. She had to depend on his torch to see him.

"I am beginning to ask myself the very same thing, my lady," he said dryly.

They stood for a moment sizing each other up. Somewhere Kara heard footsteps. She wanted to think it was Harry coming after her, but her hopes were short-lived.

"Rob, are you there?"

The unmistakable voice of Dungald. The enemy. The serpent. "Did you get them?" His voice echoed off the crumbling stone walls.

"Where do you go?" Robert asked, glancing over his shoulder.

"Above," she whispered. "To safety in the village." Of course she wanted to go back for Harry. She knew she had to find Harry. He might have been injured . . . or worse. But she had promised Harry. Duty. It was her duty to protect Isla and the baby, to protect Harry's heir.

"Then come; ye must hurry." He stepped aside to let her pass.

Kara did not move. "I don't understand."

"What is there to understand?"

"Dungald. He told you to kill us. I heard him."

"Aye, he so ordered. But who says I must do what he orders? Who tells Robert the Red what to do?" He stared at her wild-eyed, wild bearded. "No one. It's a creed I have always stood by. I don't know why I ever considered differently." He shook his head. "I do not kill women."

She swallowed hard and took a step toward him, pulling Isla with her. She didn't know what was going on for certain, but thought maybe Dungald had hired Rob to attack the castle. "Come on, Isla; this is the way."

"Nae, nae," the girl whispered.

But Kara led her forward. " 'Tis all right," she soothed. "He is here to help us. He will get us out."

Kara passed the red-bearded man. She wasn't certain she could trust him, but what choice did she have?

"To the left," he told her. "Down the long corridor, second entrance on the right. Mind your footing. We'll have to hurry."

"Rob? Rob? Have ye found them?"

Kara could hear Dungald calling. She could hear his feet pounding on the dark, hard dirt. He was behind them, somewhere in the cold darkness.

"We must hurry," she whispered.

Kara followed Robert the Red's instructions, and moments later she could feel the cold spring air as it blew into the catacombs from the outside. Another moment and they were above ground. She immediately heard the neighing of the restless horses. The sound was strangely comforting, considering the other sounds that haunted the night air. Musket fire, men's screams. The air was filled with smoke and stank of burning tar. It stung her eyes and tasted bitter on her tongue.

"Can you get astride yourself?" Rob asked urgently. "I'll have to go back and head off my friend."

"My husband is still down there; can you find him?" she begged. "Be certain he's all right . . . for I fear he is not."

"I will see what I can do," the thief said roughly. "Now go."

Kara ran for the horses left tied in the copse of trees. She would think about Harry, not about Ian, not now. What she needed to do was get Isla to safety. "Thank you!"

She glanced over her shoulder to see Robert the Red

pull on his tartan bonnet and bow. "My lady." Then he turned and ran back into the tunnel.

"Get astride!" Kara urged Isla.

Both women used the stump of a branch thrust from a tree to step up and into the saddle. Seconds later they were riding down into the village, away from Castle Dunnane.

Dry brush around the castle had caught fire and illuminated the stone walls. Clumps of men were silhouetted as they fought hand-to-hand. There was no telling who was winning, but if Gordon clansmen had spilled from the walls of Dunnane, it was a good sign. They were pushing the attackers back.

Ian lifted his sword and swung it. Metal met metal as his opponent struck again and again. Sweat beaded and ran down his face, stinging his eyes as he concentrated, making every movement count.

He wondered where Harry was. He should have been here by now. He hoped to God there had been no trouble getting the women astride and into the village. But he couldn't think about that now. He had to believe Harry had followed through on his task. There was so much confusion, so much smoke, that Harry could well be twenty feet from him, and Ian might not know it.

A united army had fallen upon Dunnane, but it had quickly fractured. Clearly these were hired men, and not well trained. They were dirty, probably hungry. Their weapons were poor. They fought, but not with heart. 'Twas always the trouble with mercenaries.

The question was, Who hired them? Dared he guess? He didn't want to suspect Dungald's hand in this, yet who else would profit so handsomely from Harry's fall? Ian sidestepped an injured man lying at his feet and swung his sword again.

A sound of horses approaching drew his attention. Not more reinforcements for the attackers, he prayed. But he recognized the leader almost immediately. "I'll be damned," he panted.

Alfred Gordon. Somehow word had gotten to Alfred and the man had brought reinforcements for Dunnane. God bless his soul!

Ian raised his sword in salute to Alfred, then brought it down just in time to meet his next assailant. He caught his opponent's arm with the tip of the blade and the man's dirty sleeve instantly flowered in red.

"They're retreating! They're retreating!" Ian heard someone shout.

The man Ian fought glanced sideways to where the voice came. Elsewhere someone hollered "Retreat! Retreat!"

The ruffian paled.

"The other men go without you," Ian said under his breath. "Tell me who you fight for and I will spare your life."

The man's chin quivered as he raised his sword to fight off Ian's next blow.

"Tell me or die," Ian threatened through clenched teeth.

"I don't know!" the ruffian cried.

"Ye don't know?" Ian thundered.

The man's entire body seemed to shake with the reverberations from Ian's voice. "We was hired! I was promised coin to fight where I was tol' to fight. Didn't nobody say 'twould be Dunnane!"

"Ye don't know who hired ye?" Ian swung his sword, knocking the other man's inferior weapon from his hands.

The man fell to his knees. "Nae, I swear on my mother's grave I dinna know!"

"Someone offered ye the coin. Who?"

"A red-haired man. Called Rob." The man clasped his hands as if in prayer. "I swear, 'tis all I know. We wasn't supposed to know."

Ian eyed the man at his feet carefully. He seemed to be

telling the truth. So who was at the bottom of this? It could be no one but Dungald. . . .

Ian withdrew his sword. "Go, and do not show your face upon these lands again or I will cut you down."

The tired, dirty man stared into Ian's face as if he did not believe him. Could not. Then he leaped up and ran, leaving his sword on the ground where it had fallen.

Ian let his sword slip to his side and wiped his brow with the back of his free hand. It was wet with sweat and blood. The fighting had ceased. With the arrival of Alfred's men, the mercenaries had realized they were now outnumbered, most definitely outskilled. Those hired men who had not fallen in the battle now retreated. Dunnane was safe.

Now to find Dungald, Ian thought, his fury increasing with every stride he took.

"Ian, 'tis good to see you safe," Alfred Gordon said, riding up to him and dismounting. Someone took the reins from his hands.

Ian nodded, continuing toward the castle walls, his gaze searching the darkness. " 'Tis good to see you, Alfred."

The man glanced at the ground. "When word came, I thought of remaining safe within my walls, but I could not. The boy—his lordship," he corrected himself, "deserved my allegiance."

Ian exhaled. He was not ready to share with anyone else who he suspected was at the bottom of the attack, but it was imperative that he find Dungald and Harry as quickly as possible. "Have ye seen the earl?" Ian asked, walking toward the front gate.

"Nae, but 'twas such mayhem when we rode in. Shall I find him for you?"

A man on the ground groaned and reached out to Ian. Ian halted and squatted to take his hand. A Gordon. "Alex," he said, glancing at the shoulder wound, noting it was not fatal.

"Run the bastards off, didn't we?" the injured man said, wincing with pain.

"That we did. I'm proud of you." He patted the man's hand. "The earl is proud of you."

Ian glanced over the dead grass littered with fallen weapons and the dead and dying. "Help comes." He squeezed Alex's hand and signaled for someone to come to the injured man's aid. Then he rose and started for the castle again.

"If ye would go in search of his lordship 'twould be appreciated," Ian told Alfred. "Also his cousin. It is he I seek most of all."

Alfred looked up at Ian. "Ye suspect he has something to do with this? They were obviously mercenaries."

"Let me just say I wish to speak with Dungald."

"Anything else I can do? Anything. I feel I owe his lordship. My behavior previously was not what it should have been."

"Get some healthy men to help bring the injured into the hall. The dead can go here by the gate. We'll carry the bodies in after the living are cared for. And find someone to regroup those still able to fight. Men need to be on the parapet to watch, should they try to attack again."

Alfred nodded. "I'll see to it."

Ian rested his hand on Alfred's back. "I appreciate it."

Alfred started to walk away, signaling to his men.

"And Alfred . . ."

He turned back.

"Should ye find Dungald, hold him; use force if ye must," Ian said gravely.

Alfred saluted and walked away.

Ian hurried toward the castle. As he made his way through the dissipating smoke, through the darkness lit only by torches thrust in the ground here and there, he stopped to speak to wounded men. He asked anyone he met if they had seen Harry or Dungald. Several had seen the cousin, but none had seen Harry. Cold fear tugged at Ian's heart as he hurried through the castle yett. He kept telling himself that Harry was safe. Perhaps he had even decided to ride with the women into the village—though that seemed unlikely, as he had been adamant that he fight beside his men.

Perhaps Harry was in the great hall looking for him.

But he was not. Inside the hall Ian found nearly as much confusion as outside. One of Alfred's men was setting up a station for the wounded. Servants were caring for the injured.

Ian stood in the center of the room, turning, his gaze moving from one face to another. His heart was pounding. Where the hell was Harry? There was still so much confusion. It was not unusual for men to go missing right after a battle, only to be found unharmed later. He refused to consider that it was not usual for the leader to be missing.

So where did he look for him now? Did he ride to the village, check on Kara and be certain Harry wasn't there? Did he find the bastard Dungald and just hold him at swordpoint and ask him where the hell Harry was?

"Ian?"

The moment Kara spotted him in the center of the hall, in the midst of the disorder, she ran toward him. She had come as quickly as she could, leaving Isla and the baby in the care of Ruthie, and ridden back to the castle. She had thought of going into the catacombs herself; only her promise to Harry to protect the heir had prevented her. By the time she arrived at the wall of Dunnane the battle was already over. It had taken her precious minutes to find Ian.

She ran to him, her step unsteady. Only the reminder of the people around her kept her from throwing herself into his arms.

"Kara, what are you doing here?"

She closed her eyes to gain her equilibrium. "I came as quickly as I could," she said breathlessly. She wanted desperately to touch him, to prove to herself that he was at least safe. That he was real.

"You shouldn't have come. You were to wait for us to come for you."

"Harry," she burst out. "Oh, God, Ian. Please tell me Harry is here with you. We got separated in the catacombs. It was Dungald. He attacked Harry. They were fighting. He wanted me dead, too. I didn't want to go but Harry said it was my duty. He told me to—"

Ian grasped her arms, not seeming to care who saw them. "Kara, you have to slow down. I don't understand."

She trembled all over. "In . . . in the catacombs, after you left us," she said, taking a deep breath. "Dungald, he turned on Harry. Harry said I had to run." Against her will, tears rolled down her cheeks, and she dashed them away with the back of her hand. She had to be strong now, strong for Harry. "I didn't want to run, I wanted to stay and help him, but he said it was my duty. And then Robert the Red was there. . . ." She stumbled. "And—"

Ian squeezed her shoulders, not allowing her to go on. "Listen to me. You must go to your chamber," he said urgently. "You'll be safe there until I get my hands on Dungald."

She shook her head wildly, then pressed her hands to her swollen belly. "Nae! I will not retreat again. I'll help you find him. I know where I last saw him. We have to go into the cellars below. We have to look there first."

She knew his first impulse was to argue with her, but when he looked into her eyes, he seemed to realize she would not be dissuaded. Short of physically carrying her upstairs, she would not go.

Ian whipped around. "You. You." He pointed, designating men. "Grab torches. Come with me." He waved to Alfred Gordon. "Alfred!"

Alfred was beside him in a second.

"Gather men and find Dungald. I want him brought here to the hall. I don't care what you have to do to get him here, bound hand and foot if ye must."

Alfred only nodded, seeming to guess what was about by the grave look on Ian's face.

Ian hurried out of the hall, Harry's men falling in behind him. He hurried through the passageway that led to the door to the catacombs. "Stay to the rear," he told Kara, pushing her back with his arm. " 'Twould really be better if you—"

"I will not stay behind!"

Ian exhaled. "Charlie." He pointed to a man. "You guard her back.

The dirty-faced clansman nodded.

Kara lifted her skirts so that she was practically running beside him. "I'll show you where I last saw him."

But when they reached the place in the tunnels below the castle where Kara was certain Harry had faced Dungald, he was not there.

"I'm certain this was the place," she said, pressing her hand to her heart, feeling it thud. "Isla and I ran that way. The reiver, Robert the Red, came from that way." She pointed.

Kara, Ian and the men stood where two passageways intersected, staring into the darkness of each arm of the tunnel.

"Now what?" Kara whispered.

"We search all the—"

A sound made everyone turn toward one of the dark halls. The clansmen raised their swords. Ian threw one arm around Kara, pushing her behind him. With the other he drew his sword.

The sound came again. Something was running. Something small. "James!" Kara cried out in surprise as the monkey burst out of the darkness. She threw out her arms and the little creature leaped into them.

"He has to be down here." Kara refused to let tears well in her eyes again as she cuddled Harry's frightened pet.

Ian turned to the men. "We split up." He took a torch from one of the men. "Go by twos. One torch per party.

Draw a line with your boot so you don't get lost. If you see anything, anyone, ye holler. Understood?"

The men nodded.

Ian turned to Kara. "Let's take the tunnel out. Mayhap he went after you."

They followed the tunnel out of the catacombs and entered the copse of trees where Kara and Isla had mounted horses only a short time ago. The sky was dark overhead, with little moonlight. Smoke still filled the air with the acrid smell of burned pitch, but it was not as heavy as before.

"Where is he?" Kara moaned. "And where is that bastard Dungald?"

Ian turned to face her, lifting the torch. She could see his dirty face etched with worry.

"Let me be certain I understand what happened. Dungald attacked Harry. But he let you go? If he was going to kill Harry, why would he let you live? You and Isla would be witnesses."

She smoothed the monkey's head. Its entire body trembled in her arms. "That was the part about Robert the Red. Dungald said he was supposed to kill me. He ordered him to kill me, Isla as well."

"You got away from the reiver?"

"He led us out. I don't know why." Her gaze met Ian's. "But he set us free."

Ian stood where he was and turned slowly, lifting his torch high. Suddenly he halted. Kara looked at him, then in the same direction. There was something lying in the grass.

Someone.

Kara stood frozen for a moment, then darted forward, dropping the monkey to the ground. Ian reached out to stop her, but she dodged out of his way.

She fell on her knees in the grass. The ground was wet and cold.

"Harry, sweet Harry," she gasped, her heart swelling with grief.

Harry lay on his back, his eyes closed, his sword on the ground beside him.

"Oh, sweet heaven," Ian moaned, falling to his knees beside Kara.

She lifted Harry's head to her lap and brushed the blond hair from his handsome face. She had cut his hair only last week.

He looked as if he were sleeping, could have been sleeping, had it not been for the bloody wound in his chest.

"Harry," Ian croaked.

Kara was too stricken for tears. She pulled Harry's head to her breast and rocked back and forth. Ian wrapped his arms around her shoulders and rocked with her.

"Harry, Harry," she whispered.

"Shhh," Ian soothed.

"Dungald must not have struck him down," she said, her throat scratchy, her eyes stinging as she choked on her words. "Look, he made it above. Perhaps he fell fighting. Perhaps it is Dungald's body we shall find—"

Ian rested his forehead against her shoulder. "Nae, he whispered, his voice as filled with emotion as she had ever heard. "Look at the grass, hinny. 'Tis a clear path. He was dragged here from down below."

Kara's gaze met Ian's. In the torchlight she saw his brown eyes filled with tears. She had not known a warrior could cry.

"Find him," she whispered from between clenched teeth. "Find that bastard Dungald and I will run him through myself."

Chapter Twenty-six

Ian ordered Harry's body to be carried into the great hall and laid upon the dais to be bathed and prepared for burial. Kara followed Ian and the men who carried Harry's body inside, still stunned beyond sensible reasoning.

As he was carried into the hall his clansmen and the servants gasped and then fell into shocked silence. Some prayed, while others hung their heads in reverence as he was laid to rest on the table.

"Has anyone seen Dungald?" Ian asked.

Kara went to stand at Harry's head and sent someone for a Dunnane tartan to cover his body.

No one had seen Dungald.

"What of Alfred Gordon?" Ian barked. He no longer wept, but any man who looked closely would have known he had cried for his slain brother.

The sound of shouting in the entranceway caught everyone's attention, and Kara looked up from the table where Harry lay.

Alfred Gordon entered the hall, men behind him, leading Dungald. He was secured by a man on each arm.

"This is preposterous," Dungald bellowed. "Unhand me! Don't you understand? I am your lord now. If the boy is dead, as you say, God rest him, I am the earl and I will not be treated thusly!"

Kara flew across the room, reaching Dungald before Ian did. "You killed him!" she shouted, shaking a fist. "You killed my Harry."

Dungald's first look was one of utter shock.

Of course he was surprised. He'd thought her dead, too, hadn't he? He thought Robert the Red had killed her in the catacomb, as he'd ordered.

The look on Dungald's face instantly changed from one of shock to feigned relief. He was a fine actor. "Kara! Thank God you're well."

She rolled her fingers into a ball and swung, striking Harry's cousin in the side of the face.

"Ouch!" He covered his cheek with his palm.

"Kara." Ian came up behind her. "Let me deal with him."

"You killed him," Kara accused through clenched teeth. She was so angry that the room was spinning.

Everyone stared at her as if she were demented. No one yet knew how Harry had died. They all thought he'd been killed in the battle. That was what Dungald wanted them to think, of course.

"Someone please bring the Lady Dunnane some water and a chair," Dungald said calmly, nursing his cheek. "She's overwrought. I believe she might faint."

Kara felt Ian's hands close over her shoulders. "Kara, let me," he whispered. "I will deal with him." He sounded as angry as she did. Angrier.

She swallowed back her tears. "You killed Harry," she said softly, meeting Dungald's gaze. "Tell them. We were in the catacombs and—"

"The catacombs?" Dungald glanced up. "Why, God help me, that's where they found him?"

"Not there," someone said. "Outside."

Dungald's eyes narrowed. He was still being held by two of Alfred's men, but loosely. "How did you know he was there?"

Everyone in the room—servants, Gordons—stared and listened.

"How did you know that was where his body would be found?" Dungald repeated accusingly.

Ian put himself between Kara and Dungald. "You are not in the position to be questioning anyone," he said flatly. But Kara would not let Ian take over. "Because I was there!" she spit, trying to get in front of Ian again. "I was there with him."

A ripple of sound rose in the room as men put their heads together, trying to figure out what was happening.

"Ian, I think this discussion should continue privately," Dungald said, looking past her. "The Lady Dunnane seems to know something of this, and yet she apparently made no attempt to get help for him." His eyes widened theatrically. "Please, madam, tell me you had nothing to do with the earl's death."

"Me!" Kara could not believe what she was hearing. "You would dare accuse me when it was you who lifted the sword to my husband!"

Dungald raised his palms heavenward, playing to the crowd. He was so damned handsome that it sickened her.

"My lady, you had best choose your words carefully so as not to incriminate yourself. We all heard you argue with his lordship."

"What are you talking about?" she flared.

"What the hell are you talking about?" Ian echoed.

Men were staring at her. Servants nodded.

"We all heard you say you wished you had never wed him. One could construe that to mean . . ." He shrugged. "That you wished his lordship ill. Worse. To kill in the midst of a fight could be considered rather clever."

Dungald was twisting what had happened that night, what she had said ages ago. How could he accuse her? She had seen him draw a sword against Harry with her own eyes.

Her own eyes, Kara thought through her daze. No witnesses but her maid . . .

"I said that ages ago," she shouted. "And I was overwrought. I didn't mean—"

"Kara," Ian whispered fiercely in her ear. "Stay calm. Don't you see what he's doing?"

She drew her lips tightly together. Suddenly she felt weak. Dizzy. Harry was dead and now this bastard might get away with it. He might put the blame on her.

"Ian," she groaned, turning to him. She felt as if she were falling, falling into blackness from which she would never emerge. "Tell them what I told you. Tell them what he did."

"Unhand me," Dungald said, and Alfred's men let go of him. Everyone seemed to be confused now.

"I believe further investigation will be necessary," Dungald announced. "In the meantime, her ladyship should be held in her chamber . . . for her own safety."

Men and women gasped. Kara knew what they had heard. A formal accusation was what Dungald meant. This was madness!

Ian lifted his gaze to Dungald. "No, wait one moment, sir," his voice boomed. "Might you tell me where you were when the fighting commenced?"

Dungald looked surprised. "Where I was?"

"I did not stutter." Ian pushed Kara gently to the side so that he might face Dungald. "Where were you when the fighting began?"

"I . . ." He blinked. "Why, I was just riding in. His lordship sent me to retrieve the patrol gone in search of the reivers. Thank God I returned in time. They had just laid siege upon the castle."

"And then?" Kara asked bitterly. "Where did you go then?"

"Where did I go, woman? I raised a sword to fight with the Gordons at the castle wall."

"Liar!" She wiped away the tears that ran down her face. "You were in the catacombs."

He looked her squarely in the eye. "And what proof have you of that?"

Kara heard rather than saw Ian slide his sword from his belt. Dungald took a step back. "Put aside your sword! You may not raise a sword to the Earl of Dunnane," he spit.

"You are not the earl," Ian shouted, as angry as she had ever heard him. "The child my lady carries, should he be male, is the new lord."

Dungald's eyes narrowed. "And what if the wife is found guilty of murder?"

Ian raised the tip of his sword beneath Dungald's nose. "Back to the subject of the catacombs. My lady says you were below."

"She is a liar!" he shouted. "My word against hers, and who would corroborate the word of a greedy, vengeful wife?"

"Me."

Dungald turned slowly, his demeanor cocky as he looked to see who stood behind him. His face went ashen. His mouth moved, but no sound came out as the thief stood defiant before him.

Everyone turned to see a red-haired, red-bearded man standing in the archway entrance to the great hall. Robert the Red, the cattle reiver.

"He was there," Kara said loudly. "Robert the Red, the reiver, Dungald hired him to lead the attack. To kill me and my maid as well!"

In one quick movement Ian pushed Kara back and lifted his sword. Dungald spun around, drawing his own weapon from his belt.

Kara covered her ears with her hands as the swords struck and clanged, but she could not look away.

"Mine," Dungald cried. "This should all have been mine. Not that snotty-nosed brat's!"

Kara backed against the dais, where Harry's body lay, to give Ian room. She clutched her hands together, wishing desperately that she could do something to help him. By God, she wanted to kill Dungald herself.

"You hired men to attack Dunnane!" Ian shouted, his voice thundering in the vaulted room. "You killed my brother. There are witnesses and now you will pay!"

"Aye, I did it," Dungald confessed amid cries of surprise and anger among the clansmen. "But I did it for my father." Tears ran down his face as the weight of his sword brought his hands down. The hand with the palsy was shaking too greatly to bear the weapon. "So kill me. Kill me now. I don't want to live!"

Ian lowered his sword. "I will not kill you now. I would not give you the honor of a quick death. Better to see you hanged in shame for your treachery," he said bitterly.

"And then what?" Dungald's nose ran. The hand with the palsy was shaking so fiercely that he could no longer steady it. "You cannot have Dunnane. Not ever. You can't even have her because you are the dead boy's brother!"

Kara saw Dungald lift his sword, but it took a moment for her to realize what he was doing. At first she thought he was going to strike at Ian again.

Ian must have thought the same, because he made a move to lift his sword in defense.

To Kara's shock, Dungald twisted the sword in his hands and thrust it into his stomach before Ian could reach him.

"Nae!" Ian shouted, letting his own sword fall to the ground as he lunged forward to Dungald.

Dungald fell to his knees, his leine chroich instantly covered in blood, dripping with blood.

Ian went down on one knee. "Nae, nae," he whispered in pity, putting out his hands to catch Harry's cousin.

Kara knew Dungald was dead before he fell into Ian's arms.

Ian's head dropped onto Dungald's shoulder. The hall of clansmen stood in stunned silence, unable to tear their gazes from the two men on the floor.

Kara covered her face with her hands and then was suddenly stricken with a pain in her abdomen. She must have cried out, because Ian turned to look over his shoulder at her.

He came to her in an instant, leaving Dungald's body slumped on the floor. "What's wrong?"

She shook her head, still in shock. She ran her hand over her belly. She felt a tightening. "A pain," she whispered. "I hope it's not the baby. 'Tis too soon."

Ian swept her into his arms and pushed his way out of the great hall. Kara looped her arms around his neck and let her head fall to his shoulder, too spent to cry. Her lower lip trembled. "He's right, you know," she whispered. "What do we have?" She stared into his dark eyes. "We can still never have each other."

"Serves him right, dealing with a man like Robert the Red," Ian said quietly.

He and Kara were in the great hall, seated before the fireplace, awaiting the arrival of Mother Anne. Clansmen wandered about aimlessly, their hearts as heavy as Kara's and Ian's. It seemed the young earl had gained a great deal of respect from his men in his last days. Harry's funeral would take place in the afternoon. "But surely Dungald had never suspected Robert would betray him," Kara thought aloud. "What reason would he have had to think the thief would not do as he had bidden him? He had paid the man off, with the promise of greater sums once he was the earl."

"I suppose Dungald thought coin could buy anything, including a man's conscience," Ian observed.

"I am still amazed," she said softly, stroking her abdomen. After a few hours' rest the day of the attack, her pains had subsided and they had not returned. She was hopeful that she would carry the baby to full term. "Even knowing what happened, I can barely believe it to be true."

"Amazed, aye, but it appears to have happened as Robert the Red explained. He agreed to take money for himself and others and then decided it was not what he wanted to do," Ian said. "He said it was because of you. Apparently Dungald had never mentioned that you had to die as well." His mouth twitched into a smile. "Apparently our Robert the Red was a thief and a murderer, but not a woman murderer." He winked. "I think he is sweet upon you."

She smiled. "I am certainly not sweet upon him, but I am glad you let him go. A man with such a conscience deserves another chance."

The sound of barking dogs brought Kara and Ian out of their chairs before the stone fireplace.

"Mother Anne," Kara said, holding out her hands to her mother-in-law as the woman approached, escorted by her priest.

"Kara, love." Anne threw her arms around Kara and hugged her tightly. As she peered into Kara's face it was obvious she had been crying a great deal. "I'm so glad you're safe."

Then she turned to her son and hugged him, too. "I came as quickly as I could," she said. "I've something of great importance to tell you."

Ian released his mother, glancing at Kara. "Mother, whatever it is, surely it can wait until your son is buried."

She twisted her small, pale hands adorned with gold rings. "Nae. Nae, it cannot wait, for that is the point."

Kara stared at the beautiful older woman, utterly perplexed. "What is the point?"

Anne lifted her voice so that anyone in the room who wished to hear her might. The Gordons quickly began to gather around.

"Harry was not my son," she said softly. "Not Richard's."

Kara's eyes widened. Richard was the previous Earl of

Dunnane, Harry's father, who had passed the title on to his son upon his death.

"Mother, what is this nonsense?" Ian asked sharply. "This is not the time—"

"Hush and listen," Anne interrupted. "Let me say what I must whilst I have the courage." She took a breath, her gaze drifting from the faces of the men who surrounded her. "I am an evil woman. Once upon a time I did something terrible. Something done out of love, but not right. Then I vowed on the Virgin's name never to tell the truth. Not so long as Harailt Gordon lived."

Kara began to tremble from the inside out. She felt Ian's hand slip into hers. Anyone who glanced down could have seen them, but he seemed not to care. Perhaps he had an inkling of what Anne was about to say.

"Harailt was not my child, not even Richard's."

Someone gasped.

"Our child died, and because I wanted so badly to give him a son he could call his own, this man brought me another child." She indicated the old priest.

"So Dungald was the true heir?" Kara said in disbelief. Ian squeezed her hand.

"Nae." Anne gave a laugh. "Were that the truth, do ye think I would be here now, dearie?" She smiled sadly. "Nae, the truth is far more complicated than that. You see, when I gave birth to Harry, that was the second time Richard and I had been married."

Another gasp rose among the clansmen.

Kara could do nothing but stare and hold tightly to Ian's hand.

"Richard and I were married when we were still young. We were in love; we ran away and married secretly and conceived a child. But our parents discovered us, dragged us home and had the marriage annulled. We were each meant for another and quickly married off and sent to the far corners of Scotland so that we might never see each other again."

Kara felt numb, numb to her toes.

Anne continued. "I gave birth to a boy thirty-six years ago this fall."

A strange tickle ran down Kara's spine. Ian's birthday was in the fall; everyone knew that. He was thirty-six.

"My new husband and I named the boy Ian. No one knew the child was Richard's, not even my dim-witted husband. Richard married his intended and a few years later she gave birth to William." She smiled, her thoughts seeming to grow distant. "Years passed and Richard and I, though married to others, kept our love for each other burning in our hearts." She clasped her hands. "We prayed we would someday be together again."

She took a breath, letting the tale told thus far sink in. "As proof that God is truly good, we were eventually able to wed again after my husband passed away, as well as Richard's wife. Richard, the Earl of Dunnane, was so good to Ian because he knew he was the son he could never claim."

Kara squeezed Ian's hand, but he did not look at her. He was staring at his mother. "Go on," he said softly.

"I was old to bear a child, but when I became pregnant I was so thrilled. Richard was so thrilled! A son we could claim together! But the baby died." A single tear slipped down Anne's smooth cheek, but she let it fall. "I couldn't disappoint him, not after all we'd been through. So Father brought me a crofter's baby under the cover of night and switched my dead child for a healthy boy. We named him Harailt. William, from his first "official" marriage, was still the legitimate heir to Dunnane, but we had our Harry."

Anne paused, taking a deep breath. For the first time Kara saw tears in the older woman's eyes. "Then our love began to drift . . . die. I don't know why, maybe because we had been through too much. Harry and I went to Edinburgh to live and Richard went about his business. William was his eldest, his true heir anyway."

"So when I was betrothed to the Earl of Dunnane's heir, I should have been—"

"Betrothed to me," Ian said, turning slowly to meet her gaze.

Kara's eyes filled with tears. Tears of joy, of sadness.

"What does this mean?" someone dared ask.

"Aye, what does it all mean?" another clansman questioned.

"It means," Mother Anne said quietly, "that I have the documentation, I have a witness, to swear these events to be true. It means that Ian Munroe is Ian Gordon, the Earl of Dunnane. It means," she said, turning her gaze to her son, "that Ian Gordon, the Earl of Dunnane, is not a blood relative to the boy we will bury today. It means that if he wishes, he may now legally wed this widow who has captured our hearts."

For a moment Kara was too stunned to breathe.

Ian leaned forward, pressing his forehead to hers, his dark eyes locked with hers. "It means ye and I, hinny, shall live happily ever after, forevermore."

Epilogue

"Ian? Ian, are you out here?" Wiping her hands on the apron tied around her waist, Kara entered the walled garden beneath the trellis of green vines and white flowers. She could hear little Harry's trill of laughter and the rumble of Ian's voice. They had to be here somewhere. "Ian?"

"Here. In the back."

Kara heard more childish giggles and shushing. Then the distinct sound of splashing water.

"Ian Munroe Gordon!" Kara said, coming around the turn in the stone path. She halted as she planted her hands on her hips.

Three-year-old, red-haired Harry stood naked, waist-deep in the stone fountain, his father seated beside him, fully dressed. Harry squealed with laughter and covered his face with his chubby hands. "I tol' ye, Papa, she would come and catch us," he bubbled, hiding.

"What do you think you are doing?"

Ian glanced up innocently. "Doing, wife?"

"Aye." She took a step closer in disbelief, fighting the smile that pulled at her lips. "What are ye doing in Grandma Anne's Italian fountain?"

"Nothing," Ian said.

"Nufing," Harry echoed impishly, lowering his hands.

"Ye look like ye must be doing something." Kara gestured.

Ian looked at Harry. Little Harry looked at his father, and both of her men burst into laughter again.

Kara strode toward the fountain, feigning as much anger as she could muster, laughing at the same time. "Get yourself from that fountain, Master Harry, before you catch your death!" She whipped off her apron.

"We was hot," Harry said, not in the least bit afraid of his mother's wrath.

Kara reached out and plucked her naked son from the running fountain and wrapped him in her apron. As she set him on his feet and tightened the cloth around his little shoulders she pressed a kiss to his wet head. "Run inside and have Isla find you some dry clothes," she told him.

The little boy nodded. "Aye, Mama." Then he turned to look over his shoulder at his father.

Ian winked. "Do as she bids afore we're both in trouble, son."

The boy nodded, then turned back to his mother. "Can I play with James when I'm dressed?"

"You may play with the monkey after you are dressed. Now go." Kara pointed.

Harry ran down the stone path toward the yett, leaving his parents alone in the garden.

"So." Kara crossed her arms over her chest, turning her attention back to her husband in the fountain.

Ian had drawn his legs up to rest his arms on his knees. A smile twitched on his broad, handsome face. "So . . ."

She took a step closer to the fountain, grinning. "You are supposed to be teaching your son proper behavior."

He gazed virtuously at his surroundings. The fountain bubbled and water swirled around him. Water poured from the cherub statue's pail in the center of the fountain, into the main reservoir, making a pleasant splashing sound. The sun shone on his back and the air smelled richly of late summer flowers.

He lifted an eyebrow. "This is not proper behavior?"

"Not for the next Earl of Dunnane, nae!" She reached into the fountain and splashed water at him.

His gaze met hers, his smile warm now, rather than playful. "I like the sound of that. Harailt Ian Gordon, the next Earl of Dunnane."

"I like it, too." She hugged herself, unable to tear her gaze from her husband's.

After Harry and Dungald had died, after Mother Anne had told the truth of the whole blessed mess, Kara had still feared Ian would not be able to claim their son. But between the annulment of her marriage to Harry and the power of the Dunnane earldom, all had been legally settled. Ian had been installed as the rightful earl and little Harry was declared Ian's legitimate son, and the next Earl of Dunnane.

For a moment they were both silent, appreciating all they had. Acknowledging what they had lost. Even after more than three years they both still missed Harry so much.

Then Ian flipped his hand, splashing Kara with water, breaking the spell.

She laughed and splashed him, trying to step away from the fountain before he splashed her again. But he was too quick for her. One moment she was standing in the grass before the impressive fountain; the next moment he was pulling her over the side into the cold water.

"Ian!" Kara shrieked. "It's cold! Let me go!"

He sat down in the water, pulling her onto his lap, trapping her. "Kiss me," he said. "Kiss me or I'll push you under." He leaned her back until her hair dipped into the water.

She laughed, looping her arms around his neck, so happy that she thought she might burst. "I'm cold."

"Kiss me and I will warm ye."

She looked up into his dark brown eyes, remembering the first time she had really noticed them, her first wedding night in Harry's bedchamber, when he had come to her rescue. She still saw the same compassion, but now she saw love. Love for her, for their son, for the life they had fought for within the walls of Dunnane.

"Kiss you?" she whispered saucily. "I believe I can do even better than that, my lord."

He pressed his mouth to hers. "I love ye, Kara," he whispered against her lips. "Forever and always."

Ever and always.

ABOUT THE AUTHOR

Colleen Faulkner lives with her family in the Delaware area and is the daughter of bestselling historical romance author Judith French. Colleen is the author of twenty Zebra historical romances and is currently working on a contemporary romance trilogy for Zebra's Bouquet line. Her first contemporary romance for Bouquet, *Maggie's Baby*, will be published in February 2000. She loves to hear from readers, and you may write to her c/o Zebra Books. Please include a self-addressed, stamped envelope if you wish a response.

<u>BOOK YOUR PLACE ON OUR WEBSITE</u>
<u>AND MAKE THE</u>
<u>READING CONNECTION!</u>

We've created a customized website just for our very special readers, where you can get the inside scoop on everything that's going on with Zebra, Pinnacle and Kensington books.

When you come online, you'll have the exciting opportunity to:

- View covers of upcoming books
- Read sample chapters
- Learn about our future publishing schedule (listed by publication month *and author*)
- Find out when your favorite authors will be visiting a city near you
- Search for and order backlist books from our online catalog
- Check out author bios and background information
- Send e-mail to your favorite authors
- Meet the Kensington staff online
- Join us in weekly chats with authors, readers and other guests
- Get writing guidelines
- AND MUCH MORE!

Visit our website at
http://www.zebrabooks.com

Put a Little Romance in Your Life With
Fern Michaels